CYNGOR CAERDYDD
CARDIFF COUNCIL
LIBRARY SERVICE

CARDIFF MOBILE ☎: 029 2078 3548	
HB59	
HB17	
HB61	
HB122	
HB71	
HB94	

This book must be returned or renewed on or before the
latest date above, otherwise a fine will be charged.
Rhaid dychwelyd neu adnewyddu y llyfr hwn erbyn y dyddiad
diweddaraf uchod, neu bydd dirwy i'w thalu.

Sinners and Saints

Sinners and Saints

Eileen Dreyer

PIATKUS

Visit the Piatkus website!

Piatkus publishes a wide range of bestselling fiction and non-fiction, including books on health, mind, body & spirit, sex, self-help, cookery, biography and the paranormal.

If you want to:

- read descriptions of our popular titles
- buy our books over the internet
- take advantage of our special offers
- enter our monthly competition
- learn more about your favourite Piatkus authors

VISIT OUR WEBSITE AT: www.piatkus.co.uk

Copyright © Eileen Dreyer 2005

First published in Great Britain in 2006 by
Judy Piatkus (Publishers) Ltd of
5 Windmill Street, London W1T 2JA
email: info@piatkus.co.uk

This edition published 2006

First published in the United States in 2005 by St. Martin's Press

The moral right of the author has been asserted

A catalogue record for this book is available from the British Library

ISBN 0 7499 0782 7

Set in Times by
Action Publishing Technology Ltd, Gloucester

Printed and bound in Great Britain by
William Clowes Ltd, Beccles, Suffolk

To JMM
You really are my hero

Acknowledgements

The list this time is a long one. I can't sufficiently express my thanks to all the people who gave their time, expertise, and assistance-not to mention all those great stories. As ever, any mistakes are mine.

One point to be made. The laws on fertility assistance are ever changing. At the time of publication, Louisiana was still the only state that forbade the auctioning of human eggs. But as fast as laws change, I decided to take my chances that it was coming.

And now, my thanks.

First, my regulars. Dr. Mary Case and Mary Fran Ernst of the St. Louis County Medical Examiner's Office. Lt. John Podolak, St. Louis City Police, and his ever-patient (with me) wife, Michelle.

Now the people who helped offer veracity for this book:

In St. Louis: Dr. Peter Ahlering, Mary Palmer, RN, and Herman Rodriguez, Sher Institute; Katie Lucas, RN, St. John's Mercy Medical Center; all the great folk at Neustaedter's Jewelers.

In New Orleans: Dr. Karen Ross (whose hospitality is unrivaled), Bo and Elizabeth, Jefferson Parish Coroner's Office; Karen Chabert, RN, Forensic Nurse Liaison, LSU Health Science Center, who gave me the seeds of Kareena Boudreaux, although Kareena doesn't hold a candle to the exceptional Karen; Det. Sgt. Dave Morales, Det. Sgt. Dennis Thornton, and Det. Eddie Klein, Homicide Division, Jefferson Parish; P/O IV Edward J. Delery, Scientific Criminal Investigative Division, New Orleans Police Department; Sgt. Gerard Dugue, New Orleans Homicide Division; Roxanne Becnel and Barbara Colley for the wonderful tour of their New Orleans, especially the Garden District in the rain; Christophe Hinton, taxi driver extraordinaire; Sunny Holliday, Gallatoire's Restaurant; Claudie Williams, Starling Books; Anna from Erzulie's; Angela Laing, Jackson Square tarot reader; Brandon Kelley, Voodoo Authentica. Thank you all. You were so gracious with your time and hospitality that I had a terrible time deciding when to finish the research and start the writing. I know I've forgotten someone. Let me know, and I promise to include you in the next acknowledgments.

To Jen Crusie for the chaos theory over Chinese food; to Andrea Cirillo; to Matthew Shear, Kim Cardascia, Joe Rinaldi, and all at St. Martin's Press for the patience and the support; especially to Jen Enderlin, who edited a travelogue into a suspense. To JMM, who was kind enough to allow me to tell this story. To the real Fred Hayes-Adams for being gracious enough to bid to have herself included. To the Divas—Karyn Witmer-Gow, Kim Bush, and Tami Hoag (who provided the perfect sanctuary)—for sanity, support, and safety. A separate thanks to Karyn Witmer-Gow for judicious editing and generous hand-holding. And, of course, to Rick for every little thing you do (except traveling without me) and Kev, Kate, and Juan. Deadline robe is off (at least momentarily).

Sinners and Saints

New Orleans Neighborhood Biweekly

Bobby's Byline

June 2 – Eddie Dupre had an uninvited guest at his hurricane party last night. As you all know, Eddie always puts on the finest celebration to kick off the beginning of hurricane season. There was a parade down Bourbon over to Royal – where Eddie lives in the Faubourg Marigny – with music, dancing, and appropriate costumes (Eddie was luminous as Dorothy Lamour).

Unfortunately, the party mood was soured when it was discovered that a nun lying passed out in the alley behind Eddie's yard not only wasn't a partygoer, she wasn't passed out. She was dead, with her face obliterated, possibly by a shotgun blast. Too, too gruesome.

Now she might not even have been a nun, but we'll never know, will we? It seems that by the time Eddie got back to the site with the police, the holy woman had vanished ... along with any evidence she'd ever been there.

Here's the best part, though, babies. It seems that when she went to her last reward, our good sister was wearing a near-flawless seven-carat emerald and diamond ring. Sure redefines those vows of poverty, chastity, and obedience. Don't you just want to know what kind of obedience earns you sparklies like that?

1

Chapter One

Omens come in all sizes. Hair standing up at the back of the neck. Crows on a telephone wire. Shapes in a cloud or a chill in the wind. A hundred innocuous things designated by tradition or superstition, and a thousand more kept in a personal lexicon.

Chastity Byrnes carried around quite a full lexicon of her own. Not just the regular omens handed down from generation to generation of Irishwomen, like birds in the house meaning death, or uncovered mirrors at a funeral meaning death, or any of the other myriad Irish omens meaning death. Chastity embraced a plethora of personal portents inexplicable to anyone but her.

Chastity was a trauma nurse, and only ballplayers and actors were more superstitious. So in addition to the usual signs of doom, Chastity dreaded quiet shifts, the words 'I think something's wrong,' and holidays.

And the number three. Chastity absolutely loathed the number three. Everything happened in threes, from births to deaths to every disaster in between.

Like the omens Chastity received that hot June day in St. Louis. She should never have ignored them. After all, Chastity paid more attention to her omens than to her bank balance. She lived by Murphy's Law as if it were the first commandment. But that hot, sultry summer day, even though she knew better, she blew off those three omens as

3

if they were parking tickets.

To be fair, they weren't easy omens to recognize, like a black cat or the hoot of an owl. They were more like odd things that made a person want to look over her shoulder.

The chaos theory.

A phone call from a brother-in-law she didn't know she had.

Lake Pontchartrain.

Innocuous in themselves, but each of them sent a skittering of unease down Chastity's back that should have had her keeping a wary eye out for trouble where there seemed to be none.

Three omens.

Well, maybe four. But the fourth could have just been Chastity's bad luck. On the way in to work that day, Chastity lost her driver's license. She didn't consider it an omen at the time. More a 'shit happens' kind of thing. But if it hadn't happened, she never would have heard about the chaos theory, and Chastity would always believe that if she'd missed that, nothing else would have followed.

The cop who stopped her was a buddy. All cops in town were buddies of trauma nurses. But he wasn't smiling when he strolled up to the window of her hot red Mini Cooper.

'Not that I'm not impressed, Chaz,' he said, an eyebrow raised at the speeds she managed. 'But this is your third warning. In three weeks.' There was that number again. 'And there are all those unpaid parking violations . . .'

Chastity ended up locking her car at the side of the highway and riding into work in a police cruiser, thirty minutes late for her shift. Which put her smack in the middle of a trauma code just in time to hear the chaos theory.

She'd been scheduled to work triage that day. She got bumped instead to Trauma Team One. Not that she minded. Chastity had joined the staff at St. Michael's especially for the trauma. Particularly the kind of trauma they saw at St. Michael's.

4

Chastity wasn't just a trauma nurse anymore. She was one of two new forensic nurse liaisons at St. Michael's. It was her job not only to save patients, but preserve any viable forensic evidence that might prove a possible criminal or civil case. She made sure abuse victims didn't fall through the cracks, rape victims got better treatment from the hospital than they did from their attackers, and unknown patients were identified. She helped police and hospital personnel work more efficiently together.

So she wasn't surprised that she didn't even get a chance to reach her locker before she got yanked into Trauma Room One to help resuscitate a sixteen-year-old gunshot wound victim.

'About time you showed up,' one of the nurses said from where she was pumping in fluids.

The room was already in turmoil, half a dozen staff members spinning and colliding around the room like random ions. Blood oozed over the side of the table, and paper and sterile wrappings littered the floor. The patient had been shot in the upper abdomen. He'd already been paralyzed and intubated, x-rayed, ultrasounded, and evaluated. A forest of lines snaked from chest, arms, throat, and penis, and blood was being recycled from his chest. The staff had probably been working on him for about five minutes.

'You're lucky to have me at all,' Chastity assured them all, slipping booties over her brand-new magenta tennis shoes. 'I was supposed to be on crowd control out front today.'

'Are those uniform?' Moshika Williams asked from her position by the boy's left chest. Moshika Williams was the trauma doc in charge. A seriously brilliant trauma fellow, she stood square and solid, and ran a code like a traffic cop on speed.

Chastity lifted a foot free of the sticky mess on the floor and spread her magenta-clad arms. 'They match my new scrubs.'

5

'Which are very . . . bright.'

'Bright,' Chastity agreed with a nod as she finished gowning up. 'Exactly. It all reflects my new attitude.'

'Your forensic attitude?'

'My happy attitude. My life is in harmony . . . well, except for the need to find a ride to work tomorrow. But otherwise, I am now in balance. Harmony, Moshika. It's the word of the day.'

'Not for Willy here. His clothes are on the counter, by the way. We didn't even cut 'em through the bullet hole this time.'

'I'm very proud of you all. You've saved the crime lab untold grief. Now, if you just haven't sneezed on everything . . .'

Gowned, gloved, and shielded, Chastity pulled out her camera and her swabs, her rulers and her paper bags to save the evidence that hadn't already been washed away in the attempt to save Willy's life.

Moshika bent over the chest tube she was preparing to insert. 'And you're in time to hear what I just learned.'

Chastity wasn't the only one in the room who groaned. The only disadvantage to working with Moshika was the method she used to keep herself calm in a crisis. Some people whistled. Some cracked knuckles or told jokes. Moshika lectured. She shared all the tidbits of random scientific information she'd been stuffing into her overheated brain, as if anybody hip deep in blood and vomit really wanted to know the latest guess about what the hell a quark was.

This time what she wanted to share with the class was the chaos theory. Bent over her patient, she waved a scalpel in Chastity's direction. 'You missed the first part of this, Chaz.'

'I'll get the notes later. Everybody smile.'

Everybody smiled. Chastity snapped shots of the slightly elliptical bullet hole just below the kid's sternum, and especially the soot ring and powder stippling that surrounded it.

6

Willy had been capped at very close range.

'Well, it's interesting,' Moshika assured her, bending back to her work. 'The chaos theory says that no experimental result can be perfectly replicated. There is always a variable that can't be duplicated.'

Chastity nodded as if she understood and hummed *Brigadoon* as she measured and swabbed and sealed. It was easier that way. Chastity hummed show tunes to keep herself focused. The fact that they drowned out Moshika's lectures was just a fringe benefit.

But then Moshika went and ruined it all. Her fingers probing the patient's chest for the tube placement, she looked straight at Chastity with those huge, bright black eyes of hers and said, 'Now here's the part that you should find most interesting. Especially considering your new attitude. It seems that according to chaos theory, just at the moment when a system attains its most perfect harmony, that's when it's really just about to spin out of control.'

The hair literally stood up on the back of Chastity's neck. Right in the middle of a trauma code, she stumbled to a dead halt. 'What the hell did you have to say that for?' she demanded.

Moshika, too busy with intercostal spaces, didn't hear. But the damage had already been done. She'd said it, hadn't she? She'd said it to Chastity, who had told Moshika no more than three minutes ago that life had finally found a certain harmony.

An odd thing to contemplate during a trauma code, certainly, but the truth was that Chastity was at her happiest during trauma codes. She loved action, she loved the rush of adrenaline, she loved the challenge of forensics. She loved living on the edge, and she could safely do that within the oddly precise ritual of a trauma code. Chastity was practicing at the forefront of twenty-first-century nursing, and she loved it.

Even knowing that she was to be separated from her lovely little car for a bit, until Moshika had opened her interfering mouth, Chastity had been happy.

Instinctively she reached a free hand into her lab coat pocket, where along with pens and penlights and laminated trauma scale cards, she always kept a small velvet draw-string bag. She wrapped her fingers around it for a minute, just for the feel of it. Just to make sure it was still there.

'Chastity?'

She could have used a better name, of course. Chastity was, after all, such a cosmic joke. Her mother had named her daughters Faith, Hope, and Chastity.

Not Charity.

Chastity.

As if Mary Rose Byrnes had either had an odd sense of prescience or a catastrophic need for denial.

'Chastity, there's a call for you.'

Chastity looked up to see the new secretary leaning in the doorway, her focus more on the disaster in the room than on the recipient of her message. No big surprise. The secretary was new, and it took a while to get used to the ambience of the place. The patient lay naked and alien-looking in the midst of bedlam. The air was rank with the smell of blood and bowels. Machines crouched at each corner of the cart, and staffers shuffled around like bumper cars in an attempt to get Willie safely to surgery before his heart gave out along with his liver and left lung.

Chastity was now helping the team do that very thing. She'd collected all the evidence she could. She'd taped the boy's hands inside brown paper bags to protect defensive or blowback evidence, and she'd collected photos and personal effects. While everybody else ran Willie Anderson to CT-Scan and then to OR, Chastity would instead pass her information and her specially taped bags to the police.

'There's a *call* for you,' the secretary repeated, her lips pursed into a moue of distaste at the wreckage in the room.

'I'll call them back later, Kim,' Chastity answered as she dropped an empty IV bag onto the littered floor and stretched across two techs and the patient to change EKG leads.

8

'Call her Chaz,' Moshika told the secretary as she finished sewing in the chest tube. 'Gives her stature.'

'Makes her sound like a made man,' a paramedic snorted.

Moshika laughed, her big horn-rimmed glasses glinting in the fluorescence. 'Considering the fact that she looks like Peter Pan, it couldn't hurt.'

So she still shopped for her jeans in the boys' department, Chastity thought. Big deal. So she wore her hair in one of those cheesy pixie cuts, and it happened to be blond. It was easier that way. She was in harmony, damn it.

She had a boxer puppy named Lilly and a flat in south St. Louis painted like a Mexican cantina. She had friends she socialized with regularly, enough money to support her habits, and a fast little car to give her the illusion of control. No surprises, no problems, no new traumas that woke her up any more than the old traumas did. She had some peace within herself, as long as she kept to her comfortable rituals and safety zones.

She had balance.

She was happy.

Which, as any Irishwoman knew, spelled disaster. The chaos theory was just the scientific spin on that old, unimpeachable Irish truth that good things never lasted.

'I'll still call 'em back,' Chastity said.

'It's long distance,' Kim insisted. 'From New Orleans. He said it's a matter of life and death.'

For a second everyone in the room stopped and looked at her.

'Yeah, okay,' the secretary said, blushing because she was still that new. 'But he says he's your brother-in-law.'

Chastity only hesitated for a second before pulling up a new Lactated Ringers IV bag to hang. 'Really? I didn't know I had a brother-in-law.'

'And that your sister's missing?'

Another lurch nobody saw. 'As opposed to the last ten years she's been missing?'

Again there was a brief silence. But then, Chastity wasn't going to explain that, either. Especially when her heart was suddenly pounding and her hands had gone sweaty.

Balance. Harmony.

Shit.

Chastity made another grab for the bag in her pocket. Soft velvet wrapped around tumbled hard edges. Reassurance. Comfort.

'You have a sister?' Moshika asked, sounding a bit affronted.

Chastity didn't face her friend. 'I never said I didn't.'

'She seems to have found a husband.'

'I heard.'

'Well, he's lost her,' Kim reminded them all.

Chastity should have done more than recognize that omen. She should have run from it. Bought a plane ticket for parts unknown and blown this pop stand before anybody knew she was gone.

Before that brother-in-law chased her down.

She could feel whispery feet tiptoe right across her grave. She could feel her life lurch imperceptibly out of balance. And no more than hours after she'd acknowledged it had existed at all.

A brother-in-law.

She checked her pocket again, just to make sure. She usually didn't need to check it more than twice a week. This had been, what, four times in an hour? Not a good sign. Not good at all.

'I'll still call him back,' she said. 'Get his number.'

'This something you want to talk about?' Moshika asked quietly as she sidled over to where Chastity was crouched by the cart doing a final check on chest tube output.

Chastity looked up at St. M's best new surgical turk. Moshika had managed to get a lot of information out of Chastity since they'd been friends, but nothing this pertinent.

10

Chastity smiled. 'And give you the satisfaction of knowing that my family's more screwed up than yours? Thanks, no.'

Moshika chuckled. 'Honey, nobody's family's more screwed up than mine. We're listed in the *Guinness Book of World Records* for most screwed-up family in existence. There are even pictures.'

Chastity bet not. Chastity bet Moshika's family was just run-of-the-mill screwed up. Not operatically fucked like Chastity's.

But that wasn't something Chastity was going to think about right now. Right now she was going to do the same thing she'd done for the ten years since she'd last seen her sister Faith. She was going to pretend she was all alone in the world, so she'd be safe, and she was going to get on with her life. Which was why she smiled again and climbed back to her feet.

'It's time to take your boy down to CT,' she said and popped the brakes on the cart.

Moshika flashed a mighty scowl, but in the end she gave in to the inevitable. Grabbing hold of IV poles and monitor, she took her place on the team and helped maneuver Willie out the door for his run down to CT. Gathering the bulging evidence bags from the counter, Chastity headed in the opposite direction to meet with the police.

For the rest of the shift, she did her best to avoid Kim, the secretary. If Kim didn't find her, she couldn't hand off that damn phone number of the brother-in-law Chastity hadn't known she had. And if Chastity had no phone number, she couldn't call to have him tell her that her sister was missing and he wanted Chastity to help him find her.

Kim found her anyway. Right before end of shift, Kim ran Chastity down in the nurses' lounge and handed off that phone number like the nuclear codes. And Chastity, fool that she was, took it. She took it in front of witnesses, so that later there would be no way to deny culpability.

11

She walked out into a purpling dusk and thought that she had a few things to say to Moshika. Because maybe if Moshika hadn't mentioned that damned chaos theory, she wouldn't have recognized the moment her harmony slipped the tracks.

Willow Amber Tolliver had shown up at Jackson Square sometime between Mardi Gras and Easter. A thin, anxious young woman with stringy blond hair and a pierced eyebrow, she wore flowing skirts and a tank top that exposed the copper bracelet high up on her arm. Her wrists jingled with cheap beaded bracelets, and her backpack was stuffed with fantasy novels.

It took only a week or so for her to join the psychics and tarot card readers who controlled the Chartres Street side of the square. At first too shy to mingle, she simply staked out a corner with a battered little card table covered in an old purple scarf. On it she lay her oversized tarot cards, an assortment of crystals, and a candle she'd bought at the Wal-Mart in Biloxi, which was where she said she was from. With a hand-painted sign that said, 'Let Madame Nola see a better life for you,' she set up her own little corner of business.

Willow didn't have much of a gift, but she was earnest. She told her customers only the good things she thought she saw in their cards and crystals. She played with any baby who came by, and petted the dogs the other street kids brought around. She struck up a relationship with another of the tarot readers, an irascible seventy-year-old ex-Black Panther by the name of Tante Edie, who couldn't tolerate most people and made it a point to frighten the customers who displeased her.

But she liked Willow. They kept an eye on each other's tables, traded food and stories, and shared the late night when the cathedral church bells chimed into darkness and their candles flickered in the desultory breeze.

When Willow didn't show up for six days in a row, it

12

was Tante Edie who notified the police. She cornered one of the uniformed officers who regularly watched the square from the unit he pulled right up to the edge of Chartres and St. Ann.

'I ain't seen the girl for a good few days,' Tante Edie said, leaning in his car window. 'You see or hear anything?'

'Nah. You know where she lives?'

'Algiers Point, I think.'

It was where most of the homeless street hustlers huddled at night. Tante Edie preferred a real house, which she'd been squatting in over to Bywater way for the last year. The last week or so she'd been thinking of letting Willow share it with her, but she'd never gotten around to asking.

'Was she in a warehouse, do you know?' the policeman asked, jotting notes on the paper his muffaletta had come wrapped in. 'There was a fire in one the other night.'

Tante frowned. 'I don't know. Anybody killed?'

'Not that I heard.'

'Can you ask around?' she asked, because this was one of the cops who would help a street performer.

'Yeah, sure. Do you think Willow's her real name?'

Tante Edie could only shrug. Who knew in New Orleans?

The officer never did hear anything. The next day a new girl took over Willow's corner with a henna tattooing stand, and Tante Edie went back to sitting alone. Willow Amber Tolliver, it seemed, was meant to fade into the lore of the Quarter, just like most ghosts before her.

It was inevitable, really.

Once Chastity got that phone number in her hands, there was no way of holding off the rest. She tried, she really did. For four days she hid in her house, where she painted her bedroom neon yellow. She took Lilly out for walks in the park down the street. She worked extra shifts, and she tested her limits in the clubs on Washington Avenue, where she went to be pummeled by thumping rock 'n' roll and drink herself into a quiet stupor.

Finally, though, she gave up and called her brother-in-law.

'You were the last person I wanted to call,' he said, sounding thin and harried.

'Not the way to entice me down there, Mr. Stanton.'

'*Doctor* Stanton.'

'Ah. Doctor, then.'

'I'm just not sure Faith wants anything to do with you.'

'Well, I'm sure. She doesn't.'

'But I can't *find* her,' Dr. Stanton insisted. 'And I don't know where else to go.'

Chastity fought a shiver of prescience. 'Why me?'

'Because you're a forensic nurse.'

Another short pause for disquiet. 'How'd you know that?'

'Your mother. One of her friends from home sent her an article in the *St. Louis Post-Dispatch* about how you helped solve some big murder case. She showed it to me.'

'I see.'

'The article said that you knew people all over the country. Police and coroners and such. It said you found missing people.'

'Identify unidentified people. There's a difference.'

'Nobody will listen to me,' he said, as if not hearing. 'I was hoping you'd know somebody down here who'd listen to you.'

As a matter of fact, she did. She didn't tell him, though.

'What about my mother? Doesn't she know where Faith is?'

After all, it had been her mother who'd disappeared with Faith the first time. Who'd decided that Chastity had no right to know where either of them were. Well, evidently while Chastity had been tied to St. Louis like a sacrificial goat, the two of them had been in New Orleans enjoying gumbo and jazz.

14

How nice for them both.

Suddenly Chastity realized she was hearing a very awkward silence on the other end of the line. 'You didn't know,' Dr. Stanton was saying. 'Of course.'

Well, that sent her stomach sinking. 'No, I guess I didn't. What?'

'Um, your mother passed a few months ago.'

It was Chastity's turn for the uncomfortable silence. Tears. How ridiculous, after all this time. She looked down, to find her hand clenched around her drawstring bag. She fought the need for details, fought the urge to apologize, when it couldn't have been her fault. At least not this time. So she emptied the contents of the bag and spread them across the table she'd bought from a bankrupt Mexican restaurant.

'I have no desire to ever see New Orleans,' she said.

Her brother-in-law never said a word. Chastity could hear his need in the rasp of his breath, though. In the weight of the silence that stretched taut across the miles. She listened and she fingered her cache, the garnets and citrines and clear water aquamarines that tumbled across her table like pirate's treasure.

Her treasure. Amethysts and tourmalines and one small emerald the color of spring. The treasure she'd accrued from the late night shopping channels she watched when she couldn't sleep.

Glittery, colorful, solid.

Hers.

She kept staring at it all, touching it, watching it glitter in the kitchen lights, as if it could tell her something.

It told her something, all right. It told her she was an idiot if she thought she was going to avoid this.

'All right, Dr. Stanton,' she said, rolling a garnet beneath her fingers. 'I'll come help you look for my sister.'

Which was how, four days later, she found herself confronted with her third omen. The omen that finally frightened her beyond escape.

15

Lake Pontchartrain.

Chastity didn't really know what it was when she saw it. She only knew that as the plane circled New Orleans for a landing, she looked out her window and saw water.

Everywhere, nothing but water.

And only one, endless bridge.

Chastity hated water. She hated it worse than she hated late night phone calls. Worse than she hated the words 'It can't get worse, can it?' Worse than she hated her own history.

No, not hated.

Feared.

Chastity was paralyzed by water. She couldn't so much as take a bath. She couldn't sleep some nights because she woke to the sounds of lapping water and laughter, and it made her cry out into her empty bedroom. She couldn't bear to look at that much water in one place.

She did, though. She sat in that claustrophobic little seat looking down on an endless expanse of metallic, shifting water, and suddenly she knew for a fact that she'd made a mistake. She should never go to New Orleans, no matter what was at stake.

It was too late, though. She was already there.

16

Chapter Two

She didn't like him.

Chastity liked most people. She'd always made it a point to. But as she climbed out of the taxi to find her brother-in-law standing on the porch of a house the size of a midsized hotel, she decided that it was a good thing she hadn't been able to see him when he'd asked for her help.

'Chastity?' he asked, walking forward into the hot, sticky sunshine, a hesitant smile on his face. 'Is it you?'

Chastity accepted her overstuffed backpack from the taxi driver and wondered if she could ask her brother-in-law to wait a bit for an answer. She wondered if, maybe, she could just climb back into the cab and turn back for home.

'It sure is,' she said instead, angry at her brother-in-law for making her sound stupid.

Angry at him for being a square-jawed, well-groomed, middle-aged white man with thick, graying hair. Angry at him for things he certainly couldn't control. Like being a doctor. Like being unable to pick her up from the airport because of an emergency.

Like making her suffer this trip in the first place.

It hadn't been bad enough that she'd had to fly over Lake Pontchartrain with its flat, ominous sheen. On final descent, the plane had seemed to skim every bit of water in the state.

And not just rivers or lakes.

17

Swamps.

Miles and miles of swamps, glinting in stuttering flashes as the sun probed between bushes and trees to find the water lurking below. Water opaque with decay, thick with old secrets and sin. Water terrified her. Swamps damn near sent her into meltdown.

And then, to add insult to injury, when she landed, her brother-in-law hadn't been there to meet her. Instead he'd sent a dour Eastern European gentleman holding a lit cigarette and a sign that said CHARITY BURNS, who'd shoved her into a worn, fuggy sedan to be driven right past New Orleans and across a bridge that arced high over the Mississippi River.

They'd ended up here, in what had to be the only subdivision in New Orleans that looked exactly like the one in which Chastity had been raised in St. Louis. Except for the fact that it had evidently been created whole cloth out of the middle of another damn swamp. And Chastity had paid thirty dollars to get here.

Which was why Chastity knew she had to try and overlook the fact that she didn't like her brother-in-law for reasons he couldn't control, and stay long enough to get her sister found.

Slinging her backpack and purse over her shoulder, she resettled her laptop and stepped up on the sidewalk. She even smiled for the man who'd talked her into coming down into a hot, steamy New Orleans summer when she'd been so in harmony back in the hot, thick St. Louis one.

'Here,' he said, reaching her halfway down his lawn, 'let me get that. Don't you have any other luggage?'

Chastity wasn't sure why, but she hadn't expected his accent. Soft, courteous, with just a hint of New Orleans and a bit of the Deep South. If he hadn't been a surgeon, he could have made a great butler.

He sure had the house for it. A jumble of rooflines, as if one wasn't interesting enough, and at least five architectural styles, all crouched over a tiny, pedestrian porch with pillars. It even had a lawn landscaped within an inch of its life by somebody who thought that all plants should come in threes.

Three. Chastity seriously wanted to rip out at least one of each and see if the whole yard tilted on its axis.

Instead, she let the good doctor take hold of her two-pound laptop instead of the forty-pound backpack and smiled as if she meant it. 'Thank you, Dr. Stanton. That'd be fine.'

She saw the taxi heading back through the gate to this walled-in compound and thought fleetingly of missed escapes.

A gated community. In New Orleans. Chastity wondered how in hell Faith had managed to find it. Then she wondered why, but only briefly. She knew why. Just as she knew why Faith had married her successful, gray-haired surgeon.

The question, of course, would be why she'd left him again.

'Come on in out of this heat,' Dr. Stanton urged as he turned for the front door. 'I can't tell you how much I appreciate your coming down all this way. Especially since the first thing I did was miss your flight because of surgery.'

Chastity caught the self-deprecating smile he flashed as he held the door open, and found herself surprised. Endearing, she thought. He looked endearing. She didn't know many surgeons who could manage it. She didn't know many who'd waste their time on it. She almost said something to that effect.

She never got the chance. She'd just stepped into the arctic chill of Dr. Stanton's house, when everything went wrong.

Chastity shuddered to a stop. Suddenly she couldn't breathe. She damn near backed out of that fancy doorway and ran straight for the swamps.

That smell. She'd recognize that smell in hell.

19

Bleach and lavender. It had the power to bring her right to her knees. How stupid was that?

Then she saw what was past the entryway and almost brought up her lunch.

'Chastity?'

But Chastity couldn't pull a single coherent thought out of her suddenly paralyzed brain.

From the smell of bleach and lavender, for God's sake.

That and the living room. The living room that looked exactly like the one she'd never been allowed into as a child. Pristine white couches and gleaming cherrywood tables, squared to the walls like soldiers at attention, never to be touched or relaxed upon or comforted by.

'Chastity, my dear, is something wrong?'

Chastity felt a hand on her arm and almost bolted like a startled horse. She sucked in a breath, trembling. She was a trauma nurse. She was trained for shock and disaster. She could control herself long enough to get safely out the door. She shoved her hand into her jeans pocket and only then realized that her drawstring bag was in her purse.

Oh, this was starting out well. If she ever made it as far as the bedrooms in this house, she'd probably have seizures.

'My,' she managed with a wry smile as she stepped carefully away, 'I didn't realize Faith liked our old house so much. This looks ... amazingly like it.'

Dr. Stanton looked around the arid splendor of his home as if seeing it for the first time. 'Really? I didn't know.'

Chastity was still staring at the crystal lamps and precisely arrayed silk flower arrangements. The uninspired Italian landscapes and curio cabinet that held the very ceramic flowers her mother had protected all through Chastity's childhood like sacred relics.

'Mother didn't tell you?' she asked, feeling every ghost of her twenty-six years whispering in her ear.

Dr. Stanton shook his head. 'No. I guess she didn't. You don't seem very comfortable, Chastity.'

20

Chastity almost told him exactly how uncomfortable she was. But that wouldn't be fair. It seemed that Dr. Stanton had never been filled in on the particulars. And Chastity wasn't at all sure she was up to correcting the oversight.

At least not among those plastic-covered brocade cushions.

'Call me Chaz,' she suggested with a strained smile. 'Chastity is only for when my mother was mad at me.'

Chastity Ann, actually, spoken with that die-away air, as if Chastity were sucking the life out of her mother like a vampire.

Again, Chastity was surprised by the threat of tears. Her mother was dead, and Chastity had lost her last chance to make amends. Yet another sin dropped into her box of atonement.

'I'll tell you what,' Dr. Stanton said, sounding anxious. 'How 'bout getting settled in? I can show you your room.'

In this house? Not likely. Just the thought made Chastity break out in a fresh sweat.

No, she had a better idea. She had a contact in town who had offered not only technical support, but room, board, and transportation. Chastity had held off accepting until she knew just what her situation here would be. It looked like she didn't have to wait any longer.

But that was for later. Right now, Chastity had to get some information. And she wasn't going to get it standing in this nightmare of a hallway.

She sucked in another breath. 'Uh, what's the kitchen like?'

Dr. Stanton brightened considerably. 'Why don't we go look? I have some sweetened tea you might like.'

And then he was leading the way past all that suffocating white carpet to the hardwood hallway beyond. The familiar layout had a central hall with living room and dining room to the right and closed den and an overwrought oak staircase to the left. Chastity marched by them as if she saw neither.

21

The kitchen and family room were spread across the back of the house with the master suite opening up beyond. Fortunately, the doors to the master suite were closed, and the kitchen was a high-tech wonder that bore absolutely no resemblance to the Byrnes childhood shrine. Chastity took the first good breath she'd managed since stepping through that front door.

The kitchen looked like something out of *Bon Appetit*, all gleaming metal, gray granite, and glass cabinets. Plopping her bag onto the center island, she settled herself on a chrome and leather stool.

'You the chef, Dr. Stanton?'

'Max,' he insisted as he opened the steel refrigerator. 'You must call me Max. We're family, after all.'

Well, if Chastity had had any question about that before now, one look at that living room would have settled it.

'Max,' she amended with a slight nod.

'And no,' he answered with a smile, pulling out a frosted glass pitcher. 'Faith is a wonderful chef. It's one of the ways she wooed me.'

Chastity had trouble pairing the words *Faith* and *woo*, or even *Faith* and *chef*. But then, Faith had always been an enigma. A codebook Chastity had never cracked. Who knew what secrets she might have unleashed once she'd broken free of that house?

That house she'd gone to such trouble to re-create.

There was so much Chastity wanted to know. Stupid, little things Max Stanton wouldn't understand. Painful things that wouldn't make Chastity sleep any better, but might help provide imperfect plugs to stop up the gaping holes in her own life.

'How long did you say you two have been married?' she asked.

'Six years. We met at a charity function, and I just wanted her to be mine. You understand.'

No, but he didn't want to hear that. He was wearing that wistful, fretful look that betrayed the hours he'd spent alone in this house waiting for his wife to come home.

'You said that Faith is your second wife.'

He pulled glasses from the cabinet and then rearranged the rest. 'Why, yes. She helped me raise my two boys.'

'You had custody?'

'My wife died.'

'I'm sorry. You've never had children with Faith?'

His smile was easy as he set everything on the island. 'I'd long since had a vasectomy. My boys were enough for us.'

Chastity had seen those boys displayed in tasteful frames on the baby grand piano by the front window. Handsome, toothy kids with All-American smiles and thick hair.

'They're at university,' he continued. 'Brand at Texas Christian and Louis at Stanford. I told them to stay where they were. They couldn't do anything but fret here, anyway.'

Chastity nodded. If worse came to worst, she could always get the boys on the phone. 'And Faith has been gone how long?'

He paused, the pitcher poised over tall frosted glasses. 'Two weeks. I'm frantic.'

Not frantic enough to muss his hair. Chastity accepted her glass with a smile and sipped her tea. She guessed it wasn't time to tell him that she didn't drink it sweetened.

'You said you'd talked to the police,' she said.

'Yes. But they don't seem to take this seriously. They say that people go missing here all the time. They say that people *come* to New Orleans to go missing.'

Chastity thought that was just what had happened. 'You're sure they're wrong?' she asked in her best nurse voice. 'Could Faith, maybe, have just wanted some time off? A sabbatical?'

He leaned against the gray granite counter, his handsome brow furrowed, his surgeon's hand clasped around his sweating glass. 'You said that before. On the phone. Why would you ask?'

Because in their time, each of the Byrnes girls had run away. Chastity just figured it was Faith's turn.

'You said my mother died recently, didn't you?'

He looked even more uncomfortable than Chastity felt. 'Yes, she did. She'd been ill for quite a while. This last year she'd been at Holy Cross Resthouse, a wonderful facility.'

She should ask where that was, Chastity thought. Go talk to those people who had cared for her mother last.

She didn't. She wouldn't. She could only do so much, after all, and her bowl was full. Hell, her tub was full.

'I told Faith to let you know,' he said. 'But she refused. She said . . . she, well . . .'

'It's okay. I'm sure I know perfectly well what she said.'

'But why?' he demanded. 'I've never understood.'

For a very long moment, Chastity just sat there. Just waited for the instinctive panic and shame to pass. She sipped at the treacle in her tea glass and wondered what Faith had ever told this man about her family, and what Chastity should fill in.

'I'm the black sheep,' she finally said, not ready yet for the harder truths. 'The troublemaker.' She gave him a bright grin, hoping it didn't look like a rictus. 'Everybody has her place in a family. That's mine.'

'What about your other sister, Hope.' His words were hushed. 'The one who died.'

For a moment, Chastity could do no more than stare, sick and stunned. Well, at least she wouldn't have to fill in every sin she'd committed. Faith had obviously gotten a start on it.

Hope had been the best of them. But Chastity didn't know this man well enough to share her sister with him. So she sipped her tea and ignored the look of naked curiosity in his eyes.

'The point I was trying to make,' she finally said, 'is that Faith and my mother were very close. It's not uncommon for that kind of loss to send someone like Faith off for a few days.'

It was even more likely for Faith, who had always protected their mother instead of the other way around. Who had forgiven her, rationalized for her, paved her way to guiltlessness. If there was nothing to protect anymore, then the need to remain and fight might have died as well.

But then, Chastity didn't know how Faith had negotiated the last ten years. She only knew how *she* had, and it had been tough enough.

'Did Faith take anything with her?' Chastity asked, just as she'd asked on the phone. Repetition aided memory. Clarified mistakes, exposed lies. 'Clothing, jewelry?'

'No,' he said, his voice tight again, just like on the phone. 'Nothing.'

'How about credit cards? Debit cards, ATMs. Cell phone.'

He shook his head. 'I even showed the statements to the police, just as you said I should. She hasn't used them.'

Not a good sign, any of it. Chastity knew he realized it. He didn't need to hear it again.

'How about medicine? Any prescriptions she needed refilled?'

He shook his head. 'No. She's healthy as a horse.'

'Her car?'

'She was in between cars. We were looking for a new one.'

'And you've talked to her friends?'

'Yes. They all seem surprised.'

Chastity nodded. 'You said that the missing persons report wasn't filed from here.'

'Well, I did make it here. But the policeman who spoke to me said that they had to file it where she was last seen.'

'And that was where?'

'The Eighth District, up in the French Quarter. She went to Friday lunch at Gallatoire's. Just like always.'

'And who drove her?'

'I did. She was going to take a cab home.' He seemed to think about that for a minute. 'A cab.'

'And how long before you realized she wasn't home?'

'Well, the next morning. We had several emergencies that night, and I couldn't break free. I left messages, thinking she was just . . . I don't know. With friends.'

'You're a cardiothoracic surgeon?'

'At Tulane.'

Chastity nodded. 'I'll need to talk to her friends, Max. Check out her hobbies and schedules. And I'll need to go through her things. Is that all right?'

No. Not for either of them. Chastity didn't want to look, and he didn't want to let her. But he nodded anyway and then smiled. 'I knew you'd know what to do.'

'No, Max,' she said. 'I really don't. This isn't at all what I do at work. I collect evidence and notify families. I'm not a detective.'

Well, she did more than that. But she just didn't want him to see her as a panacea. Faith might not come home, no matter what Chastity did. And Chastity would never force her.

'But you know more than I do,' he said. 'I can't thank you enough. I know it must have been hard to get off from your job.'

'I had a bit of vacation saved up.'

About four years' worth. She *liked* working.

'As for Faith's personal . . . things,' he said, 'they're in her little office, right off the master suite.'

Another place Chastity was sure she didn't want to see.

'And except for my mother's death,' she said, 'nothing unusual happened recently?'

Another shake of the head. Another pursed, bemused frown.

'She hasn't seemed different to you?' Chastity asked. 'More unhappy? Frightened, maybe?'

'She's been sad, of course. She and your mother . . .'

'Yes, I know. And I know this is difficult, Max, but was everything okay between the two of you?'

'Yes.' He looked sincerely surprised. Truly befuddled.

26

'Never better. It was a second honeymoon, with the boys grown. You know?'

This time Chastity just nodded and pretended.

'What has Faith told you about herself?' she asked. 'Before you met, I mean?'

A real conversation stopper, that. The good doctor stared at her as if she were speaking in tongues.

'What do you mean?'

'I'm wondering if something came back to haunt her.'

Chastity was certain something had come back to haunt Faith. She was just hoping something *else* had come back to haunt her.

'Wouldn't you know?' he asked.

'Not for the last ten years. Until you called, I had no idea where Faith and my mother were.'

Another slow shake of his head. 'Faith was an event organizer,' he said. 'She helped plan the charity event where we met. She's so perfect at it, you know. But the last few years she's been devoted to the boys, to me, to your mother.' He seemed to fold a little. 'She's so lovely. Organized. Charitable. She has friends in the neighborhood, and through the hospital auxiliary and the Arlen Clinic, and the boys' school, of course. I've never known her to say an unkind word about anybody . . .'

'But me.'

'Not unkind. She just wouldn't talk about you.'

'That's too bad. It might have helped find her.'

If she wanted to be found. Chastity didn't know. With no activity on Faith's credit cards or cell phone, though, she wasn't as sure anymore that Faith had gone of her own free will.

Chastity was now standing in the kitchen, marveling at the gleam of it and trying to decide where to go first, when the doctor's beeper chirped. Unclipping it, he checked it and frowned.

'Excuse me . . .'

'Duty calls?'

27

He flashed her a rueful smile. 'I've been waiting to hear on a patient in with an angiogram. Will you be all right if I go?'

'You're heading up to the city?' At his nod, Chastity set down her tea. 'Would you drop me off so I can hire a cab?'

'You could use either of my cars.'

This time the rueful grin was hers. 'No, I can't. I'm short a driver's license for a few weeks. And you can't be at my beck and call while I run around town. I have a lot of people I'll need to talk to. A cab'll be fine.'

'They're expensive.'

'My trust fund is full.'

Evidently Dr. Stanton hadn't expected that.

'I'm not sure if Faith knew,' Chastity explained. 'Our grandmother Dexter left me survival money.' Because the old woman had been the one to find Chastity on the street. Because she'd offered her a safe place to stay. Because she'd finally felt guilty that it had come to that. 'I'm not broke.'

For a moment, Dr. Stanton held her gaze. 'How old were you?'

'When all hell broke loose? Sixteen. Why?'

He just shook his head and cleaned out his glass.

Ten minutes later Chastity was sitting in the buttery soft seat of his BMW heading back through that electric gate toward the swamps and the bridge that arced high over the river.

Dr. Stanton went out of his way to drop Chastity off at a taxi stand in the French Quarter. Not that anyplace else in the city wouldn't have attracted taxis, but Chastity gently guided him to the stand in front of the Royal Orleans on St. Louis, where she thought a certain cabby might be waiting.

Max never asked why Chastity felt compelled to drag along her overstuffed backpack and laptop, and Chastity had no intention of telling him. At least not until she'd contracted with her ride and contacted her friend for a place to stay. She waved Max off with no small amount of relief, and turned to consider her next move.

For a moment, away from that awful house and that terrible water, Chastity wasted that moment just to take in her surroundings.

The French Quarter certainly didn't disappoint. Bustling, boiling, the narrow, cobbled streets churned with life. Cars and bikes jostled with horse-drawn carriages. Pedestrians ranged from suited businesspeople and tattooed shopkeepers to tourists draped in bright beads and carrying to-go cups at five in the afternoon.

The buildings were pink and blue and green, and looked as if they were spun from marzipan and iced with grillwork balconies. Marble-fronted hotels dripped flags and geraniums. Tinny music echoed from some storefront, and overfull trash bags blocked the sidewalk. Chastity could smell fresh bread and raw fish and rotting vegetables, and tasted the slow, seething energy of the place on her tongue.

She found herself wanting to wander off down one of those tight, cluttered little side streets and find out what life was like there. She wanted to hum and sway in her jeans and pretend that life wasn't waiting outside this odd fairyland.

Maybe when she was finished with Faith . . .

She deliberately turned away. She had a cabbie to find.

There were about six cabs in a row along the street in front of the hotel. Most were a bit battered, all were well used. The cabbies mostly waited outside, watching the street scene and exchanging news over cigarettes. Chastity walked past a rasta man who reeked of ganja, two hard bleached blondes who disagreed about the proper placement of a Harley tattoo, and a hefty black woman who coughed with a suspiciously tubercular rasp.

Finally, though, she saw who she'd been looking for. He was a white guy, maybe in his thirties. Tall and lean, with choppy black hair, light eyes, and a quiltwork of old burn scars that ate up most of his neck, left cheek, and left arm. His left hand was a claw, wrapped in a permanent burn brace. His mouth drew south on that side just a bit. He was leaning against his rig as if he had nothing better to do, sucking on a Camel and watching the pretty girls go by over the tops of his dime-store sunglasses.

She shouldn't be doing this. One look at him was all Chastity needed to know. Even with an endorsement, this guy was more than Chastity thought she could handle. Darker, harder, and too good-looking, even with the scars. If she had any sense, she'd hire somebody else.

But then Chastity caught sight of the sticker on the back window of his cab. IAFF. International Association of Fire Fighters. If she couldn't trust a firefighter, who could she trust?

'What's the going rate?' she asked, letting her backpack slide to the sidewalk.

He didn't perk right up. Simply turned her way, still leaning there in his cotton shirt and battered jeans and thousand-year-old eyes.

'Where you goin'?'

Chastity shrugged, doing her best to ignore a fresh set of shivers and an increased heart rate. Damn, she really should just walk away. She knew better. She really did.

It never mattered.

So she sucked in a breath and did her best to ignore the fireworks that were going off inside. 'Everywhere. I need somebody to be my chauffeur the next week or so while I go around town searching for my sister.'

'Hire a real chauffeur.'

'I want somebody who understands the town, speaks English, and doesn't stand out. You understand the town?'

'Sure. I was born here.'

'You do your fire duty here?'

That brought a big, shit-eatin' grin to his face. 'Firemen ain't the only people get burned, baby.'

'Bet they're the only ones who keep an IAFF local sticker in the back window of their hack. You know what union I belong to?'

Another grin. 'You gotta be a nurse.'

She grinned right back, a coconspirator, even if he'd never worked her neck of the woods. Nobody got along better than trauma nurses and firemen. Nobody respected or relied on each other more. Chastity would have had to be deaf, dumb, and blind not to see the street on him.

Besides, she'd been led here like Balthazar to Bethlehem.

'Trauma,' she acknowledged. 'Know any multisyllabic words? Read books? Editorials?'

'What? You auditioning me?'

'I gotta spend a lot of time in a car with you, fireman. I want to know I can survive it.'

He crossed his arms over his chest, just like a kid staring down a challenge. 'How's German expressionism? Chauvinism? Nihilism? Contrarianism?'

'That your personal philosophy?'

'Ever since my last day on the job.'

'And you wouldn't mind driving me around to the police and the coroner's, places like that?'

'I don't have any outstanding warrants, if that's what you mean. And if you know where you're going, why ask me?'

'I'm temporarily short of a driver's license.'

His intact eyebrow lifted. 'Speeding or alcohol?'

She grimaced. 'The speeding ticket set me up. The parking tickets put me away.'

His grin was a little lopsided. 'You say your sister's lost?'

'I don't know. She might know right where she is. But her husband doesn't, and he's worried. Asked me to try and find her. And since the missing person report was filed in the Eighth District, which I'm told this is, I thought I'd start here.'

'I gotta get off the meter.'

'Like I said. What's the cost?'

'What you offering?'

'Money,' she said. 'Only money.'

His chuckle was a lot easier than it would have been if

31

he'd known what was going on inside her pants. But Chastity needed this fireman. She trusted firemen, even if they weren't working the rigs anymore. At least he wouldn't get all hinky about how she was going to handle things. And, she thought, doing her best to ignore her body's hijinks, if absolutely necessary, she thought she could trust him with her secrets.

Then he opened the back door with a flourish worthy of a Ritz doorman, and she was hooked.

'Climb in, baby. We goin' on a ride.'

Chastity slung her stuff into the backseat and scooted in, careful not to show how grateful she was. 'I also need a place to crash.'

'The brother-in-law isn't putting you up?'

'He would. I won't.'

Her fireman just nodded. 'What you have in mind?'

'Well, I hear my friend Kareena Boudreaux has a place nearby.'

The fireman forgot to close the door. For a long second, he just stared at her, his scowl even fiercer when edged with the scar tissue that ate up the side of his face. 'You been lookin' for me all along?'

Chastity smiled. 'Kareena said she might have a cousin who drove cabs. Said he might have been a firefighter, so I could trust him.'

Still he just stood there. Chastity felt the pull of pheromones, and thought that this was the last chance to get out of that cab before she got herself into trouble. Bigger trouble than looking for her sister. The kind of trouble she'd sworn off five long years ago.

Still, he didn't smell like lavender or bleach. He didn't have gray hair. And he was a fireman.

Chastity sucked in a big breath to calm her maidenly flutters. 'Please,' she said. 'Kareena said I could trust you.'

His scowl darkened, but only for a moment. Then, abruptly, he nodded. 'As long as she's not doing *me* any favors.'

Finally Chastity laughed. 'Trust me, fireman. I'm no favor.'

Which seemed enough. He slammed the door shut and climbed in the front. Chastity let go a sigh of relief. She knew better than to think that things were better. At least they seemed more manageable. They had to be. She couldn't survive what was coming otherwise.

Opening her purse, Chastity took hold of her velvet drawstring bag. No question. She was about to take a hell of a ride.

Chapter Three

'Where you want to start?' the cabbie asked, glancing into the rearview mirror.

Chastity took another look out the taxi window to see an elderly lady in pearls and biker shorts walking a black cat on a leash. She heard that faint, tinny music again, like something you could barely remember. She saw the clouds piling up toward the river and knew they were in for rain. She smelled another whiff of decay, as if it had followed her into the cab to remind her that secrets lay hidden on perfectly dry land.

'I don't suppose we could start with a three-hour session at a local bar listening to great jazz and getting completely tanked?'

He grinned into the rearview mirror. 'Of course we can. It's usually where I start when I have to go looking for *my* family.'

'They get lost often?'

'Not nearly often enough.'

'Well, what do they call you when you do find them, fireman?'

She got a pretty decent lopsided grin off that one. 'I don't think I'm up to having you call me that,' he demurred. 'The name's James. James Guidry.'

She leaned forward, reached out a hand. 'A pleasure, James. Chastity Byrnes.'

She was met by a profound silence.

'Yes,' Chastity allowed without moving. 'You may entertain any objectionable reactions you want. Just don't share them with me.'

'B-U-R-N-S?'

'My only saving grace. B-Y-R-N-E-S.'

'Thank God.'

'And I prefer to be called Chaz,' she said. 'It lessens the incidence of having my failure to live up to a perfectly good name rubbed in my face.'

'Okay.'

He reached over the seat with his left hand. A bit of a challenge in itself, Chastity knew. She clasped that terrible, rubbery raw claw and shook.

Then, leaning back, she took stock of the cab. Clean, tidy, and free of all the knickknacks that tended to accumulate in a cab. Except for a small framed picture hanging over the backseat. A kind of charcoal sketch of the Marine Corps symbol.

'You a marine?' she asked.

'Nah. A friend.'

Must have been a good friend, she thought.

'So,' he said, starting the engine. 'Is it a bar you want? A little early for the good jazz.'

'Well, James,' she said, 'much as I'd really like to, I need to get settled, I need to contact those police to find out they don't know anything more than they did before, and then I have to figure out what the hell I have to do next.'

'They didn't make you a trauma nurse cause they liked the color of your hair, baby.'

'Yeah, well, James, they made me a trauma nurse. Not a missing persons detective.'

'We'll figure it out. Where first?'

Chastity considered the fact that her brother-in-law was probably elbow deep in somebody's thoracic cavity right about then, and that she was going to try and do her passive-aggressive best to avoid staying with him. She

thought of what she needed from that house, and how she
didn't want him to see her rifle through it.

'I guess the first thing I need is a picture of my sister.'

'You don't have one?'

'Nope. Not since she was twenty.'

'How old is she now?'

'Way past twenty.'

Chastity knew she'd picked the right cabbie when James
merely nodded and put the car into gear. 'Seems reason-
able. Where is it we're looking for your sister's picture?'

'At her house. The River Run development south of the
river.'

'West of the river, actually. East, south, north don't do
you no good in this city. It's lakeside, riverside, uptown,
downtown. Other side of the river's considered west.'

'Well, then, it's a good thing I have a cabbie who knows
that stuff, huh?'

'I guess it is. You said River Run?'

'Yeah. I have a key and all the security codes.'

His laugh was wry. 'Interesting place.'

'I'd rather go to hell,' she retorted more hotly than she'd
intended. 'It's in the middle of a damn swamp. Did you
know that?'

'Sure. You know why they have walls?'

'Because they're exclusionary and generally terrified of
the rest of the populace of the area?'

'Because they need to protect themselves from the wild
pigs that have the run of that area.'

'Pigs?'

'Killed a guy a couple months ago.'

Chastity actually smiled. 'Ah. Allegory. My favorite
literary device.'

James chuckled. 'You *are* going to be fun.'

'Not if I find my sister I won't.'

She was going to have to find her sister. Then, for the
first time in ten years, she was going to have to talk to her.

Ten years.

Ten years of silence and rage and betrayal. Ten years of Chastity being the bad guy and Faith being the victim. Ten years when the people Chastity had loved the most had disappeared from her life as if she'd never existed.

Well, she existed. And she was going to have to face her sister.

But first, Chastity had to find her.

He waited in the shadows. There weren't many. The sun was high, and humidity gathered like a shroud over the land. But in a swamp, there were always places to hide. Places to watch. He was sweating hard from the exertion, and breathless with anticipation. He'd worked hard today, and it was about to pay off.

Across the water a young gator sunned himself on a log. The moss hung limp and thick from the trees, and the air hummed with insects and heat. A pair of raccoons edged closer to the water. There was a tour group coming down the bayou on a covered flatboat, and the raccoons knew they'd get fed marshmallows so the tourists could snap their pictures.

He was in the perfect place to see, tucked in behind the elephant ears that grew to the size of a man. Far enough upwind that the wildlife didn't notice. He'd planned this down to the last detail, after all.

Not twenty feet away, a cypress stuck its thick knees out of the water, catching any debris that floated past. A plastic soda bottle bobbed in the water where some crawdadder had left his line. And there, not fifteen feet away, rose the homemade white wooden cross some family had left tucked in at the edge of the water to remember where their child had died in the swamp. Either that or the tour guides had stuck it there for a good story.

He watched that white cross. He waited in the shadows, crouched in the thick foliage, for the tour boat to reach it.

They had to find it.

If they didn't, all his hard work would be for nothing.

37

He watched that cross and the bloated white thing that floated just next to it, swaying a bit in the sluggish current as if waving to get the attention of that boat that crept up the bayou.

He held his breath.

'And here,' the guide called, 'this where poor ole Jean Claude Robicheaux, he had the unfortunate experience to mix his alcohol and a visit with a gator—'

'What's that? By the cross in the river.'

'Oh, it nothin' . . . oh, my God. That's a body!'

Tucked back in the foliage, he smiled. It was time to go.

'She looks just like you,' James said.

Chastity lifted the framed picture from the back of the piano and shrugged. 'All of us looked alike.'

Nobody had had Faith's eyes, though. Not the color – all of them had those creepy pale blue eyes, like they were blind or psychic or something – but the intensity. That bright hard light of certainty. It was what Chastity remembered most about her oldest sister. It was what had finally split the family apart.

Chastity looked for that intensity in this slick studio shot of a woman she didn't know anymore, and wasn't sure if she saw it. Faith was smiling just beyond the camera, all teeth and high chin and perfect posture in her doctor's wife attire.

Pearls. She was wearing pearls, just like June Cleaver, just like that tiny, wrinkled woman in the Quarter with her cat. Faith's hair, a shade darker than Chastity's, was coiffed into an elegant chignon. No Peter Pan locks for Faith. No bright wide grin, like Hope once flashed. No impudence or whimsy or rebellion, which had been Chastity's specialty.

Once Chastity might have known how to find her sister. But looking at that stiff, formal matron in her hands, she just wasn't sure anymore.

And she still had to go through Faith's closets.

'Tell you what,' she said, turning from the carefully arranged family of men on the piano. 'I think I should settle in tonight. Talk to the cops in the morning and maybe come back then.'

James shrugged. 'Your dime.'

Chastity looked back toward where the master suite lay, and all but shuddered. She didn't think she could bear to find out tonight what her sister might have re-created back there. She didn't really want her sister's secrets after all. So she tucked the photo under her arm, wrote Max a note on a drug company notepad, and skated out of that house like a fleeing felon.

God, she wished she were home. She wished she were in her trauma lane where she knew what to do. Where everything was clear and explainable and quantitatively measured. Chastity was great at bodily trauma. She just sucked at life lessons.

And yet, she'd walked right into one. Hell, she'd walked into the big one. And she couldn't see any way to get out anytime soon.

Back they went over that damn bridge, which sucked the air right out of Chastity's lungs. She knew the Mississippi. She had the Mississippi where she lived, and every once in a while she actually crossed it. But she didn't have to cross it the way it was here, a sprawling swath of water that seemed to take up all the earth. If she ever came back to New Orleans, she'd never cross that bridge again. But first she'd have to cross Lake Pontchartrain to leave.

She'd been doing so well in her life, Chastity kept thinking. She'd been productive and content and contained, like a controlled nuclear reaction. She hadn't been perfect. Who the hell was? But it had been a long time since she'd been forced to rub her face in every failing she possessed. Every tic and tremor and memory that could sneak up so fast you found yourself belted into a hot red car trying to outdistance them.

She wanted to go home. She wanted to run away before

39

she had to find out just why Faith had run away.

Even though she knew.

She knew, and she knew even more that Faith would need her at the end of the run, if only to be held by somebody else who understood. To be reminded that she was strong enough to survive. To remember that she wasn't alone after all. Even if Chastity was the very last person on earth she'd ever wanted to hear that from.

'So, where you from?' James asked as they swept back off the highway into cluttered housing and uneven streets.

Chastity looked out the window and smiled at the whimsical makeup of the neighborhood. It looked as if somebody had shaken up a box of houses and stores and churches and tumbled them out over the wide, tree-lined streets. All a bit worn-looking, listing a little, giving ground to the huge live oaks and ubiquitous magnolias that ate the sidewalks and shaded the streets.

'St. Louis,' she said.

'Ah, New Orleans lite.'

'I'll let you know.'

'You've never been here before?'

'I've never been out of St. Louis before.'

She got quite a look in that mirror. 'You're kidding. Not even to Chicago? Everybody from St. Louis goes to Chicago.'

'Everybody but me.'

He shook his head. 'You're missing a great city.'

'Well, now that I've made that big break from home, maybe I'll try that next.'

But then, Chicago sat on another lake. A lake even bigger than Pontchartrain. Maybe she'd try Wichita first.

'I'd be happy to give you recommendations.'

Chicago. Oh, yeah. 'You obviously like it.'

'Did my fire time there. Ten years.'

'You kidding? You're from a place like this, and you go to Chicago to be a firefighter?'

'I'd go anywhere but here when I was young. If you

40

don't get away from New Orleans right away, you just never manage to escape.'

'Didn't take, huh?'

'Obviously not.'

Chastity nodded. 'St. Louis is the same way. I'm obviously the one who never made it out.'

'Still time.'

Chastity laughed, thinking about what kind of a mess her insides were in after only a few hours in a new place. 'I doubt it. Where are we in the city?'

'St. Charles Avenue near the Garden District. Kareena lives off Magazine.'

'Which doesn't mean anything to me.'

'You might want to get a map.'

'I have a cabbie.'

'How do you know her?'

Chastity looked up. 'Kareena? We're both forensic nurses. She's offered to help me with the officials down here.'

James shook his head. 'I think I've been had.'

Chastity smiled. 'I know you have.'

They wove through a few side streets thick with antebellum homes and wrought-iron fences to reach the more mercantile Magazine Street, another of those artistically clogged arteries that seemed to make up most of the city. A couple of blocks on that and James turned again into a neighborhood Chastity would have recognized in her sleep.

In St. Louis, they called the area Dogtown. A blue-collar neighborhood once made up of Irish immigrants, it still boasted a disproportionate number of city cops and about 60 percent of its hockey fans. Unpretty, unpretentious, uninterested in anything that didn't involve sports, work, family, or church, in that order.

This neighborhood looked much the same, just more brightly painted and less affluent. The paint was chipped, the school yards a bit unkempt, and the streets sported more Bible Baptist storefronts than Catholic churches.

41

James pulled to a stop in front of a worn, two-story white wooden house with sky blue balconies and bright pink crepe myrtle trees that almost brushed the ground. Chastity gathered her stuff together, already feeling a bit better. Leave it to Kareena Boudreaux to live someplace Chastity would feel at home.

'Welcome to the Irish Channel,' James announced like a tour guide as he held the cab door open. 'I imagine you can figure who settled here. It's currently in the process of coming back from ghettoland. My cousin is an urban pioneer, as we like to say.'

Chastity climbed out onto a street where the sidewalks buckled and insects hummed. Hefting her bag, she turned toward the house.

Then, just barely, she brushed up against James.

An accident, no more.

For a long second, though, all thought fled and her palms went damp again. She came to a dead stop there on the cracked pavement. But not because she was afraid.

Five years of celibacy and her body didn't seem to notice in the least. She was lighting up like a prom queen at a football game. Chastity shook her head, disgusted. She swore she could smell pheromones on a dead man.

And no matter what her heart and her sweat glands were doing, she'd swear on her mother's grave that that was all there was to it. Hormones and proximity. Any more would be more than she could handle. Ever.

'Fireman,' she said, not looking at him, 'do me a favor. If you want to stay safe around me, try not to stand so close.'

He did everything but say 'Huh?'

She laughed. 'I have this little problem, and you really don't want to be part of it.'

'Meaning?'

But she made the mistake of making eye contact. He had great eyes, sleepy and sinful and sad. And that had the capacity to unnerve her in ways she couldn't explain.

42

So she shook her head. 'Never mind.'

Chastity knew he wouldn't understand, but there was nothing she could do. So she left him standing there gaping on the sidewalk as she turned for Kareena's house. She'd only taken two steps when the front door slammed open and a small whirlwind swept out.

Chastity could have been forgiven for first mistaking the woman for a child. She bounded down the stairs like Tigger, her thick umber hair flying, her bright brown eyes wide. Then she opened her mouth, and the illusion disappeared.

'James, you handsome son of a bitch,' she called in the husky voice of a siren. 'What you make my friend stand out on the lawn in this heat for? Get on up on this porch, y'hear?'

James had a great glare on him. 'You could have told me.'

Kareena stopped, hands on hips. 'You woulda said no.'

'Yes, I would have.'

Chastity let her bag drag on the cracked, uneven sidewalk. 'If it's an imposition . . .'

'It's not,' they both said at the same time without looking away from each other.

'He thinks I'm doin' him a favor,' Kareena said.

'He's doing *me* a favor,' Chastity insisted.

Kareena smiled like sunlight. 'Exactly. Now get up here.'

And finally, Chastity smiled. 'How are you, Kareena?'

Healthy as a horse, if the rib-snapping hug she dispensed was any indication. Kareena was only as tall as Chastity and as dark as Chastity was fair. She had big, liquid brown eyes and silky brown hair and the kind of energy Chastity only pretended to have on her better days. One look told Chastity just where James had come by his handsome dark looks. Kareena obviously represented the Cajun side of the family.

'Me?' Kareena asked with a twinkle. 'Happy to see you,

43

girl. Even if it is to go sister-huntin'. Aren't you lucky you happen to know the finest forensic nurse in the South? Charity Hospital's never had it so good. And guess what my specialty is, yeah?'

'Dare I hope it's missing persons?'

Kareena flashed a shit-eating grin. 'Your sister anywhere in any of the computer systems, Kareena, she'll find her.'

Chastity sucked in a big breath of relief. She hated being out of her zone. She hated not knowing anything, feeling out of touch, out of control. Kareena might just save her sanity.

'Come on in, girl,' Kareena said with a swat to Chastity's back. 'You got the Elvis room.'

She did get the Elvis room. Elvis Costello. His stand-up cutout was perched right by the tall second-story window to keep Chastity company at night. Everything else was decorated in black and white, with black-framed eyeglasses for wall art and bed linens made up to look like a plain black suit. Only Kareena.

She was the only Cajun girl Chastity knew – okay, she was the only Cajun girl she knew period – who despised zydeco music. That was because, Kareena informed her as they settled her in, zydeco was all people expected from somebody from Cut Off, Louisiana. Accordions and whiny tunes. That and shrimp recipes. Well, Kareena Boudreaux wasn't no Bubba Shrimp, and she could play an instrument you didn't wash your clothes on.

Kareena was also the smartest girl to ever come out of Cut Off, one of the best forensic nurses Chastity knew. With Kareena's help, she thought she might actually have a chance to find her sister.

'Okay,' Kareena caroled out when Chastity met her back in the big pink, white, and green kitchen after unpacking. 'Forensic conference. You gonna help us, James, or you need to go?'

'I am Ms. Byrnes's until she cuts me loose.'

Kareena set out big bowls of some kind of gumbo, a loaf

44

of dark bread, and a pitcher of gin and tonic. 'Good,' she said. 'Then we figure out what to do for this girl, yeah?'

Then, seemingly without drawing breath, she dropped into one of her pink plastic chairs and poured out their drinks. 'First thing you gotta know is that a quick search hasn't showed up anything on your sister. You got a picture can help us some more?'

Well, it seemed as if Chastity's trip to River Run wasn't wasted after all. Reaching into her nurse-sized purse she whipped out the framed photo and laid it at Kareena's place.

Kareena only took one look before shaking her head. 'Her I woulda remembered in Charity, yeah? My missin's are mostly young druggies and poor old black men.'

'So Faith hasn't been through Charity as a Jane Doe,' Chastity said as she spooned the rich gumbo into her mouth.

Kareena shook her head. 'Nope. I'll check any other hospitals around, though. You wanna do it now?'

Chastity shook her head even more forcefully. 'I want to sit here and finish my gin. And then I want a good night's sleep. It's not gonna make a difference if we get started in the morning.'

'Okay. Good. I'll dig out her missing persons bulletin. I get 'em from all over, just in case, since we the big gun and knife club round here. It'll have the contact detective listed on it. We'll talk to him. You already talk to her husband?'

'Yeah.'

Kareena stopped with a spoonful of dinner halfway to her mouth. 'And?'

Chastity thought about it. 'I haven't a clue. From what he says, life was perfect and she was content and productive until she suddenly went missing two weeks ago.'

Like anybody familiar with the vagaries of the public, Kareena lifted a wry eyebrow. 'You believe him?'

'I don't know. I just met him for the first time this after-

45

noon. I didn't even know he existed until five days ago. Heck, I didn't even know my sister still existed until five days ago. What the hell do I know about who to believe?'

'Get down,' Kareena breathed in wonder, eyes wide. 'You misplaced a whole sister?'

'Amazing, isn't it?' James said. 'I can't even seem to shake off second cousins.'

'That's cause you so cute, James. What's your gut say, Chaz?'

Chastity shrugged. 'I'll let you know tomorrow. Right now I'm still getting over the fact that he looks an awful lot like my father, who was not my favorite character in the cartoons.'

She didn't realize that she'd unzipped her purse again and closed her hand around her small velvet bag.

James took a look as he cleaned out his bowl with a hunk of bread. 'She wasn't wild about his house, either.'

More discomfort. 'I imagine my sister found comfort in the familiar,' Chastity said stiffly. 'It wouldn't have been how I'd decorate my house if I'd had the money.'

But then, she still lived in the same city where they'd been raised. Familiarity enough, it seemed.

'You want me to have my contacts check out this brother-in-law?' Kareena asked quietly.

Chastity looked up at her, food and alcohol forgotten as she tried her best to wade through old instincts and older fears. 'Yeah, sure. I mean, he's the one who asked me to come down to look for her, but what the hell? We've all seen smoke screens before.'

'He ask you to come look for her and you didn't even know he was alive?'

'Well, evidently my sister knew I was alive, she just didn't bother to tell me. Seems she knew I was a forensic nurse, too, because her husband sure thinks I can get results.'

Kareena flashed another big, bright grin. 'Well, he's sure right about that, yeah? What's his name?'

46

'Dr. Maximillian Stanton.'

Kareena let loose a low whistle. 'Miracle Max?' she demanded, eyes wide all over again. 'No shit, girl. He's got hands like Houdini, him.'

'I wouldn't be surprised. He's sure in demand.'

'Just about the highest priced talent they got over there at Tulane. Used to be at Charity, but Tulane gave him full professorship. And lots more money. Still got privileges at Charity, but we don't get those insured patients for him to bill, yeah?' Kareena's eyes got unfocused for a second as she sat there, clicking her pen and sipping at her gin. 'He married, huh?'

'Why? Doesn't he act like it?'

Kareena shrugged. 'I don't know. I don't work at Tulane. I'll sure ask around, though.'

For the first time since she'd sat down, Chastity smiled. That statement helped put her back on solid ground. She might not know New Orleans, but she sure as hell knew hospital grapevines. By this time tomorrow, they'd have everything but the size of Max's business parts. And if he wasn't quite the husband of the year he portrayed himself to be, they'd have that, too.

She set her purse down on the floor and attacked her soup. 'There and the Arlen Clinic. Is that the name of his group?'

Kareena looked a bit confused. 'Nah. He's with Southeast Surgical Group. Never heard of the Arlen Clinic.'

Chastity shrugged. 'It was something he mentioned. Something Faith might have been involved with. He said it along with the hospital auxiliary, ya know?'

'Oh, then it might be a fund-raiser thing, like a place for autism or shit like that. I can check it out, too.'

Chastity gave her friend a big, relieved smile. 'Good. That's out of the way. Can I have more gumbo, please?'

She had more gumbo. She drank more gin, as did Kareena and James. She called Moshika to check on Lilly the boxer and found out her dog missed her. And for the

47

first time since getting that damned phone call almost a week earlier, Chastity began to relax.

Of course, that night as she slept in the Elvis Costello room, she dreamed of water and laughter and woke up sweating, but that was to be expected. After all, she'd faced her monsters all day. She'd seen her mother's couches and heard her sister Hope's name for the first time in years. Even worse, she'd met a fireman who called to every self-destructive tendency she'd shoved down for five long, dry years, and she'd had to admit that one not-really-handsome man had the ability to set her all the way back.

It was another one of the annoying little legacies from her childhood, just like that water thing. One Chastity had thought she'd finally learned to control with her rituals and her prescribed life and contained adrenaline rushes. Classic and predictable; in her mind, just as pathetic. And not about sex. Never really about sex.

She'd been in therapy for ten years, celibate for five, like a drunk in recovery. But every once in a while, just like any addict, she put an open bottle out on the table to goad herself into a drink. Just to know she wouldn't do it.

The problem was, she wasn't quite so sure of herself. Which was what brought back the dreams.

It really was too bad, though, that she couldn't give in just this once and have nasty, raunchy sex with the fire-fighter. At least it would be noisy enough to block the old voices in her head for a few minutes. Sometimes an entire hour or two.

Kind of like a trauma code.

Or a ride in a fast car.

Instead, Chastity did her best to soak in the sounds of the night: the soothing drone of insects, the occasional barking dog, the off-balance whir and click of the ceiling fan. She curled her hand around her little velvet bag and closed her eyes and willed herself back to sleep.

There were monsters out there, after all, and she was going to need her strength to face them.

Chapter Four

Chastity would have been slow to get out of bed if she'd been staying with anybody but Kareena Boudreaux. After all, she'd only managed about three hours of sleep, and that on alcohol and nightmares and the hotbox of an unair-conditioned house. Not the best way to face a stifling, muggy morning.

But Kareena took away her choices. She blew through the bedroom door at seven with a cup of steaming caffeine and a litany of early morning joys that would have sent any sentient being screaming for a gun.

Chastity hated morning. She was an evening nurse. A night person. She firmly believed that people were shot at sunrise because who wanted to live then anyway? She had forgotten that Kareena belonged to the dawn school of religion.

'Shut . . . up,' she managed blackly as she downed about half a cup of Kareena's McDonald's-hot coffee.

It was worth it. If you had to actually get up in the morning you should do it on Cajun coffee. After it took off the roof of her mouth, it damn near took off the roof of her head.

'Aaaah.'

'I knew you'd come around, girl. There's eggs and boudin and grits in the kitchen. And you, girl, you in luck. My mama came up from Cut Off last week, she brought me some Evangeline Maid bread. Best bread in the world. I saved some for you. Come on and eat so Kareena can get to work and start huntin' that sister you lookin' for. What time did James say he's comin' for you?'

Chastity blinked a couple of times and lurched all the way into full sitting position, picking her St. Louis Police Academy T-shirt away from her sweaty skin.

'I can't remember. Nine or so? It always this hot here?'

'It summer, girl. You live on the river. You know how it is. Besides, we got some weird weather thing goin' on. We expecting some kick-ass hurricanes this season.'

Ignoring the instinctive clench in her gut, Chastity eased open a bleary eye. 'You sound excited about this.'

'You live on the edge to live on the edge, girl. I don' have to tell that to no trauma nurse, do I?'

'A trauma code is different from a palm tree blowing through my bathroom window.'

'It all a matter of degree, isn't it? Now come on. Get some pants on in case James come by. I don't want him gettin' all randy in my kitchen.'

'James is not going to get randy. We already had that discussion.'

Kareena actually backed up a bit. 'Is it because of his scars?' She didn't sound happy.

Chastity got the other eye open so she could glare. 'It's because I'm practicing a policy of celibacy.'

Kareena let loose a tugboat hoot that should have frightened the dogs down the block. 'No wonder you a legend in St. Louis. You ain't become a nun or nuthin', have you? Kareena could get in big trouble gettin' a nun drunk in her kitchen.'

'You're safe. I'm just getting careful in my old age.'

'For how long you do this?'

'Four years, eleven months, five days and ... three hours.'

Kareena let loose a whistle. 'You really give up *sex?*'

'I gave up a useless exercise in desperation and self-loathing until I could work that little thing out.'

Kareena gave her head a decisive shake. 'Well, girl, I got lots more gin. You sure haven't given up that.'

'No,' Chastity agreed. 'I make it a point never to entertain more than one addiction at a time. But I figure first, I have to earn the gin. It's the Catholic in me.'

'Addiction?' Kareena asked. 'Real life? Not just bad choices?'

Chastity's smile was dust dry as she thought of all the twelve steps she'd tried. 'I'm my very own *Jerry Springer Show*.'

'Whoo-eee. You just got lots of little snakes in your head, don't you?'

Chastity smiled. 'More like monsters under the bed.'

Kareena tipped her head over, resembling nothing more than a bright little sparrow. 'Any I need introducin' to before I go lookin' for your sister?'

'Probably. But I'm just not up to it right now.'

There was a long silence as Kareena's computer-fast brain assessed the variables. Then she ripped off the bedclothes and yanked Chastity up by the arm. 'Okay then, we got a place to start. You get some food in you and a shower. Me, I'll go search missing persons reports.'

But first, Chastity had a question. 'You don't really get hurricanes here, do you?'

Kareena gave her a big, happy grin. 'Do we get hurricanes? *Mais* yeah, we get hurricanes. Why you think we got so many cemeteries?'

'Because the climate sucks.'

'Yeah, well, that, too. Now come on, before you miss somethin' fun.'

Yeah. Like a palm tree through the bathroom window.

And water. Lots and lots of water.

Why did Chastity suddenly feel as if she were being stalked? Did omens stalk? Or just pile up?

Eventually Chastity did get her breakfast. She ate enough to clog her arteries, and then she took a tepid handheld shower in eighty-year-old plumbing. By the time she made it back out to the kitchen again, fairly coherent and in need of yet more caffeine, James had taken Kareena's place.

'So you made it,' he greeted her, coffeepot in hand.

She nudged his cup out of the way so she could get first pour. 'I'll let you know.'

Chastity had put on her professional slacks and a silk shirt. She had to interview police today, and shorts and a tank top didn't convey the correct message. She did wish she could have chanced it, though. She already felt as if she were trapped in a sauna. And then there was James standing there in his ratty jeans and Jazz Festival T-shirt like something out of a romance novel, and the temperature ratcheted up another few degrees. It was just not going to be an easy day all-round.

At least she had her treasure, safely tucked away in her pants pocket, its reassurance immediate.

'Kareena's gonna meet us at Charity Hospital,' James said.

Chastity just nodded.

'She's got a name for us at the Eighth. Also the Fourth, which originally took the missing persons call.'

'Fourth District? You mean that pretentious architectural nightmare of a subdivision is in the City of New Orleans?'

'The subdivision and all its pigs. Kareena says you'd rather talk to the guy in the Eighth. He's kinder and he doesn't chew tobacco ... although what that has to do with good police work I don't know.'

'It has to do with good hygiene. Kareena's a legend about good hygiene.'

James lifted that eyebrow. 'If you're a legend, it should be for something better than clean hands.'

Chastity had just about managed to ease her butt back down on a kitchen chair when her cell phone began to trill. 'Take Me Out to the Ball Game.' It only reminded her of what else she was missing in St. Louis while she was spinning her wheels down here.

52

'Mmmm-hmmm?' she answered, rubbing at the headache that had taken up residence behind her eyes.

'Is this Chastity?'

Ah, the dulcet tones of her brother-in-law. Sounding much more like a doctor than a butler this morning. Evidently Chastity had some 'splainin' to do.

'Good morning, Max. Did the surgery go all right?'

The surgery that should have lasted no more than four hours. She'd actually expected this call anytime the evening before.

'I was caught on two more cases. I thought I'd find you at the house this morning.'

Now a layer of betrayal and hurt. Chastity thought of facing that on top of bleach, lavender, and those damn white couches, and she shuddered. 'I met up with an old friend who's putting me up, Max. I didn't think you'd mind, since you're so busy. I'll be back sometime today after I talk to the police.'

'Are you sure? I mean, you don't know anybody down here. I thought ...'

'A friend of mine works at Charity. By the way, she calls you Miracle Max. You seem to have quite a reputation down here.'

There was a brief pause, as if he were trying to refocus.

'Tell her thank you. Where is she putting you up? You know, this isn't the safest city in the world. I wouldn't be able to live with myself if any harm came to you.'

'I'm down off Magazine,' she said, not bothering to mention which side. Even she could tell that the property values differed from the Garden District side to the Irish Channel side. 'I'll have my cell phone on all the time so you can reach me. And, like I said, I'll be back over some-time today.'

Please let him say he'd be gone.

'Well, I'm catching a few hours' sleep before going back into the office,' he said, and Chastity almost sighed out loud.

She did not need the grieving husband lurking like regret over her shoulder while she pawed through his wife's personal property.

'If nothing else,' she said instead, 'call me when you're free. We'll get something to eat while I explain what I've found.'

While she grilled him on what his home life was like.

Odd how her headache suddenly got worse.

Chastity didn't want to look into her own home life, much less anybody else's. She wanted to walk right back up the Mississippi until she reached her flat and her dog and her baseball tickets. The way this thing was going, by the time she got home, Lilly would think she belonged to Moshika, and baseball season would be over.

Instead, Chastity let Max offer a few more platitudes on safety and sign off. Then she sucked at her coffee as if it were the last form of sustenance on earth and stumbled to her feet so she could get on with the rest of the day.

Kareena was waiting for them outside the emergency entrance of Charity Hospital. Not an inspiring place, Chastity thought as she assessed it from behind her vampire-rated sunglasses. Familiar, though, in the way all old, state-run hospitals are. Brick and concrete, aged and weary. No frills or state-of-the-art anything, not enough room for ambulances to pull into the outdated drive that was cluttered with homeless trying to decide where else to go.

The whole neighborhood was lousy with hospitals, with University and the VA and Hotel Dieux down the block, and Tulane right across the street from Charity and about a hundred million dollars away. Charity's flip side, the private side of medicine, where Chastity's brother-in-law saved wealthy lives while the poor ones sought asylum across the street.

'You really into this chauffeur thing, aren't you, girl?' Kareena demanded as she yanked open the front door of the cab, her bright purple lab coat flapping a bit in the breeze.

Chastity just smiled. 'An old fantasy of mine.'

Kareena snorted and climbed in. 'I know all about your fantasies. If they involve a backseat, it comes with flashing lights and handcuffs.'

'That wasn't a fantasy,' Chastity retorted. 'That was a date. Now, you got anything for me?'

'Hi, James.' Kareena greeted her cousin with a quick kiss and the click of a seat belt. 'And who you think I am, girl? O' course I got somethin' for you. We headin' down to the Eighth. Meetin' Detective Gilchrist. You'll like him.'

James nodded and eased the cab into traffic.

'From what I hear, the only person you worked well with was a guy named Thibideaux,' Chastity said with a grin. 'You know, like Boudreaux and Thibideaux go gator huntin' together?'

'You want me to help, you stay away from Boudreaux jokes, you hear me?'

'I'll listen,' James offered.

'You're related to her,' Chastity objected. 'You don't mind Cajun jokes?'

'Not on the Boudreaux side, I'm not. My family has class.'

'Your family has three felons, a rodeo clown, and half a dozen barflies,' Kareena informed him.

'Like I said,' James told Chastity, 'I always know where to find them.'

Chastity reached for the paper Kareena was handing over the backseat.

'I didn't find anybody matchin' your sister's description so far in any of the hospital systems,' Kareena said. 'Coroner's office, either. Most o' their Jane Does look a lot like our Jane Does. Needle marks, tattoos, and gunshot wounds.'

Chastity read the missing persons bulletin in silence. It said that one Faith Marie Byrnes Stanton had been reported missing on May 23 by her husband. White female, 5 feet

4, 130 pounds, blond hair, blue eyes, DOB 5/15/1971, last seen at Gallatoire's Restaurant on Bourbon Street at 1 p.m. on May 21, wearing a blue dress. No identifying tattoos or birthmarks.

Chastity chuckled to herself.

'What's up?' Kareena asked.

Chastity shook her head. 'She's been shaving years off her age.'

'Sound pretty normal to me.'

'I wouldn't have expected it of Faith. She always had a kind of 'live with it' attitude about stuff like that.'

Kareena gave her a look. 'Well, she's the second wife of a pretty powerful surgeon. Plenty competition for that kind of position, don't you think?'

'Yeah.' Chastity nodded. 'I do. You get any whispers on the grapevine?'

'Yeah. He's brilliant, a perfectionist, arrogant in that kind of way that top docs are, and worth every penny he gets. No dangling for Mrs. Doctor Three as far as anybody knows, hasn't been caught committing acts of sexual harassment in the back halls. Real man for the cameras, remembers the staff with cookies and shit.'

'So, pretty typical high-profile CV surgeon.'

'Yeah, girl, that's what it sounds like.'

'No difference in behavior lately?'

'Takin' everybody's consolation kindly. Work's more sporadic since he's hunting for his wife and all. Threw an instrument tray at one of the girls right after his wife went missin', but nobody blames him. Say they understand. Besides, the girl, she deserved it.'

'But he's not usually into tray tossing.'

'Nah. Listens to Mozart when he cuts, shit like that.'

Chastity grinned. 'Pretty fuckin' boring, you ask me.'

Kareena grinned right back. 'Eighteen-carat snooze.'

Just about that time, James slowed the cab to a crawl in the French Quarter traffic, which even before noon was pretty stacked.

56

'Why don't you hop out and I'll meet you at the Napoleon House when you're finished?' he asked.

Kareena didn't need a second invitation. She was already out in the street before Chastity managed to get her purse and herself out the door. James moved off, and Chastity realized they were standing before yet another of those ubiquitous wrought-iron fences, behind which rose an ochre neoclassical building surrounded by magnolia trees and police cars.

'Good lord,' Chastity said, following Kareena through the gate. 'It looks like a bank.'

'It was a bank,' she said, charging past a bicycle cop and a couple of uniforms heading for cars. 'Among other things.'

It even looked like a bank inside, with pastel walls, antique globe chandeliers, and uniformed officers standing where the tellers used to.

'Hey, Travis,' Kareena called out as they neared the desk. 'Is that handsome Anthony Gilchrist here for Kareena, *cher*?'

The officer, on the phone, just pointed them back toward a row of offices to the right. Kareena sailed through the gate like a frigate into harbor. Chastity, thinking how long it would have taken her to get this far without Kareena, gave her own little wave to the young uniform and followed right behind.

Detective Gilchrist was young, tall, and ugly. Cursed with nondescript hair and premature jowls, he looked kind of like an underfed hound dog in wire-rims. Deputy Dawg in a tie. He greeted Kareena with a gentle smile and held his hand out to Chastity.

'I called your brother-in-law,' he said. 'Asked his permission to talk to you. He's a good doctor. Saved my daddy last year.'

Chastity couldn't think of anything to do but nod.

'He asked you to come down and look into this?'

They all settled at one of those endemic metal and veneer public office desks, which looked anachronistic amid the

57

nineteenth-century splendor. The detective fingered the razor-thin file that sat on his cluttered desk.

Setting her purse in her lap, Chastity shrugged. 'I think Dr. Stanton just feels helpless. He can't walk out of the operating theater to go looking for his wife, and he knows I'm trained in forensics. I kind of equate it with having your nurse friend by your bed in the hospital. Comfort more than anything.'

'You're active?'

'In forensics? Yeah. I'm forensic nurse liaison at St. Michael's Med Center in St. Louis city. Masters in forensic nursing, six years working trauma. I'm real familiar with Missouri law, but not Louisiana. So I have Kareena here to interpret.'

Detective Gilchrist nodded, fiddling with a pen. 'People go missing here all the time,' he said, just as he probably always did when discussing a missing person.

'I know. It's where I'd go missing if I could.' She tested a smile on him and was met by a moue of bemusement. Oh, well. Looked like they'd walked into the 'Just the facts, ma'am' school of investigation. She heard Kareena cough next to her and refused to look.

'Our mother died recently,' Chastity said instead. 'I really think that it might have affected Faith more then she knew. Faith has always been very close to our mother. But I figured it couldn't hurt to do a little legwork for Max while he's stuck saving lives.'

Only now did Detective Gilchrist think it appropriate to open the file. 'Well,' he said, scanning it, 'I'm afraid I don't have much. She was last seen at Gallatoire's, where she lunches every Friday. People did mention that they thought she hadn't recovered from her mother's death, but she didn't seem more depressed or upset than normal. Her husband can't remember any other changes besides that, but he said he thought she was feeling better.'

'Max said you checked her cards and cell phone and came up empty.'

'Yes, ma'am. We did. Wherever she is, she isn't using any plastic I know about.'

'Could it be foul play?' Chastity had to ask.

He considered that for a full minute. 'We haven't found any indication of it.'

'But Max says that she didn't take anything with her.'

He was fiddling with the pen again. 'I know. We have alerts out everywhere, believe me. But she wasn't in a high-risk category of any kind, she hadn't been threatened for any reason, and she disappeared off a public street . . .'

'Not from home in the dead of night.'

He seemed insulted. 'I would never jump to that conclusion.'

Chastity couldn't help frowning. 'You didn't even ask?'

He pulled himself up to glare at her, jowls wobbling a bit. 'I may respect Dr. Stanton, but it doesn't get in the way of the job. It was the first thing I did. He was in surgery the entire day. He made a lot of calls in between cases, both to his house and to his wife's friends, all from the doctors' lounge at Tulane Medical Center, to see if they knew where she was. Then he called us.'

Chastity nodded. 'Thank you. I'm going to go now and see if there's anything I can find at my sister's house. I can contact you if I have any further questions?'

'Of course. Please do.'

He climbed to his feet, obviously finished. Chastity followed.

'Faith was at Gallatoire's and then she was just gone?' she asked. 'Nothing else?'

'Pardon?'

Chastity motioned to the missing persons report. 'You said she was last seen at Gallatoire's. Nobody saw her leave? Nobody offered her a ride or called a cab since she didn't have her car?'

He looked down at the file. 'She hailed her own cab.'

That brought everybody to a halt.

'And?' Chastity asked.

'She never got there.'

The hairs stood up on the back of Chastity's neck. 'She never got where?'

He checked his file again. 'Well, there was some argument about that. Ms. Susan Reeves claims your sister asked to go to her home. But Mrs. Eleanor Webster, who was leaving at the same time, insisted that she really said she wanted to go ... well, uh, to ...'

Chastity all but gaped. The detective was blushing. Good Lord, she thought, suddenly wide-eyed. This was New Orleans. What on earth could make a cop blush in New Orleans?

'She wanted to go to, uh, what?' she asked.

He couldn't even make eye contact. 'A fertility clinic.'

'A what?' Chastity demanded.

Suddenly awkward, the detective didn't take his eyes from the file, still flushing. 'A, uh, fertility clinic.'

Chastity wasn't sure whether he felt embarrassed about the whole business of procreation, or just discomfited that the great surgeon who had saved his daddy might not have been able to fulfill his side of the equation.

'Which one?'

He shook his head. 'Mrs. Webster didn't hear. We checked all the ones in town, and nobody saw your sister.'

'Did you ask the cabdriver?' Chastity asked.

'We haven't been able to locate him.'

'But she did get in a cab.'

'According to witnesses, yes.'

'James'll find out who that cabbie is,' Kareena promised.

Chastity nodded. 'But why would she go to a fertility clinic? Did you ask her husband, Detective?'

'He said she'd had dealings with the Arlen Clinic a while back, but that she hadn't been back in the last year or so. We checked there, too, of course. Nobody remembers seeing her.'

'Oh,' Kareena said. '*That* Arlen Clinic. No wonder I didn't recognize it.'

'But what would they have to do with a fertility clinic?' Chastity demanded. 'Dr. Stanton told me himself that he didn't want any more kids.'

Detective Gilchrist looked affronted. 'Since she didn't go there, I didn't think it my business to ask, ma'am.'

Chastity rolled that whole concept around in her mouth a minute and couldn't come up with a comfortable taste. Instead of putting questions to rest, she'd added more.

'I think I have some phone calls to make,' she mused.

And after exchanging cards with Detective Gilchrist, she escaped from the police station.

'You got a look on your face,' Kareena said as they stepped back into the heat.

Chastity shook her head, her attention more on the information she hadn't gotten than on what she had. 'I got a feelin', Kareena.'

'Oh, Kareena loves feelin's like that. You think this fertility thing mean something?'

'I don't know. But the first thing I learned in school was to look for the thing that didn't seem to belong. And that doesn't. If Faith hasn't seen anybody at the Arlen Clinic for so long, why would she suddenly go there? It just doesn't fit.'

'Maybe she didn't.'

Chastity lifted an eyebrow. 'Just how much do the words *fertility clinic* sound like anything else?'

Besides, she could smell it again, somewhere beneath all that thick foliage.

Decay.

It spun her around every time she caught a whiff of it, because she kept thinking it didn't belong amid all the exotic scents and sights and sounds of New Orleans. But it did, of course. She more than anyone knew what kind of rot a pristine facade could hide. And no matter what was said about New Orleans, no one could accuse it of putting up a pristine front.

'Chaz?'

61

Chastity startled back to attention. They were already a couple of blocks down, weaving through the sidewalk traffic on their way somewhere. Chastity wished she knew where.

'I just don't know, Kareena. But I don't think the good lieutenant asked nearly enough questions about that fertility clinic.'

Chapter Five

When they found James at the Napoleon House, he was seated at a scruffed-up table by the French doors drinking coffee with an old black man in a red pageboy wig and a young white guy with a back full of tattoos and a boa constrictor around his neck.

It was something Chastity had noticed in this city. The per capita rate of tattoos was higher than hair follicles. The other thing she noticed was that she seemed to have been here long enough for the snake to somehow make sense. She gained points all-round when she sat right down with the group and smiled.

James finished his coffee and laid down some money. 'You finished with the police?'

'They seem finished with us,' Chastity said. 'Time to set out on our own.'

James nodded. 'Where to?'

'Is it time to eat yet?' Kareena asked. 'We could have lunch, and then Kareena has to get back to work.'

'We could eat here,' Chastity said, enamored by the idea of settling into this dimly lit, well-used room that reeked of history and tourism, to talk about freedom and personal choice with the old guy in the pageboy wig.

Kareena eyed that snake. 'No we couldn't.'

James grinned. 'He won't eat much.'

Chastity was rubbing that spot right between her eyes

again. 'Well, if we're not going to eat, I need to avoid my brother-in-law long enough to rifle through all his personal belongings. James, while I do that, would you mind getting Faith's picture copied and take it around the taxi stands and ask if anybody picked up my sister from Gallatoire's two Fridays ago?'

James pulled out a cigarette. 'It'll be extra.'

Chastity looked up, sure he was joking. She was wrong. She saw it in the carefully nondescript expression in his eyes as he lit up. Snake boy scowled at James.

The guy in the wig nodded. 'All right,' he intoned, as if answering to a truth delivered from the pulpit.

Kareena straightened like an outraged mother. 'What's the matter with you, James? You said you'd help.'

His smile was as lazy as summer. 'I said I'd drive. Questions are extra.'

'I'm disappointed in you,' Kareena huffed. 'You can't do this little thing for her as a favor?'

'I don't do favors, Kareena,' he said, as if reminding her of something she already knew. 'I'm afraid I've fallen out of love with altruism.'

He didn't move, but it seemed as if everybody in the place knew he was pointing to the scars along his face. The terrible, disfiguring scars that carried such pain and stigma.

Chastity felt a lurch somewhere in her middle, which she didn't like at all. She didn't want to feel empathy for this guy. She just wanted him to drive her around, preferably in silence.

No, damn it. That wasn't true. But what she wanted did not involve sharing sore spots.

'What did Richard Gere pay Julia Roberts in *Pretty Woman*?' she asked, eyeing the row of liquor bottles that glinted in the dusky light at the back of the room where Napoleon's bust sat watching the street. 'Would that be enough for all the extras?'

James lifted a knowing eyebrow. '*All* the extras?'

Chastity faced him down like a terrorist. 'I won't make

64

you tattoo your ass or satisfy my maidenly yearnings, if that's what you're asking.'

Now everybody in the bar was listening. Kareena laughed like a car horn and leaned against the open door.

James's smile was dust dry. 'Too bad. My ass needs a tattoo.'

'Probably the only thing left in town without one,' Kareena snorted.

The black guy nodded again. 'All right.'

'For the money Richard Gere gave Julia Roberts,' James proclaimed as if bestowing a boon, 'I'll be happy to include all the extras. What time did your sister leave Gallatoire's?'

There was a second of silence as they all reset goals.

'One, I think,' Chastity said, noticing that the snake's tongue flickered like a filament, as if tasting the smoke that curled off the end of James's fresh cigarette. 'Why Gallatoire's? Why every Friday? That seems to mean something.'

'That mean she part of that snotty-ass uptown crowd,' Kareena said. 'Miracle Max from up there, I think. His mama was Comus queen for sure. It mean your sister have to par-ti-ci-pate in the social rounds to be part of that family. Charities, school events. Friday lunch at Gallatoire's with all those rich old ladies in pearls.'

Chastity pulled her gaze away from the snake and faced James. 'I get the rich old lady part. What the hell's a comus?'

It was the snake boy who answered. 'Oldest Mardi Gras krewe, had the first big parade back a thousand years ago. Stopped bein' part of the parade when krewes had to be integrated. Social acme.'

She nodded. 'Ah. In St. Louis we call it Veiled Prophet. We have a parade and everything.'

He pointed at her as if she were the prize student. 'Exactly. Local bigwig honored as king and his daughter as queen. Big to-do, debutante balls, exclusive and restricted. That kind of shit.'

'Where's uptown?'

'Other side of Magazine from me,' Kareena said.

'Which means that Max and my sister could have lived in one of those beautiful old houses on St. Charles instead of that post-pretension subdivision,' Chastity said almost to herself.

'They coulda lived jus' about anyplace but there,' Kareena assured her. 'No accountin' for taste, yeah?'

She got heartfelt nods from the old guy and the young guy. Then the snake caught sight of Kareena and began to undulate in her direction. Kareena slid right out the French door to the street.

Chastity climbed to her feet and gave the snake a pat before following. 'I think what I really need is a translator.'

'That's what you have me for,' James said, waving goodbye to his friends. 'Now that I'm being compensated, anyway.'

Three miles away, deep in the uptown area so cherished by the ancestors of the old families of New Orleans, Susan Wade Reeves was just walking out her front door. Susan Wade Reeves was one of those women who ate lunch every Friday at Gallatoire's, just like her mother, her grandmother, and her great-grandmother before her. In fact, Susan had been introduced to Gallatoire's on her seventh birthday by her Grandpère and Grandmère Beauregard, in a dinner where she got dressed up in her lacy socks and pearl hair barrettes. All the waiters sang 'Happy Birthday' to her, and her grandparents gave her the exciting news that she was going to be flower girl at the next Comus ball, come Mardi Gras season.

Susan was, in many ways, typical of her class. The second daughter of Matthew Taber Reeves and Sarah Winsom Beauregard Reeves, she was born in a magnificent Greek Revival mansion on Prytania into old, inherited money her father had expanded with his banking interests.

66

She attended the McGehee School and Newcombe College, and served as maid at the Comus and Rex balls and queen at one of the lesser balls. Then she married the first gentleman who had called her out for a dance, John Matthews McCall, and moved with him into the garçonnierre that sat out back of the house on Prytania.

Susan still lived in that tidy little carriage house, but she now lived there alone. Susan had failed to live up to the expectations of her parents and her class. Instead of breeding a new generation of daughters for the service of society, she had divorced her alcoholic, abusive husband of five years and finally admitted to everyone what she'd known from the minute she'd taken her first shower at McGehee. Susan was a lesbian.

That didn't take away her social influence or her family's interference. Susan still dressed in the appropriate uniform: well-tailored suits and pearls, classic pumps and simply styled hair. She still attended to the rituals, the balls in season and the lunches and charitable causes out of season.

She was simply considered the eccentric aunt, the good girl of the crowd, as if her lesbianism were no more than a jolly joke on everyone. She had a good career as a bond trader, and a lover on Esplanade who had never been invited to family functions, not because she was a lesbian, but because she was black.

Even more baffling to her family and friends than her sexual orientation, though, was her religious one. About the time she announced her sexual preference, Susan converted to Catholicism.

Susan loved the ritual, the mystery, the faint layer of mortification that lay on everything in the Catholic Church like sacred ash. She loved the fact that there was an institution on earth that seemed completely oblivious to the fact that they'd turned the corner into the third millennium. She even loved the incongruity of a church that punished lesbianism worse than one of the big ten when it wasn't so much as mentioned in the Bible.

What she loved most of all, though, was the pantheon of saints the Catholic Church specialized in. Saints for actors and saints for firemen and saints for people who lost their way.

It was easy to love saints in New Orleans. Saints were endemic there. There wasn't a Catholic church without its collection of saints, and there were a lot of Catholic churches in New Orleans. There was even a saint who was the city's very own inside joke. Saint Expedite, a lovely male saint who stood inside Our Lady of Guadalupe on North Rampart Street.

Saint Expedite had shown up one day in the eighteen-hundreds, sent from France as a gift to the city. Unfortunately, there was no sign denoting exactly which saint the country had sent. Only the marking on the package. *Expedite*. Now the citizens prayed to him if they needed things in a hurry.

One of Susan's favorite saints, though, was Saint Roch. There was something so Buddhist about Saint Roch, as if it was his job to maintain balance in the world. Saint Roch, who had once survived the bubonic plague by the grace of God and a faithful dog, granted wishes. Susan knew. He'd granted one for her.

But that wasn't all he did. When Saint Roch gave a boon, he took something away. It was a good reminder, Susan always thought, that nobody should think they could get something for nothing.

Susan had been drawn to his shrine over at the old Saint Roch Cemetery off Claiborne for years, where Saint Roch shared a tiny side alcove in the chapel with a statue of Saint Lucy and maybe Saint Phillipa Duschene, who looked unnervingly like Kate Smith. The three of them waited in the breathless hush of holiness in that moldy, claustrophobic little room with the forest of braces and crutches and anatomically correct plaster casts the faithful had left to represent wishes Saint Roch had granted.

Susan had prayed to him for everything from good ACT

68

scores to the reorientation of her sexuality. Some things he'd helped with, and some not. But always he'd given her a sense of satisfaction for the effort.

So today, she was heading over to the Saint Roch Campo Santo, just as she did on every Sunday she was in town, even though she didn't really need to anymore, since her prayer had already been answered. Her little plaster cast cluttered up the floor of the side altar at the Campo Santo along with all the others. But she simply liked going there to remind herself of what Saint Roch had given her. And wonder what he was planning to take away.

She wouldn't have been quite so sanguine if she'd known how soon Saint Roch was going to do just that. Or what it was he was going to take.

Bleach and lavender and stiff white couches. Chastity wondered just how many times she was going to have to walk through this little purgatory. She took a couple of slow, deep breaths, just as she would have in a room with a bad burn patient or a decomposing body. Closing her hand around her little velvet bag, she braced herself for the worst, shut the front door behind her, and waded right into the stagnant recycled air in that monster of a house.

Chastity had always known she was a coward. It was brought starkly home to her as she stood in that hallway, too afraid to move. If only she could have gotten James to do this for her. But James was off looking for taxi drivers to interview. So it was up to Chastity to play anthropologist with her sister's life.

She still stood there a moment, frozen by the smells and the precisely arranged furniture. Struck hard by memories she'd spent ten years repressing. By poisons she'd thought she'd purged.

It hadn't been true, really, that part about not being allowed in the living room. She'd sat there, once, on one of her mother's couches, the plastic covers cold and sticky against the backs of her bare legs. She'd been in her plaid school uniform, hands clenched in her lap, legs dangling clear of the floor, her breath harsh and tight in her sparrow chest as she faced her mother.

They'd gone to confession at school that day. The sacrament of reconciliation, where the priest had said they should offer their guilt to God. They should share their shame and be freed of it.

She'd tried.

'You shouldn't tell lies, young lady,' he'd warned in the claustrophobic darkness of the confessional.

Her mother just slapped her.

It was the last time she'd sat on that couch.

So here she was ten feet inside the house and already shaking. Here she was one day in New Orleans and already losing control. She sucked in a breath through her mouth so she couldn't smell anything. Focused so she couldn't remember. And then she walked to the stairs and the farthest point she could think of from the rooms that really scared her.

She tried that door to the left of the foyer first, but found it locked. Probably an office of some kind. Although she could, she didn't have time right now to pick the lock. So she climbed the stairs instead to where the boys had lived.

There were three bedrooms there in all, each with the obligatory bathroom, each decorated in varying shades of blue. The rooms had evidently been cleaned when the Stanton boys had moved out, because they contained no posters, no trophies, no fug of adolescent hormones. They could have been guest rooms at a Hyatt for all the individuality that remained.

Chastity searched anyway. Chests and cupboards and the space beneath the beds. All was tidy, clean and folded. The closets held extra blankets and barely worn tennis shoes, the drawers precisely folded famous label attire. Evidently the boys had taken the evidence of their personalities to school with them. There was nothing there left to find.

So Chastity spent a couple of long minutes just sitting on

70

a denim-blue bed to gather courage, and then walked back downstairs into the area she dreaded. Past the awful living room, the dining room decorated in grass paper and cherrywood, the family room populated by overstuffed black leather and glass tabletops. All the way to the double doors that opened onto the master suite.

Chastity wanted to close her eyes when she opened those doors. Hell, she didn't want to open them at all. But she had to find out who her sister had been these last ten years. She had to understand why Faith had disappeared, although she thought she knew.

Especially after seeing that living room.

And the dining room. Precise, perfect-looking, a real ad for Norman Rockwell. A terrible, terrifying lie.

But those rooms weren't enough. The real answers would be where Faith would have kept her private possessions. Her secrets and souvenirs. So Chastity opened the master bedroom door and prepared herself for what she was going to find.

She found nothing.

For a long moment, all she could do was stand there like an idiot, the wash of air-conditioning raising goose bumps on her arms, the hard edges of the gems in her bag solid in her fingers.

Lemon polish.

That was what she smelled back here. Lemon polish and old lady perfume. How odd.

The bedroom she'd so feared was featureless. Bland and beige and completely devoid of personality, as if nobody really lived there. The furnishings were expensive, the fabrics more so, damask swagged over the bay window and layered on the king-sized oak four-poster. But no color. No contrast. No distinction at all.

When Faith was a teenager, her bedroom had resembled a harem tent. Jewel-toned saris draped over her bed, paper lanterns that turned the ceiling light red. Lush, plump pillows piled as if she could manufacture the only comfort

she'd find. Piles of albums and walls cluttered with land-
scape paintings. Escape and protection. A song of longing
Faith never once sang out loud.

Here, there was silence and emptiness. It made Chastity
afraid.

The bedroom was the size of a football field, with that
little salon Max had mentioned taking up an alcove to the
left. Beyond that Chastity caught sight of a wall of mirrors,
marble shelving, and flowers. Faith's bathroom. Max's, on
the other side, showed Drakkar Noir and brown towels.

She knew damn well she didn't want to go into either of
those bathrooms, so she sucked in a big breath and turned
to the bedroom.

The bed was king-sized, the end tables glass and holding
a phone, a lamp, an alarm clock, and a couple of pictures
of the boys. There were two chests and a vanity, all in
thick, sculpted oak, with the vanity topped with a groom-
ing set and a bottle of perfume – old lady's perfume – all
precisely placed.

Chastity had the odd feeling that if she picked up any
item, she'd see a mark beneath, showing that it had never
been moved a millimeter. Even the bobby pins that rested
in a small copper dish looked as if they'd been lined up.

Faith had always been orderly, even in her most
outwardly extravagant teens. She'd cut food like a pathologist and counted calories like an accountant. But this was
way more.

One look at the closet proved it. Chastity opened the
doors to a walk-in the size of her own bathroom to find it
full and organized to a hair's whisper by color and size and
textile.

Textile, for God's sake. Chastity could barely get her
clothes hung up, and Faith had to rank hers like a department store. All lined up fastidiously and most smelling of
that old lady perfume. Chastity couldn't get over the idea
that her sister had grown old.

She checked shoe boxes to find designer labels. She

72

opened the jewelry case on one of the shelves to find it full of expensive necklaces, earrings, and rings. And, of course, the obligatory pearls. Every piece, she knew, the real thing. After all, hadn't she spent the last years amassing her own treasure?

Okay, so hers was of garnets and peridots instead of emeralds and rubies, but to each his own. And Chastity's treasure was her very own, which no one could ever take back or take away.

She cupped the strand of pearls in her palm, as if she could divine her sister's essence from them. Then she just put them down. They were pearls. Not a crystal ball. So she closed the jewelry case and bent to open Faith's drawers.

And suffered another setback.

She blushed. She, Chastity Ann Byrnes, who had ended up turning tricks before her sixteenth birthday, blushed.

But then, Chastity hadn't ever been Faith, which might have accounted for the surprise.

Faith's room might have been a riot of color when she was a girl, but her life had been perfectly circumscribed. Her clothes had been a bit girlish, actually. Immature, even as she'd reached her twenties. They reflected older now, classic and tailored and boring. But the lingerie Chastity found certainly wasn't.

Precisely folded away like silk slips, Chastity found crotchless panties, fishnet stockings, and more than one red leather corset, with all the less than mainstream accoutrements. And were those marabou feathers?

Good God, Chastity thought. I'm the one with the addiction, and I never wore this shit. It was straight out of Frederick's of Hollywood. If not the Marquis de Sade school of seduction.

And there went Chastity, blushing again, as if she'd never seen anything like this before. Hell, she'd seen it on the street as they were leaving the Eighth District police station. Of course, she'd seen it on a man, but that wasn't the point.

She quickly checked the other drawers, for the first time feeling like a voyeur. Sliding her hand in underneath the clothes, she searched the insides, the bottoms, and backs, and then she shut everything away again. She explored the rest of the room for books, for collections, for pastimes. Sewing or crafts or magazines.

There was nothing. It was as if she were in a hotel room, ordered and faceless and decorated in careful anonymity. Faith didn't really live in this room, Chastity thought. She couldn't.

But where else could she live?

Chastity sucked in a deep breath and came away with a faint whiff of that damn bleach. Her hand in her pocket, she turned toward the little salon that opened off the bedroom. Might as well get the rest of this farce over with. Then she was going to get the hell out of here and never come back.

Chastity grew immeasurably more uncomfortable as she picked through her sister's private correspondence. She felt worse because, again, she couldn't get a handle on anything. There were condolence cards in a pile in the corner of a glossy cherry desk, with tidy little sticky notes in Faith's perfect schoolgirl penmanship about return correspondence. There were brochures for charitable events and newsletters from schools. Normal, quiet things.

No bills. No personal notes or letters. No checkbook or savings book. No computer for e-mail.

There was a mauve leather telephone book that looked as if it had just been rewritten the week before. No erasures or scratch-outs, no notes or hasty additions. Chastity pocketed it.

Faith's purse. She must have had it with her. Chastity wondered if they'd thought to track her checkbook, which would have to have been in it.

Chastity searched through the desk and found only equipment in tidy little compartments. Paper clips, pens, pencils, stamps. Handmade stationery. A drawer with greeting

74

cards categorized by event. Birthday. Wedding. Condolences. Easter.

Good grief, did people send Easter cards?

In the last drawer, Chastity found a string of neon beads along with a beautifully feathered mask in purple, green, and gold. Mardi Gras colors. She wondered what Faith had worn them with. Or, considering what she'd found in that dresser, if she'd worn them with anything at all.

The one thing she did find out about her sister in this room was the fact that she was a catalog shopper. The entire bottom shelf of the bookcase was stacked up with them. Bloomingdale's and Saks and Talbots and Nordstrom. Jewelry and kitchen utensils, knickknacks and garden supplies and furniture. Chastity saw what looked like some fifty catalogs, and she didn't think there was a duplicate in the bunch. Amazing.

The rest of the bookcase was taken up with the kind of leatherbound classics somebody buys in bulk as decor rather than pastime, and one row of old, well-thumbed historical romances.

She was just dropping the last magazine back on the shelf when her phone rang. 'Take Me Out' ... wouldn't she just love to.

'Hello?'

'Chastity? It's Max.'

Chastity decided that no matter what had happened in her life, she was still way too Catholic. Just the sound of his voice made her feel guilty, as if she were trespassing here. Which she was, of course. But it was at Max's invitation, after all.

Sort of.

'Yes, Max. What's up?'

The sound of his voice also reminded her that somewhere in this house were Max's private papers. The bills, the receipts, all the phone and credit card receipts she'd asked him to pore over.

Should she look at them again, too, just to be sure?

'I'm heading back to the house,' he was saying. 'Would you mind meeting me there?'

'Not at all. How long before you arrive?'

'Oh, about fifteen minutes, I think.'

Chastity checked her watch and turned for the door, which was when she noticed the occasional table next to the wall. A picture frame lay on its face at its edge.

'That'd be fine. I'm here now, Max.'

'Okay, then. Bye.'

Her phone still to her ear, she instinctively reached over to right the frame. She picked it up and turned it over.

She saw what it was and dropped it.

A photo. It was just a photo. Clattering to the marble floor of Faith's bathroom that lay just beyond, it landed faceup so that Chastity couldn't pretend she hadn't seen it. It landed so that she could see herself staring up from twenty years ago.

She should have expected it, really. The moment she'd decided she had to go find her sister, she should have known she'd end up seeing this damn picture again.

Not just of her. Of all five of them, posed for some church directory thing in their good clothes and plastic smiles. Her mother, looking pale and rabbity with her thin brown hair and overbite. Faith, staring at the camera as if challenging it. Hope, so overweight that the family doctor had tried to coerce her into an eating disorder unit. Chastity, the baby. Six years old and already hollow-eyed. Already terrified of water and looking for something she'd lost.

And her father. Square-jawed, broad-shouldered, gray-haired, his eyes so pale that he looked psychic. Smiling out from all those years ago with that odd little smile of satisfaction Chastity swore she'd wiped from her memory ten years ago.

The monster under her bed.

She'd made it through the smell of bleach and lavender. She'd walked right past that sterile, institutional furniture.

76

She damn well wasn't going to lose it over a picture on the floor.

She'd been seeing a shrink for seven frickin' years. She had a suitcase full of great antidepressants back in her room at Kareena's. She should certainly be able to make it through a surprise flash from the past without embarrassing herself.

Funny. It had been another ten years before everything had disintegrated. And yet this was the picture she'd always kept in her head of all of them. Probably why it churned up her stomach so much. Because she'd been such a baby, and she could already see the devastation in her eyes.

But she wouldn't puke over it.

She would not.

Deliberately swallowing back the bile that inevitably greeted the sight of that photo, she lifted the picture and carefully set it back on its face on the table, right next to the bouquet of silk daffodils in a cup. Then she made the mistake of looking into Faith's bathroom, which waited beyond.

A sea of marble. A forest of mirrors. And in every mirror, a reflection of her father. There were at least a dozen different pictures of him, framed, collected, and kept along that empty counter. They must have been culled from every scrapbook her mother had ever put together. Saved and hoarded and cherished, he stared and smiled and smirked at her from a dozen different angles.

Here in the bathroom. Across from the bathtub, for God's sake.

Chastity barely made it to the toilet before she vomited all the way down to the gin she'd had the night before.

She vomited and then she ran out of that house as if she were one step ahead of an explosion.

She made it to the front lawn before realizing she had nowhere to go. James was somewhere questioning taxi drivers. Chastity was supposed to call him when she was finished, and she'd left her purse with her cell phone back in the house, which she was not going to walk back into today if a tornado struck and it was the only shelter left in Louisiana.

So she collapsed on the manicured lawn in the wilting thick heat, and she shook and she waited.

It was so quiet here, stifling after the thick stew of energy in the city. There were no people, no animal sounds, no grown trees to rustle in whatever breeze they got. Just humidity and silence and the encroaching shadows of those badly designed McMansions, one right on top of another. Chastity bent her knees up close. She wrapped her arms around her legs, rested her head on her knees, and closed her eyes. Then she just sat there in the sweltering silence and pretended she was anyplace else in the world.

Pretended like hell she'd never stumbled over that bathroom.

Jesus, it was one thing to deny the truth. It was another to immerse yourself in the nightmare.

'Excuse me, can I help you?'

For a second, Chastity thought she was hearing things. She was, after all, still struggling hard to keep her stomach in place and her legs from carrying her in any direction at all.

'Hello?'

But there it was again. Chastity opened her eyes to find that one of the denizens of the neighborhood had evidently come to check her out. Tucked into a bright red Mercedes convertible was a bottle blonde, about forty and showing signs of second-rate plastic surgery. Her smile was anxious and her attire a hot pink terry cloth sweat suit with rhinestones across her chest that spelled BITCH.

'You can turn up the air-conditioning out here,' Chastity suggested.

The neighbor threw off a nervous smile and gave a couple of pats to her ponytail. 'For a minute,' she said, 'I thought you were Faith. But you're not, are you? Faith would never sit out here.'

And Chastity swore she'd never go back inside.

'No,' she said instead. 'I'm Faith's sister.'

'Really?' She seemed even more nervous, checking herself briefly in the mirror, as if reminding herself she was there. 'I didn't know she had a sister. I'm Barbara Rendler. I live ... over there. It's not as nice a house, is it? I've always envied Faith her house.' She threw off a quick, confessional smile. 'Well, I've always envied her Max, really. He's so good to her. Have you seen her clothes? Oh, I'd die for those clothes. And, of course, her jewelry. Max has such a perfect eye. Faith always says she's the doll he likes to dress up. Isn't that cute?'

Chastity thought it was creepy, but she figured she'd hear a lot more by just smiling along. 'My name's Chastity,' she said. 'I'm down here helping Max find Faith.'

Wide eyes, a couple of quick nods. 'Oh, I heard. He's just so distraught. I was over a couple of days ago to check on him. How's he doing, really? He puts on such a good front, but you just know he's frantic. I mean, it doesn't make any sense, does it? Who in her right mind would leave all this?'

Another quick smile, sweet and needy and anxious.

But Chastity was suddenly distracted. It was the jewelry statement. Suddenly Chastity realized just how right Barbara Rendler was.

'Um, Barbara, could you tell me something?' she asked. 'Did Faith have more than one strand of pearls?'

'Who'd need to?' Barbara asked with a self-conscious titter. 'Especially when they're Mikimotos. Perfectly matched. Like I said, Max has great taste in jewelry.'

But Faith, photographed in those same pearls, had been at a luncheon where that necklace had evidently been the uniform of the day. And yet she had elected not to wear hers. In fact, she'd left them right there in the top tray of her jewelry box.

Sitting out on that brittle, hard lawn, Chastity reassessed the rooms she'd searched that afternoon. And she realized

79

that she was right. Those pearls meant something.

But she realized something else she hadn't picked up on before. Something she might have noticed if she hadn't been sucking down toxic chlorine fumes.

'Oh, why here's Max now!' Barbara Rendler crowed, distracting her. 'Max! Oh, Max!'

And indeed, Max had just pulled his silver BMW into the driveway. His gray hair was unmussed by heat or anxiety or hard work, his cream shirt and purple tie faultless. Chastity thought about what she needed to ask him and wondered if old Barbara would lend her a cell phone to call James for a timely rescue.

So she waited right where she was, her silk shirt sticking in all the wrong places and her stomach still uncertain enough that she had to keep swallowing, while Barbara, the jealous neighbor, hopped out of her car to meet Max as he climbed from his.

Barbara petted him like a toddler as she commiserated and promised casseroles and familiar company to keep him from brooding.

Brooding? Chastity damn near burst out laughing. She wondered whether Barbara was the one who'd donated the romances to Faith and then wondered whether Max would take advantage of her neighborly concern. But Max looked more like a doctor being importuned by a pesky nurse than a man relishing his hungry neighbor's attention.

'Chastity?'

She looked up to see him frowning at her from where he stood with Barbara's crimson-nailed hand still on his arm.

'I was saying hello to Barbara,' she told him as she climbed to her feet and tried to figure out a way not to have to go back into that house.

'Well, I'll leave you two,' Barbara chirruped and bounced on back to her car, still patting her hair and checking the mirror.

Max was shaking his head before she'd even put the car

into gear. 'She's well-meaning,' he demurred, heading up the sidewalk.

She's a psychic black hole, Chastity thought. But undoubtedly a font of information, if Chastity could figure out what else it was she needed to ask.

Max had already reached the door. Chastity's stomach did another death spiral.

'I wanted you to meet me here,' Max was saying as he held it open for her. 'The police called. They may have something.'

Chastity sucked it up and followed him into the frosty foyer, chilled all over again by the air-conditioning and the house and the memories she'd spent ten years trying to bury.

'Max,' she said, hand clamped in her pants pocket like a guy playing pocket pool, 'I need to ask you a couple of things.'

'Sure.'

He was already into the refrigerator before Chastity managed to make it into the kitchen. The kitchen that smelled like air freshener and designer coffee. Thank God.

Chastity looked around, trying to pull her thoughts together. It was when she noticed the calendar on the wall that she realized what else she hadn't found in Faith's office.

Great detective she was turning out to be. One faintly familiar smell and she missed all the important stuff. Thank God nobody thought to scent the ER air with lavender.

'Faith's calendar,' she said. 'It wasn't in the salon.'

'A calendar?' Max said. 'It's right here.'

A calendar that was basically blank, with pictures of roses taking up most of the page. Chastity shook her head, not even reaching for the tea Max had poured. 'No, her personal calendar. Date book. Faith is the most seriously organized person I know. She'd have a date book. Or a PDA.'

Max frowned again, thinking. 'Of course. No PDA. Faith never has succumbed to the technical revolution. She

81

has a small daybook she carries everywhere.'

Chastity slumped a little. 'In her purse.'

Max looked surprised. 'Yes, of course.'

'With her checkbook.'

'Yes.'

'And you haven't had any activity in her checkbook?'

He sipped at his tea and thought about that. 'They didn't ask me to look.'

Chastity nodded. 'One other thing. This may sound really stupid, but the house is so clean ...'

Not littered with fast food or unwashed dishes. Not untidy in the way a distracted man might leave it while waiting for his wife to find her way home.

Max's smile was sheepish. 'It's my way of coping,' he said. 'When I can't sleep. Faith always said that it was pointless to have a service come in when I'd be scrubbing toilets at dawn while I was trying to work out a surgery.'

'You *clean* to relieve stress?'

'It's a quirk of mine. All that time in OR, I guess.'

'Well, then, you and Faith were perfectly matched,' Chastity assured him. 'I can't imagine a more orderly person than she.'

Even so, this house continued to leave her seriously creeped out. And that was even without considering those photos.

Chastity was about to ask about the pearls when the doorbell rang. Max said not a word. He just set his glass down and walked out to the front hall.

Chastity followed, noticing that he was moving faster, more purposefully. She saw the two guys standing on the stoop in their rumpled suits and hip holsters, and knew that this was what Max had been anticipating. News. Anything to push him past the inertia of waiting.

'Detective Gilchrist, isn't it?' Max asked, pushing open the glass door.

Indeed it was, the sincere young man from the Eighth

District who'd blushed when he'd had to mention the word *fertility*. Chastity wondered what he'd get upset about this afternoon. It seemed he was tag-teaming, which Chastity thought didn't mean anything good.

Both men walked into the house.

'Yes, sir,' Gilchrist was saying. 'I appreciate your seeing us. This is Detective Dulane from Jefferson Parish, sir.'

Dulane was a squared-off, middle-aged black man with old-fashioned horn-rimmed glasses and freckles. His watchful, patient gaze took in the house and then settled on the inhabitants.

Max shook hands and led them to a couch. Chastity almost interfered, the instinct so strong in her that nobody sat on those couches. The police, evidently, did.

'This is my sister-in-law,' Max said, settling them on the cool plastic of his furniture. 'Chastity Byrnes. Have you met?'

'Yes. Hello, ma'am.' Detective Gilchrist nodded with a tip of his head. The other guy just watched.

'Hello, Detective,' Chastity said. 'Seems I just left your office.'

She got him to blush again, which meant that he was either still a young cop, or working the wrong job entirely. 'Yes, ma'am. I'm sorry, but this came up after you left.'

'I assumed as much.'

He couldn't even seem to look at her. 'I was wondering if you could identify something for me, Dr. Stanton,' he said instead, not looking appreciably more comfortable.

Chastity's stomach did a fresh slide that had nothing to do with bathrooms and old photos. Oh, God, she didn't want to be here. She did not want to know that she'd failed another sister before she'd even had a chance.

Because she knew this song, chapter and verse.

Detective Gilchrist was already reaching into his pocket, and it wasn't treasure he was going to show them.

But it was. Chastity damn near lost her breath when he

turned his closed hand palm up and exposed the evidence bag in his hand.

'Holy shit,' she breathed.

'Dear God,' Max moaned.

It was an emerald. A big, blue-green emerald the size of Chastity's knuckle, sparkling like the Caribbean in the early afternoon sun. Set into a yellow gold ring and bracketed by about a dozen equally impressive princess-cut diamonds.

Exquisite. Memorable.

'Do you recognize it, sir?' the detective asked, his voice as gentle as a man's could be.

'It's Faith's wedding ring,' Max said, his voice harsh, his hand out as if to touch it. Never reaching it. Just hovering there in front of him as if contact would make a statement he couldn't.

'Sir,' Detective Gilchrist said, not moving, that emerald still glowing in the refracted sunlight, 'can you tell me what it was doing on another woman's hand?'

Chapter Six

How interesting, was all Chastity could think. Here were the police waving around her sister's wedding ring – the wedding ring that wasn't on her sister's hand – and she couldn't seem to work up any emotion.

Not dread. Not fear. Not grief.

Because you'd think that a woman wouldn't part with a legacy like that without a serious tussle, which meant that Faith must have been involved in more than just hopping a cab out of town. And Chastity could only think, how interesting.

She should have felt something more. It was her sister, after all. But it was her sister she hadn't seen in ten years. Her sister who had evidently gone to exceptional lengths to re-create a life that Chastity had been fleeing as fast as her feet could carry her. Her sister who had married a man who looked just like the father who had terrorized his three daughters straight into hell.

Okay, so maybe it would take a little while for dread, fear, and grief to push past those photos in the bathroom. Chastity still felt way too betrayed to work up any other good emotion.

Obviously not a problem for the doc.

'What are you talking about?' he demanded, suddenly on his feet. 'What do you mean you found it on another woman?'

He'd gone so pale Chastity thought he'd keel over on the spot. She knew she should go out and get him a nice big glass of tea, but she couldn't seem to move.

Gilchrist considered the ring that dangled inside that bag, as if seeing it for the first time. 'Well, that's the puzzle, sir,' he said, evidently spokesman for the day. 'You see, this ring was found on an unidentified body in Bayou Segnette over in Jefferson Parish. When he recognized the ring from your missing persons report, Detective Dulane here notified us.'

If possible, Max got paler, his face tight and small somehow. 'Bayou Segnette? How could Faith ... I don't understand.'

'That's what I'm trying to tell you, sir. The woman we found isn't your wife. At least, the coroner doesn't believe so. This woman seems younger than your wife.'

'Seems?' Chastity couldn't help but ask. 'Does she look so much like my sister you're not sure?'

Detective Gilchrist didn't blush this time. He flinched. 'Um, you see,' he said, looking down at that wedding ring in his hand as if it would give him direction, 'the woman had been in the bayou a while, and ... '

Chastity nodded. 'Ah.'

'Then how can you be sure?' Max demanded. 'I mean, Faith cherishes her wedding ring. She would *never* give it up.'

Chastity took another look over at that decadent, seductive emerald, and suddenly, in a flash of belated memory and insight, thought of how, in fact, Faith could have given it up. She assessed the flashes of blue, the deep, sweet clarity of the stone. She considered the fact that for an emerald, which almost always had inclusions, it looked just a shade too perfect. She wondered offhandedly just how much that ring had cost. How much a person could get for it if she, say, finally wanted to run away from home.

She should have thought of this before, but all of Faith's jewelry had been right there in her box. All precisely laid out like stock on a jewelry counter. Chastity had seen it and hadn't even considered such a possibility. For some reason, though, it was the first thing she thought of when she saw that emerald.

But just how did she ask?

'Are there any identification marks on the ring, Max?' she asked. 'An inscription, maybe?'

Max stared at her as if she had no right to interrupt. 'Our initials. The date of our wedding.'

Gilchrist was already nodding. 'They're there. We checked.'

Chastity sat back and wondered when she could talk to the cop alone.

'But what does this *mean*?' Max demanded, pacing. 'Why would this woman have Faith's ring?'

'Well, that's what we're trying to figure out. Uh, just to make sure, would you mind our collecting something in the house that might have your wife's DNA on it? A hairbrush? Toothbrush?'

He got another tense silence, and then Max sat down.

'Her DNA. Then you're not sure.'

'We don't want to make a mistake, sir.'

Max nodded, a sharp, frantic movement. Chastity held her breath, terrified that Max would ask her to go back into that bathroom to look for a hairbrush. Before she could even offer, though, Max lurched to his feet and stalked from the room.

Chastity pulled herself together at warp speed. She needed information more than a meltdown right now.

'What else?' she asked Gilchrist, sotto voce.

Gilchrist took a nervous look toward the back hallway, where Max could be heard, and turned to the other detective, the black guy from Jefferson Parish, who finally came to life.

'The victim took a shotgun blast to the face. She's blond like your sister, and the same basic body type. But . . .'

He shrugged and Chastity nodded. 'There's not enough

left to do dentals or anything?'

'We'll be in touch with the family dentist, just in case.'

She nodded. 'You're sure there's nothing else, though. No clothing tags or tattoos or anything. I mean, everybody else in this city sure has a tattoo.'

'The body was unclothed,' Gilchrist said. 'No tattoos. Nothing definite about the soles of her feet. Well, you know . . .'

What was left of them.

'You don't think she's homeless, then,' Chastity said.

It was the first thing you checked on an unknown victim. If their feet were calloused and dirty, chances were they weren't into regular footwear. It made identification both easier and harder.

'No, but we can't take the chance.'

'Of course. And is she at the New Orleans coroner?'

'No, ma'am. Jefferson Parish. We're west of Orleans Parish. Bayou Segnette, where the victim was found, is in our jurisdiction.'

Chastity nodded. 'Your coroner use a forensic pathologist?'

He didn't seem in the least insulted by the question. 'We have three.'

'Can I talk to the pathologist involved?'

'His name is Willis. I'll let him know you might be in touch.'

'Thank you. Is there anything else? Anything I can do?'

Dulane shrugged. 'If you can find anything else out from Dr. Stanton that might point the way to who this woman might be . . .'

'You don't think it was a thief? Burglar or something?'

His eyebrow lifted. 'If you'd made off with that thing, do you think you'd wear it long enough to get shot in?'

Chastity had to smile, thinking of the cache in her pocket. 'Actually? Yeah. I would. At least long enough to pretend it was mine before I had to give it up for the rent money.'

88

The cop thought about that for a minute before he nodded.

Chastity squirmed. 'Um, Detective ... '

'Here.' Max was back, a tortoiseshell brush in his hand that was part of the set Chastity had seen on Faith's vanity. Dulane pulled out another evidence bag and stood to let Max drop the brush in. Then Max held out his own hand to Gilchrist, as if expecting a trade. His eyes on the brush, Gilchrist didn't notice at first.

'Thank you for bringing my wife's ring, Detective,' Max said, still standing there.

Gilchrist looked up at Max, and then he stood up. 'I'm sorry, sir. We can't give this back to you yet. It's evidence.'

Max went from paper white to mottled red, and suddenly Chastity could easily see him tossing instrument trays around.

'Do you know what that ring is worth?' Max demanded, his voice hard and sharp. A surgeon's voice. 'I'm not just giving it up to the property room of the New Orleans Police Department!'

Give them their due, neither detective so much as flinched.

'I'm sorry, sir,' Detective Dulane said, taking the ring back from Gilchrist and carefully holding it alongside the brush. 'I have no choice. I promise it'll be well taken care of. And it'll be in Jefferson Parish, not Orleans. At least for the present. I'd be happy to leave my card, if you have any questions.'

Chastity, well used to jurisdictional hot potatoes from her work in the much-fragmented St. Louis region, could see the frustration build in Max as he tried to follow the cop's logic.

'Max,' Chastity said in her best tension-defusing voice, 'he really can't give you the ring.'

'He would if I contacted his superiors,' Max assured her, his nostrils flaring.

89

'But you wouldn't do that,' Chastity said. 'Would you? Especially if it could jeopardize our chances of finding Faith?'

He actually flinched, as if she'd yanked him back from somewhere. Chastity could see him pull himself together.

'Yes,' he said, nodding, focused on no one. 'I see. Anything else right now?'

Dulane relaxed a bit. 'The name of your wife's dentist?'

Max went white again, all but swayed. 'Yes. Of course. Dr. Bradley. Dr. Simon Bradley.'

'Thank you, sir. I promise we'll be in touch.'

Max nodded him off like an intern. 'Then if you don't mind ...'

He just turned and walked away, leaving Chastity to see the detectives out. She stood where she was, though, watching until Max had walked down that long hallway and into the master suite he'd shared with her sister. Where he'd shared those marabou feathers.

Not something Chastity wanted to think about now. Instead she girded herself because she knew she was about to scale a wall.

'You wanted to ask something before,' Dulane said quietly.

Chastity turned back to see the two of them focusing their cops' eyes right on her. Oddly enough, it was what settled her. Cops she was used to. It was this house that was going to send her shrieking into the swamps.

'Yes,' she said, eyes back on the ring. On that decadent green stone that seemed to have a life of its own. 'Um, actually, I have a suggestion.'

Two left eyebrows lifted in tandem. Briefly Chastity thought to ask them how they'd mastered the trick.

'Go get that ring appraised,' she said. 'Right now.'

Gilchrist stiffened like an outraged virgin. 'If you don't trust us ...'

Chastity gave him a scowl that should have set his hair on fire. 'Back down, there, Detective. My thought is this.

90

I'm not sure what Dr. Stanton said when he reported his wife missing, but I think there might be a chance she just ran away from home. I told you that. But until I saw this ring, I wasn't sure how she managed it. Now ... well, the fact is, she's done it before.'

Both cops all but went on point.

'Pardon?'

Chastity reached for her little bag, and let it comfort her. She didn't know why she hadn't thought to tell him this earlier. She didn't know why she hadn't told Max.

Oh, yes she did. Because she survived by pretending that most of it had never happened. And all that jewelry had been sitting right there in Faith's bedroom. Even her pearls. The pearls Faith had deliberately left at home the last day she'd been seen.

God, Chastity thought. She should have recognized the pattern.

'Ten years ago, Faith and my mother disappeared from St. Louis without a trace. They didn't take credit cards or checkbooks or their own Social Security numbers. I know, because we looked. What they did take was all my mother's good jewelry.'

In the dead of night, from one sunset to a sunrise, before Chastity got out of bed in the cheap little apartment she'd been sharing with five other people. Before anybody could stop them or Chastity could ask why. But then, she'd known why.

Chastity could see all those cop questions build up behind their sharp eyes, and knew they realized that a ten-year-old case wasn't the one that should interest them. She felt the tension in her neck ease by millimeters.

'I'm not saying that we should discount foul play,' she insisted. 'But I thought you should know.'

Dulane shot a look down the hall. 'You think she was running from her husband?'

Gilchrist was the one to stiffen this time. But then, Max had saved his daddy.

'No.' She sighed, sucked it in to keep going. 'Not neces-sarily. Like I told you, Detective Gilchrist. My mother just died. It's not an uncommon time for children to decom-pensate. And Faith sure had the blueprint to do it.'

Oddly enough, it was the quiet Dulane who smiled. A gentle, white-toothed smile that helped Chastity maintain focus.

'About my suggestion,' she said.

'It would help to know where he bought the ring.'

'Leyton's on Royal,' Gilchrist said. 'Dr. Stanton told me when he filed the report. Said it was the family jeweler.'

Dulane had a look like he wanted to whistle at the infor-mation. After everything else, Chastity wasn't surprised.

'May I also suggest taking me along for validation?' she asked. 'In case my brother-in-law questions the results. He seems like a nice guy, but he's got a real hard-on about that ring.'

'As good a suggestion as that is,' Gilchrist demurred, his cheeks pinking up again, 'and not to denigrate your creden-tials ...'

'Which I assume you checked.'

'Which we did. We can't assume your objectivity.'

They could, but they wouldn't know that. She thought a minute. 'What about Kareena Boudreaux? Would she work?'

At once both expressions cleared.

'Kareena's nuts,' Dulane said. 'Once rode a motor scooter through the Charity ER. But she's a pro.'

'Good. I know where she works.'

Chastity took a minute to brave the master suite to let Max know that she was going out with the police.

'Would you rather I stay for a while?' she asked.

He was lying fully clothed on that beige bed, his arm over his eyes, the curtains drawn. The room was as cold as a morgue, and Chastity wanted out even before she went in. It occurred to her, this time, that if there wasn't anything of Faith in this room, there wasn't anything of Max either.

'What are you going to be doing?' he asked, not moving.

'Trying to find Faith.'

'Okay,' he said, his voice taut and thin. 'I think I'd rather have some time alone right now. Thanks.'

'I'll call later, okay?'

'Yeah. Thanks.'

A child bred and raised for guilt, Chastity was assailed by it as she backed out of that room. But she couldn't feel any remorse for escaping that house.

She was climbing into the backseat of the New Orleans police unit when she realized what she'd forgotten to ask Max.

'Hey, Detective, I don't suppose you found out anything more about that fertility clinic, did you?'

It was almost a pleasure to see him blush again.

Frankie Mae Savage drove a cab. A lean, sleek, mocha-skinned woman of Creole descent with sly blue eyes and the kind of marcelled hair Cab Callaway had once worn, Frankie Mae was the kind of woman who moved with sinuous grace and hid much of her intelligence behind a quiet smile.

Frankie Mae had been born in the Seventh Ward, the early Creole stronghold that had given birth to Jelly Roll Morton and Paul Barbarin. She now lived with her mother and little boy just downriver of the rehabbed cache of the Faubourg Marigny in Bywater, where her sky blue camel-back cottage sat between a warehouse and the Saint Claude Tabernacle of Light Church. She'd been driving a cab for fifteen years and knew New Orleans better than the cops.

Everybody knew Frankie's cab. It was pristine, polished, and featured a cast of plastic statues the tourists assumed were Catholic saints. Those who knew Frankie, though, recognized them as her orishas. Frankie Mae might have regularly attended the Saint Agnes Catholic Church, but she also practiced as a voodoo priestess.

When Frankie Mae drove her cab, she carried with her

Elegua, who looked like Saint Michael and ruled the cross-roads. Ibeyi, the divine twins who gave good fortune and opportunity, posing as Saints Cosmas and Damien. And in the center of her dashboard, just as in any good Catholic car, the Virgin Mary. Except in this cab, if Frankie were actually asked, she'd admit that her blue and white madonna was actually Yamaya, who rules the shallow water of the ocean and helps with family, with nurturing, with fertility.

Frankie had a full altar to her orishas in her home, where she made sure that especially Yamaya, her guiding spirit, was gifted with watermelon and crab claws and molasses each day. But in her car, she simply carried them all along.

At the moment, Frankie Mae's cab was parked in front of the Morial Convention Center down by the riverfront. There was a big CPA conference going on inside, and CPAs were notorious about not hanging around for the lectures. Frankie watched the street and listened to classical music on her radio and thought about how hot it was.

That was how that cute James Guidry caught her unawares.

'How are you today, Frankie?'

Frankie flashed an erotic smile at James. She knew him, of course. Nobody could miss those snapping green eyes and black hair. Or that terrible mass of scars all down his side. Frankie had offered to do a rite for him, but James had politely turned her down. James wasn't a believer, but he wasn't a man to sneer, either. She mostly liked James.

'I'm doin' well, James. Doin' well. And yourself?'

James leaned against her door and raised a cigarette. Frankie nodded and he lit up. 'Well, I have a strange gig, I have to say. I'm squiring a woman around lookin' for her sister.'

Frankie leaned back in her seat. 'Could be worse, I imagine.'

He nodded, sucked in a lungful of smoke. Frankie had offered to help him with that, too, but James just smiled and told her that firemen didn't know what to do unless they had a lungful of smoke.

'Odd thing is, seems the last this sister was seen was getting in a cab.' Setting the cigarette between his teeth, he reached into his T-shirt pocket and pulled out a photo. 'Recognize her, maybe? She was picked up from lunch at Gallatoire's a couple Fridays ago and hasn't been seen since. Her family's kinda worried.'

Frankie didn't hesitate more than a heartbeat. She reached out for that photo and gazed at it as if she'd never seen the like before. 'They ask her husband he seen her? It almost always the husband, cries "Oh, where's my wife?" when he's jus' finished choppin' her up in the basement.'

James smiled and Frankie wanted to smile back, even knowing better. 'Evidently this time the husband was in full sight of about fifty hospital personnel. He's some big surgeon at Tulane. You didn't pick her up, did you, Frankie?'

'Me? Nah. I'm usually right here that time of day. Convention crowd's much better tippers, and they always lookin' to lunch someplace. Either that or the Zephyrs, they playin' in town.'

James took a long drag from his cigarette and nodded. 'Would you mind asking around for me, Frankie? Her name's Faith Stanton.'

'Sure,' Frankie promised without blinking an eye. 'Be happy to, for you, James.'

James took a long look at Frankie, as if assessing her tone of voice. Then he just nodded, tapped her door in farewell, and ambled on down to the next cab in line.

Left behind, Frankie watched him in the rearview mirror. She was pretty proud of herself, keeping so calm and quiet. She'd wait for her fare, or until James worked his way through the taxi line and moved on. Then she'd take off and find out about this Faith's sister who'd suddenly shown up. Frankie had a bad feeling about that, cause it might mean that things could suddenly fall apart.

Which was something Frankie simply wasn't going to allow to happen.

'Get down,' Kareena breathed in awe.

Kareena looked like a Grapesicle as she stood in her scrubs and lab coat in the hushed and marbled environs of Leyton's Jewelers on Royal Street. Chastity, standing alongside, fought a growing feeling of dislocation. Going from that silent, sterile house in that silent, sterile subdivision back to the clatter and energy of the Quarter was seriously screwing with her mojo. And her mojo had already suffered enough setbacks today for a lifetime.

At this time of the day, traffic on Royal was cordoned off for the people who had the money to shop there, and street performers took up the corners. Mimes and dancers and old men playing blues on electric guitars. Antiques and jewelry and art filled the stores like an overfull suitcase that had burst at the seams. The sun beat down like purgatory, the whine of guitars bounced off the closely packed buildings, and the air was thick with the smell of food and flowers and always, just for seasoning, decay.

Chastity felt her blood pressure rise. She felt her juices flow. It was the closest she ever felt to being in the ER, where the rush of the unexpected kept you humming along.

There was life in St. Louis. There was diversity and color and music. But it just didn't have the intensity it had here, as if it were all packed in a tight box and lidded down. Which felt almost like alcohol on raw skin to Chastity's already fragile equilibrium.

And then, like crossing into the eye of the hurricane, they'd stepped into the elegant, smiling Leyton's Jewelers. Reached by buzzer, the store enveloped them, as if with old silk and champagne, in age and serenity and dignified excess.

Kareena made a beeline for the colored gemstone case. The detectives stood like a set of salt and pepper shakers at the diamond counter waiting for one of the Leyton senior staff. Chastity cruised the polished hardwood floors in search of anything that cost less than the yearly rent on her flat. And this was Max's jeweler? Chastity was definitely in the wrong end of medicine.

'Of course I recognize it,' the cultured, white-haired woman said with a precise smile a moment later as she held out a hand for the evidence bag. 'It was from the Van Bronson estate. A lovely six-point-four–carat, emerald-cut Colombian emerald set in sixteen F color, VVS clarity, ten-point princess-cut diamonds. Flawless.'

'Could you have your jeweler look at it for us?' Detective Gilchrist asked, looking like he wanted nothing more than to scratch somewhere.

The woman lifted a very elegant eyebrow. 'To?'

'We need an appraisal.'

She nodded. 'Of course.'

Evidently, in places like this, questions simply weren't asked.

Chastity moved in to watch and noticed that Kareena did the same, her habitual big-ass smile conspicuously absent. Kareena was at work, and like Dulane had said, she was a complete pro.

'Do you know if the ring's been in recently?' Chastity asked. 'Oh, for cleaning or anything?'

Since anytime a piece this valuable came through that glass and grilled door, the store would recheck the provenance and the stones to reinforce their reputation for honesty.

Another nod. 'I'll check. A moment.'

'You see this green thing, girl?' Kareena demanded, pointing to a necklace that looked alarmingly like a slug on a line. 'What the hell is that thing?'

'The green thing is a green tourmaline,' Chastity informed her. 'Next to it are alexandrite earrings and a lovely tanzanite and diamond necklace. You can buy that or a new Jeep Cherokee.'

'No way. You really know this shit?'

'Late night television, Kareena. It will tell you all.'

Kareena was busy ogling the slug necklace. 'Get down.'

'You seem to know your stones,' the white-haired woman said with a faintly larger smile as she returned to the case, card and loupe in hand.

Chastity smiled back. 'Wishful thinking only. You have an exquisite collection.'

'Yes,' she said without pretension. 'We do. Now, as for this ring, we actually haven't had it in for over a year. I'm surprised, actually. Dr. Stanton is a regular customer. I can't imagine him neglecting something this valuable.'

'How valuable, if I may ask?'

Another smile, this proprietary. 'On today's market, this ring could fetch almost sixty thousand dollars. Not only is the emerald the finest, but there are at least a dozen high-quality diamonds.'

Dulane hid his astonishment better than Gilchrist, who let go a startled, 'Fuck me.'

Again, silence fell. The woman slid the ring from the bag and lifted the loupe to her eye, her posture assured and settled. She knew exactly what she'd find when she examined that ring.

Suddenly she straightened. She looked up.

'Who asked for the appraisal?' she asked quietly.

Both cops pointed to Chastity.

'You *do* know your stones,' the woman murmured.

She called to somebody in the back, and a younger, russet-haired man joined her at the counter. She said nothing, just held out ring and loupe.

He bent to the task. Everybody waited.

He straightened as well. He looked at the woman. He looked at the card on the counter. He looked at the four people clustered around the other side of his case.

'It's excellent work,' he admitted, then handed the rings back to Dulane.

'But?'

He shrugged. 'It is the original setting. The hallmarks in

98

the gold are intact. But the stones are excellent quality fakes.'

The woman looked at the man. Gilchrist looked at Dulane. Kareena looked at Chastity.

'Somebody's screwed,' she said, and everybody nodded.

Chapter Seven

'So the stones could have been replaced anytime in the last year,' Chastity said glumly as she stared into her gin and tonic.

'Not much help,' Kareena agreed.

They'd finally found that jazz place Chastity wanted to go to, a little joint on Frenchmen Street. Actually, the jazz place was next door. They were sitting at the sidewalk in a new vegetarian-and-alcohol restaurant that was cheaper, less packed, and close enough to hear the great riffs coming from clubs along the street.

The perfect place to rehab and reflect.

The night was fairly dark, with a gibbous moon that seemed to melt a bit in the humidity as it floated between buildings. The sidewalks were thick with a pantheon of pedestrians, and the energy level was way beyond Chastity's.

She was still feeling itchy and raw, easily startled and battling sudden flushes of nausea. The day had worn badly on her, and yet here she was extending it by treating her nerves to New Orleans nightlife.

It was too much. Too full. Too good. It excited and soothed at the same time, sparking in her all the way to her fingertips.

'You sure you want to be doing that?' James asked suddenly, his shot of scotch halfway to his lips.

Chastity realized she'd been rubbing up against his leg. She flushed brick red, the shame instinctive and hard.

'Sorry,' she said, her gaze out to the street. 'Bad habit.'

She could still feel his leg against the sole of her foot, of course. She could smell him, with his soap and scotch and his cigarettes. She could see the sharp angles of the good side of his face and the long grace of his good fingers.

Chastity swore she hadn't been this bad for five years. She'd hidden in plain sight, a friend to all the men around her, intimate to none. Safe and separate and sane. Yet suddenly she was prey to the worst of her urges all over again.

Why was it James who set her off? Was it this city, which was so much like him, handsome and scarred and sly? Was it the search for her sister? Or just that damn chaos theory, spinning her completely out of control?

Well, it wouldn't spin her anywhere tonight. With every ounce of will she had, Chastity shut her weakness away, right behind the anxiety that ate at her sternum. She pulled in a breath and took a drink of gin.

'You really didn't find anything out today?' she asked.

James took a considered sip of his twelve-year-old Macallan, rolled it around in his mouth, and took a hit off his cigarette. 'A lot of nothing, which makes me suspicious. You'd think somebody would have seen something. Especially if they picked up a rich lady from Gallatoire's and took her to a fertility clinic.'

'How's your brother-in-law taking the thing about the ring and that Jane Doe?' Kareena asked.

Chastity shrugged. The gin wasn't working yet. She felt frayed and frantic, still caught between the smell of a man and a memory.

'Chastity?'

Chastity shook her head. 'I don't know how he's doing. I think he's as confused as I am. Who's the Jane Doe, and how did she get that ring? Did Faith run away or was she taken? Or did she run away and just stumble over something bad? Since she wasn't wearing her pearls, I have to think she ran. It's a statement, ya know?'

Chastity itched to get her hands on the rest of the jewelry in that glossy mahogany box in Faith's closet. What if she'd missed more fake stones? What if somebody had spent months building up a little nest egg that couldn't be traced?

'You told him about the fake stones yet?'

'Yep. He screamed like a banshee. Claimed the police did it. I told him the police wouldn't have had time to substitute a fake of that quality. He took a Valium and went to bed. I'm here soaking up the nightlife and trying to figure out how we're going to find her without the police, who now think she just ran away from home.'

She was there trying to figure out a way to protect herself from old sins and older secrets.

'Either of you know a jeweler?' she asked. 'Somebody who might know who could do that kind of replacement work?'

'I might,' James said. 'I'll check.'

She nodded. 'What if Faith bought a new identity with that money? It sure as hell isn't that hard to do anymore.'

'We'd never find her,' James said, as if it were that simple.

If that was what happened, Chastity didn't think she'd mind. After all, she could certainly understand wanting to run away from the life Faith had been trapped in. Hell, just those pictures in her bathroom were pathological. After only one look at them, Chastity had damn near walked straight into a swamp. She couldn't imagine facing them every time you had to brush your teeth.

'You keep saying you expected her to run away,' Kareena said.

Chastity sipped at her drink and watched as a couple began to dance out in the middle of the street, swaying and smiling as if it was the most important thing in life. Next door somebody was singing about having a bad Monday, and across the street somebody else banged out something like boogie-woogie on a piano.

102

'Why do I like it here so much?' she mused out loud, making it a point to take her attention from the street long enough to wave for another drink. 'I shouldn't like it here so much.'

'Why not?' James asked. 'All these other people do.'

'For one, it's surrounded by water. I hate water. I should be a puddle of Jell-O right now because of all that water.'

Kareena snorted, sniffing the air as if testing it. 'You don't know the half of it, girl. Pontchartrain keeps away from the Gulf by one little strip of land east of here, just marshes and shit. One good storm, and we'll be underwater like Atlantis.'

Chastity gulped her gin. 'Gee, thanks.'

'Matter of fact,' Kareena continued, waving her drink in the vague direction of the sea, 'I heard today on the Weather Channel, we already got us our third tropical depression brewin' in the Atlantic. They already think it's gonna be a big-ass mother.'

'Third, huh?' Chastity asked, wincing. 'Figures.'

'And it's heading our way, which is even wierder. Storms really don't start gearing up till at least July, even though this is the technical season and all. And no tropical storm has hit the mainland before August since 1999. How cool is that?'

Cool? Chastity felt a fresh frisson snake down her back. It figured, didn't it? The first time she sets foot out of St. Louis in her entire life, and hurricanes start sprouting out of season.

It, too, seemed inevitable.

She hated inevitability more than the number three. More even than water. She'd already suffered way too much from inevitability.

Kareena didn't notice how pale Chastity had suddenly become. 'So this could be the storm to send us under, yeah?' She grinned like the Cheshire Cat, high on the possibility of annihilation. 'That'd just be the end of the world, wouldn't it?'

103

Chastity focused on the street rather than on the pasta she'd just finished that now threatened to make a big comeback. She'd done that quite enough today already, thank you.

'By the time any hurricane hits here, I'll be back in St. Louis remembering you all fondly,' she promised.

'Don't assume nothin', girl. This may be your destiny.'

'My destiny is to retire from my job at an advanced age secure in the knowledge that I've lived a virtuous life on dry land.'

Even James laughed. 'Why else shouldn't you like it here?'

Chastity shot him an arch look. 'You kidding? I have trouble enough controlling my bad habits. I'd get no help here at all.'

He gave a slow nod. 'Maybe here you wouldn't have to always worry about it so much.'

'Oh, I think I would. My habits aren't happy ones, fireman.'

His answering expression acknowledged the fact that her foot had only recently left his leg. 'But if you exchanged them for habits that are happy, nurse ...'

This time he looked down to that foot, which was now tapping to the sound of the piano across the street.

'Oh, yeah,' she retorted dryly. 'Why didn't I think of that? You like it so much, why did you leave?'

'I came back.'

'I guessed that. I want to know why you left in the first place.'

He looked out into the crowd, the smoke from his cigarette curling up into his hair and drifting away up into the humid moon.

'Old habits. Older ties. You're born here, you get caught in the net. You get tied down with your family and old expectations and older problems and can't change, because for all the variety here, nothing really changes. Of course, if you're not from here, you aren't caught at all. You can

104

change all you want, and nobody knows. Or cares.' He pointed with his cigarette. 'See that woman over there? The tall one with the great legs? She's an ex-wide receiver from the Cleveland Browns. Lives down here with a architect and his kids, and they're as happy as clams.'

'But my sister came all this way *not* to change.'

Her sister had gone to great lengths to move to a city of metamorphosis and not transform at all. It sent a chill racing down Chastity's spine, just to think of it.

Maybe it wouldn't have bothered Chastity so much if it had been any other city. Indianapolis or Tulsa or Louisville, which weren't different enough to notice. But New Orleans really did feel like something completely alien.

Hell, she'd only been here a couple of days and already couldn't quite feel her feet under her anymore. She didn't know if she trusted herself. She didn't know if she trusted the city.

But oh God, suddenly she thought maybe she wanted to.

But what if she moved here and ended up doing what Faith had? What if she planted herself in this thriving jungle of art and artifice, just to re-create the past that had so fractured her? Would she put up pictures of her father, too, to remind herself of what she really was?

She remembered once seeing a monster film with Boris Karloff. He'd found a way to transplant brains, and he'd transplanted the brain of his hunchbacked assistant, Igor. He'd put that tiny, warped brain into a strong, handsome body. But Igor didn't love his new body. His brain was too used to the old one. In only weeks, he was hunchbacked and shuffling again, because that was what he was used to. It was how he saw himself, and more frightened him too much.

Chastity was terrified, sitting here on a moonlit night in New Orleans, that she'd be tempted to transplant her brain down to this free and impulsive place, only to start shuffling.

'Why did you come back?' she asked.

James smiled this time, and merely cocked his head out the door into the street.

'Oh, bullshit,' Kareena scoffed, sweeping a judgmental hand at him. 'You came back cause you're in love with all that dead shit.'

'Dead shit?' Chastity asked, eyebrow raised.

Kareena huffed in indignation. 'They love their dead things down here, girl. Cemeteries, ghosts, vampires – which never even was heard of until Ann Rice, but that's another matter – dead things. James been obsessed with all that shit since he been back here.'

'Chicago isn't as receptive to it as they are here,' James said.

Chastity cast a sidelong look at James, who was still watching the street life. 'Dead things, huh?'

He just nodded. 'You become acquainted with death, you don't want him to ever be a stranger again, ya know? That way when he finally comes back, he'll surely treat you more kindly. Here in N'awlins, he's always part of the dance.'

Chastity wished she didn't understand what he was saying. But she'd been acquainted with death for a long time herself. And, like James, death wasn't really the thing she feared most. The inside of her own head was. The monster under her bed.

She got her new drink and damn near finished it in one swallow.

'So what you gonna do next?' Kareena asked.

Chastity tried to pull her brain into some kind of working order. 'The fertility clinic. Did you find anything out?'

Kareena leaned forward, intent. 'Sure. The Arlen Clinic gets a clean bill of health. Private, local, with strict adherence to health guidelines. Not a peep of a problem.'

'Any others?'

'There are six in town. A couple get low marks for charging for storing alleged embryos when what they're

106

storing is biological waste. Those are the high-volume places, advertise on television, shit like that. No real violations, though. And I did hear of a couple that are skating right on the edge. They do shit like auction off good sperm and eggs and that.'

'Auction them off?'

'Yeah, like a supermodel's an' shit. One of them, New Life, tried to place their stuff on eBay, but they got themselves slapped down. They're getting them a real hairy eyeball from the state.'

'But Arlen is okay.'

'Far as anybody know.'

Chastity nodded, her eyes on her glass, her thoughts struggling to focus. Better than thinking about what had happened all day. 'How far away is Bayou Segnette anyway?'

'About ten miles upriver,' James said. 'It's where they bus the tourists to see a swamp without having to actually go to one.'

Chastity thought about that. 'It seems to me that with all the water you guys have around here, it's a stupid murderer who dumps a body right in the middle of a tourist swamp.'

'Nobody says murderers have to be smart.'

'Well, let's hope this one isn't. Maybe the Jefferson Parish pathologist can give us something.'

Kareena perked right up. 'Which one? I know people there.'

'I bet you do. His name's Willis.'

Kareena did everything but spit in the street. 'Ooo-ee, girl, you hadda go pick that waste of protoplasm.'

Chastity immediately felt worse. 'I didn't pick anybody. You know him, I take it.'

Kareena dolefully shook her head. 'You lucky he recognized she dead, girl. They tryin' to get him outa there for years. I think he got pictures of somebody with a goat, somethin' like that.'

'Great. So I can't trust his results.'

107

'Well, he don't do the DNA, so that should be good. But he not the freshest taco on the plate. And you come from Mary Case jurisdiction up in St. Louis, yeah? Shit, she finish an autopsy, that body look like a fuckin' canoe. Willis couldn't pick a canoe outa a lineup.'

Chastity sighed. 'Which means they could have Faith on their table after all, and we won't know for sure till the DNA is done in a month or so. I'm just feeling better and better.'

Kareena had the gall to grin. 'There some things down here you just got to get used to. N'awlins, we jus' different.'

'So I hear.'

Chastity was feeling even worse. She should have listened to those omens. Kareena finished her drink and ordered another. James just tapped his foot and watched the nightlife, which was what Chastity should have been doing. At least for a bit, the driving piano across the street was louder than the blues next door.

'You keep saying you think your sister, she run away,' Kareena said, her forehead pursed. 'And you knew about that emerald. Why?'

Chastity sighed. She should know better than to try and slide past Kareena. Still, she couldn't face her. She watched the street and all those people who didn't know her. And she told Kareena about that day ten years ago when she'd gone home to find it empty.

Now she had both their attention. In fact, Kareena was looking decidedly owlish. 'But the police looked,' she said. 'Didn't they?'

'Well. Not for long. There was a note.'

After what you've done, I never want to see you again.
What she'd done.

Her stomach lurched again. Her back broke out in sweat, and she wanted to move.

'How'd your daddy react?' Kareena asked.

'Oh, he was already gone by then.'

'Dead?'

Chastity glared. 'Yes. Dead. I was the only one left.'

'But you couldn't have been more than—'

'Sixteen. Yeah. Obviously, though, I'm fine.'

James cleared his throat, and Chastity realized she was once again running her bare foot up and down his calf. She couldn't even apologize. She just pulled her chair farther away.

He smiled. 'Hey, a guy with a face like Freddy Kruger can only take that as a compliment.'

Don't, she wanted to say. *Don't you dare be kind to me.*

'Fishing for compliments?' she asked instead.

Now the singer next door was having trouble with his girl and his dog. The dancing couple had moved on, and a gaggle of giggling young women wandered by, obviously in search of the Girls Gone Wild cameras so they could pull up their tops. The humidity still hung heavy in the hot air, and there was no wind. Chastity couldn't breathe, and she wanted to cry.

'I really do like it here,' she admitted, wondering if they realized that she sounded afraid.

'Then solve this and move yourself down,' Kareena said. 'I'm sure we can find some work for you.'

She shook her head. 'I'd end up bringing my brain with me.'

They didn't even bother to answer.

'Do you know why they left?' Kareena asked.

'Kareena, stop,' James admonished. 'Ain't your business.'

'Besides,' Chastity added, her voice awfully calm for the fire that was consuming her chest, 'if you've been keepin' track, my mother's dead, and my sister's missing. Little chance to talk to them since I've been here.'

Kareena waved her off like an incorrect fourth grader. 'What about that note they wrote when they left you? What it say?'

'What it said was not pertinent.'

''Course it was. It took ten years for you to find 'em again, and that was only because her husband call you.'

'I didn't look hard, either, Kareena.' A lie, but one she'd perfected over the years. 'It was just that kind of family.'

'Then why'd your sister run away again now?' Kareena persisted, the bone firmly in her little jaw. 'I mean, right now?'

'Because my mother just died, that's why.'

'And?'

'And? And what?'

'And why did your sister run away now?'

Chastity slammed her empty glass on the table so hard it cracked. 'My sister ran away because my mother let her gray-haired husband fuck her three daughters. Even so, Faith took care of her anyway until the day she died. That's why.'

Well, she'd obviously finally had too much gin.

She also seemed to have accomplished the impossible. She'd left Kareena Boudreaux slack-jawed. Not to mention several people who'd been walking by and stood frozen in place. Even the singer next door seemed to pause, right between bad loves and prison.

Chastity felt a huge chasm open up right in the middle of her chest. Her hands started to shake, and she couldn't find her little velvet bag for comfort. She wanted to run away, but she seriously doubted her legs would work, or that she could see to get anywhere.

'What'd I tell you?' she said, looking out to the street that still seethed with music and laughter, her own voice bleak. 'This city just isn't good for me.'

James, his eyes suspiciously calm and distant, sipped at his drink. 'Think of it this way. You'll never have to see those people again as long as you live.'

Chastity gave him a startled look, but his expression didn't change. He didn't react or cry out or run away. It didn't matter. Chastity knew she'd see it soon. Or find out that he just hid it better than Kareena.

110

That flicker of pity. The instinctive revulsion at finding himself forced to witness someone else's shame.

And every time Chastity saw it, or imagined she saw it, she'd remember what she'd actually put into words for the first time in seven years, since that day she'd shattered the silence in her therapist's office with her screaming.

A brand, raised on her forehead like fire.

Shit. She should have known better than to come down here. She turned her attention back to the street and finally located her bag, right there in her pocket where she'd put it.

'Have I ever told you about the chaos theory?' she asked, throwing back the dregs of her drink and calling for another. 'It says that just when an organism believes itself to have found perfect harmony, it's really just about to spin completely out of control. I was in perfect harmony last week.'

She didn't bother to look at her friends for a response. It was much easier to pretend she was enjoying the street.

'It also says that the organism progresses through the chaos to a new harmony,' James said quietly.

Chastity laughed. 'I think that's wishful chaos thinking.'

'Not the same harmony, of course. Something better and stronger.'

'Ah. Not wishful, then. Delusional.'

Kareena, her focus still caught on the horns of Chastity's revelation, was just catching up. 'Get down,' she breathed, eyes even wider with suddenly comprehension. 'You the one who blew the whistle on your daddy, weren't you?'

All those bright pillows and saris and posters in her room, and yet Faith had never been happy. Not once. Chastity had thought that if she called the police, she might finally make Faith happy.

Silly her.

She accepted another gin from the increasingly efficient waitress. 'You get to go on to Final Jeopardy, Kareena. Want to pick another category?'

Obviously not. Chastity could see that warp-speed brain starting to smoke.

'It's where the sexual addiction came from.' Kareena said it in her professional voice, calm and quiet and empathetic.

Chastity barely kept herself from just closing her eyes and sinking to the ground. 'Pathetically predictable, huh? Like I said. I'm just a *Jerry Springer Show*.'

Just another abused little girl acting out and crying for help and getting approval the only way she knew how.

'And Faith?'

'As far as I know, consistently denies that anything ever happened.'

Kareena just nodded, her eyes quiet and strong and deep. James, next to her, looked like a sphinx. Chastity shook and drank.

'You said three daughters,' Kareena said. 'What—'

'We're moving on, now, Kareena,' Chastity said, her smile hard. 'Throw all those questions into the dysfunctional family bin and be done with it.'

Kareena actually blushed. 'Yeah, girl. You right. Kareena sometimes get too nosy.'

'If she didn't,' Chastity retorted gently, 'she wouldn't be so good at her job. Okay?'

Kareena's smile wasn't quite at regular wattage. 'Yeah. Okay.'

Chastity smiled back. She sipped her gin for a minute and willed her heart rate to slow toward normal. At least panic stricken as opposed to terrorized. Thank God for unaltruistic James. He just sat there splayed out on his chair like a disgruntled teen and let his eyes roam the street.

'Ya know what?' Chastity said suddenly, climbing to her feet. 'I want to dance. Can you dance next door, James?'

Kareena's hoot of laughter sounded equal parts relieved and anxious. 'Honey, James can't dance anywhere. He's a white boy.'

James looked affronted. 'I'm part coonass. I can dance.'

'Only to that nasty zydeco shit. You wanna dance, girl? Come with Kareena.'

So they all walked next door and danced until about three in the morning. They ended up singing along with 'Blue Monday' and catching a cab that wasn't James's back to Kareena's. James, who lived on the fourth floor over the Big Dawg Saloon on Bourbon Street, simply strolled home.

'You okay, Chaz?' Kareena asked before they parted in the hallway of her house.

Chastity smiled past numb lips, as if she'd really enjoyed the entirety of her evening. 'I'm fine, Kareena.'

'You're sure? I mean ... '

'Honey, it's old news. I just kinda surprised myself blurting it out for the edification of every tourist in the French Quarter.'

Caught there at the edge of the light, Kareena didn't move. Chastity smiled and shooed her off. 'I mean it. Now, I have to sleep off some of this gin before I get up in four hours.'

Kareena walked away. She shut off the lights, and Chastity was left to enter her own room, where her bed awaited her.

At 4 A.M. EST, the third tropical depression to gather in the Atlantic Ocean gained enough force to be called the second tropical storm of the year. Officially named Bob, it already boasted well-defined margins and a wind speed of 60 miles per hour. Meteorologists along the East Coast began to plot out possible courses and worried about the coming storm Bob promised to be. The Weather Channel geared up like it was the World Series. The Weather Channel made its money on hurricanes.

The first slivers of gray morning light sliced through the blinds in the Elvis Costello room. Rain pattered against the windows, and the ceiling fan clicked. Hunched over the rumpled, stale sheets on her bed, Chastity fingered the spill

113

of stones that glittered from within the folds of the bedclothes. She counted them again: one, two three, four, five peridots. One, two, three aquamarines. One, two, three, four, five, six, seven citrines.

She counted and she shook and she sweated, there on her small bed in a strange city, and she waited.

Finally, just as she knew it would, her cell phone rang.

'Take Me Out to the Ball Game.'

'Hello?'

'It's been a long time since you've needed to call me this late,' the calm, quiet voice said into her ear. 'Or this early.'

Tears gathered in Chastity's eyes and spilled over the gemstones she hoarded between her knees. 'I know. But you said . . .'

'That's what therapists are for, Chastity. What happened?'

Chastity closed her eyes. She gathered her treasures into her hand, and she told her therapist about the trip she'd taken and the day she'd had and the search for her sister. She especially told her about her sister.

What Chastity didn't tell even her therapist was that the very last thing she really wanted to do was find her.

Chapter Eight

'How are you doing, Max?' Chastity asked four hours later.

They had met at the Whistle Stop, a diner on St. Charles frequented by everybody from cops to businessmen. The waitresses were efficient and brisk, and the coffee strong enough to melt spoons. Chastity was drinking hers like Gatorade at a soccer game.

For the first time since she'd met him, Max looked worse than she did. Pale, drawn, and just a bit disheveled, he was fidgeting as if he couldn't hold still. Chastity battled a fresh flare of guilt. After what he'd learned the day before, maybe she should have stayed with him.

It didn't mean she could have. She'd barely made it to dawn where she was.

He shuffled his cutlery like cards. 'I just don't know what to do. What to think.'

'I know. You don't have any idea who that woman they found could be?'

If she wasn't Faith, that is.

He straightened as if insulted. 'No. Of course not.'

Chastity sucked in a careful breath. 'And you're sure that there was nothing different about Faith these last few weeks. Nothing that could have made you think, maybe . . .'

His head shot up and his fist hit the table. 'My wife did *not* leave me.'

Chastity jumped as high as the cutlery. For a second, a startled silence fell in the diner. Reaching across the booth, Chastity tried to take hold of Max's fist, to settle him. Max yanked away from her as if she were toxic.

'You *will* keep looking for her,' he demanded. 'You won't stop now. You can't.'

'Of course I won't,' she assured him, suddenly feeling at sea herself. 'I'm going to start talking to her friends today. To everyone in her address book.'

Max kept his eyes on her, his thankfully brown eyes, as he seemed to pull himself together. Gather his poise. He even managed a brief smile.

'Excuse me,' he said with a stiff shrug and leaned back. 'I didn't mean to snap. It's just ... those police are convinced she ran away, aren't they? Especially now.'

'They might be. But I'll keep on looking. I told you I would.'

He nodded, looked around as if checking responses at the other tables. But everybody else was already back to their own business.

'That's all I need,' he said. 'If I can count on you, I know I'll be okay.'

Again he paused. Straightened a little. Assumed that gentle, smiling self she'd first met. 'What else can I tell you, Chastity?'

No wonder they liked him in surgery if he could control his tantrums this quickly.

'Chaz,' Chastity corrected him. 'You can tell me about the Arlen Clinic, Max.'

Again, his impatience slipped loose. But just in his eyes. 'I already told you about it.'

'No. You just told me the name. I'm not from here, Max. I didn't know what it was. And I certainly wouldn't have guessed from what you said that it was a fertility clinic. One of the witnesses at Gallatoire's said Faith asked to go to one. Do you know why?'

Chastity caught another brief flash of irritation in his

eyes, right before he donned a gently smug smile. 'Well, it's not what you think. We had a friend who couldn't conceive. Faith donated ova for her. At the clinic. It gave her the idea that it was a nice thing to do for infertile women. She ended up donating for about, oh, three years or so. Off and on.' He smiled, the proprietary smile of a proud husband. 'She loved giving that kind of gift. But when her mother got so ill, she decided to stop. I can't imagine why anybody would have thought she went back.'

Chastity frowned down at her coffee. 'But isn't she too old to donate eggs? I thought the cutoff was, like, thirty-two or three.'

Max frowned a bit. 'The cutoff is thirty-five at Arlen. And your sister turned thirty-four last month. It's why she retired when she did.'

Chastity looked up to see Max sipping his coffee, perfectly certain of what he'd said. Okay, she wondered. Did she tell him the truth about that, too? Did it matter so much that he know his wife was really thirty-eight and shouldn't have been donating anything faintly reproductive for at least the last three years?

Chastity just didn't have that much courage. Besides, it wouldn't make any difference in the long run.

'Can you call the clinic and give your permission for me to talk to them?' she asked. 'Just in case Faith did go there.'

He shrugged. 'Of course. Oh, and I'll call the bank and see if there's any activity on her checkbook. Is that right?'

'Yes.'

He focused on her a second, that laserlike eyeball that only a surgeon can master. 'My wife wouldn't leave me, Chastity.'

Nothing like a surgeon for certainty.

'She might not have been leaving you, Max. She might have just been running away from overwhelming stress. But I'll find her, I promise. I'll make sure she's okay.'

He reached over and patted her hand, an utterly avuncular motion. 'I'll never understand what was wrong between you two.'

Chastity managed a travesty of a smile. 'Someday I'll tell you.'

In the meantime, she needed to get moving. She could see James out in his hack reading the *Times-Picayune*. If he was going to earn that Richard Gere money, they had people to see and fertility clinics to investigate.

'I'm not sure I approve of him,' Max said, following her gaze.

'He's an ex-firefighter,' Chastity said, the only defense she figured James needed. 'Obviously invalided out from a bad fire. I have no problem trusting him.'

Max considered her for a minute, those sharp brown eyes of his betraying nothing. Then he just nodded and pulled out his wallet.

'I really do wish you'd stay west of the river. It's much safer there.'

'Except for those wild pigs,' Chastity couldn't help but say.

Max didn't seem amused. 'I feel responsible for you.'

'Well, Max, don't.'

That didn't sit well, either. But Chastity had stood up to too many doctors to let that bother her. Gathering her purse, she climbed to her feet.

'I'll call you later today, okay?'

They left it at that, and Chastity walked out, most of her breakfast still on her plate.

It was almost time for lunch. Melanie Magee knew that because little Mrs. Carrera in the first row was beginning to fidget. It was a too-bright, too-hot, too-summer day outside, and the air-conditioning at the Metairie Retirement Community wasn't keeping up with it. Melanie felt sticky and limp beneath her makeup and wardrobe. The old people didn't mind, of course. They didn't have enough body fat left to withstand any climate less than tropical.

118

Melanie knew she had enough body fat. Plenty, in fact, for the average healthy twenty-four-year-old postgrad student in history. A postgrad student who was at the moment dressed up as Elvis.

'Thank you very much, Mr. Evers,' she huffed in her best Elvis voice. 'Now then, everybody, let's just pull another ball and see who gets bingo, all right?'

Bingo with Elvis. It was Melanie's newest, hottest gig to help defray the astronomical cost of her doctorate. Twice a week she toured the local retirement communities in a white jumpsuit, handing out bingo cards and singing 'Blue Suede Shoes' on a Mr. Microphone.

Then, in the evening, she did her k.d. lang impersonation down at the Lotusland Club in the Quarter, where she was the ringer in the gender illusion show that made people wonder even harder who the real women were.

Melanie had no problems with her gigs. They paid well, she made people smile, and she had plenty of time for research and reading. She still lived with her parents in Metairie, the most boring place on earth in comparison to New Orleans proper. But her parents worried, and Melanie was a good girl.

Melanie did have a secret, though. It had to do with how else she made money. Even her boyfriend, Kevin, didn't know, because for the moment it wasn't his business. Besides, it wasn't illegal, and she was putting a much bigger dent in her loans doing that than she did prancing around in an Elvis outfit.

'Uh-huh,' she huffed in her best baritone as she held up the next ball. 'I'm shakin' all over, baby. It's B 15.'

'Bingo!!' Mrs. Ignacio warbled from the back row.

Melanie was just about to pick up the mike to serenade the winner, when her beeper went off. Reaching into the hip pocket she'd sewn into her white jumpsuit, she checked it.

911. The package has resurfaced. Meet me.

'Oh, shit,' she muttered.

Well, maybe she was doing something a little illegal.

'What's that?' Mrs. Ignacio demanded, impatient for lunch.

Melanie pasted a big smile on her face and slid the beeper away. 'Well, now, Mrs. Ignacio, you just won ten dollars and that fine bottle of hand lotion. Now, Elvis has another gig to play, so enjoy your lunch. You all come back now, y'hear?'

And after packing up all her supplies as quickly as possible, Elvis left the building. She had something vaguely illegal to do.

From the outside, the Arlen Clinic looked like no medical facility Chastity had ever seen. A lovely blue, green, and white Victorian house complete with turrets and leaded glass windows, it took up the corner of Delachaise near the Touro Infirmary and looked like an upscale B and B. Lots of trees, a big porch with wicker furniture, and lush flower beds to line the sidewalk.

Of course, most B and Bs didn't sport a line of protesters out front. Not to mention the police car and crime scene van.

'Well, now, this looks interesting,' Chastity mused as James pulled them to a stop behind the cop car.

'Breaking through a line of people chanting slogans costs extra,' James informed her from the front seat.

'Be content, fireman,' she said, pushing open the door. 'This doesn't really look like a tear gas kind of crowd.'

Not yet, anyway. The line was a bit straggly, some serious middle-aged women, a mother or two with children, and a young man standing along the edge of the lawn with hand-drawn placards.

Genetic Monsters.

Murderers.

Every Baby Deserves a Chance.

Chastity hitched her purse over her shoulder and prepared to breach the line. A uniformed officer took up one of the wicker chairs on the clinic porch, but he was well settled in. It seemed that Chastity was on her own with this bunch.

She barely made it to the front walk of the clinic before the intense young man planted himself in front of her.

'What are *you* doing here?' he demanded, looking indignant.

He was the one with the Murderers sign. Painted in dripping red, as if the word weren't message enough. In his late twenties, he was good-looking, buttoned-down, and close-combed as a marine.

Chastity lifted an eyebrow. 'Minding my own business, why?'

He stopped within millimeters of her toes. Chastity wondered if he wanted her to step back. She didn't.

He leaned forward. Actually, he leaned over. He had about six inches on her. 'I know you, and I know what you do. And in the name of God, you're going to stop.'

'No kidding,' Chastity responded, wondering if she should recognize him from the night before. 'Which thing that I do am I supposed to stop?'

'I *know* you,' he insisted, as if she should understand.

'Yes.' Chastity nodded. 'So you said.'

'Am I going to have to carry you across that picket line?' James asked from the taxi.

'Nah. This nice young man's gonna let me by now. He knows if he doesn't, that policeman up on the porch is going to get upset.'

'Murderer,' he hissed, giving ground. 'You and all your kind. Selfish, thoughtless murderers. Your judgment is here.'

'If it's all the same to you,' Chastity said, walking by, 'could it wait till I'm finished? I hate to miss an appointment.'

'I knew I didn't need to get out of the car,' James groused.

The uniform climbed to his feet as she approached and asked for ID.

'I'm here to meet Dr. Petit,' Chastity said, flashing her hospital ID as if it were an FBI shield. It had taken her all damn morning to score this interview. She wasn't about to miss it now. Not after she and James had swung by every other fertility clinic in town to find that nobody recognized Faith's name or face, but that everybody seemed to want a blond-haired, blue-eyed egg donor.

'Nurse, huh?' the cop said, squinting. 'You don't got a driver's license?'

'Not this week.'

He nodded, unconcerned. 'You're not here to throw blood on anybody or anything, are you?'

'I couldn't fit it in my purse.'

That made him laugh, so he waved her on by.

That homey B and B illusion lasted all the way through the entryway and into the large, bay-windowed front parlor. All soft colors and bright flowers, it had high ceilings and pastel rugs on gleaming hardwood floors. Overstuffed couches and lamp lighting.

The fantasy was quickly marred by all the *American Baby* and *Mother* magazines lying about. The obligatory Mary Cassatt prints on the wall. The rather utilitarian reception desk crammed against the far wall that was staffed by a smiling woman who reeked of efficiency and confidentiality.

'I'm here to see Dr. Sidney Petit,' Chastity announced. 'I'm Chastity Byrnes.'

Well, at least Chastity knew the receptionist was human. She caught the flicker of humor in those comfortable brown eyes. 'Of course. Have a seat.'

Chastity strolled instead to the window to see that for all the light coming in, somehow there wasn't much to see outside but trees. Another graceful illusion that provided privacy from prying eyes. Fertility was a personal business, after all.

'I'm telling you, we need more security,' she heard behind her. 'They could have gotten in.'

Chastity took a slow turn to see the tallest, biggest, baldest lab-coated man in the world whispering to a petite brunette in a business suit and flats. A woman with short brown hair, a roundish face, and a jaw that was just a little short.

The doctor. Chastity could spot them a mile away. The big guy looked furious. The doctor was patting his arm as if he were a toddler, her irritation just barely in check. The receptionist sat there as if she didn't notice what was going on three feet away.

'It never would have happened,' the doctor said. 'Your security precautions are second to none, Eddie. Now, the police are finished. We need to get back to work.'

She looked up then to find Chastity standing by the ficus tree in the parlor. A bright smile lit her pleasant features. In contrast, when the bald guy caught sight of her, he looked horrified. Chastity could have sworn he went white for a second, before Dr. Petit stepped forward.

'Ms. Byrnes,' she said, hand out. 'I'm Sidney Petit.'

Chastity took her hand and shook. Good clasp, dry palms. Relaxed eye contact. A woman comfortably in charge.

'I appreciate your seeing me, Dr. Petit,' Chastity said. 'If this is a bad time . . .'

Dr. Petit just kept smiling. 'I'm sorry you had to wade through all that. But don't worry. We're about all finished.'

Then, turning away from the doorway, as if to sever attention from the motley crew beyond her lawn, she motioned Chastity farther into the building.

'You've come about Faith, of course.' She seemed to heave a sigh, then shook her head. 'We're happy to help in any way we can.'

She would. Chastity could see that. But the big guy over by the reception desk wasn't quite so sanguine. He was back in scowl mode, his posture rigid with outrage.

'Eddie?' Dr. Petit called over to him. 'This is Faith's sister Chastity. You'll want to meet her.'

123

Eddie hesitated, his face all but hidden for a second. Then, as if bracing for something, he lumbered over with a hand out.

Dr. Petit smiled. 'This is Eddie Dupre, our embryologist here at the Arlen Clinic. He and Faith got to be good friends.'

Eddie's hand was damp, his gaze unable to settle on Chastity. He topped her by a solid foot. 'Nice to meet you. I have to ... uh ...'

Dr. Petit patted him again. 'Eddie's a bit distracted today. Somebody broke in last night. Tried to get into his laboratory. We've been dealing with police all day.'

'Not to mention protesters,' Chastity acknowledged. 'That a normal thing for you?'

'They're the ones who tried to break in,' Eddie said, his voice hot again. 'They were trying to get the babies.'

'The babies?'

Another smile from the doctor. 'The cryopreserved embryos. We store them here, in Eddie's lab. There is a possibility it was protesters ...'

Chastity nodded. 'Ah. The Murderers signs out front. You destroy the unwanted embryos, which they consider children.'

Dr. Petit offered a small sigh. 'We're actually much more responsible than most labs. We never store more than six extra embryos per request, and we have an embryo adoption program for the extra embryos. But, well, it's still such a new science that of course there will be questions.'

'There will be *terrorists*,' Eddie insisted. 'That man outside is the one who did this. That Lloyd Burgard. Mark my words.'

'If he's the guy with the Murderers sign,' Chastity said, 'I have to admit that he does lack basic manners.'

Dr. Petit smiled. Eddie didn't.

'If you could stop by in a bit, Eddie, to talk to us,' Dr. Petit suggested, then turned to Chastity. 'I know Eddie invited your sister to his annual hurricane season party.'

124

'Hurricane season party?' Chastity echoed a bit blankly, thinking that nobody in this city took disaster seriously.

'She wasn't there,' was all Eddie said. 'The police already asked me.'

Then he just stalked off before Chastity could ask more.

Dr. Petit shook her head. 'Usually Eddie is very friendly.'

'If Eddie is Faith's friend,' Chastity said, 'it's doubtful he has a good opinion about me.'

For a second, Dr. Petit just looked at her. Blinked. Probably fought a thousand questions. 'Why don't we go on back to my office where we'll be comfortable?' she finally said.

Dr. Petit led Chastity back toward the heavy oak door through which Eddie had disappeared. They stopped just before it, where a small elevator had been tucked into an alcove.

'According to reports,' Chastity said, 'my sister came here two weeks ago last Friday. But the receptionist didn't recognize her when the police asked. Would you have been here on that day?'

Just about to punch a button, Dr. Petit stopped. 'I was. But I can promise I never got as far as the front desk. It's a scheduled procedure day.'

'Meaning?'

Dr. Petit's smile was patient. 'We only perform procedures during a two-week period every month. The other two weeks we prepare the next clients and clean and check the surgical suites and laboratories. That Friday was dead center in the middle of the two-week procedure cycle. I never so much as saw my office, much less the front hall.'

Chastity nodded. 'I see.'

'Would you like a tour?' Dr. Petit asked. 'It might help you understand what Faith was involved with.'

Chastity considered the offer, then nodded. 'Yes. Thanks. We don't get much call for fertility information where I work. If this was important to my sister, though, I need to know.'

125

Dr. Petit turned toward the oak door. 'Oh, it was. By the time Faith left us, the staff had taken to calling her Sister Mercy.'

'So she was a regular?'

Dr. Petit nodded again and ushered Chastity through the oak door into the more traditional medical environment beyond. Oh, there were carpets where staff manned desks and changing rooms that looked more like dens. But surgical tables were tucked behind glass partitions. Centrifuges and lab equipment took up one wall, and hospital doors had signs like Equipment Room and Laboratory.

'Faith first came to us about three years ago,' Dr. Petit said. 'A friend of hers couldn't conceive. Had tried IVF – in vitro fertilization – without success. Her eggs simply weren't viable material. Faith offered her own eggs, and her friend had a lovely set of twins. After that, Faith put herself on our registry for donors and she became very productive. We had ten successful pregnancies from her.'

'Ten,' Chastity answered. 'Isn't that a lot?'

'Yes. Usually a woman doesn't donate more than four times or so. Our limit is twenty, to prevent commingling. But Faith really felt it was a mission, and wanted to help as long as she could.'

'And you felt she was healthy enough at her age to do it?'

'Of course. She had a physical. A psychological interview ...'

'Really? How thorough?' Considering Faith's background.

'Well, it's a phone interview,' Dr. Petit said. 'But they're very thorough.'

Chastity stared. 'Over the phone?'

'It's standard. And, of course, Faith had already proved that her eggs could produce a viable pregnancy. That's very desirable.'

'Um, is that how you get most donors? Doing it for friends?'

126

'Oh, no,' Dr. Petit said as she resumed the walk. 'It's just one way. Some women donate extra eggs after a successful IVF, or begin to donate for others. And we do a lot of advertising, much of it in college newspapers and magazines around the tristate area. Our best candidates tend to be college students.'

'Good heavens. Why?'

Another smile as they stopped by the surgical suite. 'They're healthy and young. They're interested in the money. Right now, a donated oocyte is worth about five thousand dollars, plus expenses, and takes only about two weeks out of a young woman's schedule. Maybe ten doctor's visits, one week of ultrasounds and blood tests to assess health and readiness. A couple of days completely out of commission. And you can do it safely every two months. That's a pretty good return, don't you think?'

Chastity found herself staring. 'Five thousand? That much?'

And she'd blithely turned down all those offers from the other clinics she'd swung by.

Dr. Petit smiled. 'It's a seller's market, if you will. The demand is huge and rising. In fact, only recently, Louisiana became the last state to allow the auctioning of human eggs. Depending on the reliability of the donor, the physical and mental characteristics, a woman can name her own price. My heavens, if your sister were younger, she could have made a fortune. Not only is she beautiful, blond, and blue-eyed, but she scored thirty-three on her ACTs, had a perfect four-point-oh average in grad school, and was profi-cient in piano and tennis. Do you know how attractive that is?'

Of course she did. Chastity had been compared to that standard her whole life. Well. The first sixteen years or so, anyway.

'You don't auction?' Chastity asked, trying to focus.

'No,' Dr. Petit said. 'We prefer not to go in that direc-tion. We have a reputation for honesty, service, and accountability. A woman gets a partial refund of her fee if she doesn't have a successful pregnancy. Women know they can rely on us. You can't always say that about auctioned eggs.'

Chastity shook her head, a bit stunned. 'I'm totally unprepared for the future, aren't I?'

Dr. Petit smiled. 'What did *you* score on your ACTs? I think you could do very well yourself.'

Chastity laughed, not really surprised by the offer. 'Sorry. Faith is the scholar in the family.'

Faith also hadn't been living on the streets when she'd taken her ACTs. Besides, the other talents Chastity could claim probably didn't rate high on prospective parents' wish lists. She couldn't imagine anybody checking off the box that said *Want my daughter to be able to tie a cherry stem into a knot with her tongue.*

Dr. Petit shrugged. 'You still have your sister's beauty. It's quite a draw.'

'Thanks, but not today. I already have a pretty full plate.'

Dr. Petit nodded, content, and scanned the corridor before her. 'All right then. The tour. We here at Arlen are a full-service fertility clinic. IVF, sperm donation, to dona-tion of both egg and sperm and implantation. We collect sperm in this room here ...' Opening the door onto a comfortable little cubbyhole that contained a couch, sink, and stack of *Playboy Magazine*, she turned to Chastity and grinned. 'We call it the Oval Office.

'We harvest eggs over here in the procedure room' – the one with the surgical table and crash cart – 'under minor sedation. Usually we can retrieve twenty to thirty mature eggs at a time. We never keep more than six. You see the window here into the laboratory next door? The eggs are passed through to Eddie and his staff, who thoroughly eval-uate them for viability before performing the ICSI – intracytoplasmic sperm injection – in which one sperm is immobilized microscopically and injected directly into the

128

oocyte. Then, after letting the embryos mature for three days to the blastocyst stage to make sure they're viable, Eddie loads two in a catheter, three if the patient is over thirty-two, and we do the implantation procedure, again here in the procedure room.'

Without waiting for Chastity's reaction, Dr. Petit stepped on down the hall, punched the security code in the lab door, and pushed it open.

'Please don't go in,' she said. 'But here you can see the electron microscopes, the incubators, and the liquid nitrogen tanks in which we store the sperm and cryopreserved embryos.'

Chastity looked. She'd seen labs before, even though this one was a marvel of efficiency in a small, tidy space. She'd seen incubators. She hadn't, however, seen where frozen babies lived.

She wasn't sure what she'd expected. Wall units, maybe, like in the morgue. Something big and unmistakable and important-looking. Something worth the contents.

Instead, crouched beneath the lab counters, like big discarded soda cans, sat two squat metal canisters that looked like nothing so much as R2D2.

'You're kidding,' Chastity said. 'That's it?'

Dr. Petit smiled. 'They're safe. So safe that once we verify viability and cryopreserve them, embryos have an eighty-five to ninety percent survival rate, once thawed. The rate of successful pregnancies is nearly the same as unfrozen.'

'That being?'

'Here? All told, we have a sixty percent success rate.'

'Both tanks are babies?'

'No. One is for sperm only.'

'How many IVFs do you do a month?'

'Right now about twenty. The demand is growing, though.'

Chastity took a last look around the lab. 'Don't you worry about getting stuff mixed up?'

Dr. Petit smiled. 'Every minute. That's why our procedures are so strict. Why we spend so much time preparing and organizing between schedules. We are very, *very* careful.'

Chastity nodded slowly, her focus still on those unprepossessing little canisters. Suddenly she could understand how the guy out front could object. It seemed almost disdainful to put tiny humans in those cans, like sardines or tuna. She wanted to object herself, and she had no real problem with IVF.

'How long do you keep them?'

'We can keep them up to six to eight years. But, as I said, only six per client. And only if we're sure they're viable.'

'But then you do destroy some.'

'If the client wishes.'

Chastity nodded. 'And Faith had ten of the little devils.'

Did she have more still here? Chastity wondered. Tiny fertilized babies left dreaming in the cold? Did it bother Faith to think of them there, waiting for nothing? To think that she'd made babies she'd never get to hold or nurse or dress?

It would have bothered the hell out of Chastity.

But then, it was something Chastity would never have to worry about. Another legacy from her formative years. Which was why, she realized suddenly, she was so jealous of her sister. Once again.

Story of her life.

'And Faith retired from the baby business because she'd reached the maximum age?' Chastity asked, her focus still on those cold white containers.

'Well,' Dr. Petit demurred, 'no. Come on to my office and we'll talk about it.'

That got Chastity's attention. Dr. Petit closed the door and led Chastity back down the hall, past where Eddie was busy playing with his centrifuge, past the nurses in their lab coats and slacks, past the Oval Office, to the oak door.

130

'Then why did she stop donating?' Chastity asked when she finally sat in a comfortable mauve armchair across from Dr. Petit's desk.

Chastity would have recognized the room anywhere as a GYN's office. More Mary Cassatt and a three-dimensional model of the female reproductive system on the bookcase. One of Chastity's instructors had called it the Moosehead. Perched up there like it was, it looked as if Dr. Petit had bagged it instead of studied it.

Dr. Petit fiddled with the Cross pen in front of her. 'As you can imagine, we have to give hormones to our clients, not only to stimulate the production of eggs, but to coordinate our donors' and recipients' cycles. This can, of course, cause symptoms not unlike PMS. But at Arlen we've never had anyone really react badly.

'On rare occasions, though, the donor can develop ovarian cysts, or OHSS – ovarian hyperstimulation syndrome. It can produce a range of symptoms from exaggerated PMS to kidney damage. We monitor that kind of thing extremely closely. It was what Eddie was doing today. Testing hormone levels in our donors and recipients, not only to know when each is ready, but to screen for problems.'

'And there were problems with Faith.'

Dr. Petit shook her head, her attention again on her pen. 'I'm not even convinced it was the hormones. Usually if we have problems with a client, it's some outside stressor. Money, family, that kind of thing. And I knew her mother was very ill. But in the last few months here, Faith grew increasingly anxious. Her emotions became friable and her health seemed to suffer. Although we couldn't find any diagnosable variation of hormone levels, and her donation was a success, we had to make a unilateral decision to stop. For her own good.' Another head shake, another frown. 'That last month, she seemed frightened. Suspicious. It simply wasn't like her.'

Something else Max hadn't mentioned. Had he even

noticed? Or had Faith only betrayed her disintegration to these women?

'Not that she wasn't still our Sister Mercy,' Dr. Petit amended anxiously. 'She was. It was why we were so worried about what happened to her. No one that kind should suffer.'

'How did she react?' Chastity asked. 'When you told her.'

Dr. Petit sighed. 'She tore my office apart.'

Faith? *Faith* had done that? Chastity had never so much as heard her sister raise her voice.

'Did she say *anything* to you that might have explained why she was so upset?'

Dr. Petit turned back, already shaking her head. 'We all tried our best to understand. We had several meetings on it. She just said she couldn't stop, that we were being cruel to her.'

'Did you talk to her husband?'

'Yes. He believed it was the death of her mother that made her so fragile. We felt he was probably right. It was a terribly traumatic time in her life.'

'So until those last few months, Faith didn't seem to have any problems.'

'No. I told you. And, as I said, we had quite a bit of background on her. The screening was extensive.'

'Not extensive enough, evidently.'

'Ms. Byrnes . . .'

Chastity gave a quiet smile. No confrontation here. But the clinic hadn't done enough to screen Faith, and they had to know it. 'Dr. Petit, how old do you think my sister is?'

'Pardon?'

'Her age.'

'Well, it was one of the things we did consider. She's now thirty-four. We thought that reaching the end of her donor years might be affecting her.'

Chastity kept her voice very calm. 'She's not thirty-four. She's thirty-eight.'

132

Dr. Petit all but stopped breathing. 'Pardon?'

'My sister is thirty-eight years old. She was born in 1967. I'm just surprised that you didn't double-check that.'

'You're sure?'

'I've known her longer than you.'

Dr. Petit looked flummoxed. 'Why would she lie?'

Chastity shrugged. 'If she wanted to do this so badly, why not?'

'But we never had somebody lie before.'

'How can you be sure? You know, with the rewards going up, you just might not be able to rely on honor anymore. You obviously don't check out the data.'

Dr. Petit actually sagged a bit in her seat. 'No,' she admitted. 'Not really. I mean the important thing is to screen for communicable disease and genetic history, and we test for the first and can for the second depending on the recipients' wishes. And, like I said, your sister had already had a successful pregnancy. She was a dream candidate.'

'But that was just her eggs.'

'No, not the eggs. Her own pregnancy.'

Chastity shook her head. 'I'm sorry, Dr. Petit. You're mistaken. Faith has never been pregnant. I'm afraid she lied about that, too.'

It was Dr. Petit's turn to look patient. 'Ms. Byrnes, I'm an OB/GYN. I might not be able to tell if a woman's lying about her age, but I can certainly tell if she's lying about having delivered a baby. And your sister wasn't lying. She has had a child.'

133

Chapter Nine

Chastity found herself sitting there openmouthed and numb.

A baby. Faith had a baby?

'No,' she said instinctively, 'she couldn't have. She only has stepchildren.'

Dr. Petit shook her head. 'But she did. The impression I got was that it was before her marriage. That the baby was given up for adoption. Your sister did assure me that it was a full-term, healthy baby, though.'

Chastity blinked. 'You couldn't be mistaken?'

Dr. Petit allowed an eyebrow to raise. 'Not about that. No.'

'Yes. Yes, of course.'

Chastity tried to assimilate the idea of Faith having and giving away a baby. Yet another thing she didn't know about her sister.

Good God, did Faith have a dorsal fin Chastity didn't know about? A stigmata, or the power to bend spoons with her mind?

Could *that* have been the real reason Faith and her mother had skipped from St. Louis like debtors outrunning a loan shark? Had Faith been pregnant? Could Chastity's mother have heaved that load of guilt on Chastity when it hadn't been her fault at all?

Chastity knew she never should have set foot outside her safety perimeter. She never should have returned Max

Stanton's phone call. She'd been so certain of who she was back in St. Louis. She hadn't liked it much, but she'd recognized it, had drawn it in strong colors and clear black lines. Now everything was melting and morphing, and the world just didn't look familiar anymore. As if she were trying to focus through water.

It took her breath, that thought. Because, of course, in a way, she really was trying to see through water.

For a long moment Chastity just sat there staring at the mahogany grain on Dr. Petit's desk. Trying like hell to play catch-up, when every time somebody opened their mouth she stumbled farther and farther behind. Sank deeper into the dark.

'We really did try and help her,' Dr. Petit said gently. 'But after that last month, she simply didn't come back to see us.'

Chastity physically pulled herself together. It took a couple of long breaths, a clearing of her throat, but she yanked herself back into the interview.

'She must have been close to several of the people here.'

Dr. Petit settled, as if relieved. 'Well, Eddie, of course. A few other donors whom Faith recommended to us. And several of the women who had children because of her.'

'That's normal?'

'No. Not really. In fact, we never even tell our donors if their donations are successful. It is up to the recipient to decide if she wants to contact her donor. The vast majority of donors want no part in knowing. But Faith?' Dr Petit shrugged. 'It was more personal to her than simply the money.'

Yeah. Chastity just bet.

'How do you get them in touch with each other?' she asked. 'I mean, how does somebody contact a donor?'

'Our Web page. We have a password-sensitive page for our clients with all the donors and all their information on it. The recipient chooses, and then we make the contact.'

Chastity nodded. 'Could I talk to any of the women who

came in contact with Faith? They may be able to help me find her.'

'I'm sorry.' Dr. Petit, settled back into her chair and picked up that much-worried pen. 'Our files are completely confidential. I can't give you any names at all.'

But come to think of it, Chastity had Faith's address book. Maybe some of the names she needed were tucked away in there in Faith's precise, unerased handwriting. Maybe one of them would offer up information to help the woman who'd given her children.

Of course, would those women trust Chastity with their information? If the look on Eddie Dupre's face had meant anything, Chastity wasn't at all sure they would. Her sister might not have shared anything with her, but she'd evidently shared her loathing for her younger sister with her friends.

'How long has it been since Faith's been here?' she asked.

Dr. Petit looked out the window onto the roof of another Victorian next door. 'Oh, I'd say about four months. Like I said, after that last day, she just hasn't been back.'

'So you haven't seen her since before Mother died?'

'I know some of our people went to the funeral. She hasn't been here, though. I made sure to ask when the police came to question us.'

'One more thing, Doctor,' Chastity said, all but holding her breath. 'Do you know if anyone from here has gone missing?'

'Missing?'

'Well, somebody in the last few weeks you've lost touch with. A client or donor who missed appointments. You know.'

Who might look just like Faith.

Dr. Petit looked seriously bemused. 'No. Nobody's missed any appointments.'

'And of course, you don't keep regular track of your donors. Since they're on the Web page and all.'

136

'Not unless they're needed. No. Why?'

'Because the police found an unidentified woman wearing my sister's wedding ring. She'd been murdered.'

'And you think . . .' There was serious outrage in the woman's voice, as if the murder were a personal insult.

Chastity shrugged. 'I don't think anything. I don't want to overlook anything, either.'

The kind, smiling Dr. Petit was suddenly very angry. 'I can guarantee you it isn't one of our clients.'

'I hope you can,' Chastity said, wondering if she should suspect what could be perfectly legitimate anger. 'Would you let me know if there is anybody?' she asked. 'It might be important.'

'I'm sorry . . .'

'Then let the police know. Detective Dulane of Jefferson Parish, or Detective Gilchrist of the Eighth District.'

The doctor just nodded, still not comprehending, still defensive. Left with nothing else to say, Chastity picked up her purse and stood to leave. Dr. Petit followed suit.

They were all the way down to the front desk before the doctor spoke again. 'She's thirty-eight? You're sure?'

That brought Chastity to a stop. 'I'm sure. It seems she shaved a few years when she moved down here. I'm sorry.'

The doctor sighed. 'So am I. I have to tell a few of her beneficiaries. It's the honest thing to do.'

Yeah, Chastity thought. We certainly all want to be honest.

'Do you think I could talk to Mr. Dupre now?' she asked.

Dr. Petit smiled again. 'Of course.'

But it seemed that Mr. Dupre had already gone to lunch. And Chastity had a feeling that they'd be ice-skating in Jackson Square before he let her find him again.

Chastity had just reached the front salon when the door swung open and a stocky brunette strode in.

'What is it, Jane?' she demanded of the receptionist. 'I got a message—'

Spotting Chastity, she stumbled to a halt. Her eyes widened. 'Oh . . . ' scuse me.'

That was when Chastity realized that the girl was wearing a white sequined jumpsuit with a shoulder cape. And that her hair was slicked high off her forehead, just like Elvis. Having absolutely no idea what to say to a girl dressed as Elvis, Chastity just nodded and pulled the door open. The cop on the porch, now rocking and smoking, waved her on by. James was again reading his newspaper in what was undoubtedly a no-parking zone under a big live oak. The straggling line of protesters caught sight of Chastity and renewed their efforts at vilification.

'I know what you are called!' that young guy again shouted, pointing at Chastity's chest.

Well, she thought dryly, at least she wasn't totally lost. She had absolutely no desire to see this guy naked and sweaty. Probably because he was already sweaty, and it wasn't a good look for him. He was in a suit, for God's sake. On a sidewalk in hundred degree heat with a protest sign in his hand. Hadn't he ever read the etiquette books on protesting?

'You know what I'm called, huh?' Chastity said, trying to stroll by as if he weren't crowding her. 'You must tell me. But be forewarned. If the words "whore of Babylon" leave your lips, I'll beat you to death with your own sign.'

'I thought I'd dealt with you,' he accused her, his eyes intense and certain.

Who was it Eddie Dupre had said this guy was? Lloyd Burgard? Chastity was going to have to Google him when she got back to her computer, see if he came up on any police beat items. He was seriously batshit. And the last thing she needed right now, while she was dealing with everything else, was seriously batshit.

'Can we do this some other time?' she asked, trying to get by.

'I thought you'd seen the light. But you haven't, and your penance is nigh. Pestilence and storm and the wrath of the wind!'

138

So God spoke to this guy in hurricane. Great.

'Oh, hell, honey,' Chastity snorted. 'My punishment has been commencing for twenty-six years. You got nothing to say to me.'

Even so, a shiver snaked right down her back. Somehow that creepy little psycho had just walked across her grave.

'I have the word of God to say to you,' he insisted, following her. 'Vengeance is His, and he will mete it out to the wicked. And so he has judged *you*!'

'Are you going to engage in pointless bickering all day, or are we going to get some lunch?' James asked, not looking up from where he was evidently engrossed in the sports page.

'I could have him accuse *you* of something, James. It might alleviate your boredom.'

'Thanks, no. I'm sure that driving a hack through New Orleans is judgment enough.'

Chastity opened the back door and slid in. After last night, there wasn't a chance in hell she was sharing the front seat.

'Where to?' James asked.

'Food. Does that paper say what the Cardinals did last night?'

'They won. They say they're sorry to have done it without you.'

'You have the eyes of Satan!' the weird little guy cried out.

'Finally,' Chastity said, leaning back in her seat. 'Something we agree on.'

She was just about to close the door, when she heard his bemused voice as he turned away. 'You were older last week.'

'You okay back there?' James asked.

Chastity didn't so much as open an eye. 'This gonna cost extra?'

'Talk's free, nurse. You look like you didn't much enjoy your visit.'

'I didn't, fireman. I didn't.'

She just couldn't shake that damn feeling of prescience. Some of the best prophets had been crazy, after all, crying out there in the desert where nobody believed them. She wondered if her crazy person had just prophesied for her. That she had, indeed, been judged, and this trip was just her personal route to hell.

Via wind and water. Hotcha, this was sure her day.

'"By the pricking of my thumbs,"' she found herself saying.

'What?'

She shook her head. 'Let's go.'

The rest of the quote was 'something wicked this way comes.' Chastity closed her eyes because, oddly enough, sitting in the back of a cab on a hot summer day in New Orleans, she believed it. And she was afraid she wasn't talking about hurricanes.

The cab had reached the corner of Magazine when Chastity shot up in her seat. 'Oh, shit, James! Turn around!'

'You forget something?' James asked, throwing his cab into a quick U-turn.

'I wasn't paying attention. Didn't you hear what he just said? He thinks I'm Faith. He thinks he's been visiting judgment from God on Faith. And he was doing it last week.'

But by the time they made it back to the clinic, Lloyd Burgard was gone.

'Please,' Chastity asked one of the kinder-looking women out on the sidewalk. 'Can you tell me where he went? It's important. My sister's missing, and he may be able to tell me something.'

'One of the other clinics,' the woman said, resting her Genetic Monsters sign on her shoulder. 'Lloyd always makes the rounds in the afternoon.'

Well, at least he'd really been there. Not some figment of her imagination or angel of death sent to seriously annoy

140

her. For a minute there, Chastity had actually wondered.

'Do I look familiar to you?' she asked the woman.

She looked, smiled, and shook her head. 'Afraid not.'

Nobody else recognized her, so evidently Lloyd had been the only one out to save Faith. The protesters all knew him, but nobody really claimed him. All they could tell Chastity about him was that he was sincere, devoted, and addicted to digital photography.

'And he was trying to save my sister only last week,' Faith said, climbing back into the cab. 'And evidently not here.'

'What do you think?' James asked, tossing his cigarette out the window and starting the car. 'That this guy is taking the vengeance of the Lord into his own hands?'

She thought she shouldn't have the shivers over this guy.

'Well, they think he tried to break into the lab to steal the babies this morning. That's what the cops were here for.'

'My horizon is expanding by the minute. What next?'

She thought about it. 'Do you do computers?'

'I don't even go through the self-serve lane at the grocery store.'

Chastity sighed, looking out at the passing storefronts as James turned onto Magazine and headed downriver. She knew she had to meet Faith's friends sooner or later. She had their addresses in her backpack. But first, she thought she'd try familiar territory.

'Do you know where the Jefferson Parish coroner's office is?'

He did. It was back over the river, which Chastity hated all over again. Tucked back in an industrial park, the coroner's office was new, clean, and well designed. Chastity wished she could have said the same for Dr. Martin Willis. A short, portly man with a tonsure of ginger hair and eyes like a Boston terrier, he looked as if he slept on his couch and bathed in the office bathroom.

One look at him sent Chastity's spirits skidding. His attitude finished the job. Kareena had been right. Dr. Martin Willis wasn't going to win any awards for his work or his attitude.

'You want me to *what*?' he demanded.

Chastity had been very careful in presenting her credentials. She had questioned him carefully about his findings on the woman in the bayou. She'd been deferential, no matter how slipshod she thought his approach. She'd been appalled, but she'd been quiet.

'A full autopsy,' she said, hands curled in her lap where she sat in a very uncomfortable straight-back chair, 'with X-Rays.' She wasn't going to tell him that it hadn't done a damn bit of good to do only the head, as he had. Hell, Ray Charles could have told them how that woman died. But there might just be a clue to who the woman was.

Like whether she'd had children or not.

'My sister was para one gravida one,' she said, telling him that her sister had delivered a live pregnancy. 'I'd like to know if this is she.'

'Well, so would I, missy. But I have other things to do. Other people die down here, you know. Besides, why bother when we're already waiting for the DNA?'

'Because with the best effort in the world it will still take a good three weeks to get results back. It would really be helpful to find out sooner if there's a match.'

Dr. Willis climbed to his feet. 'The parish coroner is satisfied with my findings. You might as well be, too.'

And he walked out.

Chastity rubbed her forehead where her chronic doctor headaches lived and went in search of James.

'Do you know where the homicide cops live?'

'Sure,' he said, looking up from the paper. 'Climb in.'

And he drove her to the other side of the parking lot.

'Yes, Ms. Byrnes?' Detective Dulane asked. He had school art taped to the wall behind his desk and family shots scattered on his desk. Chastity wished he had her sister's case.

142

'How much pull do you have with the coroner's office, Detective?' she asked.

There was a slight, stunned silence. 'I'm sorry ...'

Chastity laughed and sat. The detective's chair was much more comfortable than the pathologist's. 'No. I am. I was just hoping you could convince Dr. Willis to complete his autopsy on that floater from the bayou. I was just there, and he doesn't seem to know she has anything from the neck down. I'm grateful that he found out the lady had no drugs or alcohol on board, and that she died of a surfeit of double-ought buckshot and had no calluses on her feet. But it would sure be nice to know if she'd given birth.'

'Your sister ...'

'Had a child, according to the fertility clinic where she donated her eggs.'

'You've been busy, Ms. Byrnes.'

'I suck at wailing and wringing my hands, Detective. Now, what do you say?'

Again, that silence as he doodled on his desk blotter. 'I'll see what I can do.'

'Thank you. I know I'm dipping my toe in your pool, but I just can't let this go unquestioned.'

'Yes, ma'am.'

'Thank you, Detective.'

She noticed that the detective did not thank her back.

For the rest of the day Chastity and James sought out the people in Faith's directory. It was an alphabetical journey, from Ardoin to Cadro, where they had to stop because they ran out of time. Chastity met with Suzies and Emilies and Mary Catherines. She made it a point to visit them in person because she wanted to see these women's reactions. She had James drive her to their homes in the Garden District, in Lakeside, and in Metairie. The women wore tennis attire, or pearls and slacks, or designer T-shirts and shorts.

To a woman, they were the friends Max had talked about who had met Faith through the hospital auxiliary or through the boys' schools. They had helped Faith plan charity functions and bridge tournaments and Mardi Gras parties. They smiled when her name was mentioned and looked bemused when asked about her whereabouts. Not one had seen Faith anywhere but Gallatoire's in at least six months. 'Her mother, you know. Faith didn't want to leave her.'

The more Chastity heard that tune, the less she liked it. There were new snakes crawling up her back, and Chastity couldn't quite get a name on them yet. But there'd been something wrong long before Faith had decamped. As if those pictures in Faith's bathroom didn't say that very thing.

When Chastity got back to Kareena's she called Moshika. She got an answering machine and left a few pathetic 'woofs' on it for Lilly, feeling homesick and unsettled. Then she logged on to her computer for a little investigative time.

First she accessed the Arlen Clinic Web page to find that the design matched the clinic's. Pastel comfort and quiet support. Miracles performed for a fee. She found the donor page, but couldn't come up with a password.

Next she Googled Lloyd Burgard, but he was even more of a bust than the clinic. If Lloyd was his real name, he was either a rookie at rabble-rousing or an ineffectual one. Not only had he not made the news, he'd wasted his digital photography. Lloyd had no Web page. Hell, everybody had a Web page these days. Either Lloyd was too crazy to have figured that out, or not crazy enough.

As a last resort Chastity called Detective Gilchrist, to ask him if he'd check up on Lloyd. She could hear from the detective's tone of voice that he had already consigned her sister to the circular 'ran-away-from-home' file, and she couldn't say she blamed him much. But there was something here that didn't fit. Something that tugged at Chastity's sense of impending disaster.

She wanted to know about that baby. She wanted to know why Faith had moved so far not to move at all. She mostly

144

wanted to know what place their father had in Faith's bathroom, and that wasn't something she could make Detective Gilchrist understand.

They met at the back of Lafitte's Blacksmith Shop on Bourbon, a building purporting to be the blacksmith shop owned by Jean Lafitte. It certainly looked as if it had survived that long. The roof sagged, the walls peeled, and the doors didn't square. The only light in the place came from candles on the tables. It was a convenient place for somebody who didn't want to be noticed.

They bent over their drinks in the back where the air was cooler and the shadows deep.

'We have to move now.'

'She agrees?'

'It doesn't matter. We simply have to take over.'

'Why?'

'Because the police went to see Eddie.'

'Eddie? Good God. Why?'

'They found a body. With the ring on it.'

A small sound, like the flutter of a bird against a cage. 'They can't know for sure who it is.'

'They will. And when they do, we'll be the first ones suspected. She had the ring.'

'And you think, what? We should just march into the police station and tell them what we did and why?'

There was an uncomfortable silence in the dim corner. Outside, the afternoon summer thunderstorm had just passed, leaving the sagging old room in almost complete darkness, except for the random flicker of candles and the glow of the ATM machine by the bar.

'Why couldn't we?'

'You think they'd believe us?'

Another silence, punctuated by a distant rumble of thunder and the closer growl of a Harley gliding past the open windows.

'So what now?'

'For now we get back to business.'

'And the sister?'

There was a laugh. 'Leave it to Eddie. He says he wants to take care of her.'

'Will he?'

'One of us will. We don't have a choice, do we?'

Chapter Ten

Chastity woke to another still, sullen morning. The temperature and humidity hovered in the nineties. The wind had died completely, and the sun beat down without respite, even though clouds always seemed to be massed at the horizon.

On the little TV Kareena kept on the kitchen counter, a swirl of orange took up the screen. Tropical storm Bob lay off the north coast of Puerto Rico. With sustained winds of 70 miles per hour and a surface pressure of 986, Bob was building into what might be a meteorological miracle. A very big hurricane in the middle of June.

Kareena was thrilled. First estimates were that Bob would sweep across southern Florida and into the Gulf of Mexico. If the jet stream held, it would usher the storm right into New Orleans.

Chastity felt the approach of all that water build right in her chest. She watched that hypnotic curl of color on the TV and knew that it was zeroed in on her. She didn't care what anybody else thought. Lloyd had prophesied it the day before, and he was right. She was about to be punished for whatever was left to punish her for.

'You said that Faith decided to retire from donation,' she said to Max, cell phone to her ear as she sat at Kareena's table making inroads into the Boudreaux coffee supply. 'The clinic said they had to ask her to stop.'

There was a slight pause. 'I didn't want to put it like that.'

'*Was* she having problems with depression, Max?'

Another, longer pause. 'She was grieving for her mother.'

'Was Faith seeing a psychiatrist?'

'No. Heavens, no. She said she knew more about their business than they did. After all, her masters is in psychology.'

'So she isn't on any antidepressants?'

'No. I told you. Check her bathroom vanity, if you want.'

Ah yes. The bathroom. 'Who put the pictures of my father all over Faith's bathroom, Max?'

Max all but hiccupped with the sudden change of direction. 'Pardon? What does that have to do with anything?'

'I'm not sure, but it could be important. Who, Max?'

'Why, Faith, of course. She still adores her father.'

With that, every other question on Chastity's list vanished.

'Chastity?'

Chastity stared off into the sea of lime green that was Kareena's kitchen walls. She thought of a million and one tiny, forgettable incidents from her childhood that she could never forget. She thought of the thick stew of distrust, shame, and competition her father had brewed among her family. She thought of poor Hope, caught in the middle and squeezed to death.

She thought of how comfortable she'd been no more than a week ago. How she'd managed to control all that noisome waste from her past with ritual and a small bag of rocks.

Chastity wondered if she'd actually thought this search would make it better. It hadn't. It was making it worse. Everything she'd been shoving down into the dark was starting to bubble up around her like a toxic soup.

'Faith hates her father,' she said, and still wasn't sure she believed it. Faith had been Daddy's girl. It had been up to Hope and Chastity to vie for his attention.

And they had.

'Oh, no,' Max said. 'I'm sure you're wrong.'

When it sounded as if he were about to expound on that, Chastity shied. 'Did you know that Faith had a child, Max?'

Max sounded bemused. 'Yes, Chastity. I did. It was before me. A mistake she rectified.'

A mistake. What a tidy word for what must have been a devastating time in Faith's life.

'Why didn't you tell me?'

He hesitated. 'You think it could mean something?'

'She was going through an emotional crisis, Max. Everything could mean something. Had she been in contact with the baby?'

'No. She never expressed an interest in it after telling me about it. She simply felt I should know.'

'And you don't know when it was born or anything?'

'No. I'm sorry.'

Maybe, faced with the end of her reproductive life, Faith had become obsessed with her own child. Well, Kareena was looking for a birth certificate. She'd find out.

'One last thing, Max. Faith's address book. As far as I can tell, nobody from the Arlen Clinic is in it.'

Not even Eddie Dupre. Chastity hadn't noticed until she'd sat down the night before and read the thing beginning to end. All in all, she'd counted six Suzies and four Emilies. But no Eddies. If Dr. Petit was telling the truth, that shouldn't have made sense.

'Well, she didn't really see those people much after she stopped going,' Max said. 'She thought it important to devote her time to her family and her mother. You're not quitting.' Not a question so much as a statement.

Chastity sighed. 'No, Max. I'm not quitting.'

Not when there was a dead body somehow involved. Not when none of her questions had been answered. Certainly not when all these new questions kept piling up.

149

So Chastity hung up, slipped on her sunglasses, and prepared to spend another fruitless day interviewing women who planned social events, all the while feeling like she was making things worse instead of better.

New Orleans had no centralized homicide bureau. Subscribing to the 'local cops know their own neighborhoods best' theory, the department let each district handle its own cases. The only exception to that edict was the Eighth, the French Quarter district, since any homicide at the core of the tourist area was such a potential red ball. Homicides in the Eighth were caught by the Cold Case squad up at police headquarters in Duncan Plaza.

If not centralized, the information was at least coordinated. When a call came in anywhere in the city, Cold Case recorded it in The Book, a large ledger that sat on a wall desk in the Cold Case office. A pin marked the site on the large district-by-district map on the wall. Then every Tuesday morning at ten, the lieutenants from each district gathered at the Cold Case squad room to compare notes, just to make sure they hadn't overlooked anything.

On this Tuesday the curious case of the fake-emerald-bedecked body in the bayou over in Jefferson Parish was presented by the lieutenant from the Eighth District at the behest of Detective Gilchrist. They made mention of it this Tuesday because the case reflected on a person who was still missing from New Orleans, who had a high-profile husband, and who had a forensic nurse sister who was down there nosing around.

It was just a heads-up. After all, the current opinion was that the missing person had tossed her now worthless ring once she didn't need it anymore, and the Jane Doe had found it just in time to wear to her funeral. Notes were taken, opinions rendered, and jokes shared, especially about the nun-in-an-emerald-ring-at-a-hurricane-season-party aspect of the case. Sergeant Obie Gaudet, one of Cold Case's vets, was given the file, just so they could put a name on it and be done. Then they moved on to the triple homicide from the B. W. Cooper Housing Project, which would eventually be tagged to some yos from the Magnolia Projects. Business as usual.

Back in Jefferson Parish, Detective Dulane sent a missing persons alert out on the wire. He checked every convent in town that might be missing a nun, and ran by the shelters. He contacted the *Times-Picayune* to run an article asking for information that might lead to the identification of a young woman found in Bayou Segnette who might be connected with Mrs. Faith Stanton of New Orleans.

Now it was time to meet with Dr. Willis. Chastity Byrnes was right. They needed a full cut on this woman. There were just too many unanswered questions to leave any stone unturned. Or any organ uncut. Pulling his weapon out of the drawer, Dulane snapped it into his holster and headed out to cross the parking lot.

He had a feeling about this floater. He had a feeling about Ms. Byrnes. He didn't want to be the one she made look stupid.

'You're kidding,' Chastity said when James pulled to a halt before a nondescript marble building set in the middle of noisy, vulgar Bourbon Street. 'This is Gallatoire's?'

'They were here first,' James said.

They'd spent the last three days tracking down the names in Faith's address book. Today, they were to talk to Susan Wade Reeves, who had seen Faith get into that cab. And it being lunchtime on Friday afternoon, they knew just where to find her.

Chastity really wasn't in the mood for this. She'd just gotten off the phone with Kareena, who'd told her with apologies that there was no record to be found locally of an infant born to Faith Marie Byrnes. There was, however, a record of Lloyd Burgard.

'That boy's a four-star paranoid schiz. A regular at our

151

psych unit. He keeps stoppin' his meds because the New Orleans Saints tryin' to steal his soul.'

'The football Saints?' Chastity had asked. 'What I've seen of them, they couldn't steal a lateral pass.'

'Oh, yeah. They stealin' souls, stealin' identities, stealin' that boy's shorts, all I know. But that Lloyd, he crazy.'

'But what do the Saints have to do with fertility clinics?'

'Ah, that's what's so beautiful. See, the Saints, they say to Lloyd, "You save some bebes over at those bad places, we not steal your soul." So Lloyd, he try and save him some bebes.'

'Uh-huh. Anything else?'

'Yeah. Bob ain't a tropical storm anymore. An hour ago, they made him a hurricane of his very own.'

Chastity fought a fresh set of shakes. She knew an omen when she heard it.

And that was how she walked into Gallatoire's.

Chastity wasn't sure what she'd expected. Pristine white tablecloths, deep carpet, hushed, reverent tones. The inside of Gallatoire's resembled nothing more than an ice cream parlor. With high ceilings and tile floors, the place echoed with conversation and laughter. The walls were covered in green fleur-de-lis wallpaper, and the tables were bare and comfortable. The waiters wore white jackets, but they were all singing 'Happy Birthday' to one of the tables, and the rest of the room seemed to be participating. It was loose and easy, the way Chastity always imagined a good family would be.

'I'm sorry. Ms. Reeves just left,' the maître d' said with a hesitant smile. 'Excuse me, don't I know you?'

Chastity did her best to smile back. 'I'm Faith Stanton's sister.'

The maître d' actually patted her arm like a nanny. 'Of course. I'm so sorry. The police talked to us, but we simply couldn't offer anything. She seemed fine. In fact, better than I'd seen her in a while.'

Chastity paid attention now. 'I'd heard that she hadn't

done well since my mother's death.'

'She got so ... quiet. But she came. Every week. Dr. Stanton made sure of it.'

'Did she eat with anyone in particular?'

'Why, no. It depended on the week. Mrs. Stanton, of course. Dr. Stanton's mother. Friends, acquaintances.'

'Is Mrs. Stanton here today?'

'No. Not during the summer. Mizz Ellen is in Italy. But Mizz Webster's here, if you want to talk to her. The police did.'

'Webster. She was also there when my sister got in the cab.'

'Yes. She's right over there. And sweet as they come.'

Mizz Webster was the size of a hummingbird. Gray-haired, bright-eyed, and as bubbly as a debutante, she patted Chastity's hand the entire time she talked to her. Yes, she knew dear Faith. No, she hadn't had lunch with her that last day. Yes, she thought for sure she'd heard the words *fertility clinic*. Which one she didn't remember, and she'd been trying to recall, especially since she'd heard that her dear Faith had gone missing.

'Would you remember seeing the cabdriver?' Chastity asked.

Mizz Webster was already shaking her head. 'He was colored, dear. And he had statues on his dashboard. But then, everybody has statues on their dashboard down here.'

Chastity left with Mizz Webster's best wishes and an invitation to tea, but no real sense that she'd made progress. She found James parked at the corner watching the street life.

'How many cabdrivers are black and have statues on their dashboards?'

He never looked back as she slammed the door. 'At least a third.'

'Great. I need a new favor.'

'It's a good thing I'm naturally curious. What?'

'I need you to go in with me on these interviews. I'm

missing stuff. Forgetting stuff. I just realized I hadn't even thought to talk to Max's mother about Faith's well-being.'

'You want to do it now?'

'Can you drive to Italy?'

'I could sure try.'

'How 'bout we talk to this Susan Reeves on Prytania first? It's probably on our way.'

The house was everything Kareena had promised. About a block square with porches and colonnades that would have made the Greeks weep with envy. Lush landscaping with huge magnolias, live oaks, crepe myrtles, rhododendron, and jasmine, all tucked behind a high wrought-iron fence to remind folk just where the demarcation between fantasy and reality existed. All on a street that seemed to be erupting around the roots of the huge trees that reigned there.

Susan Wade Reeves resided in the smaller coach house to the rear. Small being relative. This one had two stories and could have sat about four coaches and a Hummer.

'I'm just not sure what I can do for you,' she said in response to Chastity's introduction.

The three of them settled in the salon, a small, tidy room with priceless antiques and fresh flowers. Susan sat on the couch, framed by the front window. Chastity and James were perched on matching Chippendale chairs, like supplicants before the master. Chastity wasn't sure it was accidental.

But the effect was lost when Chastity realized that Susan Wade Reeves looked ... well, twitchy. Unsettled. It could have been because she couldn't quite keep her eyes off James, which shouldn't have been a surprise. Clad in his Grateful Dead T-shirt and baggy-assed jeans, he was lounging in his straight-back chair as if he were in a club, his scars livid in the sunlight that poured in behind Susan Reeves's head. He even made it a point to lay that clawed left hand on his thigh, where nobody could miss it.

Maybe she should have brought him to all her interviews, Chastity thought. If he could keep people off center like this, she might get more information than she had.

'You had lunch with Faith at Gallatoire's,' Chastity said to Ms. Reeves.

Susan Reeves pulled her attention back to Chastity. 'Well, yes. But that's all. We worked together on some charities.'

'Did Faith say anything odd to you?' Chastity asked. 'Something maybe you wouldn't think was important at the time?'

Susan Wade Reeves exuded the quiet control Chastity had seen in all the women she'd interviewed. Her clothes were careful, her dark brown pageboy precise, her makeup reserved. She smiled like a debutante and ruled the room like the social doyenne she was. But her hands were tight in her lap, and her smile was pasted on like a mask. And she couldn't quite keep her eyes off James.

'I really can't remember her saying anything specific,' she said. 'We were discussing the fall fund-raiser for Hope House. I was pleased because it was the first time Faith had really participated since her mother passed.'

'She didn't mention plans after lunch?'

'No. I'm really not close enough to her for that. As I said, we simply talked about our projects.'

'I see,' Chastity said. 'You told the police you heard her tell the cabdriver she wanted to go home.'

'Yes, I did.'

'But why would Mizz Webster believe she heard that Faith wanted to go to a fertility clinic?'

Susan Reeves blinked a couple of times, twisted a signet ring on her pinkie. 'The only thing I can think of was that Mizz Webster was talking to quite a few people at the time. Everyone feels obliged to say good-bye to her, you know. She's that kind of lady.'

Chastity could hardly argue with that. 'Do you remember what the cabdriver looked like? What company it might have been?'

She seemed to think a moment, her focus on the red tulips on her coffee table. 'No. I'm sorry. I was talking to people myself.'

'You don't know about her work with the Arlen Clinic?'

'The Arlen Clinic?'

'A fertility clinic in town. Faith spent some time there.'

'No.' She flashed a brief, tight smile. 'As I said, I know her from lunch. It's really the only time I see my old social set.'

'Oh? Why's that?'

For the first time, Chastity got an honest reaction. Ms. Reeves laughed. 'You want the truth, Miss Byrnes, I'm as queer as Alice B. Toklas. That just doesn't sit well with some people.'

'My sister made you feel uncomfortable?' she asked, surprised. Faith was the last person Chastity would have thought would make an issue over lesbianism.

Ms. Reeves ducked her head. 'No. To be honest, she didn't. But then, more women eat at Gallatoire's than just your sister.'

Well, at least Chastity still knew *something* about her sister. 'Can you think of anyone else I could talk to who might know more?'

Ms. Reeves offered another smile, this one wry. 'It's too bad Max's mother isn't in town. She could tell you everything. She kept close watch on that family.'

'Why's that?'

'Well, no offense, but your sister wasn't her idea of a proper wife for Max. She wanted a Comus queen for him. Well, he had a Comus queen, didn't he? His first wife, Arabella. She was the perfect daughter-in-law for Mizz Ellen. But she died, and then Max made his own choice.'

'You seem to know more than you think about Faith.'

Ms. Reeves shook her groomed head. 'About Max, really. He grew up nearby. Our mothers are good friends. And I heard all about it when poor little Arabella succumbed so tragically.'

156

'Succumbed? Cancer?'

'Depression. She accidentally overdosed. No real surprise. She was a fragile little thing. I always thought Faith was more up to Mizz Ellen's weight.'

'How long ago?'

'Oh, the boys were small. Probably ten years or so, I'd guess. Nobody was surprised, really. Except Max. Amazing, isn't it?'

Again Faith felt as if she were playing catch-up. She battled an urge to look over at James. He sat perfectly still next to her, his eyes half open, as if he were barely paying attention.

'And you're sure you don't remember Faith speaking of the Arlen Clinic. Of wanting to go there that Friday.'

'I remember that Faith wasn't wearing her pearls. That sticks with me because I never saw her without them. They were Max's wedding gift to her. I know that because Mizz Ellen informed us all that Max didn't think his family pearls good enough. Truth was, Mizz Ellen wouldn't give the family pearls up a second time.'

'Did you ask Faith about them?'

'She said they were being restrung.'

'But she didn't say anything else? Anything that might have seemed odd? Anything that said she was troubled or afraid?'

'No. Like I said, we simply didn't have anything in common.'

There was something Susan Reeves was not telling her, Chastity knew it. But she'd run out of questions. She'd just gotten to her feet to leave, when the front door slammed open. Chastity couldn't miss Susan Reeves's reaction. She jumped to her feet, her mouth already open, when a toddler came bounding across the room.

'M-o-m-m-m-y!' she shrieked, throwing herself into Susan's arms.

'I'm sorry, Mizz Reeves,' a thin black woman apologized as she shut the door. 'I couldn't keep her any longer. She missed you.'

157

But Chastity barely heard the woman. Her own focus was fixed on the bright-eyed little two-year-old who was babbling nonsense for the mother who had picked her up and held her in her arms.

The two-year-old little girl with almost white blond hair and blue eyes so pale she looked as if she were blind or psychic.

Faith's eyes.

Chapter Eleven

Chastity sat back down with a thump. 'You want to tell me again how little you know about my sister?'

Instead of answering, Susan Reeves focused her attention on her daughter. The little girl was dressed in a bright pink T-shirt and shorts, pigtails and sandals. A normal little girl. A bright, happy, healthy little girl.

'I think not,' she said.

'I'm not going to hurt your daughter,' Chastity said.

Susan Reeves kept smiling. 'You're so sure about that?'

'I'm not sure of anything except that I want to make sure my sister's all right. And that I won't intentionally harm anybody.'

Susan Reeves stared at Chastity with that patrician over-the-nose look that probably sent most lesser beings scurrying. Most people didn't face down gangbangers and neurosurgeons on a daily basis, though. Susan Reeves broke eye contact first.

'You can imagine what my family thought when I told them I wanted a baby,' she said, her voice soft, her eyes suddenly alive as she made faces with her daughter. 'Especially considering the fact that my lover is black. Well, and a woman, of course. Since my family tends to dark coloring, my mother made sure people would wonder.' She shrugged. 'We all finally compromised. I made sure my baby was as white and pretty and smart as possible, and my mother agreed that she would accept her as a member of the family.' Nuzzling her baby's neck, she chortled at the high shriek of glee she got in response. 'Who could not love this little munchkin?'

Chastity couldn't manage an answer to that. She couldn't take her eyes off Susan Reeves's little girl. Faith's little girl. That little girl who looked so much the way Hope had, once. Eons ago when she could still smile.

Chastity had pictures of her somewhere, that sister who had been six years her senior. Who had already been fragile and fey by the time Chastity was born. But in those pictures, Hope had looked out at the world with just this delight, this saucy grin.

Faith had to have seen Susan's daughter. How could she have stayed away? How could she have told herself it was just an egg? Just a gift? Chastity wanted to grab that little girl out of her mother's arms and hug her so tight she squealed. She wanted to soak in the exuberance that still lived in those pale, pale eyes.

Maybe, though, this was the better way. Live on through genetics, but let somebody a lot healthier raise the child.

'My sister is missing, Ms. Reeves,' Chastity said quietly, her eyes on that baby as Susan handed her back to the black woman in the crisp white uniform. 'You need to be honest with me.'

'Mommy will be in in a few minutes, munchkin,' Susan said to her little girl, and then waited until she left.

Then, almost wearily, she sat back down.

'I really didn't know Faith donated eggs until I saw her on Arlen's donor page. And you tell me, Ms. Byrnes. If you're looking for the whitest, smartest little girl you can find, where better to go than your sister Faith?'

'Were you one of the friends she made at the clinic?'

'No. I know she did make some. But it seemed uncomfortable. And I really wasn't sure how Max felt about it.'

'Max seems fine.'

160

Susan laughed. 'He probably bet on the outcome each time. Max loves a good bet.'

Chastity went a bit still. 'Pardon me?'

Susan just shrugged. 'I've known Max forever. It's just part of his nature. I think it's why he's a cardiovascular surgeon. His mother wanted him to be a cardiologist. Socially acceptable and available for family functions. But I think Max enjoyed the risk.'

'Have he and Faith been getting along?' Chastity asked.

Susan shrugged. 'I rarely saw them together. Faith certainly never said anything.'

'And the clinic. Why wouldn't you talk to me about it?'

'Because my daughter is my business. No one else's.'

'Is there anything you can tell me now?'

Susan Reeves had a very cool smile. 'I have a beautiful eighteen-month-old, and four more just like her waiting for me when I decide she needs sisters or brothers. I'm perfectly happy with the Arlen Clinic.'

'Faith didn't talk to you about her connection with it?'

'No. Not really. It was too uncomfortable for both of us.'

Chastity nodded and gathered her things once again. 'I thank you for your time,' she said. 'If I may, I might call again later.'

Susan Reeves got to her feet. 'I really can't tell you anything more.'

Chastity and James followed. 'Could you maybe tell me the names of any of the people Faith made friends with at the clinic?'

Another pause. A calculation Chastity could actually see.

'Well,' Susan said, 'I do know that there was Willow Tolliver. She's one of the psychics down at Jackson Square. She's been a donor, I think. And Eddie Dupre. He's the embryologist. Faith has talked about them both.'

Chastity nodded because there was nothing else she could do. She was certain she wasn't hearing the entire truth from Susan Reeves, but she didn't know what else to say. So she

161

climbed to her feet and bid Susan good-bye. Just as they reached the polished mahogany front door, though, she turned one last time.

'Would you share the password for the donor page?'

Susan frowned. 'They've undoubtedly changed it.'

'Even so.'

Ms. Reeves shook her precise brunette head. 'No. I'm sorry.'

For a moment Chastity fought the urge to insist. But she couldn't blame anyone for the desire to protect. So she nodded, as if it were all right, and held out one of the cards she gave out to victims' families.

'My cell phone number is here,' she said. 'If there's anything you remember or find out that might help find Faith. Please.'

It took a second's hesitation, but Susan accepted the card. Chastity turned back toward the door. She'd just about stepped through, when Susan Wade Reeves spoke up.

'You might consider your Bible, Ms. Byrnes. You know, all that begetting.'

Chastity pulled to a stop. She faced the woman, and saw just a brief flash of something in her eyes, something that spoke for her daughter and the woman who'd given the gift of her.

'Thank you.'

Then she and James walked back out into the thick, evocative yard where shadows lurked beneath bright, tropical flowers.

Chastity was still so focused on Susan Reeves that she didn't pay attention as James stopped at the edge of the yard.

'Know anybody in a black sedan?' he asked.

She looked up, blinking. 'Pardon?'

He pointed to where a black sedan sat about a block down. 'I think he was following us.'

But just as he said it, the car started and turned down one of the side streets.

'Does paranoia cost extra?' she asked.

'Caution. Comes with the package.'

For some reason, that didn't make her feel better.

No one who met Dr. Winnifred Hayes-Adams would have taken her for a desperate woman. Fred, as she was known to her friends, was a scientist, a brisk, lab-coated innovator in the world of bioelectronics. She helped design and implement the newest generation of monitoring equipment that beeped and whirred and blinked throughout hospital hallways.

Fred had a Ph.D. in biophysics, master's in biology and engineering, and a Phi Beta Kappa key. She tested off the range for intelligence and played three instruments. Fred had been married for fifteen years. She was nearing forty years old, and she was becoming frantic to get pregnant.

She and her husband had gone through a full range of fertility testing. She'd tried IVF unsuccessfully four times. She'd considered a surrogate mother, a surrogate father, and more than one international adoption agency.

In the end she'd turned to New Life Associates. Not because they were the most reputable. She'd been to the most reputable. Because they promised the best bang for the buck. New Life didn't just offer donor eggs. They offered top-of-the-line donor eggs. For a certain amount of money, Fred and her husband could design their child the way they might a new kitchen. And Fred, who regarded science with the passionate fervor of a religious zealot, knew that this was the way to go for her.

The problem was that Fred had gotten in a bit of a jam. She'd found not just the ideal donor, but the perfect donor. The clinic was all set to start the testing, and here she was doing her best to jeopardize that. After all, she hadn't known she was going to find the perfect donor just when she'd promised to help a good cause. She hadn't realized that her cause *was* the perfect donor.

She should have been at the clinic getting her blood work

done. Gazing wistfully into the computer image of the mother of her future twins. Instead, she was dressed like a college senior looking for the apartment of a man who did very illegal things.

Expensive, illegal things.

Almost as expensive as the eggs she hoped to score.

And she was doing it for the second time in four weeks.

Clad in jeans and T-shirt, Fred marched down a side street two blocks from Loyola University. She had to hurry. The weather was moving in, and she didn't want to be found here.

She never figured to be breaking the law at the corner of a campus. It was something that belonged downtown, near the projects. A place given to shadows and whispers, like in the movies. But the people near the projects didn't have the capability to produce what she needed. What she'd promised to obtain.

She still couldn't quite figure out how she'd volunteered to do this. She was a straight shooter if there ever was one. Church, work, marriage.

Baby.

She just hoped she'd be able to finish this without obstacle. She was already going to have to delay. But if she were caught today, there might be a chance that New Life's operation would receive unwanted scrutiny. And Fred didn't want that.

Not yet. Not till she had her baby.

Babies.

Fred would have twins. Even a desperate woman could be efficient.

'Pick another Bible verse,' Chastity said, her attention on her computer screen. 'And move farther back.'

They'd been at this for a couple of hours now, sitting at Kareena's kitchen table with coffee and sandwiches as they tried to pull a password from a very long book. Chastity had been feeling bad enough when she sat down. She felt worse now. Hot and claustrophobic and as twitchy as Susan Wade Reeves.

James sat alongside, doing nothing more than helping, and she wanted to throw him to the ground. A perfectly normal stress reaction for her once upon a time, and God knows she'd been dealing with some stress.

It was worse this time because it had been so long. And because James wasn't a nameless one-night stand. She liked him. He almost made her feel safe.

Which was the most stupid thing she could ever think. Safe, after all, was no more than an illusion.

The table had been set with the gold-rimmed Sunday china. There was a tablecloth, snowy white and pressed, and they all sat around it, enveloped by grass cloth and the sparkle of the chandelier. Chastity had asked her friend Frances over to dinner, and they were all gathered there, stiff and proper and polite, like a TV family in technicolor.

'You're so lucky,' Frances said with a smile full of braces. 'This is such a cool place to live, and your parents are great.'

Everyone smiled. Even Hope, who looked like hell. Hope, who was only fifteen and three hundred pounds of dimpled gray fat. They smiled, knowing that later, after Frances was gone, after the doors were locked to keep people from seeing, he would creep down the hall.

'Yes,' Chastity said with a perfectly straight face, because she didn't know what else to do. 'We're very lucky.'

And she felt ashamed. Hot and claustrophobic and small.

'Try Genesis,' James said alongside her.

Chastity jumped, yanked back to the present. She could still smell that dining room. She could hear the careful clink of glasses and the small talk that had seemed so safe. So normal. But it hadn't been. It had been the code for terror.

'Chastity?'

She closed her eyes a second. Pulled herself a bit farther away from James so she could concentrate on what they were doing.

165

'Yeah, okay. What Genesis?'

'Book five, verse one.'

'How do you know the Bible so well?'

His smile was enigmatic. 'I had a lot of time to read once.'

Chastity considered him a minute as he munched on a sandwich. 'Why do you drive a cab, fireman?'

He didn't seem in the least disconcerted. 'Kind of tough to steer a rig with one hand.'

'And yet you're driving.'

'Yep.'

'No dreams of careers or education or advancement?'

'The only dream I had was to be a fireman. Like most kids. Can't do that. Do this.'

'Must make life a lot easier if the only people you have to interact with sit in the backseat, though.'

She thought she'd get chagrin. Instead, she got a slow, knowing smile. 'Immensely. Now, how 'bout Genesis?'

He was right. It was Genesis 5. Actually, the password was Gen51, or Genesis 5:1, the start of the recitation of all the generations of Adam. As Susan Wade Reeves had said, all that begetting. A clever password for a fertility clinic's donor page.

And quite a page it was. Slick and commercial and laid out like a catalog, as if the women were advertising beer instead of eggs. Bright, smiling faces, compassionate words, promises of immortality for a mere five thousand dollars plus expenses.

Not all were beautiful, but every one had some kind of recommendation. IQ, talent, fertility. Blondes, brunettes, Hispanics, African Americans, Asians. All types and sizes.

It creeped her out.

But she had a sister to find. And one of these women might be able to help her. Like, maybe, Willow Tolliver.

Chastity found her right there on the fifth page.

Willow Amber Tolliver claimed two children and high grades through junior college. Athletics, art, and a sweet

166

disposition. She could be contacted through the Arlen Clinic.

She was a blonde.

A pale blonde with anxious blue eyes. No tattoos or disfiguring marks. Chastity couldn't take her eyes off that photo.

James didn't say a word. Just studied alongside.

'Is it me,' Chastity asked, 'or does she look an awful lot like my sister?'

'Yeah,' he said, setting his coffee mug down. 'She does.'

Chastity looked a bit longer, her stomach in a sudden twist.

If Susan Reeves wasn't lying, it was a connection. It was also quite a coincidence. Only Chastity didn't believe in coincidences.

'James,' she said, her focus on those pale blue eyes, 'do you think Susan Reeves gave us Willow's name on purpose?'

'You mean, she wanted you to specifically check Willow out for some reason?'

Chastity sucked in a breath. 'Like, maybe she knows that Willow is missing.'

James looked at the picture. Then he looked over at Chastity. 'You think she's the body in the swamp?'

'I think it's somebody to rule out.' She was sitting there just staring at that young girl with the pale blond hair. She needed to call Kareena. See if there was a missing persons report on Willow Tolliver. She needed to call the coroner and find out if their victim was a natural blonde. As far as she knew, Faith still was. She wasn't so sure about Willow.

'I had the feeling Susan Reeves wasn't telling us everything,' she said. 'Or maybe that she was speaking in some code.'

'Like telling you your brother-in-law gambles.'

She looked over to see that James was watching her. He made her feel twitchy again. 'You caught that, did you?'

'Yeah. I don't think she's a great friend.'

167

Chastity turned back to the screen. 'I need to talk to her again. But first I need to talk to Kareena.'

'Willow Tolliver,' Chastity said five minutes later. 'Thirty-year-old white female, blond and blue. No scars or tattoos.'

'From New Orleans?' Kareena asked in her professional voice.

'Must be a transplant. This doesn't give any contact info, and I'm sitting in an illegal Web page.'

'Shut up, girl. I don' need to know that.'

'I have a couple other questions then. Can you find out if Max Stanton gambles? Oh, and could you check with Jefferson Parish and see if Dulane talked them into another post? I think it's better coming from you. I've annoyed that man enough.'

'Sure, girl. I got nothin' else to do.'

'I'll buy you a drink, Kareena.'

'Damn right you will. Especially since I'm gonna tell you that your crazy little Saints fan lives with his sister over on St. Patrick, out by Metairie Cemetery, you should happen to be that way. But Kareena didn't tell you. That would also be illegal.'

'Thanks, Kareena.'

'Yeah, well, we got thunderstorms comin' through. Wait till they pass before you go. Always floods for a while after.'

Great. Another stressor. Chastity took a look out the kitchen window and saw the clouds churning up from the trees. 'Floods? It floods here?'

'Oh, yeah, girl. Every time. But you just wait till Bob. He come in, *then* you'll see a flood.'

Not what Chastity wanted to hear, either. Bob was already on the TV full-time. Chastity swore that Kareena had rigged the damn thing to show nothing but the Weather Channel. And she could smell James again, which was making all that pressure in her chest worse.

'We go party tonight, girl,' Kareena said. 'You feel better.'

168

'Ya know what, Kareena? You're on. I'll even have a Hurricane and name it Bob.'

She hung up and looked back at the screen. 'I have a feeling this is getting more and more out of control.'

James, scanning pages, just shrugged. 'You didn't expect to find your sister in a Wal-Mart buyin' T-shirts, did you?'

'I expected to find that she'd run away. The rest of this is just complicating things.'

'Inconsiderate.'

Chastity just glared.

He took another sip of coffee. 'You think she's alive?'

'Faith? I don't know. I don't seem to know anything anymore.'

'Well then, let's find some stuff out.' He leaned back over the donor page, scanning faces. 'Elvis is here, ya know.'

Chastity settled her chin atop her arms on the table, her energy suddenly spent. 'He's donating eggs?'

'She is. That girl who was at the clinic yesterday.'

Chastity just shook her head. 'I really want to know what they're looking for in their genetic material.'

'She's a Phi Beta Kappa working on her Ph.D. in history and political science.'

'Yeah, fine. So she has some hobbies.'

James just smiled. 'She also looks hot in a jumpsuit.'

The bitch was taking too long. What the hell did she think she was doing, wasting time like this? If she wanted to find her sister, she had to get out onto the streets. She had to talk to more people. She had to *try*.

If she didn't, he wouldn't have a chance, either.

He'd been so sure he'd taken care of it.

So sure.

He hated feeling this uncertain. He hated *her*. He hated all of them.

But it was all right. He was back on the right track again. He just had to stick it out.

169

The rain had passed, as it always did, right at rush hour. The streets were still awash, so that the traffic sounded like high waves on a beach. There wasn't any fresh movement from the white house with the blue porches. Out in his black car, he made a decision and started the engine.

If only the bitch wouldn't take so long.

Chapter Twelve

On the stroke of six the rain swept off in a burst of sun and a rainbow. The humidity didn't ease, but the streets glistened in the slanting sun, and the floods Kareena had predicted shrank to puddles. Sitting in James's backseat as they splashed their way up Canal toward Metairie Cemetery, Chastity fought a monster headache. She was on the phone with Max, and he wasn't cooperating.

'I'm exhausted, Chastity,' he said when she'd tried to offer him an update. 'I came home about noon and crashed. I'm not working tomorrow, though. You can come out here then, can't you?'

Which meant that she was going to have to go back to Faith's house after all. 'Yeah. Fine, Max.'

Hanging up the phone, she slammed down three Excedrin and the rest of the go-cup of coffee she'd liberated from Kareena's kitchen.

'The Burgard home,' James announced as he pulled to a stop before a faded, unattractive little tract house with molting trees and a sagging porch.

Chastity sighed. 'I hope Lloyd's home.'

He wasn't. His sister was. Older than Lloyd, she was a thin, tense woman who seemed to have had the color all sapped out of her. She never opened the screen door more than a few inches.

'Lloyd isn't here,' she kept saying as she stood half

171

hidden in the shadows of her foyer.

'Please, ma'am, do you know where he is?' Chastity asked, leaning closer. 'It's very important.'

Chastity saw Lillian's posture stiffen. Heard the intake of breath, and understood. Lillian Burgard knew disaster when it showed up at her door. Lloyd was off his medication again. Lloyd was causing problems, maybe violent ones. Lillian was about to go another round with the medical system, just to lose. Again.

Chastity reached out to Lillian's hand where it wrapped white-knuckled around the door. 'I'm sorry,' she said, meaning it. Willing Lloyd's sister to know that she understood. That she hurt for her, because she knew what kept Lillian in the shadows. Chastity might have had to deal with her own demons. Lillian Burgard would spend her life consumed by her brother's. 'I really don't mean any trouble for Lloyd, Miss Burgard. It's just that he might have seen my sister.'

Lillian Burgard did no more than nod, the tears too close now.

So Chastity pulled out another card. 'My cell number,' she said, wishing this woman would let her stay. Let her offer comfort, because she had a feeling nobody was left who would bother. 'If there's anything I can do. You can call me anytime.'

Another nod. A struggle for control.

'He has the car,' Lillian Burgard finally said. 'My Toyota Corolla. I haven't seen him for three days.'

Not good news on any front.

'Has he mentioned the name Faith Stanton?' Chastity asked.

Her stricken eyes said it all. 'Nothing specific,' Lillian insisted. 'Just that he thought for sure that God's justice had been meted out. That it was her fault, and the fault of her kind.'

'It's okay,' Chastity assured her. 'We'll find him, Miss Burgard. We'll do our best to help him.'

172

'We're finding your sister,' James reminded her a few minutes later when they were back in the cab. 'Isn't that more than enough for one day?'

Chastity rubbed at her neck and sighed. 'Not when they're connected, it isn't. Where should we go next?'

'I can give you a lovely tour of the cemeteries up here. There's Metairie, which used to be a racecourse, and Greenwood and Cypress Grove, where the trees are growing up right through the graves ... that's one of my favorites. It's shady and cool, and you can smell the cypress and magnolias—'

'And dead people. I thought Kareena was kidding when she said you were obsessed with death. She wasn't, was she?'

James looked seriously affronted. 'Nobody should leave without seeing the cemeteries. They probably say more about this city than the Quarter. They're sure as hell better cared for. God knows the art's better. Some of our best statues are on tombs.' He grinned then, a mischievous twinkle that was suspicious. 'Why, out at Lake Lawn, you can have them take your ashes and make pictures with 'em for you. Kinda like an eternal Etch A Sketch, yeah?'

Chastity sighed. 'And you find this amusing?'

'You know that picture in my backseat? The Marine Corps?'

Chastity all but climbed out of the car. 'Oh, no.'

'My friend Boots. Great old cabdriver. Fought at Tarawa.'

There was nothing to do but laugh. 'I should have known.'

'And did I tell you that there's a cemetery founded by the Fireman's Benevolent Society? Now how thoughtful is that? I felt it was a sign I should never have left home.'

Chastity just shook her head. 'Do you realize that that is the greatest number of words I've ever heard out of your mouth?'

James was still smiling, his face pulling oddly on his

burns. 'Come on, trauma nurse. You gotta admit that it's elegant. Cradle to grave and beyond, all in the same six-mile radius. We celebrate *everything* in this city. You want, we can get beer and sandwiches and have a picnic on my plot. It's right at the top of the rise under a big ole magnolia tree. Or by the big fireman statue at the entrance to Greenwood. It's a particular favorite of mine.'

'Maybe when we have time, fireman. As you so eloquently reminded me, we have to find my sister.'

'And Lloyd Burgard.'

'And Lloyd Burgard. And Willow Tolliver, and Eddie Dupre.'

'You do put in a full day, nurse.'

'I'm just keeping you honest, fireman.'

Just to make sure, they made another pass at the fertility clinics. The rain, it seemed, was mightier than civil protest, because nobody was out. Eddie Dupre had already left Arlen for the day, but evidently hadn't made it yet to his house on Royal. Just one more dead end in a maze that kept on growing.

Chastity and James didn't make it to Jackson Square until well after dusk. The air was still close and hot, the sky low with scudding clouds. On the streets beyond, Chastity knew there was light and noise and music, but here at the edge of the Quarter, a kind of hushed quiet reigned. The cathedral, white and spectral in the dusk, seemed to hold the rest of the revelry back, and the trees in the square sheltered them from the traffic on Decatur.

Chastity stopped at the edge of the square, enchanted. She wasn't really a mystical person. She'd given up her faith with her virginity, long before she could comprehend either. If she could, though, she thought, she might look for it again here in the dark, where the trees dripped shadows and the church bells tolled into the night. Where usually raucous voices quieted to a murmur, and the only real lights were the candles that flickered on the psychics' tables.

If there was magic, she thought, it was here. And damn it, she didn't have the time for it tonight.

'Willow?' an older, tattooed white man said as he peered up from beneath a big straw hat. 'Went home to Mobile, didn't she?'

'Biloxi,' the woman at the next table said.

A city ordinance that restricted the psychics to one side of the square kept them bundled up here right across from the cathedral doors. The tattooed guy sat two tables in, where he advertised communion with the spirits and Indian fetishes. The woman, bedecked in flowers and enough beads to string a curtain, advertised psychic healing. She had nothing more to offer on Willow, though. Willow, it seemed, had wandered into their midst and then wandered back out. Nothing unusual about that. Half the people here had done the same, time to time.

'You want to know where she went,' the psychic healer said with lots of teeth and kohl-rimmed eyes, 'ask Tante Edie, down at the other end. She and Willow kinda became friends.'

Chastity had already turned, James on her heel, when the woman coughed.

'But be careful.'

James laughed. Chastity hesitated only a moment before heading on down the line.

She really liked it here, she thought, feeling the unbearable tension of the day begin to writhe away into the air like the humidity.

'See dat card dere?' a harsh, deep voice demanded at the far corner of the fence. 'It da Deat' card. Mean change. Mean you gotta change you dead-end, waste-o'-you-life job, you pea brain. You a Pisces, what da hell you bein' an accountant for? You got no head for detail, do you? Well, *do* you?'

It didn't take Chastity long to track down the voice. Some poor schlump in Hawaiian shirt and jeans was sitting at the end table like a first grader getting his knuckles rapped.

'No. I don't.'

'Sit up straight! I know you jus' a fish, but even fish got a spine! Go back to school. Fin' a job doin' research in a jungle somewhere you don' have to sit in no office. Now get outta here!'

The person taking up the other chair at the table made Chastity want to laugh. She was a human hummingbird, all bright colors and quick movement. No, Chastity decided, she was in hummingbird disguise. Beneath all that color lived a walnut doll. Wrinkled, hard, and brown, with black eyes that glittered from the flickering candle she'd put before her on the bare card table.

She had a classic layout of tarot cards spread out before her, old, big cards that seemed well used. She had twenty rings on her tiny fingers, all flashing and gleaming as she moved. She had a brindled Great Dane draped across her feet and a big cardboard sign resting against the table that said TANTE EDIE SEES ALL.

'James,' the little woman announced in her deep voice without looking up, 'you come back for more abuse, did you? I'm not gonna tell you again you got no place up on dat hill wit' dose other dead people.'

Her chortle was the kind Disney used to frighten children.

James just smiled. 'I brought somebody to meet you, Tante.'

'What, don' you like her or somethin'? You do have a tormentin' soul in you, boy.'

Tante was smiling to herself as she raked in the tarot cards. She'd just made a deck when she looked up.

Then she stood up.

It was hard to tell the difference. She still barely topped the table. The Dane, displaced, rolled on his back and watched.

'What are *you* doing here?' Tante demanded, her musical accent noticeably absent.

Chastity felt a definite frisson slither down her back. 'You know me?'

176

Tante squinted in the shadows, her head tilted. 'No,' she admitted. 'But I know your twin. I seen her here.'

Chastity sat herself down in the folding chair the guy in the Hawaiian shirt had just vacated. 'She's my sister,' she said.

Tante sank back into her own chair, her dark eyes wide and staring, her tarot forgotten. 'She's dead, then. Isn't she?'

'My sister?'

The little woman looked truly distressed. 'My Willow. You're here to tell me she's dead.'

'I don't know. Is she missing?'

'These last two weeks and more. Just didn't show up one day. I told the police, but you know how it is. Wasn't even sure it was her real name. I mean, who the hell'd name their kid Willow, 'cept somebody in a commune?' Tante shook her head and sighed. 'But she's dead. Looking at you here, I can tell.'

Chastity couldn't take her eyes off that sharp black gaze. She couldn't say why she didn't laugh at the certainty in them. 'Willow was friends with my sister?' she asked. 'Faith Stanton.'

'I know who she is. She came here one day, after lunch with her friends. Takin' a little time for herself away from her mama. Met Willow, and ended up helping her get the money to get back to her kids. Willow thought the moon hung on that woman.'

'You're sure Willow didn't get back to Mobile.'

'Biloxi. I'm sure. And her cell been disconnected.'

'My sister is missing, too, Tante,' Chastity said.

Tante sat quietly a moment, just watching Chastity. Then, without a word, she reached across the table and grabbed Chastity's hands. Chastity would swear to anyone who asked that she felt nothing. She wouldn't lie to herself. She tried twice to pull away.

'Did you know any of Willow's friends from the clinic?' James asked from where he stood at Chastity's shoulder.

177

Tante never blinked. 'Yeah. Some. Girl did shows at the Lotusland. Don't know her name, though. Guy named Eddie, looks like a big gay Frankenstein fresh from the tanning bed. He'd make sure Willow ate sometimes. And Frankie Mae, of course.'

James stilled. 'Frankie?'

Chastity was still trying to ignore the shock of contact with those gnarled little hands.

Tante pulled her gaze from Chastity and dropped it on James. 'James, sure you already talked to the cabbies. Didn't you talk to Frankie Mae Savage?'

'She said she didn't know nothin' 'bout no missing white girls.' James didn't sound pleased.

Tante's grin was more frightening than her chuckle. 'Where you think she got her baby boy? Ain't no cabbage patch in Bywater. And no matter how much you pray to Yamaya and all them other pagan people Frankie got in the front of her cab, you ain't gonna get a baby after you has your ovaries taken out. Frankie had hers yanked, she was twenty.'

Chastity turned to James. 'You know her?'

He was not smiling. 'I do.'

'Is she by chance a black woman with short hair and a cab full of statues?'

'That would be her.'

Chastity nodded. Finally, a question answered. 'Do you know anything else, Tante?' she asked, facing the little woman once more. 'Anything at all that might help find my sister? Something she or Willow might have said? Something that didn't seem to make sense, or didn't fit?'

'I know how it's done, girl. And no. I can't remember anything unusual. Except, maybe, Willow saying something about what I didn't know about fertility clinics would surprise me. I asked what she mean, and she just shook her head. 'There are some not nice people out there, Tante' was all she said. I tol' her to take care.' Tante huffed a bit, shook her head. 'She didn't, did she? Oh, and she said once

178

your sister hated cameras. Didn't make sense to me, but it seemed to make a lot of sense to Willow.'

'Cameras? At the fertility clinic?'

'I don't know that, child. Seemed to have somethin' to do with it, though.'

Chastity's head was beginning to spin. She was ready to leave. To meet Kareena for some playtime. To rest from the relentless energy in that little woman's hands.

Evidently Tante Edie wasn't ready to let her go.

'You'll find her,' she said, her voice suddenly flat. 'I don' know if you'll find her good or find her bad. But you will. There's somethin', though . . .'

Chastity just waited. Tante tilted her head again, frowned.

'Huh. It's usually fire you got to wade through to get to the end. With you, it's water.'

Chastity opened her mouth, but nothing came out.

'You got to deal with your daddy,' Tante said. 'You don't, you got no chance to get through.'

Chastity stared. 'How do you know that?'

Tante huffed again. 'Didn't you read the sign? What do you think I do here?'

'I'm sorry. I guess I just don't understand.'

'No,' Tante agreed. 'I don' think you do. I'm not sure you gonna make it, girl. I'm just not sure at all. But face your daddy. It's all you can do.'

And then, like pulling a plug, Tante took her hands back and waved one at James. 'Now take this girl dancin', James. And not to those jazz places, where they only sing about bad times and lost things. You take her to Mulate's or that bowlin' place so she can do some happy dancin' with a good Cajun boy.'

Chastity was climbing to suddenly uncertain legs when Tante swung back around on her. 'And you. This boy can give you good ya-ya, you want.'

Chastity thought she might have actually blushed. She didn't bother to tell Tante that there was no such thing as good ya-ya.

179

'You don't know somebody named Lloyd Burgard, do you?' she asked instead, trying so hard not to laugh.

Tante glared as if insulted. 'Ain't no jokes here, girl,' she said, pointing a sharp finger at Chastity. 'You balanced on the edge of somethin' fierce. But it don't matter what your name is. You deserve a good time. Let him give it to you.' Then she snorted like an overheated horse, startling her dog. 'If he can remember how, that is.'

Chastity did not let James give her good ya-ya.

But only barely. And it made her sweat like a suspect, just thinking about it.

She did, however, try to get hold of detectives Gilchrist and Dulane. She called them from the square so she could pass on what information she'd gathered. All except that last part from Tante Edie, of course. Hell, *she* didn't even want to think about that.

She got no further with either than their answering machines. So sitting there in the still shadows at the edge of the square, she left them three nominations: Willow Amber Tolliver as possible ID for their beringed body, Lloyd Burgard as psych detainee of the week, and the Arlen Clinic as possible coconspirator in whatever was going on.

She could just imagine their reactions when they played back the messages. Well, at least she hadn't told them that she'd have to wade through water to deal with her father.

Did that nasty old woman just live to terrify her customers? Chastity shook all the way to Mulate's.

Then, her first gin at Mulate's neatly dispatched, she called Susan Wade Reeves.

'Yes?' Susan asked after the preliminaries.

'Willow Tolliver,' Chastity retorted, a finger in her ear to hear over the fiddles and accordions. 'You knew she was missing.'

Chastity couldn't swear to it, but she was pretty convinced there was dead silence on the other end of the phone.

'We need to talk, Susan.'

Another silence, longer. Then a half laugh, almost a nervous sound. 'Okay, Faith's sister. I'll tell you what. Noon tomorrow. Saint Roch's Cemetery, the Campo Santo. Somebody ought to be able to direct you to it. We'll meet there.'

'Why there?' Chastity asked.

Another laugh. This one surer, more wry. 'Because I'm going to give you something, but I'm taking something away. Bye.'

And she hung up.

'We're meeting Susan tomorrow,' Chastity announced, shutting her phone away. She saw her velvet bag in there, nestled right in the bottom of her purse. The urge to open it and spill her treasure out on that plastic red-checked tablecloth was overwhelming. She shut her purse instead.

'At her house?' Kareena asked. 'Can I come this time?'

'At Saint Roch's Cemetery. Something about giving and taking away.'

James laughed, his face lighting in its dust-dry delight. 'Ah, Saint Roch's. Perfect. It's one of my favorite places.'

'Of course it is, James.'

'Well, if it's a cemetery,' Kareena said, 'I'll let you two handle it. Kareena, she only like her dead people fresh, yeah?'

'There's a great story to Saint Roch's,' James offered.

'Which you can tell her on the way there at noon tomorrow,' Kareena insisted. 'Tonight is for live people.'

'Amen,' Chastity agreed, and ordered her next drink.

The band started a new set, something nasal that involved lots of accordion and foot-stomping, and the waitress took orders.

'A fertility clinic,' Chastity mused a minute later, raising her new drink for a taste. 'What could go on at a fertility clinic that could scare my sister into disappearing?'

Kareena considered the question. She sipped her beer, wincing when she saw a guy on stage running a spoon up

181

and down his washboard tie in rhythm to the accordion and fiddle. 'You don' think fertility clinics couldn't cheat people jus' like everybody else in medicine?'

'Like everybody else in the free world,' James amended.

'There was that one guy,' Kareena added, 'ran a clinic using all his own sperm instead of the husbands', remember? He only got caught 'cause so many of his bebes got cystic fibrosis from him.'

Chastity nodded, elbows on the table. 'My sister was too old to donate. Maybe they knew all along.'

'Bad eggs. Oh, that's a good one. What about all those extra bebes? What they do with 'em?'

'Put 'em in a tin can under the sink.'

'Read up on the Web,' Kareena suggested. 'You know there's somebody out there postin' stuff about how bad fertility clinics are.'

'Yeah. I think I'll do that. Maybe I should do it now.'

'Not now. You need to have some fun now. Didn't that Tante Edie tell you that?'

'She told me to wade through water to deal with my father. I'm not listening to that crazy old woman.'

'She told *me* to give her good ya-ya,' James said.

Kareena hooted. 'You gotta stop givin' that ole lady bribes, James. Tante wanted you to dance, girl. We gonna make you dance.'

Not only did Chastity dance, but Kareena ended up singing, right up there with the washboard player and a fiddler she seemed to know from home, some song called 'Jolie Blonde' that was evidently sung entirely through the nose. Chastity found herself clapping and whistling along.

And with Tante Edie's words hanging right over her shoulder, she forced herself to have a good time. She danced, she laughed, she talked about anything but what was important, and she let the place and the music seduce her. She inhaled the smell of James like pot at a rock concert and hung on to her control by her fingernails. She beat her fears back and she did her best not to make too

182

much of the fact that James seemed to like to dance with her.

But she did have fun. She made friends with people she didn't know and danced down the street like a tourist and almost forgot what awaited her in the morning. She even splashed in a puddle without wetting her pants.

Damn, she loved this city.

James was right. She had ghosts in her pocket and a murderer at her periphery. She had to find one sister and exorcise another. She had to deal with her daddy and rescue her sanity. But for right now, for this few hours in the dark with people she didn't know who smiled at her, she could celebrate it all. The night and the music and the friends she'd gathered here in foreign climes.

Even that whiff of decay in the corner.

The whitewashed walls of Saint Roch's Cemetery rose like battlements against the decay of the surrounding streets. Angels guarded the wrought-iron gates, and a late model Lexus sat at the curb. Susan's, Chastity hoped. James parked the cab behind it and ushered her out.

'This is a great little cemetery,' James enthused. 'A veritable jewel in the middle of the hood.'

James was right. The cemetery was a tidy, well-worn cement city crowded with classic, flower-bedecked New Orleans tombs and crowned by a tall, narrow chapel at the rear. A tall crucifix bisected the main avenue and shared a berm with a cement child who rested on an eternal bed.

'My favorite place is the side altar in the chapel,' James said as they walked through the gates. 'See, people leave all kinds of things for Saint Roch there. Mementos of prayers answered. Some of them are pretty . . . unique.'

Chastity had never seen James move with so much purpose. He waved at the caretaker, who waved back from his shack by the gate, and marched down the cement boulevard to the chapel as if on his way to a football game. It was hot and bright out so that the tombs seemed to gleam white and hard against the eyes.

Inside the chapel, the darkness pressed right in on them. Chastity didn't like it. With few windows, high walls, and no air, it redefined the term *claustrophobic*. There were four pews inside and a glass coffin bearing a beaten Christ to hold up the altar.

But again, James was right. It was the side alcove that was really eerie. It was gated and closed, arched, with a grilled window at the back. After all the rain, mildew claimed the corners and peeled the paint so that it smelled stale and small and close.

It wasn't just that, though. There was something else. Something that resonated from all those plaster casts that hung from the walls and cluttered up the floor. Arms, legs, hearts, hands. Eyes and ears and faces, all haphazardly piled up as if displayed at a flea market. Remembrances from people who were so wretched that in a town that teemed with grant-giving saints, they'd finally come to one who might give a boon, but then took something away again. The room reeked with the smell of desperation.

'Where is she?' Chastity asked, sweating to be gone, her gaze skittering away from all that futile hope nailed to a wall.

'Did you see the army of baby angels on the floor?' James asked, his attention still on something back in the chapel. 'All ranked there on their bellies, hands folded, with their little gold wings tucked up? You know what those are for, don't you?'

Chastity only saw one, tucked into the left corner beneath a bouquet of crutches. It was facing the wall, as if being punished.

She so didn't want to be here. She couldn't breathe in a place like this. She didn't want to look at what people had left. She didn't want to identify with any of them. And she sure didn't want to spend any time with those statues.

There were three of them, crammed in like second-class passengers in steerage. Saint Roch, she guessed, a grim-

184

looking guy with a dog. Some big woman in black who looked like Kate Smith. And Saint Lucy, a saint any girl with a working knowledge of *Lives of the Saints* would recognize. After all, nobody else held her eyes out on a plate. Another one of those ancient martyrs who'd died protecting her virtue. Which, it seemed, was the only way women got their martyrdom in those days. Chastity would have told ole Luce to let him have at it, then bash his brains in with a rock.

But only one angel baby. Left alone amid the dust and mold.

'I don't see . . .'

Then she did see. There on the floor behind the statues.

A pile of wings. A pyre of angel babies glinting in the dusty sun.

A cairn of hope and prayer piled up like refuse in the corner.

Chastity instinctively wanted to turn away. She knew just by catching a glimpse of them that they were wrong. In the wrong place, in the wrong shape, tumbled about where no seeking penitent would place them.

She was a forensic nurse, after all. She knew how to recognize disaster. And she knew damn well she was looking at disaster.

And then she saw the shoe.

The foot.

Sticking out from beneath those fat little cherubim, a leg that belonged to no statue Chastity had ever seen.

Ah, there it was, she realized. That familiar perfume of decay. But this time, Chastity knew what it was from.

'James?'

'Do you like the statues?' he asked, still not paying attention. 'My favorite is Kate Smith over there. I keep expecting her to sing "God Bless America."'

'James?'

He must have heard it that time, because he turned. Chastity pointed. She could see the hair now, not so tidy

185

anymore, flowing out from beyond Kate Smith's feet, beneath angel elbows and knees.

And beyond that, blood.

Susan Wade Reeves had been killed and buried right there beneath the angel babies.

Chapter Thirteen

'I knew I shouldn't have wasted my time being happy last night,' Chastity said.

At least two hours had passed. The sun had come out and now beat down on the half-dozen police units blocking the north lanes of St. Roch Avenue. The crime scene van was pulled right up into the cemetery proper, and yellow tape ringed the chapel. The coroner's investigator had come and gone, leaving the evidence unit to try and pull something from the thousand or so artifacts that crowded that tiny room.

Right now orange-jumpsuited prisoners from the city lockup were preparing to transport Susan Reeves's body down to the city morgue. Chastity and James and the cemetery caretaker sat out on the cemented mound of stone that held up a ten-foot crucifix in the center walkway, waiting out in the sun to be questioned again.

'Bein' happy's never a waste of time,' James assured her as he sucked on his fifth or sixth cigarette. 'It's more of a luxury, you ask me.'

'Great. I'll go cross-stitch that for my living room.'

James just smiled.

'I don't know how it happened,' the caretaker protested yet again. 'I would have heard!'

Susan had been shot in the face. Her purse, watch, and cell phone were missing. Her 2004 Lexus waited for a tow.

The caretaker knew her, of course. Susan had been coming to the Campo Santo for years. She'd even left a baby angel behind once. But the caretaker swore he hadn't seen her since he'd opened the gates at eight that morning.

Chastity felt sick. Not because of the dead body. Dead bodies were her business. The minute she recognized Susan, she'd pulled open that gated door, squeezed past the saints, and knelt down, pressing her fingers against Susan's cold throat to make sure there was no pulse left. She'd assessed the body just as she would in her ER, for injuries beyond the obvious.

There had been no struggle to speak of. Susan's hands and arms were free of defensive wounds. Her clothes, except for the fall, were tidy. No rips, not so much as a hair out of place, no obvious blowback on her hands or arms. There wasn't any room for movement in the alcove, and all the statues were in place, the floor free of scuff and drag marks.

All the same, Susan Reeves had been terrorized.

She'd been shoved up against the wall. There was dust and plaster in her hair and across her back. There was a defect in the plastered wall where a bullet had probably passed through Susan's brain, and a splatter of blood and brain across the dusty plaster behind Saint Kate Smith's broad shoulders. There was soot at the edges of the wound, which meant that the shot had been point-blank.

But worse, much worse, there was the clear imprint of a muzzle against what was left of Susan's cheek. A laceration, the skin tearing in an almost perfect semicircle, the ridge that was the sight pointing to one o'clock. No pulling or tearing. Simple, straight-on pressure.

Susan hadn't just been shot. She'd been forced back against the wall and had that gun pushed so hard against her that it had cut her. And it had been done deliberately enough that bruising had been raised.

Her murderer had pushed against her so close that he would have seen her pupils dilate. He would have smelled the sweat that still pearled on her upper lip. He would have heard the rasp of her breath in the close, fetid air of that tiny room. And then, while those cold saints looked on, he'd pulled the trigger.

Susan's face was gone, from lip to ear. The back of her head was mush, and her eyes still stared at nothing in stunned silence.

She'd been shoved in the corner and buried in angel babies. And then, as if to punctuate the act, she'd been left with one right in the center of her forehead.

The dead body didn't upset Chastity. The fact that it was Susan Reeves did. The fact that she'd died so terrified it still resonated off the walls. The fact that nobody seemed to wonder why.

'Please,' Chastity had begged the Fifth District homicide detective when he'd arrived. 'Just talk to Detective Gilchrist from the Eighth. He knows I'm looking for my sister. I think Ms. Reeves was going to give me some information.'

The detective, a tired, blunted, middle-aged guy, obviously did not want his life complicated more than it was. 'You're telling me Ms. Reeves was murdered because of some fertility clinic.'

'It has something to do with it. Yes.'

'And it has nothing to do with the fact that this is a neighborhood where white folk shouldn't even turn off their engines?' He shifted on obviously sore feet. Rearranged his increasingly damp bulk. 'I been on ho-micide for ten years, ma'am. I never seen anybody killed in a conspiracy. Not in this neighborhood. When we go lookin' for suspects, usually the simplest answer is the right answer.' Even his red cop mustache was damp.

Chastity straightened her shoulders. 'Talk to Detective Gilchrist. That's all I ask.'

She just couldn't get the image out of her head. A yo might have shot Susan Reeves. Might have stolen her purse and rings. He might even have terrorized her and then tried to cover her up with whatever was handy so that she wasn't found so quickly. But Chastity didn't think he would have taken the time to position one of those little angel babies precisely in the middle of Susan's forehead, so that her staring eyes could watch it.

What was it Susan Reeves had meant to tell her? Could somebody have been threatened by it?

Twice while Chastity had been waiting, her cell phone had rung. Twice she'd let it take a message. She thought it was Max. She just wasn't in the mood for Max yet. Besides, she didn't know what the hell to tell him.

Chastity sat there staring at her hands. They were shaking, she realized, a bit surprised. She hadn't realized she was shaking. She knew her stomach was, of course. Her head was threatening to split right open, and she could smell James again. Thick and hot, a scent that had no business in the sunshine. What it did to her was meant for the dark, for slick sheets and sinning.

At least in a normal life.

'Move over,' she snapped at him.

He barely raised an eyebrow, but did so. 'What about *him*?' he asked, subtly motioning to the caretaker on her other side.

The caretaker was petting the head of the child's sleeping effigy that had been laid at the foot of the ten-foot cross.

Chastity shook her head. 'Even an addict has standards.'

'We could just get it over with, ya know,' James said, not looking at her. 'Some good ya-ya, like Tante Edie said.'

'Thanks, no. I haven't been into audiences in a while.'

James laughed. Chastity didn't.

He turned to consider her, and his voice was quiet. 'You okay?'

Chastity stretched her shoulders. 'What's going to happen to that little girl?'

That really got his attention. 'There are some things that

are definitely beyond the scope of even this taxi service.'

Chastity laughed so hard she snorted. 'You think I want to take that child *home*? Believe me, I know perfectly well what kind of parent I'd make. I want her to grow up happy and healthy.'

Angel babies.

Susan Reeves had come to Saint Roch to ask for a child. He'd given her one.

And then he'd evidently taken something away.

Chastity found that she was shivering all over now. 'Do you think we can go yet?'

'You that anxious to talk to your brother-in-law?'

'I'm that anxious to get out of the sun. My nose is getting red enough to do Barnum and Bailey.'

'Well, I'd suggest we go back in the chapel ...'

'Not if you shoved a gun in my ribs.'

'You don't like my cemetery?'

'It's not your cemetery, James. And no. I don't. If the other cemeteries are like this one, I don't think I want any tours.'

'Well, usually other cemeteries don't come with their own crime scene van. Except Saint Louis 1, of course. But that's just the neighborhood.'

'Ms. Byrnes?' the detective asked, trudging up to them. Chastity hoped he was close to serving his thirty. He just didn't have any gas left in him. 'When did you last talk to the victim?'

Chastity didn't move from where the rocks were gouging her ass. 'About nine o'clock last night.'

'Uh-huh.' The detective nodded and jotted in his note-book. 'And you got here, when?'

'About two and a half minutes before you got your call.'

Another nod. 'About noon, then. Yeah?'

Chastity gave up looking at him. She reached into her purse and rescued her little velvet bag, closing it in her shaking hand. She could smell that chapel again.

Well, it was better than bleach.

191

Not by much, though.

At least she had James to offset it, although that didn't settle her any more than the chapel smell did.

'About noon.'

'And you didn't see or hear anything unusual?'

Should she include the dead body in that list?

'No,' James said for her. 'Nothing.'

'And you didn't notice anybody else come in?' the cop demanded of the caretaker.

The little man flinched as if he'd been smacked with a truncheon. 'No. I ... no. I was recementing one of the tomb doors over there at the back. I had my headset on. I'm sorry.'

He really seemed to mean it.

'Well,' the cop said, consulting his dog-eared notebook, 'she died sometime this morning. We're canvassing the neighborhood.'

They were canvassing a neighborhood that made it a point not to notice anything. Chastity shifted against the hard stone and fought the urge to say something the cop would never forgive her for. He walked back to the clot of cops by the chapel, and she kept sitting there.

Chastity knew she should be thinking of what to do next, what this meant to her and her sister and the fact that Faith was still missing. But it seemed that the image of Susan Reeves crumpled in the corner of that chapel took up all of her brain, pushing the rest back into the corners.

She didn't know what to do. She didn't know what to think, except that somehow she should have known how to prevent Susan Reeves's death. So she just sat there.

'Do you think I'm responsible for this?' she inevitably asked.

Since she was already responsible for everything but 9/11.

'It could just be a bad coincidence,' James offered dryly.

Chastity sighed. 'Or a figment of my imagination.'

The detective walked back from his friends. 'You can go

now,' he said, flipping his notebook closed. 'I have your numbers.'

The detective ambled away. The caretaker popped up as if spring-loaded. James and Chastity followed in far more exhausted fashion.

'What do we do now?' Chastity asked.

James gave her a little smile. 'Isn't that my line?'

She slung her purse over her shoulder. 'Kareena's,' she said. 'I'm in need of some bright green walls and coffee.'

'And another look at that hurricane.'

Chastity shook her head. 'You're not helping, James.'

'Sure I am,' he said, walking up behind her.

He set a hand on her shoulder. A touch, nothing more. A fleeting contact. And yet she spun on him as if he'd just attacked her. Her breath left. Her heart stuttered. She damn near landed on her butt, she backed away so fast.

James stared at her as if she'd turned to smoke, his hand still out.

'Don't—' Chastity dragged in a breath. Shook her head again. Fought the urge to vomit. 'I'm sorry. It's just . . .'

His eyes widened. 'You don't like to be surprised.'

She tried to smile. 'Not like that.'

A hand on the shoulder, a brush of hot breath on her neck. A stumble into the darkness. Into the water. She couldn't explain it, even to ease his discomfort. She couldn't bear it, either.

But he nodded. He dropped his hand. 'I'll never sneak up on you.'

And damn if it wasn't the compassion in his eyes that nearly undid her.

So she nodded even more briskly, thanked him, and walked out of the cemetery, sweating. It was getting worse.

Where was she going?

He couldn't keep following her. He couldn't wait.

The pressure was building up in him to act, to do something, to cleanse himself with her.

Because she knew.

She knew where the other one was. She knew and she wasn't going to tell unless he made her.

He didn't have *time*.

He knew they were following him. He'd seen it. He knew they'd catch him soon, soon. They seemed as impatient as he. More impatient, maybe. He saw what they did, and they would know it.

They would know and they would stop him.

It didn't matter. Nothing mattered but finishing this. Finishing this now.

Bitch.

Slut.

Whore.

Detective Dulane was sitting in his unmarked, wolfing down a hamburger before heading back out on interviews, when the call came through from the coroner's office.

'You wanted something on this floater?' Dr. Ross asked.

Dulane set down his burger and riffled through the paperwork on his front seat to find his notes on the Jane Doe in the bayou.

'I just wanted to make sure,' he said. 'You did the entire post?'

Ross huffed. 'You have to ask. Good thing I did, too. Well, good for somebody, I'm sure. Not that little girl in my garage.'

Dulane came right to attention. 'What?'

'You got a fondness for Saint Jude, Francis Xavier?'

Dulane stopped scanning the scant information on the page before him. 'He's a nice guy, I guess. Why?'

'Well, our Jane Doe had a real intimate acquaintance with him.'

'How intimate?'

'Intimate enough that if I weren't such a good pathologist, I'd think she was trying to give birth to him.'

Dulane's wise old eyes opened wide. 'To Saint Jude.'

194

'To a lifelike eight-inch replica, to be sure. Isn't this the girl was dressed up as a nun?'

'Allegedly.'

'Well, there's no allegedly about her acquaintance with Saint Jude.'

By the time Dulane got in touch with Gilchrist, just to fill him in, the cops at Jefferson had retagged his Jane Doe as Judy Doe in honor of Saint Jude. The statue was sent to evidence, and Judy was sent back to the cooler to await identification.

It took Chastity no more than five minutes to realize that the addition of James to her interviews wouldn't be quite as successful with her brother-in-law. Max treated James like some housekeeping tech who'd broken sterile field.

'You want him to be here while we talk about your sister?' Max asked, eyes narrowed and hostile.

'He knows more than you do by now, Max.'

At least Max was beginning to look familiar to her. He was acting more like a surgeon than a tour guide. He was testy and impatient and haughty. He was, finally, in character.

It didn't make Chastity feel any better. There was no way she could, in this godforsaken wasteland of a house. She felt more claustrophobic here than in the Campo Santo, and that said something.

'Susan Reeves is dead, Max.'

Max stopped halfway into the kitchen, his face completely blank.

'Who?'

'Susan Reeves. You grew up in the same neighborhood. She was a customer at the Arlen Clinic. She's been murdered.'

For a second, Max just stood there as if trying to translate to a second language. 'Susan? Susan the dyke? She's dead?'

That one almost took Chastity's breath away. 'What?'

195

Max waved her off. 'It's what Susan's always called herself. What do you mean she was murdered?'

'She was going to meet us and talk about Faith. Somebody killed her.'

Max just made it into the kitchen before thunking down on one of the stools. 'I don't understand.'

Neither Chastity nor James sat. 'I don't understand, either, Max. But you need to tell us more about that clinic. About Faith's time there. About anything and anybody at all.'

He looked up. 'You think the clinic . . . '

'I believe that the girl in the bayou was another egg donor.'

He straightened like a shot. 'What? Who?'

'A girl named Willow Tolliver. She's been missing, too. Did you know her?'

He looked bemused, bewildered. 'No. No, I don't recognize the name. She . . . she looked like Faith?'

'Very much so.'

He stared down at his granite countertop as if mining for answers. 'You've found out a lot.'

'Not enough. Can you think of any more names? Anybody Faith talked about, or had over or called? The only name from the clinic I could find in her address book was Susan's.'

'Really? I would have thought she'd stay in touch with at least some of those people. It meant so much to her and all.'

'Do you recognize the name Frankie Mae Savage?'

'Frankie . . . Frankie. No. I remember an Eddie, but no Frankie.'

'Yeah. Eddie Dupre. He's the embryologist over at the clinic. Have you ever met him?'

'No. I checked out his credentials, of course, when Faith decided she wanted to donate. I checked out everybody at the clinic. They all passed with flying colors. I simply can't imagine that there's anything wrong with them.'

'Two women connected with that clinic are dead, Max.'

He nodded absently, his attention still on that counter. 'Yes. Yes, I understand. But who's this Frankie?'

'A cabdriver. A client at the clinic. Somebody thought they saw Faith getting into her cab that afternoon at Gallatoire's. You sure you wouldn't have any more information on Faith?'

'No. I've tried hard to think. But I don't know where else Faith would have kept any other personal information. You went through her things already, didn't you?'

'Yes. I've checked everything I found there without much success.' She sucked in a breath for calm. For focus. 'What about *your* records, Max? Would you mind if I went through them?'

He looked up, still puzzled. 'What for?'

'Well, you pay the bills. Something might have shown up on her credit card statements, or her cell phone bill. Long distance. Repeat numbers. Something like that.'

'But I would have known . . .'

'Not necessarily.'

Again a pause. A consideration. Then, abruptly as always, Max got to his feet. 'Of course. Whatever it takes.'

And then he just walked out of the kitchen.

He led them back toward the front of the house, right by those awful couches and that bleach smell to the doorway at the other side of the foyer. The one that had been locked before.

It was still locked. Max whipped out a set of keys and bent to the door. Chastity came to an uncertain halt behind him, the house working its peculiar sorcery on her. Damn, her heart rate hadn't been this bad when she stood over Susan Reeves's body. Her hands were shaking again and she wanted to vomit.

Why couldn't he keep his records at work? At a Denny's? In Cleveland?

'You lock your office?' she asked, her chest tight and her hands scraping across her pants legs to wipe off the sweat.

It had already been too long a day. She wanted to go home.

'It's habit,' Max said, turning the key. 'From when the boys were little. They used to make a huge mess of my things.'

He opened the door and ushered Chastity in. James, silent and watchful, waited in the foyer.

It took Max only a few moments to find the records he wanted. Last month's statements from the credit cards, from the phone company. While he did, Chastity tried to hold her breath. That smell seemed so concentrated in here. It seemed to wrap itself up inside her head and sear her eyes.

Bleach and lavender.

In a regular, nondescript office with oak and cream walls, a trophy case packed with Little League awards, and a computer.

'Here we go,' Max was saying. 'Cell phone.'

He held up the statement. Chastity did her best to focus on the list of phone numbers. She was having trouble, though.

'Can you mark any numbers you know?' she asked. 'I can call the rest and check them.'

She wanted to look for a pattern of some kind. Long distance numbers, repeaters, numbers Max didn't recognize.

'Sure,' Max said, pulling it back before she even had time to check, 'but I recognize all of them. And the only number I see a lot of here is Chuck's. But he's been calling a lot since your mother died.'

There was the oddest buzzing in Chastity's ears. A humming, as if external sound were suddenly very far away.

'Chuck?' she asked, her voice distant to her own ears.

Max looked up, bemused. 'Yes. Chuck. Your father.'

Chastity blinked. She listened to that dial tone in her head. She realized she was shaking again.

198

'No,' she said, certain. 'That's not right.'

'What do you mean?'

'He can't have called. Faith wouldn't talk to him.'

Max laughed. 'Talk to him? Chastity, he's here all the time. I told you. Faith adores her father.'

'Here?' Chastity demanded. 'Here where?'

'Well, he lives here now. In New Orleans. Didn't you know?'

Louder. The noise was louder. And there was her heart, thudding in her ears like footsteps. Running. Running hard.

'I thought you said he was dead,' James said quietly behind her.

'I *wanted* ...'

'Why, look,' Max said, moving a bit to his left and reaching for something on his desk. 'See? This is from Mardi Gras.'

And there he was, right in Max's hand. Smiling. Gray-haired and square-jawed and handsome. With jowls and creases and a sallow cast to his skin, as if he hadn't seen the sun in a while.

Charles Francis Byrnes.

Smiling out from the picture as he stood with his arm around Faith's shoulder.

Chastity gulped in some air. She stepped back. She straightened like a marine on parade. And then she did the only thing she could do.

She laughed.

She laughed and she kept laughing until somebody sat her down and shoved her head between her knees.

Chapter Fourteen

Bourbon Street was at its tawdriest. Neon winked and skipped and spun all along the street. Crowds milled in and out of a dozen clubs that had once offered good jazz or mediocre blues, but now only played mediocre covers of bad rock or canned zydeco. Bored hawkers waved customers into strip joints or transgender clubs, and cops kept to their cars.

At the corner of St. Louis and Bourbon, a taxi pulled to a halt. 'This is as close as I can get,' the driver said.

Chastity handed over the fare and opened the back door, her hand shaking and the sweat already soaking through her halter top. Her feet hurt from the four-inch heels she wore, and fishnet stockings abraded her ass. The leather miniskirt she'd borrowed from Kareena's closet barely covered her crotch.

'You okay?' the cabbie asked, his voice a bit disconcerted.

Chastity knew just what she looked like. Pale and perspiry and trembly. A woman at the end of her tether. She climbed out of the cab without a word.

The crowd surged around her, shouting and laughing. At one corner a dozen Harleys thundered into motion. Cheap beads winked in the flashing lights, and pretty young women stumbled into stupidity. It was close to ten o'clock, and the crowd wanted to feel as if they were sinning for a lifetime. It was the perfect place for a woman intent on disaster.

She'd lasted all day. From the moment James had dropped her off back at Kareena's, neither of them saying a word about what had happened at Max's, her hands already shaking so hard she could hardly put a key in the lock. Long enough to get Kareena back out of the house so she could go to hell in her own way.

She couldn't last any longer.

She kept seeing the courtroom. That formal, ritualistic scene straight out of a *Law and Order* episode, frozen in flashes. The sound of air-conditioning. The rustle of paper and the smell of dust. A shaft of sunlight hitting the defense table, illuminating her father as he did his best impression of Spencer Tracy in *Boys Town*. The acid that roiled in her stomach as she told the truth nobody wanted to believe. The deathly cold humiliation as her father's lawyer filleted her for the pleasure of the jury.

'How can we believe you, Ms. Byrnes?' he asked in a voice a parent would use for a fractious child. 'Don't you have a history of lying? Of running away from home? Of drug use and dangerous sexual behavior?'

She did. All of it.

Faith was sitting in the front row, holding hands with their mother and glaring. The Faith glare. The 'How dare you do this to us?' glare. Hope was there, too. Poor Hope, who by then had completely disappeared beneath her fat.

Chastity couldn't get that scene out of her head.

She marched down the middle of Bourbon Street, Kareena's stiletto heels clacking on the blacktop, the humid air wrapping around her bare arms and legs. Nobody noticed her. Nobody interfered as she counted buildings and windows.

There it was, right in the center of the 400 block of Bourbon. The Big Dawg Saloon. ZZ Top blared from the speakers, and partyers pushed in for their drink orders. The woman behind the counter looked like Carol Channing's slutty sister, her aged, crepey breasts pushed to impossible heights by a red bustier, her wide blue eyes rimmed in bluer glittered shadow and Tammy Fae Baker mascara. Chastity reached the open door and looked up. She counted windows. She stood there, knowing she shouldn't take another step.

'Can you tell us, in your own words, Miss Byrnes, what your relationship is with your father?'

Hope was the one who sat in the witness stand this time. Faith had already testified. She'd called Chastity a liar. Chastity didn't think Hope would say anything different. All Hope wanted, after all, was peace. She sat there, hunched over as if hoping no one would see her, her hands writhing in her lap. She kept her eyes down, too terrified of her father to face him. To confront that genial smile that camouflaged the monster.

Even before Hope spoke, Chastity knew her sister had used up her last reserves of courage just to make the walk up to that chair.

Not quite all, evidently.

Hope never looked up. 'Everything Chastity said is true.'

In the movies, a statement like that would have caused an eruption in the courtroom. Instead, there was silence. Profound, stricken silence.

And a moan from Hope.

'Can I help you, honey?' the Carol Channing look-alike asked.

Chastity stepped right inside the Big Dawg. 'You bet,' she said. 'Something overwhelmingly alcoholic in the biggest go-cup in New Orleans. Oh, and a set of those purple, green, and gold beads.'

The beads went over her head. The Hurricane mostly went down her throat. When she felt properly prepared, she walked out to the next doorway, where a grilled gate hid a set of stairs. The grill was unlocked, but she knew it would be. Taking a slug of alcohol, she climbed four stories into the littered darkness.

'James, open up,' she commanded with a couple of good raps on the plywood door at the top of the stairs. Fourth floor. A perfect view of all the amateur desperation out on the street.

James answered the door wearing nothing but gym shorts. Chastity thought she was prepared to see the extent of James's old injuries. She wasn't sure she was prepared for the rest of him.

He was buff. Pecs and a six-pack and strong, hard thighs on a swimmer's frame. And, of course, a tattoo, high on his right bicep. Homemade and obscene and whimsical. A fire hose as a phallic symbol. And all gleaming just a bit with sweat from the heat.

Chastity grinned like a girl getting her first glimpse of Christmas. 'Oh, good,' she said with a leer at his naked chest as she stalked in. 'You value expediency.'

James backed up into the uncertain light of his living room and let her past. 'I was wondering when you'd show up.'

Chastity stopped long enough to run a finger down his sternum, just to the right of the worst burns. 'You're not going to tell me I'm predictable, are you, fireman?'

James didn't move. 'I kinda expected this. Yes.'

She sighed and started pacing. 'You do know how to insult a girl.'

Before he shut the door, he took a peek out into the hall. 'Where's Kareena?'

Chastity waved her hand. 'Oh, she had a hot date. I didn't want to interfere.'

'So she doesn't know what happened today.'

'She would have missed her date. I couldn't do that.'

'Do I recognize Kareena's clothes?'

Chastity spun around once, arms wide. 'She has great taste, huh?'

Then, before James could deter her, she dropped her purse on the floor and set to pacing through the rooms.

The apartment was a surprise. Not the stark, basic decor

203

that looked as if it had been rescued from a Dumpster. Chastity knew enough men to recognize that decorating scheme. Single male uncommitted.

James had two rooms with a kitchenette and tiny bathroom. A faded brown couch, three big green throw pillows and a sound system, a two-person formica table and unmatched metal chairs. A mattress lay on the bedroom floor, and sheer curtains blew fitfully at the open windows that faced the street below. His chest of drawers listed, and his closet door stood open and draped in jeans.

But none of that surprised Chastity. His bedroom ceiling did. His bedroom ceiling, where every night the neon from Bourbon Street washed the walls like frantic tides.

Chastity caught sight of it and stopped her pacing. She found herself walking right through the bedroom doorway, not sure she believed what she'd seen there in the dark.

She thought the ceiling might be light blue. She wasn't sure, especially with the neon shuddering over it. What she was sure of, though, was the decoration. Because there, in a shabby apartment on Bourbon Street, re-created in painstaking detail in fluorescent paint, was the night sky. Constellations crossed the ceiling in miraculous order as if there were no ceiling. No roof at all.

For a moment Chastity could do no more than stand in the doorway, awed. 'I didn't know you were a romantic.'

'I used to go camping.'

He was standing behind her, right in the bedroom doorway. The ZZ Top downstairs morphed into Bruce Springsteen, and across the street some bad band was trying to wail out some Thunderbirds.

For a second, just to be sure, Chastity flipped on the bedroom light. The night sky magically transformed to day. White, wispy clouds and sunshine. It meant something, she was sure. She just didn't know what. She only knew that it made her more anxious, more hungry. More skittish. So she sucked down her drink, set it on the TV by the door, and shut off the light.

204

'Well, fireman. I hear you want some ya-ya.'

She thought he sighed. 'You want to talk about your father?'

Chastity spun around on him, her heart stumbling all over her chest. 'No, I don't want to talk about my father. I want what Kareena's getting tonight.'

He was standing there in his shorts, the shadows collecting along those terrible scars. He wasn't smiling. Chastity wanted him to smile. She wanted noise and heat and a good, mindless fuck. So she reached out and rested a hand on his left shoulder.

'That doesn't extend to vital areas, does it?' she asked, motioning to what lay beneath her hand.

The scars stretched all the way down his side. From cheekbone to thigh. Red, raw, motley, as if somebody had tried to lay a patchwork quilt over his old injuries and it had fused to him.

'I thought your father was dead,' he said.

She laughed. 'No. I just wanted him to be. I pretended he was.'

It was the only way she'd kept her sanity.

'And he was here all along?'

'He was in prison. Fifteen-to-twenty-five.'

He never did believe he was going to be convicted. Even as they walked him out in handcuffs. He'd looked back at his daughters as if he were Joan of Arc going to the stake. Chastity's mother spit in her face.

'And when he got out?' James asked. 'What then?'

Chastity started walking again, as if pacing those two rooms could distance her from what had happened that afternoon. 'He was supposed to be considerate enough to disappear into the ether, where he couldn't ever bother us again. Bother *me* again. Obviously Faith didn't think it was as much of a bother as I did.'

She couldn't breathe again. If she did, she just smelled James, and if she smelled him, she knew she was going to simply tip him onto the floor. She was shivering with the need of it. The need of him. Sweaty and hot and frantic. Chastity suddenly felt like a little girl, and God, she hated that worse than anything.

'Come here,' he said, his voice quiet.

She chuckled, the sound high and thin. 'About time.'

She walked right into his arms, and he pulled them around her.

And then, he just stood there.

Chastity lifted her face for the kiss of a lifetime. James avoided her like a pro.

'What's this?' Chastity demanded. 'Zen sex?'

'Shhhhhh.'

He was holding her. Bending his head over hers so she couldn't reach him with her mouth. He wrapped his arms around her so tightly she could feel that scar tissue. She could feel the strength in him, the hard leanness.

The trap.

Suddenly she was trying like hell to get away.

'What are you doing?' she demanded, bucking like a toddler in a tantrum. 'Come on. I'm ready to throw caution to the wind. I'm ready to throw your gym shorts out the window. What's the matter with you?'

James never so much as flinched. He just held her. 'Hasn't anybody ever done this for you before?'

'Not unless a blow job was involved. Let me go!'

He walked her right over to the couch and eased down onto it, still wrapped tightly around her. 'Nope.'

And he held her.

Chastity didn't know what to do. She felt like a bird caught in a chimney. She knew her heart was going to explode, right there in her chest. She wanted to cry, and damn it, she didn't cry in front of anybody. Not *anybody*.

'Let me go.'

'In a minute.'

'You said you wanted sex!' She was shrill. She knew it. She couldn't stop. 'What the hell's this?'

'We'll have sex when it's for fun, nurse.'

206

'Sex is never fun, fireman.'

'No, you've never had it for fun. You told me so yourself.'

She was shaking so hard she thought she'd fly apart. 'I can't ... don't humiliate me like this.'

'It's comfort,' he said quietly, his face right against her hair. 'Normal people do it all the time.'

Her laugh was brittle and sharp. 'They can't. It's too terrifying.'

'I know. First time somebody did it to me, I clocked 'em.'

She tried to pull back. He didn't let her. 'You clocked Kareena?'

He chuckled. 'Actually, I did. First time she saw me after the burns, and I couldn't bear anybody touching me. Not because it hurt. Because ... '

Nobody knew better than Chastity. 'Yeah.'

'But you know Kareena.'

'Yeah, I know Kareena.'

Kareena was a toucher, a patter, a woman who nursed with every inch of her. Chastity touched in her job. She held. But it had never been natural, and she was always afraid her patients knew it.

It wasn't natural for James, either. She could tell. But he wouldn't let go. And suddenly Chastity realized that she wasn't fighting anymore.

She couldn't believe it. She was settling. She was calming, right there where she couldn't get away. She was breathing better, and she found herself just wanting to close her eyes and settle against his chest like a tired child.

Was this what families felt in her ER when she held them? When she softened the blows she leveled on them by wrapping them in strong arms? They talked to her, she knew. They poured out grief and anger and surprise, right along with the tears that stained her shoulders. They gave her more trust in response to a simple act of compassion than she'd ever given another human in her life.

For a few moments, she actually thought she could do it, too. Could allow herself to be comforted just like a normal person. For a few moments, she held still.

But only for a few moments.

The panic resurfaced, and it was sharp and suffocating. Her heart slammed against her chest. She couldn't think of anything but escape. The minute James let down his guard, Chastity launched off that couch like a catapult.

She could tolerate anything, it seemed, but compassion. Compassion, she'd learned a long time ago, came at a price.

'Thanks, fireman,' she said, tottering on those four-inch heels as she tried to find her balance. 'Really. But I gotta go.'

James climbed to his feet. Chastity backed away.

'You can stay,' he offered. 'I have cable.'

Nobody had ever said anything so nice to her in her life. 'I'd just buy something I can't afford.' Her laugh sounded really shaky.

'Then let me drive you back to Kareena's.'

'You're not the only cab in town.'

'Chaz ...'

She looked at him. At those once-distant eyes that glittered in the odd lighting of his apartment. At the devastation his body had suffered, that most days nobody even noticed anymore. She fought a fresh wash of lust and a worse one of shame, because they always came paired that way.

'Don't worry, fireman. I was only going to come here, where it was safe.'

His smile was wry. 'It's not as safe here as you think, Chaz.'

She smiled, because of course she'd felt how hard he'd gotten, just holding her. 'Oh, shit, James,' she sighed, 'but I think it is. Immutable laws of physical nature notwithstanding. I'm sorry. I shouldn't have imposed on you this way.'

She shouldn't have bared herself that much. Now she felt

208

frayed and raw, and she didn't know how to escape.

His shrug was a thing of ease. 'You're dressed up to go out. Wait a minute and let's go on down to Frenchmen Street.'

Chastity thought of that empty, echoing house back in the Irish Channel, and the fact that she'd stolen Kareena's clothes to go get laid. She thought about the temptations the rest of this city had to offer a woman with an addiction, and how easy it would be to find somebody who'd be happy to help her look for them.

She thought that James, with his obvious scars, was the person she could be with right now.

Chastity turned for the door and stopped, still in the shadows. 'Ya know, it's really embarrassing. You reach a certain age, and you think you've finally become mature. Put other people's concerns ahead of your own. And then, in one day I see a dead woman who's left behind a child – who happens, in the grotesque scheme of things, to be my niece – and a fresh picture of my father. And what do I throw a tantrum over? I ask you, fireman. How mature is that?'

'You're asking the wrong person, nurse. I have tantrums over parking spaces.'

She grinned to his door, which was as scarred as he was. 'I'll meet you downstairs.'

He nodded. 'Tell Carol you get a Hurricane on me.'

Chastity actually laughed. 'Her name really is Carol?'

'Yeah. She used to work the strip clubs. Now she owns Big Dawg. She also makes a great chicken soup.'

Chastity nodded and opened the door. Turned back. Did something as maudlin as just kiss James right on that scarred cheek of his. Then she walked out.

Chastity was standing in front of the stairs to James's apartment watching the pedestrians when she felt a hand on her elbow. She knew it wasn't James. Even Superman didn't change that fast. For only a moment, she considered just walking off with whoever it was. Disappearing into the night and taking her consequences where she wouldn't have to face James again. She started to turn so she could at least address the person.

Then she was pushed from behind. Hard.

'Hey!' she yelled, trying to pull away. 'What do you think you're doing?'

Her attacker grabbed hold again and propelled her toward the alleyway between the buildings. As Chastity struggled to stay on her feet, she caught sight of his face in the streetlight. She gaped like a fish.

'Good God. What are you doing here?'

It was Lloyd Burgard.

Lloyd the crazy person, in his suit and tie and precise haircut. 'Shut up,' he commanded.

Then he shoved her so hard into the alleyway that she dropped her cup and slammed against the far wall.

'I can't wait . . . wait any longer,' he insisted. 'You have to show me.'

Chastity scraped her hands against the bricks. She twisted her ankle on those damn shoes. Her legs were suddenly sticky with the dropped Hurricane.

She straightened, thinking fast. She'd had too many surprises in too few days, and way too much alcohol in the last few hours. She was reeling with it.

'Show you what, Lloyd?' she asked, backing up against the wall. Trying hard to make eye contact.

But his eyes were in the shadows. He was standing there at the edge of the alley, silhouetted by the neon, and she could hear the rasp of his breathing. She caught a gleam of something wet at the corner of his mouth.

Her very own angel of judgment. And he'd finally come for her. She sure couldn't think of any other reason Lloyd Burgard should have appeared on Bourbon Street at midnight.

At this particular midnight.

'You know, your sister Lillian is looking for you,' she

said, trying hard to control her voice, to seem nonthreatening and friendly.

Lloyd wasn't buying it. 'Don't you understand?' he demanded, crowding her against the next building. 'You escaped your punishment. How did you *do* it?'

The alley smelled like piss. Like rotted food and stagnant water and rum. Chastity was no more than ten feet from people, but nobody turned her way. She had to get out of that alley.

'How did I do what?' she asked.

'Escape the angels of death.'

For just the briefest moment, Chastity's attention faltered. Wouldn't it be really funny, she thought, if he weren't crazy? If he really were the angel of judgment, and death *was* after her?

She shook it off, though. She knew, in a split second, that things had just changed again. That Lloyd was telling her something wrapped and coded in his own language.

'What angels, Lloyd?'

He waved a hand at her, and his voice was sharp with impatience. 'They pulled you out of the cab. I saw it myself, and I said, 'Thank you, Lord, because I don't have the strength to carry out the will of the saints.' But you're *here*. Why are you here?'

'You saw the angels of death pull me out of a cab? Where, at the clinic?'

'Where you sold your children into bondage. I followed you, even when you went back. But they didn't return. They didn't—'

'What angels, James? What did they look like?'

As she talked, Chastity inched her way closer to the street. Lloyd, caught in his delusion, didn't notice.

He blinked at her. 'They did not introduce themselves,' he said, intense and sincere. 'The saints have said I am not worthy.'

Great.

'Can you tell me what they looked like?'

211

'The dark angel, or the light?'

'Dark how, Lloyd?'

'Divine in his darkness. Deadly. Dying, dangerous dark . . .'

She was losing him. She tried inching toward escape and prayed James would get his pants on in time.

'Where did they take her, Lloyd? The angels.'

'Into the car. Into the silver car.'

Susan Reeves's Lexus was silver.

'She had no choice,' he said. 'I knew that. The Lord had finally visited his wrath on her and they took her away, right in front of their eyes.'

'Whose eyes?' Chastity asked. She'd almost made it. Two more steps and she could at least stumble over a drunk. 'The clinic? Was it at the Arlen Clinic?'

He blinked again and frowned. 'Of course not. At New Life.'

Chastity stopped moving. 'New Life? My sister never went to New Life.'

'Oh, lying tongue! How can you say that? I *know*. I *saw* you!'

New Life? Chastity struggled to pull that information up. It was one of the clinics, she remembered that. It was . . .

'But I have you, and they can't torment me anymore!'

Chastity reacted just a second too late. She should have known what to expect. She'd dealt with enough paranoid schizes in her life. She should have kept her eyes on his hands.

'Lloyd . . .'

She was raising her own hands when she saw the knife. It glinted purple and green in the neon, just like her beads, and it moved faster than she. She screamed at the top of her lungs.

She got her arm up over her chest. The knife caught her across the wrist. She tried like hell to slither away, but Lloyd grabbed her other arm, and crazies were the strongest people on earth.

She screamed again. She pulled at the hand that held her

212

and damn near dislocated her shoulder.

Nobody heard her. It was Bourbon Street.

Chastity saw the knife coming again and twisted away. It caught her dead against the scapula. She felt it scrape along her shoulder blade before Lloyd pulled it back for another try.

She screamed again. He stabbed again. A rib. She yanked. He pushed. She went down, right into the puddles of piss in Kareena's leather skirt. Her head smacked like a pumpkin against the bricks.

Lloyd was haloed in neon like a saint, and Chastity couldn't move.

'Vengeance is mine—'

Suddenly, there behind him, Chastity saw a mountain. A skyscraper. She saw the shadow of it silhouetted in the light, but she couldn't quite focus. The noise was coming and going in her ears, and she thought maybe the words she heard were jumbled.

'Here, give me that!'

The mountain grabbed the knife as if it were a toy, and literally lifted Lloyd off the ground. Then he moved, just enough for Chastity to finally see his face.

Eddie Dupre.

Chastity had been looking for Eddie Dupre for four days, and *now* he shows up?

With Lloyd still in his grasp, Eddie turned on her, his bald head shining purple. 'Just go home,' he snarled down at her. 'Won't you just go home?'

'You followed me?' she thought she said.

'I followed *him*.' He shook Lloyd like a rat. 'He's been threatening my babies. But you need to get out of here before something even worse happens to you.'

Something worse than lying in piss on Bourbon Street with three knife wounds and a head injury?

Chastity started to laugh again, but she couldn't enjoy it, because suddenly it hurt. And then Lloyd got enough purchase to rear back and kick her right in the head.

Chastity didn't worry about the piss anymore.

213

Chapter Fifteen

'Can I *please* rinse off?' Chastity asked again.

She was in the Charity ER, sitting in a cubicle like a rube who'd been rolled for her lunch money. She was sore and stitched and still reeling from that last kick to her head. And everybody was grinning at her as if she were the latest in reality shows.

'I smell like piss and maraschino cherries,' she whined, thinking how mad Kareena was going to be when she saw what had become of her leather. 'It is *not* my favorite cologne.'

'You're lucky you don't smell like dirt and flowers,' James said, from where he was holding up the wall with Detective Gilchrist.

An old wall. A well-worn place, Charity ER, that looked like a rabbit warren and sounded like a rock concert. It was a zoo in here tonight, with prisoners and victims and the general detritus of humanity cluttering up a maze of narrow, wandering hallways.

And Chastity Byrnes, who should have known better.

Any other time she would have loved her visit. There was such a stew of life here. One of the nurses wore pearls with her Grapesicle scrubs, and there was a Day-Glo rosary hanging like a stethoscope over an oxygen outlet. The wheelchairs were made of wood, and the hallways were so narrow they could barely fit.

214

The noise was worse than Bourbon Street, but this was a symphony Chastity relished. A street scene she loved. The sights were familiar; the smells were comforting, even if they were blood and ambulance exhaust and Betadine. It was probably stupid, but for the first time since she'd come down here, she felt at home.

Wearing a patient gown and piss.

Well, and the Mardi Gras beads she'd bought. The nurses had made it a point to drape those back over her, as if they didn't make her look like an even bigger idiot.

'So Lloyd Burgard followed you to Bourbon Street to stab you?' Detective Gilchrist asked again from where he was bent over his cop notebook and pen. His suit was rumpled again, and he looked tired.

'He said he's been following me for days,' Chastity said. 'He's a bit confused. He thinks I'm my sister.'

They'd been through this already. Chastity had told the detective everything Lloyd had told her. She'd emphasized the fact that it was possible Lloyd had seen her sister's abduction. The fact that Lloyd was at that moment restrained and shrieking about professional football and judgment day did not encourage Gilchrist to trust Lloyd's observational powers.

'He might actually have seen something,' Chastity said again.

Gilchrist shook his head. 'I'll talk to him when he's medicated. And even if he does talk, who says what he saw was real? Or that he didn't kidnap your sister himself?'

Chastity tried to shake her head, and then thought better of it when the room spun even faster. 'No, I don't think so. He spoke as a witness, not as a participant. Considering how complex his delusion is, I think he would have been perfectly willing to claim responsibility if he'd really taken Faith.'

'He also says the New Orleans Saints have been sending him messages through his toaster.'

Absolutely true. But not something Chastity wanted to

215

hear right now. She wanted Gilchrist to believe her. To take this off her hands and give her an easy answer. She wanted all this over before it could spin into something immeasurably worse.

Chaos really did threaten, and she didn't know how to stop it.

'You really don't want to press charges?' Gilchrist asked.

'Not if he's committed. I promised his sister.'

'That was before he tried to make you a kebob,' James reminded her from where he still leaned by that plastic Day-Glo rosary. He was in jeans now. They were stained along with his latest black T-shirt from where he'd helped Eddie restrain Lloyd.

'He needs to be treated, James. What about Eddie Dupre?' she asked Gilchrist. 'Did you talk to him?'

'Yeah. He said that he'd been following the suspect. Said he thought Mr. Burgard had been trying to break into his lab to steal babies, and just wanted to catch him at something illegal so he could be put safely away before he did any harm.'

Chastity scowled. 'Doesn't that behavior register on your weirdness meter, Detective?'

Gilchrist shrugged. 'Just a bit obsessed himself, is our Eddie. Says nobody at the clinic takes him seriously about the safety of the . . . uh, babies.'

'He's also a friend of my sister's.'

'I know. We've already talked to him about that.'

Chastity came as close to snapping to attention as she could. 'You have? What has he said? He won't talk to me.'

'That she wasn't at his party, and that he never saw the ring on the dead body.'

It betrayed how battered and sore Chastity was that it took her a second to pick up on that. 'Dead body?'

Gilchrist actually looked surprised. Chastity had a feeling he hadn't meant to tell her that. His jowly face darkened.

'That unidentified woman in the bayou,' he finally admit-

216

ted. 'With the ring. There was a report that she was seen in his alley. Dressed as a nun. During his hurricane party.'

Chastity kept blinking, as if that would clear things up. 'A *nun*?'

'It was a costume party,' James offered, fighting a grin.

Chastity glared. 'How do *you* know?'

His grin grew. 'You kidding? That party is famous. I would have tried to get in if I hadn't been busy with a convention.'

Chastity huffed at him, then turned back to the uncomfortable detective. 'What happened after they noticed her?'

Gilchrist shrugged. 'By the time the investigating officer responded, she was ... uh, gone. Showed up later in the swamp.'

Chastity blinked again. 'They discovered a nun wearing an emerald the size of a Fig Newton and then just *lost* her again?'

James chuckled. 'You sound surprised. Doesn't stuff like this happen in St. Louis?'

Chastity glared at him. She wasn't sure that it was the head injury that was making her dizzy anymore. 'Have you checked out Willow Tolliver, Detective?'

'Nothin' more than the original missing persons report. A warehouse where the homeless squatted burned around the time she disappeared, but it was empty. Word is, she went home to Biloxi.'

'I know. But she had friends at Jackson Square. Tante Edie. Couldn't you ask her to see if she can make an ID?'

Gilchrist shook his head. 'Nothin' to see. Not enough face, no tattoos, birthmarks ...'

Chastity sighed. 'And she was in the water awhile. Yeah.'

'Well,' Gilchrist said, flipping the notebook closed. 'I'll let you know if anything else comes up.'

Chastity all but sputtered. 'Comes up? Detective, since we first met, another woman from that clinic is dead, and I've just been attacked.'

217

'And we have the guy who did it. As for that woman at the cemetery, I talked to the investigating officers from the Fifth. Nobody in the neighborhood saw anything unusual. No other cars driving up, no extra people. It means it was probably just a local robbery, like they think. The rest' – he shrugged, still looking faintly uncomfortable – 'it's probably a coincidence, ma'am. I'll let 'em know about Lloyd Burgard, though, just in case.'

It *wasn't* a coincidence. Chastity didn't know how she knew that. Hell, right now she didn't know how her name was spelled. But she felt it, right in her chest. Everybody was working far too hard to ignore a perfectly recognizable pattern. Chastity just wished she knew what the pattern was.

'You'll share this information with Detective Dulane from Jefferson Parish?' she asked.

'Yes, ma'am.'

'And you're going to talk to someone at the Arlen Clinic? And New Life Center? Lloyd says he saw Faith taken outside New Life.'

'You were wearing *my* clothes!' a new voice intervened.

Chastity suddenly felt immeasurably worse. Detective Gilchrist, obviously waiting for a diversion, slid out of that cubicle like a cat burglar.

'Well?' Kareena demanded, hands on denim-and-sequin-clad hips.

Chastity couldn't even manage a smile. 'I thought you were doing the horizontal hoedown with somebody named Earl.'

'I would have if I hadn't gotten about eight nine-one-ones on my beeper. Everybody but the mayor wanted Kareena to know you was here. And in my clothes!' Kareena was all set to stalk right up to her, when she wrinkled her nose. 'You piss yourself in my good clothes, girl?'

'No. I fell out on Bourbon Street.'

That seemed to be all Kareena needed to hear to laugh. 'A woman shouldn't wear fuck-me pumps, she not trained in 'em.'

'I'm just out of practice is all.'

'You could have asked me, ya know.'

Chastity couldn't face her friend. How could she explain what had happened when she'd seen the picture of that gray-haired man in her brother-in-law's hand that afternoon? How fast a perfectly controlled person could decompensate and end up doing the ho patrol down on Bourbon.

'You weren't there,' Chastity said. 'I'm sorry.'

'You will be, my clothes smell as bad as you do. You a mess, girl. And you stank.'

'Yeah. I know.'

'They keepin' you?'

'Not if I have to walk out of here in my bare feet.'

'You'll have to do that anyway,' James told her. 'You broke Kareena's shoes.'

Kareena just shook her head like a nanny. 'You damn lucky, what Kareena hears. He had three good tries at you, girl.'

Chastity started to shake again. Every time she closed her eyes, she could see the flash of purple and green along that knife blade. She could hear the odd grunting sound Lloyd had made as he'd lunged. And she could smell the stench of sewer that still clung to her. Heck, her life had been just a bouquet of pleasant stimuli since she'd been down here.

'So, who you gonna investigate next?' Kareena asked. 'You know, after the room stop spinnin' and all.'

Chastity closed her eyes. 'Nobody,' she said, wishing with all her heart it were true. 'I think I'm gonna investigate nobody.'

For the next three days, that was just what she did. She lay curled up in fetal position on her bed in Kareena's house trying to pretend that that last day hadn't happened at all. She left assurances of her health with Max, and greetings for Moshika and Lilly on Moshika's answering machine. Then she ignored her own phone when it rang.

She brewed coffee and sat at the kitchen table watching Hurricane Bob inch his way toward Florida and learning more than she ever wanted to about surface pressure and the Saffir-Simpson Hurricane Intensity Scale.

The scale Chastity knew was Fujita. Tornadoes. She could measure them like an Olympic judge, and knew just how to react. She knew that no matter how bad, the damage would be there and gone so fast that she wouldn't have to live for endless days being taunted by the building storm as warnings increased and the news threatened destruction and loss.

Tornadoes swept through like rage. Hurricanes, it seemed, were bent on much more calculated destruction. They courted, then threatened, then stalked. A more malevolent entity entirely, Chastity decided. And Bob, who shouldn't have been there at all this early, was stalking her.

Chastity felt the slow, certain approach of all that wind and water, right there in her chest where all dread lived, and for once she couldn't seem to care. It helped that she could add Vicodin to her round of medications. Sometimes, she decided, listening to the rain once again spatter at her window, it was just a good thing to be a bit hazy. Sometimes it was better if you could just hide away from what was coming.

A hurricane was coming. Even if it was still wandering around the Caribbean, it was coming right for her. She knew it right where she knew when disaster approached in her ER and in her life.

But the hurricane only made it all worse.

Because she had much bigger things to be afraid of.

James did not share the vigil with Chastity. Instead, he went looking for Frankie Mae Savage.

James Guidry was a patient man. He'd learned how to be the hard way. But his patience vanished like pocket change the minute somebody deliberately lied to him. Especially somebody he'd thought he could trust.

James trusted very few people anymore. But Frankie Mae Savage had been one of them. Frankie was an honest cabbie. She didn't steal fares, she helped old ladies, and from all accounts, she raised a good family in a marginal neighborhood. James had respected her.

Until she'd looked up at him with that age-old smile of hers and told him she didn't recognize Faith Stanton.

Until she'd lied.

Now, he was furious.

And it had nothing to do with the fact that somehow he found himself feeling responsible for an out-of-town nurse who couldn't find her sister. It certainly couldn't be because he still shook when he thought of the moment he'd stepped down onto Bourbon Street to see that crazy asshole aiming his shiny black shoe right for Chastity Byrnes's head.

Rages like that were a thing of the past. James had vowed a long time ago that he would never again suffer the kind of impotent fury that pushed a man into action before he thought.

He made damn sure of it, every day of his life.

So he was just finishing a job, like he was getting paid to. He was going to find out what Frankie Mae Savage knew about Chastity's sister. And why she hadn't thought to share it with him.

There was only one problem with that plan. Frankie Mae, it seemed, did not want to talk to him. James spent three days looking for her. He haunted taxi stands, he harassed the dispatcher at the office, he knocked on every door along Piety down in Bywater, where the dispatcher said Frankie Mae lived.

Frankie had disappeared.

James kept his voice level when he asked for her. He ignored the stares and shudders that always accompanied a first look at his scars. He even flirted with some of the little old ladies who cleaned the Saint Claude Tabernacle of Light Church on a Friday morning. But he got nowhere.

221

Frankie didn't leave a message. She hadn't consulted neighbors or bosses. She'd just vanished into the ether, as if she knew that James would come looking for her.

By the third day of his search, James figured that even if Frankie did come back home, she'd make damn sure she didn't talk to him. He had not left many instant friends in his wake. Frankie's mother had slammed the door in his face. Her next-door neighbor, a tall, stately black man with a dead-animal toupee on his head, had simply shaken his head at James's behavior. Only the volunteer cleaners of the Saint Claude Tabernacle of Light Church had remained kind. But James had a feeling that those smiling, sweet ladies would serve tea to the devil himself if they thought it would help.

It wouldn't help him. He'd been lied to. And Chastity Byrnes deserved some answers.

Not that that mattered to him.

Dixie Livingstone didn't live in the Bywater neighborhood. She didn't belong to the Saint Claude Tabernacle of Light Church. She could have told James where Frankie Mae was, though. That was because Frankie Mae was sitting in Dixie's passenger seat as the two of them returned to the city from out on Chef Menteur Highway.

Dixie knew that what they were doing was dangerous. She knew that she couldn't talk about it to nobody, not even her own husband, Warren Lee. *Especially* not Warren Lee. He just wouldn't understand how his wife, who spent her days driving a cab just like her friend Frankie, was helping people break the law. He really wouldn't understand that she was using his hunting camp to do it.

Sounded a lot more romantic than it was, really, that hunting camp. Made a person think of deer heads and servants and dogs and shit. Truth was, Warren Lee's camp was a rickety wood box on stilts out on a marshy strip between Pontchartrain and Lake Borgne, where the Intercoastal Waterway made fishing easy, and the swamp

222

grew pigs and deer and nutria. Warren Lee just loved to disappear of a weekend with his men friends and shoot things out in the marshes and catch fish from his little john boat.

The only time Dixie had ever been to the camp was to decorate. That meant that she ran string through Handi Wipes and hung them as curtains. Then she stocked the jury-rigged bathroom with cleaning supplies she figured Warren Lee would never use.

She'd been right. She and Frankie had just come from the camp with its two bare rooms out in the saw grass, and it looked like the pigs lived there instead of the hunters.

But it didn't matter. Since Warren Lee was double-shifting for the overtime, it was the perfect place to hide something. And Dixie had helped Frankie do just that. Now they at least had a couple of days to figure something else out before they had to worry about that hurricane heading their way.

Cause if that hurricane did hit, Warren Lee's hunting camp would smash itself into kindling, and there'd be no more pigs roaming the grass.

But that was okay. There were still a couple of days before they had to worry about that, and by then Frankie'd think of something.

She'd have to. There were already two people dead, and that bitch of a nurse was getting too close. The nurse they'd thought Eddie Dupre was going to take care of.

Couldn't ever depend on a man. They'd just have to see to it themselves.

Well, Frankie Mae would. Dixie just didn't have the stomach for that kind of thing.

Chapter Sixteen

'Where are you goin'?' Kareena demanded.

Chastity stopped a second as she struggled to get her arm into the sleeve of her one good silk blouse. It was the fourth day of her recovery, and her stitches itched. She had a knot the size of a regulation baseball on the back of her head, she was stiff as a quarterback on Monday morning, and the bones Lloyd Burgard had nicked with his knife screeched every time she moved.

She'd spent three days trying not to think about her sister, and it hadn't worked. Trying to pretend she didn't know that her father was not just alive, but close by. She'd called her therapist and upped her antianxiety meds, and still the coming storm clawed at her chest. She'd spent hours staring at that swirl of yellow on the TV, and couldn't help thinking how appropriate the symbol was for a balanced, harmonious life spinning out of control.

She just couldn't breathe anymore, and she knew that things were only going to get worse. After all, compared to the chaos Chuck Byrnes could sow, a hurricane was just a weather snit.

'I'm going to a funeral.'

Kareena lifted an eyebrow. 'Yours?'

Again, Chastity reached around and flinched. But this time she managed to slide her arm successfully into the sleeve and covered the bandage on her left wrist.

'Susan Wade Reeves.'

There was a moment of heavy silence as Chastity closed her blouse and Kareena closed her mouth.

'Yeah? Why you wanna do that?'

'I have to find out what happens to that little girl. Susan said her mother didn't want her.'

Kareena actually looked stunned. 'Well, *you* can't have her.'

'I know that. I just . . . I feel like there's something more there I need to find out.'

'You need to make yourself feel better, that woman dead. That's what.'

'It's something I can do, Kareena. It sure as hell seems as if there's little else I can control right now.'

'James lookin' for that cabbie for you.'

'I know. And he can't find her. Maybe there's something to see at the funeral.'

'And maybe you should ask you daddy. You sure you don't want to know where to find him?'

Chastity deliberately focused on her buttons. 'No.'

'You need to talk to him, girl. Even Tante Edie says so.'

'Then let Tante Edie talk to him. I'm not going near him without a gun. Maybe a knife. No, an ax, just like Lizzie Borden. Who I need to talk to is Eddie Dupre. The people at New Life Center. The police. I do not need to talk to my father.'

'He's in the sex offender database, girl. We can find him.'

'You find out where he is, I'll just have to kill him.'

Big words from a woman who sank straight to sex every time the man was mentioned. Just the idea of seeing her father face-to-face set Chastity to shaking so badly she almost couldn't get the last button closed.

'You're stronger than that, girl,' Kareena insisted, her voice quiet. 'Kareena knows.'

From where she stood, Chastity could see all the bright colors of Kareena's house. Pinks and greens and blues and

225

purples, a big jumble of crayons in a dilapidated box. A haven of joy and exuberance. It was the difference between Kareena's house and Chastity's. Chastity painted with bright colors in defiance of her life. Kareena did it to celebrate hers.

Chastity felt so unbearably tired all of a sudden. Old in ways she thought Kareena could never imagine. Her father was here. The monster had crawled out from under the bed, and she was going to have to face him, just like Tante Edie had said.

God, she wanted to climb back into that bed and pull the covers over her eyes. She wanted to hide for ten more years. For twenty, until he was dead and she was safe.

But she wouldn't be safe, and she knew it.

Not until she finally faced him.

It was what had really kept her curled up in that house. Not pain. Not confusion.

Fear.

And not the fear she'd lived with for the last ten years. That had been residual. The itchy, uncomfortable, healing scar kind of fear that had gradually begun to wear away with therapy and drugs until water was the only thing that still terrified her.

This was the kind of fear she hadn't felt since the day her father had been escorted from the courtroom in handcuffs.

Belly-crawling, breath-stealing, I-can't-open-my-eyes fear. The kind of fear that robs your strength and sets you to shaking because you know that your worst nightmare is about to start all over again. That no matter how hard you fight, those footsteps you hear padding down the hallway late at night are coming for you.

But Chastity had learned a long time ago how to survive this kind of fear. You just did what tiny little thing you were able to. You controlled what you could. And you spent your days pretending that those footsteps never destroyed your nights.

'I have to go to a funeral,' she said.

Another moment of silence. Then Kareena nodded. 'We'll all go.'

They did, with James actually sporting an oxford shirt and khakis, and Kareena in a flowered dress. They drove in James's cab, first to Sacred Heart Parish on St. Charles, and then up to the end of Canal Street where Metairie Cemetery took up the only real ridge in the city. They watched as Susan Wade Reeves was laid to rest with all the ceremony and dignity of an old aristocratic family.

The service was familiar, the tone bemused, the emotions held in strictest check. The sermon was about unfair death and random violence, which made Chastity shift in her seat. Unfair death, Chastity could agree with. She just didn't think that the violence delivered on Susan Reeves had been random.

The cemetery was beautiful, the grass green and the trees lush. It was a solemn, sweet place, even if just beyond the trees Chastity could see the roof of a nearby restaurant, and it had a twenty-foot plaster crawfish climbing out of it.

The family stepped out of limousines, and friends clustered in groups separated by the roles Susan had assumed in her life. Chastity, Kareena, and James stayed by the cab and watched. Chastity watched the funeral. Kareena watched the crawfish and said how hungry she was.

It was only after the three of them followed everyone to that monstrous house on Prytania that Chastity finally caught sight of Susan's little girl. She sat wide-eyed and silent on an overstuffed couch in a back room, held in the arms of the black woman. The little girl looked confused. The black woman was weeping.

No one else was.

'Shit, girl,' Kareena breathed in astonishment at the sight. 'No wonder that little girl make you so nervous. Genetics is just scary, yeah?'

'Oh, yeah.'

'What you do now?' Kareena asked, tearing her attention away from Susan's daughter so she could finally catch a

227

look at the decor in one of the Prytania houses.

'I don't know,' Chastity admitted. She just couldn't take her eyes off Susan's daughter.

'What are you doing here?' a strident voice suddenly demanded to Chastity's left.

It wasn't a loud voice. Chastity knew that because no one else turned around except her and Kareena. But Chastity knew who owned it from the first syllable.

She was tall and patrician, a brunette with a pageboy that owed its color to expensive treatments. A queen clad in the very attire Chastity had seen on Susan Reeves. She had Susan Reeves's glacial blue eyes in an older face, and the obligatory pearls around her neck.

Susan's mother.

'You can't have her,' she said, stalking forward. 'You have no right!'

Chastity blinked, bemused. She obviously shouldn't have taken that last Vicodin.

'Pardon?'

Susan's mother stepped closer, a brittle, angry light in her eyes. 'She's my granddaughter,' she hissed, not even bothering to note who might overhear. 'I don't care who you are or what your part in this was. You gave away your rights when you signed that contract. Margaret Jane is *Susan's* little girl.'

It took a second, but finally at least one rock lifted off Chastity's chest. 'The way Susan talked, I wasn't sure you'd want her. Margaret Jane.'

'Not *want* her? Who could not *want* her? But I told you that when you were here before.'

Chastity absorbed the surprise like a punch to the head. Oh, a very bad time to take Vicodin.

'My sister,' she said, trying to remain as calm as possible. 'You mean my sister, Faith. You saw her here?'

It was Mrs. Reeves's turn to reassess. She peered hard, squinting just like an old woman who refused to wear her glasses. 'Yes, of course. I'm sorry. I saw those eyes ...'

Chastity nodded. 'Yes. I know. But I'm not Faith. My name is Chastity Byrnes. I'm Faith's sister.' Always good to reinforce basic information. 'I'm here because my sister is missing, and my friends are helping me look for her.' She grabbed elbows and drew Kareena and James close, needing the support. 'This is Kareena Boudreaux, who is forensic nurse liaison at Charity Hospital. And James Guidry, her cousin, who is also helping us.'

Mrs. Reeves assessed them all with precision and restraint. 'But what does that have to do with any of us?'

Chastity sucked in a calming breath and tried to focus. 'You said you saw my sister. Can you tell me when?'

'Oh, heavens. Two weeks ago? Ten days? I didn't speak to her, you understand. I just saw her. At Susan's.'

Chastity held her breath. 'Did she look all right?'

Mrs. Reeves looked bemused by the question. 'Well, I'm sure I don't know. She was just arriving. Another young lady was dropping her off.' She smiled, suddenly. 'As a matter of fact, the only reason I really noticed was because the young lady reminded me of Elvis Presley. She was all in white.'

'Susan never spoke to you of why my sister was here?'

Mrs. Reeves blinked. 'Susan has her own friends. I never pry.'

Which stopped the conversation cold.

'Now if you'll excuse me . . .'

'Mrs. Reeves.' Chastity reached out. Laid a hand on that tailored linen sleeve. 'Please. It's really important. If you can remember anything Susan might have said about my sister. Anything that might help us find her. I spoke to Susan, but she never got the chance to help me. She . . .'

Mrs. Reeves was still looking uninvolved, as if Faith's problem had nothing to do with Susan. Chastity knew she had to break through the denial.

'Susan was supposed to meet me at Saint Roch's the morning she was . . . the morning she died.'

Mrs. Reeves blinked. Then, imperceptibly stiffening, she

blinked again. 'Susan was robbed.'

Chastity held herself together. 'No, ma'am. I don't think so.'

An eyebrow lifted. 'You think she's dead because she was going to talk to you?'

'I'm afraid she's dead because she had something to do with my sister's disappearance. I'm also very afraid that my sister is in the same kind of danger.'

'But why?'

'I don't know that. I know they were both connected to the Arlen Clinic. I know that Susan was going to tell me something, and is dead. I also believe that another woman who knew my sister from the clinic is dead. Unless I find my sister, I can't tell you how any of these things connect. Or who killed your daughter.'

Chastity hated to see how pasty and small Susan Reeves's mother suddenly looked. Mrs. Reeves didn't so much as falter, though. 'Susan would never do anything illegal. She would not hurt anyone.'

'I'm sure she didn't.' Chastity handed out another card. 'If you remember anything, couldn't you call? It's all I ask.'

Mrs. Reeves accepted it without a word and turned to go.

'Mrs. Reeves,' Chastity said, stopping her. 'Susan loved her little girl so much. I'm glad you have her.'

Tears suddenly glistened in the older woman's eyes. She straightened until it looked like she would snap and gave a nod, nothing more.

'I'd like you to take my card, too,' Kareena said quietly, handing it over. 'If I can help in any way, please contact me.'

Chastity didn't think Mrs. Reeves was going to last much longer. Her back was so taut it should have snapped. But she bowed a head at Kareena and took the card. Thanked her. And left.

'So what do you think our chances are she'll say something else?' Chastity quietly asked.

'I think she said more than she ever meant to already,' Kareena said.

Chastity nodded. 'Maybe we can come back.'

James, stiff in his good clothes, said not a word.

'Elvis, huh?' Kareena asked under her breath. 'Was Marilyn with him?'

'There is a girl who looks like Elvis,' James finally spoke up, just as quietly. 'She's an egg donor. At Arlen.'

Kareena stared. 'Get down.'

'Faith was here ten days ago,' Chastity said. 'Faith was here at Susan's.'

'Who's now dead,' Kareena said.

'We need to find somebody to talk to from that clinic.'

'Well,' James offered, 'I'm not sure if you noticed, but it doesn't look as if there are any of them here.'

Certainly no Eddie Dupre. No black cabdrivers or Elvis impersonators. No Dr. Petit.

'I'm not sure why they'd feel compelled to come,' Chastity said. 'Although it would sure have made it easier for us.'

'You also need to talk to that brother-in-law of yours,' Kareena said. 'He been trying to get in touch, girl, and you been avoiding him.'

Chastity took one last look at the little girl who should have been her niece and turned away. 'Well, we've tasted all the hors d'oeuvres here. Let's go.'

But just as they reached the front door it opened, and a petite, wet-eyed black woman stalked in followed by what looked like the lesbian brigade.

Ah, Chastity thought. Safety in numbers. She was about to say something when the young woman in the lead saw her and stopped, gape-jawed. It seemed to be that kind of day.

'What did you do to her?' the woman demanded, her voice shrill. 'Susan helped you and now she's dead.'

Half a dozen people were suddenly on a vector to intercept. Chastity didn't hesitate. She grabbed that woman's

231

arm and marched her right back out the door. All her friends followed, protesting.

'That's what I want to know, too,' Chastity said as they came to a halt on the gracious, pillored porch. 'My name is Chastity Byrnes. I'm Faith's sister. Faith, who looks a whole lot like Susan's little girl?'

The woman pulled out of Chastity's grasp and stared at her. 'I'm sorry. I made a mistake.'

'It's perfectly natural. You're Susan's lover?'

Tears again, brutally controlled so that the woman stiffened almost as much as Susan's mother. 'Jane Brightwell. What did your sister do to Susan?'

'My sister is missing, Jane. I'm trying to find her.'

Jane stilled. The crowd around them just watched, cluttering up the porch.

'Can we go someplace?' Chastity asked quietly.

Jane shook her head. 'No. I need to get in there and establish my place in Margaret Jane's life, or I'll never get another chance. Besides, I really don't know that much.' She sighed, wiping at a couple of tears that had run over. 'Susan wasn't one to share everything. Even Margaret Jane is more Susan's child than mine. I do know she tried to help your sister. I only saw her here once.' Suddenly she smiled. Chagrined and wry and sad. 'My God, do you know how much you look like her? Like Margaret Jane?'

Chastity fought the Vicodin and the frustration and the feeling of some awful deadline in her head. 'I know. The sight of that little girl set me back ten years. But Jane, did Susan ever say why she was helping my sister?'

Jane shook her head.

'She did mention one thing,' she said. 'She said that if it were up to her, she'd shut down that fertility clinic with her own hands. She said that they took advantage of vulnerable people. I think it had something to do with your sister.'

'The Arlen Clinic?'

Jane straightened like a shot. 'Of course not. They were wonderful. It was New Life. New Life Associates, some-

232

thing like that. I think Faith was involved with them somehow. And that something was going really wrong. I know that Susan was afraid for her.'

New Life. It was the second time she'd heard about that place in four days. Lloyd Burgard had claimed that Faith disappeared from New Life. And Chastity didn't believe in coincidences.

'Did Susan think she was in danger herself?' she asked.

Those dark eyes got darker. 'Last week. We hadn't had a chance to visit. I called. She said she couldn't talk. That she was involved with something that was getting beyond her control. She said she'd tell me later when she figured out what to do.' Jane fought again for control. For grace. 'She never got the chance to.'

Chastity pulled out another card. 'If you need me,' she said, closing her hand around Jane's. 'We're going to find my sister, and we're going to find out why Susan is dead. I promise.'

It was easy to make a promise. Chastity tossed them around at work like candy, if it could make her families feel better. *You'll feel better. You'll come around. We'll do the very best we can to save your sister-brother-mother-son.* She knew better than to believe her own promises.

She believed this one, though.

Jane's smile was a bit wobbly, but she nodded and offered a card of her own.

'Now,' Chastity said, pocketing it, 'I think you better go in there and fight for your daughter.'

The groups parted, and Chastity led James and Kareena off the porch, Kareena once again rubbernecking like a tourist.

They'd barely shut the doors to the cab, when Chastity leaned forward. 'How are we going to get information on New Life?'

Kareena glared at her over the back of the front seat. 'Aren't you tired or something, girl? You just got outta bed, ya know.'

233

'I'm exhausted, Kareena. But now it seems I really need to find out about New Life.'

Kareena sighed. 'Should get something soon. Lot o' people lookin' into them.'

'Yeah, but I mean in relationship to Faith. Do you think she went there when they threw her out of Arlen?'

'They didn't exactly throw her out,' James said.

'She had to stop, and it seems she didn't want to. Or couldn't.' Like sex, Chastity thought briefly. Self-destructive behavior that began to define a person's life. Something that sounded so good when you started. 'But what was going on that scared Susan Reeves? And if she didn't like New Life, why didn't she report them?'

For a second, the only sound in the cab was the rattle of James's air-conditioning.

'What if there was something going on that involved both of them?' he asked. 'New Life *and* Arlen? Would Susan jeopardize the chance for more children?'

'Maybe she thought she could keep everything under wraps till she could figure out how to secure those eggs.'

'Eddie Dupre?' Kareena asked.

'It's worth a shot. But first we need to find out what went on at New Life that made a dead woman upset.'

'We can't,' Kareena said. 'We got no jurisdiction, girl. Especially when it's reproductive rights. Nobody can get into those files without a court order. Shit, Kareena's already six feet into illegal with all the stuff she been gettin' you.'

'I know, Kareena. And I don't mean to get you into trouble. I'm just thinking about how to get in the door. I need enough to give the police a reason to get court orders.'

Both of them turned on her.

'Did I mention that breaking and entering is also beyond the scope of my voluntary activities?' James asked.

But Chastity had another idea altogether. 'Who do I look like?'

Kareena squinted. 'Peter Pan?'

234

'Fuck you. I look like my sister. Haven't you seen all those people yelling at me because they think I'm her? What if I just walked into New Life out of the blue? Don't you think I'd get an interesting reaction?'

'Looking like that?'

'No.' Chastity sucked in a deep, shaky breath. 'Looking like Faith. She's got an entire wardrobe nobody's using right now. And a lovely set of pearls, just going to waste.'

James was frankly staring. 'You'd go back into that house?'

Chastity imagined he could see the sweat that had suddenly popped out all over. 'Yeah. I think I have to.'

'You're not even thinkin' to ask her husband?' Kareena asked.

'I'm not sure he's getting the whole story. I think I need a firsthand look.'

James gave her another look. Then he just turned around and put the cab in gear. Next to him, Kareena jabbed him in the ribs.

'James?'

'Yeah?'

'Our girl's back, huh?'

'I'll tell you something, though,' Chastity said, slumping back into the hot, hard seat. 'Either Faith looks really good right now, or I'm looking bad. She's a lot older than I am, ya know.'

It was Lloyd Burgard's sister who called the police. Lloyd Burgard had been on a locked psychiatric ward the last four days, first restrained, then sedated, and finally, today, simply groggy and quiet. But every minute of every day that Lloyd wasn't howling about his mission from the saints, he was begging for his camera. Lloyd kept his memory in that camera, especially for the times he disappeared into his delusions.

Finally convinced that it couldn't hurt, the nurses called Lillian Burgard and asked that she bring Lloyd's camera for him.

Lillian found the camera in the glove compartment of her car. The car she'd had to pick up from a police impound lot for illegal parking in the French Quarter. She knew Lloyd's penchant for photography. She'd even bought him the camera and helped him learn how to use it. She referenced the pictures stored in its memory herself, just to see what Lloyd had been up to while he was in one of his fugue states.

That day she clicked through the pictures to see shot after shot of Ms. Byrnes. Walking, talking, sitting at restaurants. She saw the protesters Lloyd had adopted, and she saw a big, bald guy. And then, toward the end, she saw the murder.

She recognized the chapel, of course. Hadn't she been to Saint Roch seeking help for Lloyd? Hadn't she left flowers and prayers and a rosary made of crystal to hang around Saint Roch's neck?

But this picture was of Saint Roch's feet. And Lillian couldn't mistake what was lying there.

So she called the police.

'I'm so sorry,' she whispered to the homely, polite Detective Gilchrist who had talked to her after Lloyd attacked Ms. Byrnes. 'I think my brother has done something terrible.'

The detective looked at the picture and sighed. It was definitely Susan Wade Reeves, shoved behind those statues like trash. It was her blood on the floor and her eyes staring up at the camera. And Lloyd Burgard had caught it in full color.

'I'm sorry, too, Mizz Burgard,' he said, and he was.

Chastity Byrnes had asked him to put Lloyd Burgard on a psycho watch a good twelve hours before the murder, and he'd blown her off. He really hadn't wanted to look too closely into her sister's disappearance, certain as he was that she'd just run away from home. But he should have at least looked up Lloyd Burgard. If he had, he might have been able to keep Miss Reeves from dying.

236

At least he had an answer for Ms. Byrnes now. He just wished she'd be content with the information and go home. He didn't count on it, though. After all, her sister was still missing.

The New Life Center paid its homage not to maternity, but to technology. A low, square building that looked more industrial park than medical center, it was tucked in at the end of a strip mall neighborhood in Metairie.

James and Chastity had been there before in their searches. Chastity thought the place was as inviting as a dentist's office.

'You want we should go in with you?' Kareena asked.

'You come, Kareena,' Chastity said, making a final check on her clothing and pearls in the mirror of Kareena's compact, as if she were going on stage. 'I need the support.'

'Well, you don't have to worry about passin' for your sister,' Kareena said. 'You look just like her.'

Chastity sighed. 'I smell like her, too.'

Old lady perfume. Chastity thought she was going to gag. She was so tired she felt like frayed rope, she hurt from head to toe, and when she looked into the mirror, she saw her older sister.

She wore Faith's tailored, midnight blue silk dress, Ferragamo pumps, and pearls. She had the oddest feeling that she'd just wrapped herself into a straitjacket.

'Let's get this over with before I puke all over Faith's nice clothes.'

'Before you get arrested for boosting all your sister's jewelry, you mean,' Kareena said.

'I didn't boost all of it. I carefully chose suspect pieces to get appraised. They'll be back before Max knows they're gone.'

Pieces that were now sitting cheek by jowl with her own paltry treasure, the kind that glittered but didn't cost.

'He'll know, he catches you in those pearls.'

237

'Unless he has business at New Life, which I doubt,' Chastity said, 'I don't think there'll be a problem. Now let's go.'

The two women climbed out of the cab and walked up a perfectly level sidewalk. They were in the suburbs, after all. No tree roots eating the pavement, no jungle-inspired landscaping and wrought-iron fencing. This part of Metairie looked like the interchangeable strip-mall-and-fast-food landscapes that blighted most of the rest of the country.

Chastity felt the sweat break out along her back. It was hot here, muggy and noisy with traffic. And yet the minute she opened the door to the center, she stepped into a kind of techno-oasis.

The wood floors were pale, the colors retro aquas and browns, the furniture architecturally inspired. Lights were strung on industrial wire, and there was a sound of soft white noise coming out of the sound system. Fertility for the twenty-first century.

The last time she'd been here, nobody had recognized her. The receptionist had been young, cute, and a bit vacant.

There was another of her breed behind the desk today. A blue-eyed blonde who might have been the first designer baby born here. She looked up from the magazine she was perusing and gave Chastity another of those empty smiles.

'Hi. Can I help you?'

Again, nothing. No recognition. No revelation. 'Um, Faith Stanton,' Chastity said.

The girl immediately stood up. 'Oh, so *you're* Mrs. Stanton. Everybody's been worried about you. Wait a second.'

And left.

'Well, that's one question answered,' Chastity said, rubbing at the ache in her neck.

Kareena turned toward the waiting area. She'd just been about to sit down when she whistled. 'Shit, girl. Look at this.'

238

Chastity looked. There on the coffee table was a flat-screen computer monitor with a program running. On the screen was a progression of faces, one morphing into another like one of those *National Geographic* specials of the peoples of the world, except that these people were all stunningly beautiful. Women, men, children, blacks, whites, Latinos, mixed races, all smiling, all fading into someone else, someone even more beautiful, more compelling.

'Hell of a sales tool,' Chastity agreed. 'This is the place that auctions off eggs, isn't it?'

'Yeah.' Kareena couldn't take her eyes off that screen. 'Normal people with big hips and skinny lips just got no chance here, do they?'

Chastity shrugged. 'It's a product, Kareena. Like cat food.'

'I don' think I want my baby to be no cat food, girl.'

They were both bent over that screen when the door behind the reception desk swung open.

'Mrs. Stanton, my God, where have you been? Your client has been frantic to start her treatments. You should have been here *days* ago. Especially since you already have half the fee.'

Chastity looked up then to see a thirtyish brunette with too little body fat and too much energy barreling toward her. The name tag on her pearl gray lab coat read *Mary Webster*, *RN*.

Mary Webster finally caught sight of Chastity's face and skidded so hard that her rubber soles squeaked against the wood.

'You're not Mrs. Stanton.'

Chastity straightened. 'I'm her sister. Chastity.'

The nurse actually looked around. 'Where's Mrs. Stanton?'

'That's what I'm trying to figure out. She's been missing now for close to four weeks, and you seem to be among the last people to have seen her. Obviously she's donating her eggs here.'

'*Selling* her eggs,' Kareena muttered. 'Like cat food.'

Mary tightened with displeasure. 'What's the problem with that?'

'Besides the fact that she was overage and lying about it?' Chastity asked.

The nurse's reaction was telling. She wasn't surprised at all. Ah, one of the questions that needed looking into at the New Life Center, obviously.

'I'm sorry,' Mary Webster said stiffly. 'Our relationship with our clients is confidential. There is nothing I can tell you.'

'Not even the last time you saw her? Or if she personally seemed troubled, or afraid, or depressed? I don't care about her eggs, Ms. Webster. I care that Faith's husband can't seem to find her.'

Ms. Webster's eyes lit. 'Ah, Dr. Stanton. It should have tipped me off right away, of course.'

'Tipped you off?' Chastity asked.

'Yes. I should have realized right away that you weren't Mrs. Stanton.' Ms. Webster smiled with a certain amount of triumph. 'Faith Stanton never comes here without her husband.'

Chapter Seventeen

It was Chastity's turn to stutter to a halt. 'I beg your pardon?'

Mary Webster wasn't smiling anymore. 'If you're Mrs. Stanton's sister, you should have known.'

'Dr. Stanton brought his wife here?'

'She won't come without him.'

Chastity just kept feeling the need to blink. 'When was the last time you saw her?'

'My assistant spoke to her toward the end of May to say that she had a new client. We've been expecting to see her for the last seven days. We've been worried sick.'

'But she seemed all right?'

'Why, yes. Why not?'

Max had been here? Max had walked his wife into a place that auctioned off her eggs like farm equipment? A place that was under investigation? A place Faith might have been that last day?

'Has Dr. Stanton been here asking about her?'

'No, of course not. We've talked to him, of course. But he has no reason to come without her.'

'Describe him for me,' Chastity said. 'Dr. Stanton.'

The nurse seemed confused. 'Handsome man. Square jaw, lots of gray hair.'

Now Chastity couldn't even get a breath in.

'How old are you?' the nurse asked, her smile growing.

It took Chastity a full few seconds to pull herself back into the conversation. 'Excuse me?'

'You're a natural, you know. Just the kind of genomes we're looking for.'

'No, thank you. I'm not interested.'

'Not even for twenty thousand? I'm sure an auction could go that high. You're a beautiful woman. And if you're related to Mrs. Stanton . . . '

It was Kareena who responded. 'Twenty thousand? *Dollars?*'

The nurse smiled again. 'We don't get many natural blondes anymore. I mean, I assume . . . '

'No,' Chastity said, feeling this place crawl over her skin. 'Really.'

'You could at least *think* about it,' Kareena urged. 'Think what you could do with twenty thousand.'

Chastity turned on the nurse. 'Faith got twenty thousand dollars for her eggs?'

That was evidently one question too many. 'I'm sorry,' Ms. Webster said, sliding behind her professional wall of secrecy. 'That information is, of course, confidential.'

And that was the last they got. Except for Kareena's insistence that Chastity at least take a brochure.

'Twenty thousand!' she caroled as they walked out the door. 'We could go on a cruise somewhere. Shit, girl, we could go on a cruise *everywhere*!'

'What do you mean *we*, Kareena?'

Kareena's smile was huge and unrepentant. Chastity was still just trying to breathe.

James waited for them with the air-conditioning on. 'Well?'

'We need food,' Chastity said, slumping into her seat.

'And alcohol,' Kareena added. 'You notice that snotty bitch don' want Kareena's eggs? She got no taste, her.'

'I'm sure your eggs are wonderful, Kareena,' James soothed.

Kareena hooted in derision. 'They gonna give Chastity

242

twenty thousand for *her* eggs. Kareena, she probably end up payin' *them*.'

'Twenty thousand?' James demanded, stunned. 'Why?'

''Cause her collar and cuffs match, that's why.'

Chastity burst out laughing. 'I promise, Kareena. If I change my mind, you'll be the first one I invite on the boat. Now, can we go someplace where I can change out of my Faith suit? I feel like I'm stuck inside Mary Tyler Moore.'

'And a jeweler to assess that stash you stole from your sister.'

'I didn't steal it. I borrowed it. I'll bring it back right after we find out whether it's real or not.'

'Well, we better do it soon. All you need is for Miracle Max to go try on those pearls and find 'em gone. We gonna be wearing pretty orange jumpsuits.'

Miracle Max.

It only took mention of him to change Chastity's mind. Suddenly she sat up a little straighter. She sucked in a breath that wasn't quite steady.

'No,' she said, realizing she wasn't going to change back into herself quite yet. 'What I need to do is go to Max's office. Where is it, Kareena? Do you know?'

Kareena turned around to gape at her. 'His office? You gonna walk into his office lookin' like his wife?'

'Yes. Yes, I think I am. I want to know why he didn't tell me about the New Life Center.'

Kareena shook her head. 'And I bet you want me to go in there, too.'

'Think of it as an adventure.'

'I'll think of it as my license, he get mad.'

They went anyway. Kareena used the time to fill James in on what they'd discovered at the fertility clinic. Chastity sat in the backseat thinking about what she'd learned so far that day and feeling spun around all over again, as if she weren't just underwater, but sucked down by a wave.

Her sister had started selling her eggs. For a lot of money. To a place that was under investigation. Not only that, she'd been arranging this with her husband, who hadn't bothered to mention it to Chastity. And then, with only half a payment in her pocket, Faith had disappeared.

Faith had been afraid. Susan Reeves had been afraid. Of New Life? Chastity certainly hadn't liked it there. She hadn't liked Mary Webster's pinched face or her aggressive behavior.

'Did you see any cameras in there, Kareena?' she asked suddenly. 'Tante Edie said that Faith hated cameras.'

'I didn't see nothin', girl.'

'You don't see cameras anymore,' James said. 'You can put them in a button. Haven't you seen that *Oprah* where the mother keeps track of the babysitter through the smoke detector?'

Chastity just shook her head and focused on trying to breathe. She should never have gotten out of bed that morning.

By the time she opened the door to Max's office, Chastity wasn't in the mood to be impressed. And she certainly wasn't.

Max's office looked a bit utilitarian, decorated with uncomfortable chairs, pastel prints, and out-of-date magazines. And, of course, a receptionist who waited behind frosted glass.

The receptionist's eyes lit up when she slid that glass back to find Chastity standing there in her Faith clothes.

'Why, Mrs . . . wait. *You're* not Mrs. Stanton.'

'No,' Chastity said, suddenly too impatient to be polite anymore. She'd been lied to, and she was going to find out why. 'I'm not Mrs. Stanton. I'm her sister. And I need to talk to my brother-in-law. Right now.'

'He's seeing patients,' the woman bristled.

'I imagine he is. He's just going to have to squeeze me in between a couple. Tell him I'm here, please.'

Propelled by the rather rabid look in Chastity's eye, the receptionist fairly leaped to her feet and back out of her cubicle. Taking that as an invitation, Chastity opened the door into the inner sanctum and stalked through.

'Are you sure this is a good idea?' Kareena asked, following right behind. 'He mad at you, he can arrest you for those pearls.'

'He's not half as mad as I am,' Chastity assured her, outpacing the receptionist toward the back of the offices. 'And I'm not sure he's ever seen me mad before. I don't think we need to worry about those pearls.'

Max's reaction was everything Chastity could have hoped for. His office was not only open, but empty of patients, so Chastity just walked on in. Max had been sitting at a big mahogany desk, his starched white lab coat gleaming in the halogen lighting. One sight of her in Faith's uniform brought him right to his feet.

'What are you doing?' he asked, his voice raspy.

'Dr. Stanton, I'm sorry—' the receptionist gushed.

'It's all right, Nancy,' he said, never taking his eyes off Chastity. 'Close the door, please.'

Actually it was Kareena who closed the door, right before she took up her position in front of it. Chastity sat herself down in one of the pressboard and metal chairs that faced Max's desk.

'I'm just about to ask you why you didn't say anything to me about Faith's visits to the New Life Center,' she said.

Max sank into his chair like a ship with a leak. 'Visits? What visits? And what's the New Life Center?'

He was surprised, Chastity thought. But not confused.

Chastity tilted an eyebrow. 'It seems that ever since she retired from the Arlen Clinic, Faith has been auctioning her eggs to New Life Associates, a fertility center. In fact, she should be there right now to start her hormone regimen for a new client.'

'Fertility center? *That* New Life?' He laughed, waving her off. 'Don't be ridiculous. I'd never let her go there. Among other things, they sell fertilized eggs to stem cell researchers without the clients knowing. Who says she went there?'

245

'Why, they do, Max. That's why I'm dressed for trick-or-treat. I wanted an honest reaction when I walked in there. For just a minute they thought I was Faith and chastised me for not meeting my responsibilities. Especially since they'd already paid me half my fee for this client. Ten thousand dollars, I think.'

'*Ten* . . .'

'That's just what Kareena thought,' Chastity heard behind her. She didn't take her eyes off her brother-in-law, who seemed perplexed and upset. And unbearably tidy.

It suddenly made Chastity think of that locked door in his house. Everything important contained and locked away.

'When she left Arlen, I was sure she retired,' he insisted. 'You're telling me she was going to the New Life Center instead? What could she be thinking?'

Chastity was fast losing her patience. 'Well, here's the interesting part, Max,' she said, leaning forward. 'Faith never went alone. The nurse at New Life seemed really impressed that Mrs. Stanton never came without her husband.'

Max was on his feet like a shot. 'What the hell are you talking about? I never would have allowed her to set foot in that place, much less taken her myself. I told you what I thought of it.'

Chastity willed herself to stay calm. It was hard, but she kept her place. 'Then how could the nurse describe you? 'Handsome man. Square jaw, lots of gray hair.' Sound familiar to you?' Now, deliberately, she climbed to her own feet. 'You want to tell me why you forgot to mention it?'

He glared. 'Don't be absurd. I told you I've never been there. They obviously made some kind of mistake.'

Chastity glared right back, one eyebrow lifted. 'I think it would be tough to mistake you, Max.'

For a second, he simply stared. Then he gave her another shake of the head, but this time it was accompanied by a patient sigh. 'Chastity, come on,' he said, 'you're not that dense.'

246

Chastity saw the lifted eyebrow. Heard the sigh. She found herself bristling. 'You're not winning points, Max.'

He sighed again. 'It was your father,' he said. 'You know perfectly well how much we look alike.'

She'd meant to surprise Max. He'd just managed to turn the tables on her. In a heartbeat she lost her certainty. Her balance.

Her breath.

Suddenly she didn't know what to say. She just knew she smelled Faith on herself and she couldn't bear it. She had never considered her father. Truly, never. It was inconceivable.

'No,' she said, hating the breathy sound of her voice. 'You wouldn't say that if you knew the whole truth. You couldn't believe that Faith would let him that close. Would trust him that much.'

Max smiled, and it was unbearable. 'I know perfectly well,' he said, lifting a hand. 'Of course I know. You think Faith would keep something that important from me? She forgave your father, Chastity. She moved on. I don't think you have.'

Chastity wasn't sure she was going to be able to stay on her feet. She'd started to shake. She could feel sweat trickle down her back, as if she'd been running hard. She could feel the bile rise in her throat, and wondered how much time she had before she disgraced herself. 'You knew?'

'Of course I knew.'

'Why didn't you say anything to me?'

He shrugged, his focus still intent on her. 'That was all behind Faith. I saw no reason to bring it up.'

Chastity fought the urge to just laugh. She was losing ground here, too battered to think. Too stubborn to leave. She was foundering in old memories, and that wouldn't find her sister.

'Will you come with me to the clinic?' she asked, holding on to her purse like the last lifeboat on the *Titanic*. 'Will you come talk to them with me?'

247

Max lifted an eyebrow. 'You should be asking your father that, Chastity.'

'I'm asking you, Max. It's the least you can do to find your wife.'

He suddenly looked sad. 'You have to face him sometime, you know. You also have to face what you did, or you'll never move on.'

'What I did?'

How had they gotten so far off the track? How did she get them back on?

'Well, yes, Chastity. You killed Hope.'

'What?' Chastity managed.

'What?' Kareena echoed more strongly behind her.

Max never faltered, never looked away. 'It's true, isn't it? Faith told me. You killed Hope.'

And just like that, Chastity was swamped. Blindsided, when she'd thought she was making progress. Suddenly she was on her feet, reaching into her purse. She was rooting for her bag of shiny rocks, as if they'd help her.

Finally, she couldn't think of a thing to do but hold her bag of worthless stones and nod. 'Yes,' she said. 'I guess I did, didn't I? Thank you, Max.'

'Chastity . . '

But Chastity didn't wait for more. She'd had enough, and she was still dressed like Faith, and she couldn't breathe anymore. So she walked right past Kareena and out the office door.

She might have made it all the way to the taxi, if the elevators had been quick. If she hadn't been so anxious she all but ran down the four flights of stairs to safety. If she hadn't been shaking so badly she lost her grip on her little bag. She tripped, and her gems scattered over the concrete steps like bright rain.

She was shaking like a street sign in a high wind, and she couldn't seem to stop. She was sweating again, and trying to figure out why. All Max had done was bring up

248

Hope. He'd done it before. Hell, she'd done it before. But *she'd* evidently had one too many revelations, because she couldn't keep the images of the past from flashing before her like bad movie previews.

Water. Still, red water.

Dull, unfocused eyes just beneath the water, watching forever.

The flat, unbearable weight of inevitability.

Chastity's legs just gave out on her. That was okay, she thought, landing on one of the stairs. She had to rescue her gems.

'Girl, you all right?' Kareena asked. 'You all white and starey and shit.'

Her attention on trying to pick up every last stone from where they winked in the harsh, unnatural light, Chastity gave a sharp nod. 'Yeah. Gimme a minute.'

'Here. Let me . . .'

'No!' She actually shoved Kareena away, then gasped for breath again. 'I need to do it myself.'

Kareena backed away. Chastity carefully plucked each stone to safety, a precise exercise that let her calm. It took a minute, but her heart rate began to ease and her brain righted itself. She counted citrines and went over the scene she'd just played, and she suddenly realized that something had been wrong.

Really, really wrong.

The last small aquamarine in her fingers, she looked back up the stairs. 'I never got an answer out of him.'

Standing alongside, Kareena looked back up. 'What?'

Her stomach was lurching again. 'I didn't finish talking.'

'Sure looked finished to me.'

But Chastity shook her head, her gems safely back in the palm of her hand. 'No. He distracted me. I asked him to go to New Life, and suddenly we were talking about Hope . . .'

Chastity sucked in a deep breath, trying to bring order to her thoughts. She was chilling from the sweat along her back, and she couldn't let loose of the gems. But all she could think of was that somehow Max had distracted her. That maybe he'd waved a red flag at her, and he'd done it on purpose.

'Excuse me,' she said, and climbed unsteadily to her feet. 'I have a conversation to finish.'

Even with her heart racing like she was on meth, she stalked back through Max's office without stopping. Fortunately for all concerned, Max was sitting alone at his desk making notations.

'You never answered me,' Chastity said without preamble, her knuckles white around her purse. 'Will you go to the clinic?'

He stiffened. 'You still don't believe me,' he accused.

How did she know that would be his response? Why was she suddenly so afraid?

'Come with me, so there's no question.'

'I have a schedule here, Chastity. I can't just leave.'

'Will you call and give them permission to speak to me?'

'I wasn't with my wife this time. I have no right to give permission.'

'They don't know that.'

'They will the minute they hear my voice. I told you. Talk to your father. Now, I have patients to see. I'll talk to you tomorrow. We'll go then. We'll even pick up your father.'

Chastity braced herself against the sharp panic that statement incited and nodded. 'Do you know his address, Max? My father, I mean. Since he's been over to your house so much.'

He glared, but scribbled a quick note and handed it over.

'You did know that fast,' she said.

'It's a rental property I own.'

'You did that for my father?'

'I did it for my wife.'

Chastity had nothing else to say. She took the information and walked out, her legs still unsteady and her head aching.

'You recognize this address?' she asked Kareena as they walked back down the stairs a second time.

Kareena looked and whistled. 'He ain't doin' your daddy no favors, girl. This up midcity, in the hood.'

Chastity nodded. 'Well, I certainly don't want to go into a bad neighborhood. I'll give this to the police and be done with it.'

'We're not goin' to see your daddy?' Kareena asked, handing the note back.

'No. You never gave me an ax.'

'Probably because I didn't want to spend my night in the waiting room at the city lockup. You really kill your sister?'

'Yes.'

'You did not. I know you better'n that.'

'But I did. I killed Hope.'

She'd just wanted to go to the movies. It had been five days since her father had disappeared, handcuffed and convicted, into the back of the county courthouse. Five days since her mother had told her that her job now was to watch over Hope, since she was the one who had made her sister get up and humiliate herself in public. But Chastity had watched over Hope her whole life, and she was tired. She was sixteen, and she wanted to go to a movie.

'Hope was an artist,' Chastity said, slumping back onto one of the stairs. 'Did I tell you that?'

Kareena eased down next to her. 'You didn't tell me anything.'

Chastity stared down at the harsh angles and shadows of the stairs. 'Watercolors. She painted shorelines. Bright blue skies and wispy clouds. Children playing in the sand.' Chastity smiled, thinking of the painting in her bedroom. 'It sounds sappy as hell, but they were beautiful. They were who she wanted to be.'

Kareena's voice was unbearably gentle. 'What happened?'

Chastity shook her head. 'My father happened. Hope was

251

the daughter who gained the weight. Another classic behavior. She was also suicidal and silent, but especially after the trial. After she stood up and told the world what her father had done to her.'

She smelled it the minute she stepped into that terrible house. Bleach and lavender. And something worse. Something that reeked of devastation.

'Hope? Hope, where are you?'

Hope was in the still, red water. Staring, her wrists weeping the last of her blood and her hair floating like lank seaweed.

When she heard the lapping water and the laughter in her dreams, that was what she saw.

'I gave up,' Chastity said. 'I just couldn't take it anymore, and I gave up.'

'On Hope?'

'It was my responsibility to watch her. It was my job to make sure she lived through the night.'

'And she didn't.'

'I went to a movie. She climbed into the bathtub and slit her wrists.' Chastity laughed again, a harsh sound that echoed in the stairwell. 'In the bathtub, for God's sake.'

'Did you know she was gonna do it when you left?'

Chastity looked over to see Kareena watching her. 'You know something? I'm not sure.'

It was an example of how good a nurse Kareena was. She didn't try and hold Chastity. She just laid a hand on her arm, where it wouldn't intrude. 'I think you've done your time, girl.'

Chastity's smile was terrible. 'You never do enough time for something like that, Kareena.'

'And your momma left right after that?'

'Ten days later.'

Kareena just shook her head. 'And you were sixteen. You sure had more than your share, that's for sure.'

Chastity sat on that stair, the cold of concrete seeping through the silk dress. She tasted her failure against her

252

tongue and it was familiar. Guilt and regret and loss. Fury and frustration, and Max had recognized it.

No, she knew. He'd relied on it.

'So you think Max, he knew that about you?' Kareena asked, as if she'd been sitting inside Chastity's head.

They both looked back up the stairs. 'Yeah, I do. And I think he's yanking my chain with it to distract me. He's done it before.'

'Why?'

Chastity sucked in a breath. 'I wish I knew.'

Kareena nodded. 'You think Max, he involved in this? Like the murders and shit?'

Chastity took her time, really thinking about it. 'No. You didn't see his face that day the cops came. He was literally gray with shock. But I'm beginning to think that there's something going on he doesn't want us to know about that might be important.'

That seemed to be all Kareena needed to hear. Climbing to her feet, she held out a hand for Chastity. 'Then we gotta go. We gotta find out about that jewelry, and then I'll go talk to those girls at Tulane again. Somethin' goin' on with a surgeon who's that popular, somebody's got to know about it.'

Chastity gingerly climbed to her feet. 'Thanks, Kareena. I really appreciate it.'

'Hell, girl. Don't thank me. This is the most fun Kareena's had since Mardi Gras.'

They were walking out of the building when Chastity's phone rang. 'Yes?'

'This is Detective Gilchrist.'

Finally, she thought. 'Yes, Detective.'

'I wanted you to know, Ms. Byrnes. You were right.'

For a second, Chastity couldn't focus. 'About what?'

He sounded tired. 'Lloyd Burgard. It seems he has a passion for digital photography.'

Cameras. Could that be the camera Faith had been afraid of? Had Lloyd caught her doing something she was afraid

253

to be seen doing? Could it be that easy?

'Yes?'

'His sister came to us. It seems Lloyd took a picture of Susan Reeves's body.'

The air seemed to leave Chastity's lungs. 'I beg your pardon?'

'At Saint Roch's. We're just about to serve a search warrant for his house and car. I thought you should know.'

'Lloyd Burgard was at Saint Roch's?' she demanded. 'I never saw him.'

'Seems a lot of people didn't see a lot of things, Ms. Byrnes.'

'And you think he killed her? That somehow he found out we were going to meet her there and he killed her instead?'

'Or he followed her from her home. He's been pretty fixated on the people at that clinic.'

No, Chastity thought. No, it didn't feel right. Schizophrenics stayed locked into predictable patterns. This didn't fit.

'No,' she said. 'He didn't kill her.'

'No?' the detective echoed, much less congenially.

Chastity closed her eyes and pulled up Lloyd in his business suit and his complex, complete delusion. She could see the flash of purple as it slid along the blade of that knife, and her stomach dropped all over again. 'Crazies are pretty predictable, Detective. Their weapon has to do with the delusion, and the delusion just doesn't change. If Lloyd killed Susan, I think he would have used a knife. Just like he tried to do on me.'

'I'm just doing this as a courtesy, Ms. Byrnes,' Gilchrist reminded her.

'And I appreciate it, Detective. I hope with all my heart that you find the pistol that killed Susan and the shotgun that killed Willow Tolliver. But you're not going to find them with Lloyd.'

'Ma'am, we still don't have an ID.'

254

'I know that, Detective. But I think I'm going to end up being right. And there's something else. I have new information about my sister. Lloyd said that he saw her last at New Life fertility center. I found out she was auctioning off her eggs for a pretty hefty sum there. But she only collected half her last payment and didn't show up to complete the course.'

There was a brief pause. 'Ms. Byrnes . . .'

She heard it in his voice. He fully expected to find Faith wherever Lloyd had dropped her. And Chastity didn't blame him. She just didn't want him to try and collect his arrests in one basket.

'Answer me this, Detective. If my sister were just afraid of some crazy guy who's harassing fertility clinics, why wouldn't she just call the police?'

The search warrant on Lloyd Burgard's house and his sister's car was served an hour later. The Fifth District handled it, but Tony Gilchrist invited himself along. He stood with Lillian Burgard by the front porch as computers were seized, clothing rifled, and drawers searched. He watched as they found hundreds of pictures of innocuous subjects significant only to Lloyd. Reams of yellow-lined paper stuffed into clipboards so Lloyd could set his flight of ideas down in ink. Newspaper clippings and half-full medication bottles and a stuffed bear that evidently calmed him at his worst.

They found two other knives, tucked beneath Lloyd's mattress, and a pair of pinking shears in his jacket pocket. They found no pistol. No shotgun. Nothing that tied him to the Susan Reeves killing except for a photo of her lying at the feet of Saint Roch.

The coppers from the Fifth weren't too bothered. They thought for sure they'd find something soon. They figured that as soon as Lloyd was sane enough to talk, they could get it out of him.

Detective Anthony Gilchrist suddenly wasn't so sure.

255

What was worse, he had the terrible feeling that if Lloyd Burgard hadn't killed Susan Wade Reeves, he might have seen who had.

Chapter Eighteen

The verdict was in on the rest of Faith's jewelry.

'Good copies,' Donald Lee Guidry proclaimed as he handed back the snarl of jewelry Chastity had given him.

Donald Lee was a cousin of James's. Not one of the rodeo clowns, evidently, he owned a store on Magazine that sold art, jewelry, and stationery in a tiny, crowded space between an antique store and a tattoo parlor. He took no more than five minutes to deliver his judgment.

'Everything's fake?' Chastity asked, by then aching and exhausted.

She got a shrug from the pencil-thin, blond young man. 'The good stuff. It's well done, but definitely fake. Except for the pearls. Those are originals.'

'How much would the cache have gone for, do you know?'

'Without knowing the quality of the stones, no. Enough for a couple years' good college education, though.'

Which meant that by the time Chastity made it back to Max's to finally change from her Faith clothes, she was not only aching and exhausted, but frustrated. She'd spent the day collecting pieces to her puzzle, and not one of them seemed to fit. She really needed a hot shower and a drink, not necessarily in that order. That was if she stayed awake long enough for either.

With Kareena's help, she changed in record time, rinsed her face and hands in the kitchen sink, and made it back out front in time to see James standing in the foyer, his phone to his ear.

'Okay, Frankie, tomorrow,' he said. 'And it better be good.'

Conversation over, he flipped the phone closed and straightened.

'Who was that?' Kareena asked.

Chastity wanted to get out of there. She was so tired and sore she thrummed with it. But she found herself stalled by Max's office, staring at it as if it were malevolent.

'You okay?' James asked her.

She shrugged. 'I don't know. I have a feeling I should get back into that room and finish looking around. There's something in there I think Max didn't want me to see.'

Not that she wanted to. She wanted to know what she'd missed in that room, but she wasn't sure she had the guts. After all, her father waited for her in there. And Max had made sure she knew that.

He'd anticipated her reaction. He'd known she would be susceptible to that kind of manipulation. The subtle control of words and innuendos. He'd known perfectly well how to dominate a woman who had spent her life trying to come out from under the burden of abuse.

'I wonder what kind of relationship Max had with his first wife,' Chastity mused out loud. 'And what kind of relationship she had with her parents.'

Kareena looked from Chastity to the closed door. 'You hearin' voices from in there?'

'No,' she said. 'I'm replaying a conversation from the other day. Susan Reeves said she didn't think Arabella was up to Max's weight. I think she was right. And that she wanted us to know.'

'You think Max was abusing her?'

Chastity shrugged. 'I'm beginning to think that he's far too enamored with the concept of control.'

Kareena laughed. 'Name me a big-ass surgeon who isn't.'

'He's going to be home soon,' James reminded them both.

Chastity nodded, still distracted. 'Yeah. Okay. I'd rather find people to talk to on the other side of the river anyway.'

'Funny you should mention that,' James said as he opened the front door. 'That was Frankie Mae Savage on the phone just now.'

That caught Chastity's attention. 'The cabdriver? What did she want?'

'She says somebody's going to talk to us tomorrow at three. We're going to Bayou St. John.'

Chastity blinked. 'We're going to a bayou to meet a voodoo queen? Isn't that a bit colorful, even for here?'

James's smile was dry as dust. 'Priestess, not queen.'

'A real priestess wouldn't use St. John,' Kareena huffed. 'That's just for the tourists now.'

Chastity lifted an eyebrow. 'They went there before?'

'Favorite place for voodoo worship in the old days.'

Chastity scowled. 'I hope she's not just entertaining this tourist. I really need to talk to her.'

'Frankie takes her religion seriously,' James assured her. 'This is just an easy place to meet.'

'She say anything else?'

'She said don't do anything until we see her. Not anything.'

Chastity couldn't help but laugh. 'Well, that'll be easy. I can hardly walk, much less anything.'

'In that case,' James said, 'let's blow this pop stand.'

They blew.

The next morning was the scheduled homicide meeting at Cold Case, where the Fifth District lieutenant would present the Susan Wade Reeves murder as one of his six for the week. Armed with the results of the search warrant served on Lloyd Burgard and the autopsy results Detective Dulane had shared on the floater in Jefferson Parish, Tony Gilchrist met Sergeant Obie Gaudet from Cold Case for breakfast at Mother's beforehand to put in a few words.

He still couldn't claim a murder, but he had information, and Obie was the one whose name was on the Stanton file. He hoped Obie would help make sense of everything he had. He also hoped Obie could light a fire under the ass of the coroner's office, which hadn't so much as sent a preliminary report on Susan Reeves.

He had Chastity Byrnes making tracks up his ass, and he had a nasty little niggle in his cop gut that said she might have something. He wanted somebody else to know. Especially since he'd just gone over everybody's head and put Lloyd Burgard on suicide watch over at Charity, just in case he wasn't the murderer the Fifth District thought he was.

Not that he thought the Fifth District were bad cops. They were overwhelmed cops, overworked and understaffed. They would be perfectly happy to put the Reeves homicide in Lloyd Burgard's basket so they could get back to the multiples that plagued them. Gilchrist just wasn't so sure anymore that that was a good thing.

Obie Gaudet was the best. A near legend on the force who'd trained Gilchrist in the arts himself, Obie was a twenty-year vet with coarse, near-blue-black skin, narrow eyes, and a wide nose made wider by altercations with suspects. Obie had a gravel voice from too much gin, bad breath from too many smokes, and a smile that made him look like a six-year-old. Obie listened better than a good whore.

'So you got this woman missing, this other woman dressed like a nun in the swamp—'

'She wasn't dressed like a nun when she showed up in the swamp,' Gilchrist said, drawing geometrics on his paper place mat.

'But she was havin' intimate relations with Saint Jude when they found her. And you don't think it was consensual?'

'In New Orleans? Who the hell knows?'

260

Obie nodded. 'Uh-huh. And a dead lesbian socialite dressed like a dead woman—'

'In pearls.'

Obie's eyebrow rose. 'She still had her pearls?'

'Her purse and Cartier watch were gone. The pearls stayed. None of the stolen merchandise has surfaced.'

Obie nodded. 'And an attack on the woman asking about those women. And you don't think the psycho had anything to do with it.'

'With the last attack, yes. Everything else?' Gilchrist shrugged. 'I don't want them jumping to conclusions.'

'You think this is all tied in.'

Again Gilchrist shrugged. He spent a minute shoving eggs around an already greasy plate. 'I think it should be considered.'

Obie pulled out his third Camel of the morning and lit it. 'Okay. Give it all to me again. Especially that part about how the Saints are stealin' that boy's soul. I just love that part.'

And Gilchrist did while Obie listened, as still as a statue, the smoke floating from his wide nostrils. At the end, Obie nodded and stubbed out his cigarette in his coffee cup. 'Interesting, all right. Makes you itch, right in that too-many-coincidences spot in your gut. I sure hope it isn't as complicated as you think, though.'

'Why's that?'

Obie grinned like a little boy. 'Haven't you heard? We got a hurricane comin'. It does, nobody be left in town to solve it.'

They had a hurricane coming. It was the only news on James's radio while they drove up to Bayou St. John. Bob, hovering somewhere near Cuba, had just gained Level 3 status, which meant he could tear down trees, roofs, and small buildings. There were hurricane watches out from Galveston to Biloxi, but the big news was that they'd finally determined where Bob's most likely landfall would be.

261

New Orleans.

It just figured.

He wasn't due for three more days, but there were frontal lines full of tornadoes and heavy rain to precede him. As if Chastity weren't having enough trouble breathing.

She wanted to go home. She wanted to be safely back on dry land, where it didn't flood, where her father couldn't pop up and she didn't see Hope in her sleep, where she didn't have to face James with the memory of what she'd tried to do in his apartment.

He hadn't betrayed her once. Not by word or look did he remind her that she'd fallen so hard off the wagon she'd had a big bruise on her ass before she'd ever fallen off those four-inch heels. Which only made it worse.

She really had done so much better hiding in plain sight.

'Well,' James said, catching her attention. 'At least she showed up.'

He pulled the cab to a stop along the side of Wisner Boulevard where it ran straight up along the edge of City Park. On the other edge of that border ran Bayou St. John. Chastity imagined that at one time the area had been wild and mystical. Now it just seemed well groomed, with the park on one side and some very nice homes lining the other.

The live oaks were there, of course, dripping their Spanish moss into the dark waters. The waters lay still and sullen beneath a low sky, and the grass rippled in a tepid breeze. But on a Tuesday morning, there was traffic in the park, children on the lawns, and the sound of lawn mowers to break the mood.

Despite all that, the first sight of Frankie Mae Savage could well have sucked Chastity straight back into the more occult past.

Frankie stood by her cab, a tall, thin woman who was regal in a way that seemed born in the bones of her. She wore a white T-shirt and a flowing flowered skirt that

262

rippled to her ankles. Bracelets circled her wrists, and a collection of beads hung around her neck. Her hair was short, her face preternaturally calm, her eyes old.

Chastity had a feeling that the trappings were for the tourist. The eyes, though, couldn't lie. Frankie Mae turned them on Chastity with less than a friendly welcome.

'Why are you here?' she asked, her voice as calm as her person.

Chastity lifted an eyebrow. 'If I'm not mistaken, you asked me to come.'

James walked up alongside, his own posture a bit tense. 'I hope you have some things to say to us, Frankie. I don't want to think you lied to me for nothing.'

'I lied because there are more important things than this girl's curiosity.'

'This girl's right here, thank you,' Chastity said. 'And she wants to know how you're involved. She wants to know if you know what's happened to my sister.'

Frankie focused on Chastity like a cat, and Chastity found herself wondering what Frankie really was capable of.

'Why you want to know what happened to your sister?' she asked. 'You haven't bothered to see her in ten years.'

Chastity relaxed a bit. This kind of reaction she understood. 'Ah, no. You have that backward. My sister disappeared ten years ago, and hasn't contacted *me*. If you're acquainted with her – which I assume you are – you'll know that.'

'I know that I better hear a good reason why you come all the way down here.'

'I came because I know my sister better than you do. If she needed to run away, then I might know how to help her.'

'What about her husband?'

'What about him?'

'You came to see him.'

'He asked me to help look for Faith. I started looking,

263

and I'm finding out some unsettling things. But I won't stop looking till I find Faith. Till I know for myself she's all right. She doesn't want my help, fine. But she has to tell me herself.'

For a long moment, Frankie just looked at her. Chastity counted the seconds by the cadence of the insects that lurked in the trees. She felt the weight of the air in her lungs. She smelled old water and rotting foliage and decay.

Finally, with a quick nod, Frankie evidently made her decision. 'Go home.'

Chastity blinked. 'What?'

Frankie waved a hand, her bracelets skittering about her wrist. 'Go back to your city up the river. Go now. Go without any more questions. You'll get your answers.'

'I don't think so.'

Frankie stiffened like one of those Garden District dowagers. 'I beg your pardon?'

'The spirits tell you that? Or the saints on your dashboard? Well, I'm sorry, I'm not going until you tell me where Faith is. I want to know why she's disappeared, and I want to know what you have to do with this.'

Frankie pulled herself up straight, a show of power and dignity that didn't fail to impress Chastity. 'No. I cannot. You must trust me on this, Miss Chastity Byrnes. I promise on Yamaya, my crowning spirit, who is guardian of our families and our lives, you won't be disappointed. If you just *go*.'

Chastity fought the urge to argue. 'My sister?'

'Is well. Is going to let you know what's been going on. But only after you go home.'

'But why? And what do you have to do with it?'

But Frankie was shaking her head. 'Your answers are at your own home. Go on. You want to get out of here before the hurricane comes anyway. I hear you scared of water.'

It was Chastity's turn to stare. To assess. To decide. And oddly enough, she decided that after having known this woman for a sum total of five minutes, she probably could trust her.

'Faith is safe?'

'She is safe. But only if you go.'

Slowly Chastity nodded. 'All right. But I do know where to find you, Yamaya or not.'

For the first time, Frankie Mae smiled. A brilliant, powerful smile that was at once sly and sweet. 'I'll be here, you need me.'

'What about Eddie Dupre and that girl who dresses up like Elvis? Will they be here, too?'

For the first time, Frankie Mae looked surprised. 'Eddie Dupre? What's he got to do with this?'

Chastity stared. 'I thought . . .'

Now she looked disdainful, and Chastity hoped Frankie never looked like that when her own name was mentioned. 'Eddie Dupre has nothin' to do with me, or the girl who dresses up like Elvis. You can believe me. Go home. Leave Eddie and everything else here.'

'But Susan Reeves did have something to do with you?'

A real shadow of grief crossed Frankie's handsome features. 'Yes. And now she's dead, which is why you have to go.'

Chastity believed her. So they left. James still grumbled about wasting three days searching for Frankie, but Chastity was galvanized.

'I can pack in fifteen minutes. If I can fly standby, I can be out of town tonight.'

'You might be too late already. That forecast is gonna make some people crazy.'

'Nah. They won't go till the last minute. At least that's what happens in Florida every year. Think positively, James. You're about to be paid.'

She wondered if he heard that brittle ambivalence in her voice. God, she wanted to go so badly she was breathless with it. But – how stupid could she get? – she wanted to stay. She wanted to keep Kareena like a little household god to protect her. And James?

Oh, hell, James. She hadn't let a man that close in her

entire life. Which was the most stupid thing she could do. She was barely hanging on by her fingernails as it was.

Besides, the hurricane was coming.

'What about Dr. Stanton?' James asked as he started the cab.

Chastity shook her head. 'I'll call him from St. Louis. I don't want to do anything to jeopardize my getting back.'

'You think your sister's there?'

'It sounded like that's what Frankie was saying.'

Up in the front seat of the cab, James nodded.

Chastity grinned like a freed hostage. 'And I don't even need to talk to my father.'

He was watching.

Over in the park, with binoculars, so he wouldn't be seen. He knew what they were saying, though. He knew that it was time to take care of her. He should have been afraid. He was taking too many risks. Playing it too close to home. But all he could feel was the sudden sharp taste of exhilaration.

Anticipation.

The bitch was going to pay for what she was trying to do.

For what *they* were doing.

Because he knew, with the unerring instincts that had brought him this far, precisely what she was going to do.

She just didn't know that he was one step ahead of her.

He couldn't wait to see the surprise on Chastity Byrnes's face when she saw him. When he placed the gun right against her cheek and leaned his whole weight against it.

But first, he had something else to do.

It took Chastity twenty minutes to pack up and get out. She left a message for Kareena, who was helping to coordinate the hospital's response to Hurricane Bob, and she paid James out of her grandmother's trust. Then she let him drive her to the airport, where she got a standby ticket for home.

266

She never got the chance to use it.

There was no room Tuesday night. Chastity finally gave up at eleven, when she saw the last flight of the evening pull back from the gate. She returned bright and early Wednesday morning, James and Kareena in tow. She sat in the hard plastic chairs in the waiting area and played endless hands of gin while she prayed that somebody would cancel from the suddenly overbooked flights. She told Kareena to go back to work, which Kareena refused to do, and she turned off her cell phone so Max couldn't find her.

She waited.

And the planes left without her.

Then, at about noon, Kareena's phone went off. She carried on the entire conversation in French, which left Chastity completely out. But she knew what disaster looked like, and it was written all over Kareena's expressive face.

'James,' Kareena said, closing the phone, 'we got a problem.'

James, who had been flipping through the latest *Times-Picayune*, looked up without much interest.

'That was a friend of mine from the force,' Kareena said. 'They lookin' for you.'

James lifted an eyebrow. 'Which they are looking for me?'

She sighed. 'You were looking for Frankie Mae Savage, yeah?'

The hair went up on the back of Chastity's neck.

'Yeah.'

'And you talked to her yesterday, over to Bayou St. John way?'

'Yeah.'

Now Chastity knew she didn't want to hear more. She took a frantic look at the boarding gate, as if her status would suddenly change. As if she could get on a plane before the news got worse.

But just like always, she was too late.

'Frankie's dead, James,' Kareena said. 'They found her an hour ago by the bank of the bayou.'

267

Chapter Nineteen

There was a seat on a flight leaving at 12:45. Chastity wasn't there to claim it. She was climbing into the cab with James and Kareena. They had an appointment to keep back in the city.

The scene at Bayou St. John was distressingly familiar, the players all in place. Police units, crime scene van, fluttering yellow tape. Another detective Chastity didn't know met them at the street. A Third District detective this time. Tall, thin, and wise-looking, he could have been Frankie Mae's twin. He wore his regulation suit rumpled and his tie pulled, the New Orleans crescent and star tiepin dangling from it like a forgotten stepchild and his holster riding his left hip.

'Mr. Guidry?' he asked James, ubiquitous notebook out. 'How did you hear about this, sir?'

It was Kareena who stepped up. 'Cristophe Paissant, he call me, Kareena Boudreaux,' she said with a big Kareena smile. 'Said you might want to talk to James. Aren't you Louis Sanchez? Mario's little brother?'

Chastity listened even as she evaluated the scene. Out at the edge of the water, just beyond where she'd stood the day before, technicians were clustered around something on the grass. Something she knew was Frankie Mae Savage. Frankie with her wise eyes and graceful hands.

One of the techs snapped a few more pictures and stood

up. Nearby, the orange-clad prisoners with the body bag and stretcher stood smoking cigarettes. The live oaks whispered in a sultry wind, and across the park, children played. Chastity could still hear lawn mowers.

'Yes, ma'am,' the detective was saying to Kareena. 'I'm Mario's brother. I appreciate your coming down here, Mr. Guidry, but I'd rather we talked at the station.'

James couldn't seem to look away from the crime scene. His eyes looked suspiciously blank, his posture stiff. 'Third District?' he asked. 'Oh, I don't think so. I'll talk to you here.'

Detective Sanchez cast his own quick look over to where the technicians gathered on the grass. 'It'd be more comfortable.'

James snorted. 'I don't like razor-wire compounds, Detective. Call me finicky. I'm happy to talk to you, but let's do it here.'

The detective sighed. 'For now.'

Chastity should have picked up on that, but she was distracted. Somebody had moved, and she saw what lay beyond.

Frankie lay on her back, faceup, her arms thrown out as if she were making snow angels. She wasn't wearing her voodoo priestess attire today. Jeans and T-shirt and jump boots. Cabbie livery. She looked smaller, less dignified, her mouth sagging, her eyes open and opaque. Her right cheek was missing, and Chastity had the terrible feeling that if she got closer she'd see the clear, circular imprint of a muzzle just below Frankie's eye.

Then she noticed what lay around Frankie in the grass.

'What's that?' she asked, interrupting the detective as he flipped pages. 'Mashed into the ground around her.'

Everybody looked. James and Kareena actually sucked in identical breaths.

'That what I think it is, James?' Kareena asked in a whisper.

James kept staring. 'Offerings,' he said. 'Fish and cornmeal and melons. To Yamaya, maybe? She was Frankie's crowning spirit.'

'But they're smashed and tossed around like a vandalized kitchen,' Chastity said, the sight of it crawling in her gut.

The destruction had drawn not only flies, but wasps and bees that droned thickly in the heat. They settled and swarmed over the food that had been crushed around and over Frankie. And on something that lay scattered over her forehead. A small cloth bag, torn and leaking flakes of something that lifted and spun in the breeze. Placed deliberately, just like the angel baby.

Chastity suddenly felt cold.

'What's that on her head?' she asked.

James didn't move. 'I can see blue corn. Can you tell us, Detective? Is there lavender and chamomile in there? Maybe magnolia blossoms?'

'I smelled lavender,' the detective admitted quietly.

James nodded. 'A gris-gris bag. For fertility and harmony.'

'You know a lot about it, Mr. Guidry.'

James shrugged. 'I talked to Frankie some. Some of the other practitioners in town.'

'What does it mean?' Chastity asked, hoping they didn't make her smell the lavender. Wondering if it were some kind of cosmic joke she failed to see that it was lavender of all things that Frankie thought would protect her.

'Probably means it's something to do with voodoo,' the detective said. 'I can't remember the last time we had a ritual killing like this, but I'm sure there are records somewhere.'

'No,' Kareena said. 'If it were ritual, she wouldn't have been shot. And different things would be left. A reversing candle, graveyard dirt. And they might have smashed eggs, but not watermelons. That's a peaceful offering. This is a deliberate desecration of something sacred to her.'

Chastity couldn't get her mind off those angel babies.

Susan Reeves had prayed to Saint Roch to give her a baby.

Frankie Mae Savage had prayed to Yamaya.

270

'Ms. Savage's mama says you've been up there looking for her, Mr. Guidry,' the detective said, his voice calm. 'That you seemed pretty upset.'

James eyeballed the cop. 'Not upset enough to smash melons.'

'You talked to her yesterday?'

'*I* talked to her yesterday,' Chastity said. 'I've been looking for my missing sister, and we thought she might know something.'

'Did she?'

'She said I should go home to St. Louis, and I'd find my answers there.'

'That upset you, Mr. Guidry?'

James stood so still all of a sudden, almost as if he meant to disappear. 'No. She explained herself just fine.'

'Can you tell me where you were this morning? Say six a.m.?'

Chastity looked between the two men. Then she caught the look on Kareena's face, a dawning horror that spoke volumes, and she knew she was missing at least half this conversation.

'You want to know if I tracked down Frankie Mae and shot her because she did what Ms. Byrnes asked her to and gave her information about her sister?'

'I want to know if you lost your temper because it took three days to do it.'

James was smiling now, and that was even scarier than the stillness. 'No, Detective. I didn't lose my temper. I haven't lost my temper in seven years. But I imagine by now you know all about that.'

Chastity sidled closer to Kareena. 'What the hell's going on here?' she whispered.

'Just a minute,' Kareena said without looking away from her cousin.

Her cousin who was locked in an eye-fuck with the cop. The kind of eye-fuck Chastity suddenly recognized all too well.

271

'I was still asleep,' James said. 'I usually work evenings, and I don't like to get up early. And before you ask, yes. Alone.'

'You own a gun, Mr. Guidry?'

'You know perfectly well, Detective, that an ex-felon can't own a weapon.'

'Not legally.'

'I don't like guns. But you should know that, too. And Ms. Savage wasn't killed with anyone's bare hands.'

Chastity swung her attention back to Kareena. 'You two have some explaining to do,' she hissed.

Kareena returned her look glare for glare. 'What happened before has nothing to do with what he was doing for you. Besides, that isn't what we should be worrying about right now.'

Kareena was right, of course. Chastity sucked in a breath and caught a whiff of lavender. Her stomach clutched. Over lavender. Which she could smell over fish and the metallic tang of blood and viscera. At least it got her attention back where it should be.

Frankie Mae.

Frankie Mae, who lay staring up at the fleeting sun as if surprised by it, her bag of protective herbs scattered over her like a curse, her beliefs trampled and demeaned beneath somebody's heel.

Just like those angel babies.

It wasn't rage Chastity saw here, no matter how messy the scene. It was disdain. It was domination and degradation. Deliberate desecration, as if death weren't enough of a message.

It was something that set Chastity's stomach to churning, like that smell of death at the corner of every block in New Orleans. Faint, familiar. Frightening.

'Detective?' she ventured, her attention still on the splash of melon that had dried on Frankie's ankles.

'Yes, ma'am.'

'I can't verify where Mr. Guidry was this morning, but

I think I can tell you pretty conclusively that he didn't have anything to do with this murder. This murder wasn't about somebody losing their temper.' She sucked in another breath, her brain beginning to tumble. 'It was about somebody sending a message.'

Now everybody was looking at her.

'And who are you, ma'am?' the detective asked.

Chastity rubbed at her forehead. She sure wished New Orleans had a centralized homicide bureau. Then she would only have had to flash her credentials once and be done with it. 'My name is Chastity Byrnes. I'm a forensic trauma liaison nurse from St. Louis. I've been in New Orleans looking for my sister.'

His eyebrow lifted. 'A forensic nurse ...'

Kareena scowled. 'I know you don't have a problem with that, Louis. Not if you want to maintain a smooth working relationship with the forensic nurse at Charity, anyhow.'

He damn near smiled. 'You vouch for her, Kareena?'

'I wouldn't be here, I didn't.'

He nodded. Then he turned to Chastity. 'What was it you wanted to tell me, ma'am?'

Well, here she went again, Chastity thought.

'It's kind of complicated,' she admitted, wondering how to condense this to Cliffs Notes. 'But there was another murder about a week ago over at Saint Roch's Cemetery. Susan Wade Reeves.'

'We got the report on that,' he said. 'Yes.'

Chastity nodded. 'Susan Reeves was found in a similar situation, shot in the face at point-blank range with what looked like a large-caliber handgun. She also had symbols of her personal faith scattered around her. One was placed right on her forehead, as if the killer wanted it to be the last thing she saw. And pardon me for asking, but is there a perfect round imprint of a muzzle avulsed into Frankie's cheek? I can't see from here.'

Suddenly the detective was paying attention. 'How do you know?'

273

'Because that's what they found on Susan Reeves. I think the same person murdered both these women, and did it in a way to demean them. Maybe to demean their desperation. They both sought religious intercession for their infertility. They also both sought help at the Arlen fertility clinic.'

'And you found this out because?'

'Because the sister I'm here looking for is also connected with the clinic.'

The detective stared at her a moment. 'You know about Ms. Reeves, Mr. Guidry?'

'I was there when Ms. Byrnes found her.'

The detective stood there quite silently for a minute. Then he deliberately clicked his pen closed and slid it back into his shirt pocket. 'I think we'd better all go to the station now.'

James actually paled.

Chastity felt terrible. 'I thought I was helping,' she said.

Instead, the detective ushered James into the back of the unit himself.

James was right. There was razor wire.

Well, some. Like a pockmark on a pretty face, the Third District was an unkempt compound on Moss at Esplanade, on the very same Bayou St. John where Frankie Mae still lay. The site overlooked the bayou, with Spanish moss licking the ground and a cemetery taking up the other side of the street.

Several divisions were housed there, including traffic. The Third District station itself was an uninspiring single-story yellow brick building that looked more battered than the housing projects.

Inside, it was regulation cop shop. Much more familiar to Chastity than that reconditioned bank in the Eighth District. Not more comfortable, though. By the time Kareena parked James's cab among the units and led the way into the station, she wasn't the only one who was feeling frantic.

274

'James doesn't do locked doors well anymore,' Kareena said. 'Not since Joliet.'

'Which you're going to explain to me.'

Kareena waved her off. 'Kareena was sure James had told you. Though why, shit, I don't know. He never talk about nothin'. Sure not that unfortunate five years.'

'In prison.'

'In Joliet.'

'And you're going to tell me why.'

Kareena waited until she'd maneuvered them by the first phalanx of officers into the waiting room by the intake desk.

'I guess you think James, he get those burns on the job, yeah?'

Chastity's butt hit a chair with a thud. 'Yeah.'

Kareena shook her head. 'Got 'em in prison. He wasn't very popular, our James. Just a regular pain in the ass, yeah? He should never have been there in the first place, though.'

'Because?'

Kareena sighed, shot a blinding smile at one of the detectives who walked by. He smiled back and kept on walking.

'One of the women at his firehouse, she had a bad husband. The kind that hurts people, ya know? James finally saw to it that ole boy, he found out what it was like to be on the receiving end of those punches and kicks.'

'You don't get Joliet for a couple of roundhouses.'

'You do if the guy has the unfortunate luck to fall back and hit his head a iron pig doorstop. Got him a subdural the size of Texas and a place in the Everlast Cemetery. Got James ten to fifteen for manslaughter. He served five, two of 'em in the infirmary, after the fire in his cell.'

'That somebody set?'

'Got in the face of one of the gang leaders over a kid who couldn't defend himself. Gang leader figured James needed a lesson. It's why he don't do locked doors. He has to know he can get out.'

275

Chastity felt the new weight of James settle on her chest like grief. 'Yeah.'

She remembered the ceiling in James's bedroom. The sky, precisely reproduced in a run-down apartment. It made her hurt for him in ways she just didn't want to. It made her want to help him. Take away some of that distrust and isolation, even though she knew perfectly well how ill equipped she was to take on that kind of project.

It explained why he wasn't so fond of altruism, certainly.

Shit. Her world had just spun a little further out of control.

'Please tell me these guys aren't lazy enough to pin these murders on a handy ex-con,' Chastity begged.

Kareena scowled mightily. 'If they ever want any good time with Kareena as long as they live, they better not.'

Chastity sat for a while and then she paced and then she sat again, while Kareena called in to check on Hurricane Bob, as if he were a sick relative.

'We gettin' the first line of thunderstorms tomorrow,' Kareena said. 'The precautionary evacuation announcement goes out in the morning. You want Kareena drive you back to the airport so you can get out? Go find your sister?'

Chastity didn't even have to think about it. 'Not till James is out of here.'

It did occur to her, though, that if Frankie meant that Chastity would find her sister in St. Louis, then Faith might already be there. So she pulled out her own cell phone and tried to track down Moshika, who had her dog, and might find her sister.

'Where the hell have you been?' the doctor demanded when Chastity finally found her. 'Do you ever answer your phone?'

Chastity was a crack trauma nurse, a state-of-the-art forensic nurse, but she couldn't have figured out the extra features on a cell phone if the fate of the free world were at stake.

'I'm sorry. I've been trying to call you, too, but all I've

gotten was your answering machine.' As if that would absolve her.

'Did you know there's a hurricane coming your way?' Moshika demanded. 'We've all been worried about you.'

'Did you know there's a hurricane coming, Kareena?' Chastity asked, absurdly tickled by the question. Then she turned back to her outraged friend. 'I'm sorry, Moshika. Things have been a bit ... complicated here. Yes, I know there's a hurricane coming. I'm going to be out on whatever plane leaves before then, I promise. But I wanted to ask a favor.'

'Your puppy is fine, by the way. You remember her. Lilly, who didn't eat for three days after you left?'

Chastity sighed. Yes, please, she thought. More guilt. 'I'll be home soon, Moshika. But until I get there, I wanted to warn you that somebody who looks like me might come looking for me.'

'Now I know you need remedial classes in phone technology. I've been trying to tell you. She's already been here.'

Chastity straightened like a shot. 'Really? When? The last couple of days? Do you know where she's staying?'

'She was here a week ago, Chastity. She's gone now.'

Chastity gaped like a fish. 'A week? What are you talking about?'

'I'm talking about a woman, claiming to be your sister Faith – you know, the one you went looking for – walking into this ER looking for you. I'm talking about us trying to get hold of you. I'm talking about her leaving again. She didn't seem very happy about it. Apparently, you were supposed to be here, not there.'

Oh God, Chastity thought. She could have avoided all of this. She might have somehow prevented these murders and kept James out of trouble and never had to face the fact that her father was out of prison. Faith had been at her house all along. Chastity felt sick all over again.

'Did she leave a way to get in touch with her?'

277

'No. When I told her you were in New Orleans, she just disappeared again. She was cursing a blue streak, though. Said some words even *I* didn't know.'

'Faith? Faith used obscenities?' Faith who used to be the one to wash Chastity's mouth out when she'd committed the same crime. 'Okay, Moshika, listen. I'm kind of stuck here right now. But Faith might be back. If she shows up, call. I'll give you my friend Kareena Boudreaux's number.' A number she never would have thought anyone in St. Louis would need. 'Please. Don't let her leave again.'

'I got no special powers, Chastity.'

'You have a magnetic personality, Moshika.'

'This is gonna cost you in ways you aren't even prepared to anticipate yet.'

'You can spout every theory Stephen Hawking has ever proposed, Moshika. I won't so much as blink.'

Chastity hung up, more anxious than ever. 'My sister was there. In St. Louis.'

Kareena nodded. 'Yeah. I heard.'

Chastity rubbed at her neck. She ran agitated hands through her too-short hair. 'When she heard I wasn't there, she left again. Do you think she's come back here?'

'She got anyplace else to go?' Kareena asked, her attention on the door back into holding that refused to open and produce James.

Chastity huffed. 'How the hell would I know?'

'She was looking for you. Maybe she'll come here now.'

Chastity sat in one of the hard plastic chairs, overwhelmed by how many ways she'd lost control of her life. 'How will we know?'

'What about askin' Eddie Dupre?'

'I'm not so sure. Frankie didn't seem to think he had anything to do with what was goin' on.'

'Okay, then, Elvis. We could track her down.'

Chastity sighed. 'I have a feeling we'll have to.'

Her attention still on the door, Kareena nodded. 'After we have James in our hands.'

It was Obie Gaudet who got them out of there. The two of them were still sitting in the waiting room two hours later when the well-worn black detective shambled up and introduced himself.

'You're the woman who's single-handedly agitating the entire New Orleans force,' he said to Chastity, then smiled like a kid. 'Not to mention a good portion of Jefferson Parish.'

'Yes, sir,' Chastity said, still wary. 'I imagine I am.'

'I'm Sergeant Obediah Gaudet, from Cold Case Department,' he said, easing what looked to be a sore body into a chair alongside Chastity. 'We help out the district homicide departments if they need it. Detective Gilchrist told me about your theories.'

'Is Mr. Guidry still under suspicion?'

'There are still some questions the detectives here want to ask him. I'm just following up Detective Gilchrist's information.'

'Does James have a lawyer yet?' Kareena demanded, giving him the once-over. 'Nobody'll talk to us, and James's last lawyer still livin' in Illinois, yeah?'

'No,' Sergeant Gaudet admitted. 'I don't think so. He's mostly sitting in interrogation staring at people.'

'He been charged with anything?'

'Not that I'd heard of.'

Kareena sighed and yanked out her phone. 'I thought so. Time for a little forensic nurse intervention.'

Kareena headed away to make her calls, and Gaudet returned his attention to Chastity.

'I think the murders are linked,' she said.

'There seems to be some resemblance,' he agreed. 'We now have a preliminary ballistics report back on Susan Reeves, and it seems to be the same caliber weapon as was used on Frankie Mae Savage. We won't know for certain if it's the same weapon until her post is done tomorrow, though. She also had that muzzle imprint on her cheek, just like you said.'

279

'Is there any other information from the Susan Reeves autopsy?' Chastity asked.

Gaudet lifted an eyebrow.

'I'm sure Detective Gilchrist told you that I'm a forensic nurse,' she said, tired of introducing herself everywhere she went. 'So I'm conversant with the particulars.'

'Probably not the particulars here, though.'

'No full postmortem?'

'No results. They got . . . uh, temporarily misplaced.'

Chastity stared.

'I have someone on it,' Gaudet said. 'But I don't think it's going to make much difference. You picked up the vital similarities.'

'And they're not going to lose Frankie's results?'

He didn't so much as shrug. 'We'll have something soon, Ms. Byrnes.' Then, pulling out his cop notebook, he began to flip pages. 'Personally, I wish I could say your friend Lloyd Burgard was responsible. It'd sure make it all easier on us. Unfortunately, he's not around to kill anybody anymore.'

Chastity nodded. 'I'm hoping that when he's better medicated, he might be able to tell us something. He might have seen what happened to Susan.'

Gaudet looked up from where he was scanning his notes. 'I thought you knew.'

Just how many times could Chastity's stomach tumble without her just losing her lunch? 'Knew what?'

'About Lloyd Burgard.' Gaudet went cop still. 'He's dead.'

If Chastity hadn't already been sitting on one of those hard plastic chairs, she would have hit the floor. 'What?'

Gaudet assessed her reaction and softened. 'I'm sorry. I thought somebody might have . . . ' He shook his head. 'Mr. Burgard hung himself in his room last night.'

Chastity couldn't seem to form words. She couldn't get past the image of crazy Lloyd, so sure he was saving his soul. Thin and pressed and paranoid. Praying for salvation

280

and only getting restraints and locked doors.

'I thought you knew,' Gaudet repeated.

Chastity just shook her head. 'They're sure it's a suicide?'

'We're looking into it.'

She nodded, not knowing what else to do.

'He must have seen something,' she said. 'He *must* have.'

Gaudet shook his head. 'If he did, he was never able to clearly describe it.'

And now he was dead.

In a hospital.

Chastity wondered just how many of the doctors involved in this little investigation had privileges there? She wondered why just that thought sent her pulse skyrocketing.

'If you don't mind,' the sergeant was saying, 'I'd like to talk to you about what's been going on.'

So Detective Gaudet took her back into one of the interrogation rooms and had Chastity tell her story, yet again. But this time, at least she was listened to. Gaudet didn't so much as blink when she mentioned fertility clinics. And evidently Max hadn't saved the sergeant's daddy's life, because he wrote Max's name down along with all the others, without once hesitating.

Chastity wondered if she should feel a measure of hope yet.

'So you think your sister is back here and in danger.'

'If she had anything to do with Susan Reeves and Frankie Mae Savage, yes, I do.'

He tilted his head a bit, assessing her. 'Has it occurred to you yet that you could be in danger, too? You do seem to be closely connected to a considerable amount of violence, if you haven't actually instigated it.'

Oddly enough, Chastity really hadn't considered the idea that she could be at risk. She'd been so full of outrage for Susan and Frankie and now James, so afraid of her father and preoccupied by the hurricane, that she hadn't had room for it.

But now, even Lloyd Burgard was dead, and she was the obvious link to all the deaths.

'Actually,' she said, wishing he'd never said a word, 'it seems that I'm more dangerous to the people around me.'

Which included James and Kareena.

Maybe she should go home. Give this all up to the police. Wait till Faith contacted her, if she ever did. She wanted to, God knows. And if she did, Kareena and James might be better protected from whatever was happening.

But Chastity had a terrible feeling that it was Faith who was in the real danger. Faith who was in hiding, who had touched Susan and Frankie and Willow before they'd been murdered.

Willow, whom Chastity had almost forgotten about in the course of the last few days. Who had been murdered first, her face disintegrated by a gun blast and left wearing a habit and what should have been a priceless ring.

Chastity stiffened. 'She was dressed as a nun.'

Sergeant Gaudet looked up. 'Pardon?'

Chastity looked up at him, her eyes wide with distress. 'Willow Tolliver. The body in the bayou. When Eddie Dupre saw her, she was dressed as a nun. I'm wondering if that could be some kind of message. Like the angel baby and the voodoo offerings, ya know?'

Gaudet stared at her a minute, then started flipping pages in his notebook, looking for something. 'They still don't have an ID on her, you know.'

'Is it my sister?'

'No.' He faced her with those comforting eyes. 'This woman was younger, although she had had children.'

'Yes, two. I'll go bail it's Willow.'

He nodded. 'I'll check on it.'

Chastity remembered something else suddenly, now that she was on that train of thought. Something that should have clicked the minute she'd heard about how Willow was

282

found. But then, she'd heard that when she was on an ER gurney.

'Oh, God,' she said. 'Sister Mercy. The people at the fertility clinic called Faith Sister Mercy.'

Sergeant Gaudet perked up like a beagle. 'You didn't say that before.'

Chastity glared at him. 'Do you know how many directions this thing has taken?'

His smile was sweet. 'Welcome to my world. Now, tell me what you think.'

She shrugged. 'Willow looks like my sister. Could somebody have killed her thinking she was Faith? Then all three women might have been killed by the same person. I wonder if they found a circle avulsed on her cheek.' She sighed, rubbing the bridge of her nose. 'I wonder if she had any cheek left to avulse.'

'She didn't.' He took another look at his notebook. 'Uh, your sister. Do you know if she had any affinity for Saint Jude?'

'Saint Jude?' Chastity asked. 'Patron saint of the hopeless? Why?'

'Just that there was a Saint Jude statue found with the, uh, body in the bayou.'

Chastity instinctively shook her head. 'No, I don't think so.'

But she wasn't sure. What if Faith had come to rely on Saint Jude, had prayed to him, as Frankie Mae had built her altar to her orisha? What could she have been praying for?

And, being Chastity, she wondered if maybe she should have tried harder to find her sister. Intervened before she needed a saint who only performed miracles of deliverance. Before she'd needed delivering from anything.

But that was a stupid thought. Because if Faith had needed saving, it would have been from her own father. And if he'd run true to form, he'd hurt Faith long before Chastity had even been born.

'I think I'll talk to some people at those clinics,' Sergeant

283

Gaudet said, calling Chastity back to attention. 'It does seem to figure into all the comings and goings.'

'So you don't think I'm just weaving a bunch of coincidences into a big tapestry of paranoia?' Chastity asked.

He considered his notebook a moment longer. 'Maybe. But maybe not. You say that New Life is using questionable practices?'

'Yeah. I also got the feeling that Faith was paid in cash. I wouldn't be surprised if there weren't some accounting gymnastics going on there.'

'What about the Arlen Clinic?'

Chastity sighed. 'I haven't seen anything objectionable, but who knows? All I know is that the murderer seems to have focused on these women's desperation for a baby. And they were all connected with Arlen. And at least two of them had terrible things to say about New Life. If I could get hold of Eddie Dupre, I might be able to give you a better answer.'

Gaudet finished writing and closed his book. 'You were about to head home, I hear. Back to St. Louis.'

'Yes, sir.'

His expression folded into concern. 'Much as I hate to tell a woman she can't escape a hurricane, we have at least two murders you seem to figure into.'

Chastity gaped all over again. 'Are you saying I can't leave?'

He gave a small shrug. 'You want this cleared up, don't you?'

She wanted her dog. She wanted to crawl into her nice comfortable bed in St. Louis and never leave it again. She wanted to run so far away from her father he'd never find her again.

It didn't look like that was going to happen.

The police might well answer the question of who was behind this, but Chastity wasn't at all sure they'd do it in time to keep Faith safe. If only she could figure a way to do it without involving Kareena and James.

284

'Here's my card,' Gaudet said, handing it over. 'Anything occurs to you, let me know. I'll do the same. And please. Be careful.'

Chastity responded with her own card. She should have felt better. The police were finally listening to her. They were going to look into those fertility clinics and see if they had anything to do with the murders. They were going to be able to get records and information she never could. They might find out why a fertility clinic would be involved in multiple murder.

But the minute that idea came to mind, Chastity realized that it didn't work anymore.

Maybe it could have with Faith's disappearance.

Not with the murders.

Not *these* murders.

Standing there in a utilitarian police station waiting for James and Kareena and a hurricane the size of Texas, Chastity couldn't collect her thoughts enough to understand it. She just knew that, like bad shoes and rationalizations, the theory just didn't fit anymore.

It took two hours of alcohol to figure out why.

James wasn't sprung until almost dusk. The lawyer who finally showed up was something straight out of central casting. Clad in a white Tennessee Williams suit and bow tie, he was shorter than Chastity, rounder than Paul Prudhomme, and fluent in French and Cajun charm. Chastity was sure she'd seen him in *The Big Easy*.

It didn't matter. The lawyer took fifteen minutes to produce James. His posture impossibly rigid, his face impassive as a frieze, James allowed Kareena to guide him out the door and all the way down to the Big Dawg, where they proceeded to get James completely wasted.

It was there, perched on an impossibly high bar stool that put her directly at eye level with Carol the bartender's precarious seventy-year-old breasts, that Chastity finally figured out what was wrong with the idea that somebody

285

protecting a felonious fertility clinic would murder three women.

Those three women.

In just that way.

'It's personal,' Chastity said into her gin.

James looked over from where he was seriously depleting the city's supply of Macallan scotch. 'What?'

Chastity looked up to see that his eyes were still brittle and old. She imagined locked doors did to him what bleach and lavender did to her.

She didn't want to put him through this again. She didn't want to hurt him or Kareena or Faith. She didn't want anybody else to die.

And James and Kareena didn't even know yet about Lloyd.

So she tried to distract him. 'You have that sky on the ceiling of your cell, too?'

He didn't so much as flinch. 'The penitentiary library had a good astronomy section.'

Chastity was on his left, faced with all those terrible burns and that claw of a hand. A view full of the devastation he'd suffered for an act of justice.

Chastity understood that kind of justice. She desperately wished someone had thought to visit it on her father. She knew it wasn't legal or ethical or kind. But there were times when kind just didn't answer.

She had no right to ask it of James.

'I'm sorry,' she said.

James made a lurching turn, so she could catch sight of smooth skin. 'Why? You didn't ask me to beat the crap out of that guy.'

'I asked you to put yourself at risk again.'

He glared at her a minute, as tightly locked away as she'd ever seen him. Then, amazingly, he smiled. 'Don't be silly. This time I'm getting paid.'

Even so, Chastity reached over and took hold of his scarred hand. He flinched. But he forgot to pull away.

'What's personal?' he asked. 'You said it's personal.'

Chastity shook her head. 'Nope, you're off the case. I can't do this, James. I can't put you two at risk any longer.'

'And how are you going to find your sister?'

The sister she hadn't seen in ten years, as opposed to these two people who had helped her with no questions asked. This man who had risked more for Chastity than she thought she could bear.

'I don't care. I'm going home.'

She wasn't, of course. But he didn't need to know that.

He did. He shook his head. 'Might as well let me drive. I'm gonna keep looking anyway.'

'Why?'

His grin was a bit lopsided. ' 'Cause whoever did that to Frankie pissed me off.'

She sucked in a breath, struggled with all those deaths. Deaths she had a feeling she was responsible for. They accumulated there, right beneath the weight of her sister Hope and her mother and the rest of the sins she'd ever committed. But in the end she told James what she thought about them, because she knew he wasn't being frivolous. He wouldn't stop.

'Those murders,' she said, then looked away to think. It only put her in line of sight with those massive mammary glands of Carol's, wobbling over to refill James's drink. Chastity shook her head and focused on the street scene beyond. 'They were personal, James. Don't you think so?'

'How?'

Chastity waved an unsteady hand. 'Those women weren't just killed. They were demeaned. Their most precious beliefs were degraded. The message wasn't just to stop. It was that what they were doing was worthless. That *they* were worthless.'

James blinked a couple of times. 'Okay.'

Chastity leaned closer, intent on her message. 'He got right in their faces. Eye to eye, so he could smell the fear on them. And then he calmly blew them to hell.'

The more she talked, the more frightened she became. Because she'd somehow led the murderer right to those women. She'd put them in the line of fire and then walked away, without even knowing it.

But why?

'Do you really think that any place of business could be so threatened that they'd go to that much trouble?' she asked. 'To leave a message like that?'

'Maybe if the person who's threatened takes it all personally.'

She shook her head. 'I didn't see that at either place.'

'What about Eddie Dupre?'

Chastity chewed on that a minute. 'Okay, maybe Eddie. But . . .'

'But?'

She shrugged, all the thousands of bits of information they'd collected swirling around in her chest. 'I don't know. I didn't get that kind of attitude from him.'

'Who did you get it from?'

But she wasn't ready to say that yet. Especially in a biker bar in the Quarter to a man more drunk than she. Some things should only be acknowledged in the light of day.

If they were acknowledged at all.

'We'll track down Eddie tomorrow if it's the last thing we do,' she said instead.

It was just what they did do. The next morning Eddie was the first stop on their rounds. And for a minute, it looked as if Chastity would finally be able to rely on the police to solve all her problems. That they would not only answer all her questions, but do it before Faith could possibly come to harm.

Chastity thought that because, when they pulled up to Eddie's house, the police were already there.

Not just the police. A full crime scene. Yellow tape, technicians, cameras, the whole works. But before Chastity even had a chance to fear for Eddie's life, he walked out his front door with Sergeant Gaudet's hand on his elbow.

Eddie was cuffed and arguing. The police were chattering like blackbirds on a wire. Another TV news truck had just pulled up, and the neighbors had congregated in the street. And there, blocking the street in front of Eddie's house, was a white New Orleans police van. Not the crime scene van, though.

The haz-mat unit.

Hazardous material, like toxic waste and bodily fluids.

Two men stepped out in full protective gear and lumbered right past Eddie as he was led down his lawn.

'Don't hurt them!' Eddie shrieked, tears streaming down his face. 'Don't hurt my babies!'

Which was when Chastity saw what the haz-mat guys were heading for. Propped against a little car that had been driven halfway up Eddie's lawn, as if Eddie were in a tearing hurry to be gone. One glinted silver in the dull sunlight. Another already sat in the open trunk, like a keg looking for a party.

Metal tanks, two of them, just like the ones Chastity had seen at the Arlen Clinic. The kind that held frozen embryos.

Eddie had evidently been taking his work home with him.

Could he really be the killer? Chastity wondered. Could there be a reason for him to turn on the women who had relied on him? Could Eddie Dupre really have stared down a woman like Frankie Mae Savage and then murdered her?

Stepping out of the cab, Chastity fervently hoped it was so. Because by the time she saw Eddie Dupre in handcuffs, she realized that the only other real alternative was unthinkable.

Chapter Twenty

It *should* have been unthinkable. Chastity *wanted* it to be unthinkable. But by the time she saw the police pull Eddie from his house, she'd already had the kind of morning that made her wonder.

She'd woken to another flat, still morning, James in the kitchen, and more hurricane warnings on TV. Bob was flirting with Level 4 status, and the screen was filled with shots of Grand Isle at the southern tip of Louisiana, where they were bracing for an eight-foot storm surge.

'We going to see Eddie Dupre this morning?' Chastity asked, feigning disinterest as she poured herself some coffee.

'Almost this afternoon,' James said, his eyes on the screen.

'My taxi driver wasn't here.'

Her taxi driver looked like he belonged in one of those crypts he so coveted.

'A hurricane's coming,' he said. 'Why don't you just go home?'

She glared at him. 'Same reason you can't go anywhere. We're involved in some homicides. I thought felons couldn't get cab licenses.'

'You need proof of residency and a working knowledge of English to get a license.' He shrugged, his attention on the TV. 'Of course, it helps if your Uncle Tibby's a city constable.'

'Of course.'

'Why are you so afraid of water?'

That brought things to a screeching halt. Chastity fought for air and lost. She grabbed her purse for her velvet bag and wondered what good she thought it would do her.

She was just about to ask him why locked doors frightened him, when her phone went off. Her hands were shaking, but she went ahead and answered it, even knowing perfectly well who it was.

'Yes, Max.'

'I've been calling you for two days!' he accused.

'Well, here I am.'

'Are you all right? I heard about that woman's murder this morning on the news. That cabdriver.'

Chastity grabbed her coffee and walked out into the living room where the west-facing windows kept the hardwood floors cool and shady in the morning. She looked out again to that flat, uninspiring sky. 'Yes, Frankie Mae. I'm fine, though.'

'That's good. I'm glad. What are the police saying?'

It took Chastity a second to answer that. His voice had suddenly sounded so agitated. Almost excited.

'I don't know, Max. Why should they tell me anything?'

'You were there. I saw you on the news.'

Wonderful. 'They didn't tell me anything.'

It was Max's turn to pause. Chastity imagined him huffing in frustration, and wondered if she was being unfair.

'Did she tell you anything about Faith?' he finally asked. 'Do you know where she is?'

Chastity suddenly felt cold in a room the temperature of a sauna. 'No. I'm sorry, Max.' She closed her eyes. 'I need to tell you something. I was just about to call you. I'm scheduled to fly out of here today.'

Well, that got his attention. 'Fly out?' he demanded. 'Where?'

'I'm going home. I can't stay with the hurricane coming.'

'But you can't! You promised you'd find Faith! What if

291

she's in danger? What if we don't find her before the hurricane hits?'

Chastity fought the urge to argue and won. This time. 'I'm sorry, Max. I'll come back afterward. Just not now.'

She heard him breathing over the line, quick pants of frustration. Or fury. She couldn't tell which.

She just knew that she couldn't tell him any more. That she didn't trust him, especially after that last meeting with him. After what she'd been thinking.

Those murders had been personal.

Those murders had been about power and control and domination.

And Max had proved himself a master of all three.

She didn't have a single piece of hard evidence to back up that feeling. Just the fact that he seemed to know how to distract her. That he locked away the information Chastity needed the most, and managed to keep her out of it by the simple trick of making her afraid.

He'd been so surprised to see that ring. So stricken.

But he knew how to make her afraid.

'Before you leave,' he was saying, his voice urgent, 'will you meet me here? There's something . . . something you should know. Something that might change your mind.'

'What, Max?'

'No. It's not something I can just say over the phone. Come to the house, Chastity. Come where I can talk to you in private.'

'No, Max. I can't.'

Not that house. Not where he had all the control.

'Somewhere! Meet me somewhere!'

'The Whistle Stop? Where we met before?'

'No. Not a restaurant. I don't need people gawking. Neither do you, once you find out. What about my office?'

Chastity stared out the window toward the flat sky. She thought of how adept Max was at controlling a situation. She thought of how much worse it was when he was on his own home turf.

292

'Jackson Square,' she said. 'I'll meet you in Jackson Square.'

'No, Chastity. The weather . . .'

'Jackson Square, Max. I'll be there at three.'

After she'd had enough time to get some more questions answered.

'Chastity, your father. You should know—'

Chastity held on to her composure by her fingertips. 'You can tell me at three, Max. At Jackson Square.'

He fought, but finally gave in. 'Three o'clock, then.'

For a moment after she hung up, Chastity just stood there, staring out the front window.

'You lied to him,' James said from the kitchen doorway.

Chastity shrugged. 'I need to get some answers without him looking over my shoulder. I need to know exactly why he wants his wife home.'

'You think she ran away from him?'

Chastity sucked in a breath, thinking of Saint Jude. 'I think maybe she did. I do know that I don't trust Max's motives. He just brought up my father again, right when I disagreed with him. He seems really good at that, ya know? It makes me wonder. If he's using my father to control me, what's he been using with Faith?'

Which was when it dawned on her that she'd just blown Max off too quickly. 'Oh, God.' She shuddered. 'My father. I just figured Max was yanking my chain again, distracting me from asking any questions. But what if he's bringing him? What if that's what he was telling me?'

'Questions?' James asked. 'What questions?'

She shrugged. 'Questions about what he wants to tell me. He implied that I'm not going to like it.'

'Call him back and find out if your father's coming.'

Chastity looked at her cell phone. 'No.' Whether Max had meant it or not, it had worked. Her brain was tumbling around like a rock in a whirlpool. She'd even broken out in a sweat. 'No. I can't.'

There was a silence behind her. A small shuffling, as if James were uncomfortable.

'Why *are* you so afraid of water?'

Chastity didn't turn. She kept her eyes on the sky, much as she figured James had done all those years in his tiny cell. She stood that way for a very long few minutes.

She'd spent ten years running away from that particular question. She'd wasted a fortune in drugs and therapy, and a lifetime of ritual. Lapping water and laughter. The feeling of suffocation. The world disappearing through the film of water.

Her stomach was churning again, and she didn't think she was going to be able to stand any more.

But she did. She faced the window and wrapped her hands together, as if holding on, and she told James the truth.

'My father had a big Jacuzzi installed in the master suite at our house. It was ... his playground. He called himself Poseidon.' For a moment she stood there, her throat closed up, her hands clenched, the smell of bleach so strong in her memory. 'I think the real reason he liked it so much was because if one of us objected, all he had to do was hold our heads underwater until we obeyed.' She lifted her face, as if the sun out beyond those flat clouds could find her. She dreamed of drowning almost every night of her life. 'My mother scrubbed that tub with bleach every day.'

She smelled it now. That bleach and the lavender sachets her mother had put in the underwear drawers.

'You're right,' James said after another long moment. 'We need to get you out of here before the hurricane comes.'

Chastity nodded and turned. 'Let's go see if we can track down Eddie Dupre,' she said, finishing the coffee in her mug. 'We only have till three o'clock, and then we have an appointment at Jackson Square.'

Fifteen minutes later they pulled up to that little shotgun house on Royal and found the police pulling Eddie off the

294

front porch. And for one very dark moment, Chastity prayed it was all over. That for some inexplicable reason Eddie had really murdered those three women. That his arrest would close all the books and she could go home without ever having to show up at Jackson Square at all.

'Wait!' she yelled to Sergeant Gaudet as he hustled a handcuffed Eddie to his unmarked unit.

'He doesn't know where she is,' the sergeant told her across the crowd. He nodded to the perimeter cop anyway, and the guy let Chastity and James through.

'Please, Mr. Dupre,' Chastity begged as she rounded the unmarked to stop before him. 'Don't you know anything?'

There were tearstains on Eddie's face, and his clothes were disheveled. He glared at her. 'I know that I saved her babies, and she yelled at me.'

Okay, Chastity thought. This wasn't going to be as quick as she'd hoped. 'You're Faith's friend—'

'*Was*,' he corrected her, looking as if he was going to cry again. 'She was going to turn me in. She was going to tell them that what I did was *wrong*!'

Chastity had no idea whether she had the time to ask what that was, but the sergeant, with that impish delight in his eyes, filled her in himself. 'Seems Eddie can't bear to destroy any of his embryos. Or anybody else's, either.'

'Babies,' Eddie objected. 'They're babies.'

Gaudet nodded patiently. 'He managed to sneak embryos out of most of the fertility clinics in town and keep them under his kitchen sink. Whole house is rigged to support those things. I'm just amazed nobody noticed. Meth labs are less complicated.'

'They were going to be murdered!' Eddie protested. 'I had to do something!'

Gaudet gave him a nod. 'He even got somebody to donate from your friends at New Life.'

Eddie scowled. 'They have no scruples. Three-fourths of what I collected from that place was nonviable waste matter. Can you imagine what they've been storing as

295

viable embryos for those poor dupes who go there? *And* charging them for it? They should be sued.'

Chastity blinked a few times. 'But then, why were you so mad at Lloyd Burgard? He just wanted the same thing.'

'Because he didn't know what he was doing. He could have killed *hundreds* of infants by damaging the storage containers.'

Chastity took a quick look over to where the haz-mat guys stood considering those shiny metal canisters. 'Boy, are you gonna have a legal toffee-pull on your hands.'

'Tell me,' the sergeant said.

'If he was that angry at Faith . . . '

Gaudet shook his ugly head. 'Sorry. His alibi is solid for both murders. And he was the one who called in the nun.'

'Was it really Willow Tolliver?' Eddie asked. 'I thought she went back to Mobile.'

'Biloxi,' Chastity said instinctively. 'Even if you didn't talk to Faith recently, Eddie, didn't you hear anything? About where she'd gone? Or why?'

'No. Nothing. I figured she left because she'd just had enough. All you have to do is look at that ostentatious wedding ring she never took off except to have the stones changed to understand. You know it's fake as a three-dollar bill, now, don't you?'

'I know.'

'Then you know that he gambles. Good. I never did like him. Faith had so many chances to be a mother herself, and he wouldn't let her.'

Chastity froze. 'You mean Max? Max exchanged the stones in her ring to do what? Cover gambling debts?'

Eddie huffed. 'You think *she* did it? Not likely. Not when he had her mama over in that Holy Ghost place, all snug and everything. Not when he held it over her head like the sword of Damocles. She wouldn't ever risk doing *anything* that would jeopardize her mama. Because he would have put that old woman in a pisshole faster than you can blink, if he got mad.'

296

He was taking her breath away. He was giving her reasons that Faith would have run away. 'Was she afraid of Max? Eddie, was she afraid of him?'

'Like you care. You're the one who broke her heart the last time. Don't think I'm letting you do it again.'

And with a lift of his head, Eddie Dupre stopped talking, except to exhort the haz-mat guys to be careful. Sergeant Gaudet seemed to hear the same thing Chastity had, though, and nodded to her.

'It's easy enough to check out. I'll be in touch.'

Chastity stood there a second, terrified suddenly to take the next step. But Eddie had been her last chance. And Eddie wouldn't have had privileges at Charity to allow him to walk blithely into a locked ward and, just maybe, murder an inconvenient witness.

'Have you heard any more about Lloyd Burgard's death?' she asked Sergeant Gaudet.

Gaudet raised an eyebrow. 'No. I've been doing fertility clinics. The people at New Life were the ones who turned on ole Eddie here. Seems they don't want any more problems than are comin' to them. I think they might be closing up shop.'

Chastity nodded. 'Does Eddie have an alibi for Lloyd?'

Gaudet considered her for a long moment. 'I'll certainly find out.'

Chastity didn't move. 'Lloyd was in a locked ward,' she said, not really wanting to say it. Not wanting to take this step, even in her own head. 'You might want to double-check who had access to him. Who might have seemed out of place on the ward.'

Gaudet squinted at her. 'You goin' somewhere with this?'

She shook her head, too afraid suddenly to say it out loud. 'Lloyd was on suicide watch. Somebody should have noticed if anybody stopped by to see him. But they might not notice medical people so much.' She sucked in a breath to try and ease the sudden constriction in her chest. 'I think my brother-in-law still has privileges at Charity. You might want to see if any other doctors involved in this case do, too.'

Gaudet stopped a minute to watch her. He nodded again, and then stuffed Eddie into the cruiser. Chastity and James walked back to the cab.

'You think Max killed Lloyd Burgard?' James demanded.

Chastity didn't face him. 'I think we shouldn't overlook any possibility.'

'You sure you aren't just paying Max back for being controlling?'

'I'm trying to think of all likelihoods, fireman. I haven't been doing that very well until now. Are you taking his side?'

'I'm playing devil's advocate. What makes you suddenly so suspicious?'

'He sold Faith's emerald,' Chastity said as she slid into the front seat. 'Max sold her emerald to gamble.'

James started the engine and waited. 'Last I heard, it's not a felony.'

Chastity shook her head, impatient. 'He knew all along that that stone had been switched, and yet he put on such a show when we told him. Accused the police of doing it.'

'Closer to a felony, admitted. Still, understandable. Tough to be the perfect husband when you're caught in that big a lie. It doesn't mean it has anything to do with her disappearance.' He considered that a minute. 'Although it might be another reason for her to go.'

Chastity sat there for a few minutes listening to the shudder of the air-conditioning and thinking back on that afternoon when Detective Gilchrist had sat down on Faith's good couch. Of how gray Max had grown at the sight of that ring.

A person can fake surprised. Ashen is a lot harder to pull off. Max's surprise had been all too real, and if he'd been the one to put Willow in the bayou, he shouldn't have been surprised.

298

At least the police were helping out now. At least Chastity didn't need to face her monsters quite alone. Sergeant Gaudet was no long-timer just waiting out his pension. He was really interested. If she wanted, she might just be able to retire to Kareena's house and wait for him to answer all the questions himself.

For him to find Faith.

Chastity sighed. She was already here. She might as well get some of the answers she knew she was going to need.

She reached over and fastened her seat belt. 'I think it's time we stop by the Holy Cross Resthouse. See what they have to say about Faith and Max and my mother.'

If Chastity had simply seen the nursing home, she never would have questioned the impressions she'd gotten of the last days of her mother's life. It was a showy place, with landscaped gardens and a lobby that looked like a hotel. Chastity could even have overlooked the faint odor of urine and decay in the air. This was, after all, where people came to die.

But Chastity took that extra step, and Max lost his merit badge. Chastity tracked down the nurse's aide who had cared for Mary Rose Byrnes in the last years of her life.

'Her daughter Faith?' the little woman asked, her tired brown eyes surprised. 'No, I'm sorry. I wouldn't know how to get hold of her. We didn't see her much, even when her mother was here. And she was with us for three years.'

Chastity stood there stone-faced, wondering if she should have anticipated this. 'What do you mean?' she asked anyway. 'My sister devoted her life to my mother for the last six months of my mother's life.'

The aide was tiny, round, and slow-moving. She wasn't confused, however. 'She might have wanted to, ma'am. He wouldn't let her.'

'He?'

'Her husband. He only let her come when he drove her, and that wasn't often. Especially toward the end. She didn't

299

have a car of her own. No cash for a cab. No way to bring her mother those little things that make dyin' easier. It troubled her somethin' mighty.'

Chastity had known fear. She'd known guilt and frustration and pain. She couldn't ever remember battling the kind of anger that was building in her chest. Against Max. Against herself.

'You're sure?' she asked anyway.

'Yes, ma'am. He didn't like your mother much, I'm afraid.' The aide looked behind her, as if afraid Max would show up. 'But then, he didn't seem to like your sister much, either.'

'I should have come here first,' Chastity snarled as she climbed into the front seat of James's cab.

She had no problem with libido this time. She was still so incandescent with rage that she didn't have time for pheromones.

James started the cab. 'Possibly.'

'No. Definitely. *Damn* him.'

'Max?'

'Of course, Max. He knew how much trouble I'd have coming here. He knew I'd stay away as long as I could. He *counted* on it. I think I need to talk to Sergeant Gaudet again.'

'Because Max wouldn't let his wife see her mother?'

'Because everything Max has said to me has been a lie. Because it's a pattern that I should have recognized about eight conversations ago. Come on, fireman, you know what an abusive relationship looks like. Faith had no car. No ability to go anywhere without him taking her. No contact with friends except for one lunch a week, which he took her to and picked her up from, which supported the myth of the perfect, upscale family. I wonder now if she really has a checkbook or a PDA or anything that would help her maintain her independence.'

'You know this kind of thing better than I do.'

300

It took Chastity a second to answer, because suddenly she wanted to cry, and that wouldn't do. 'Yes,' she said. 'I do. It's my job, damn it. I can smell an abusive spouse faster than three-day-old fish.' She took a couple of breaths, blinked away the tears. 'Except when it's my own brother-in-law, evidently.'

'Just from what that aide said? Maybe he wasn't nice to her. Maybe she was lying.'

'Maybe she was. But I don't think so.' Another breath, to steady herself, as images tumbled again. 'He uses abusive language, James. All the time. My family. My house. *My wife.* He only calls her Faith when he's paying attention. Otherwise, he calls her by his possessive. He uses the language of abuse and control. And damn it, he's been doing the same thing to me.' She wrapped her hands tightly around her purse, around the treasure that seemed wasted all of a sudden. 'And I let him.'

'You seem more upset by that than anything.'

'I forgive many things, fireman. I do not forgive someone who preys on another person's weakness to control them.'

'I wouldn't call you weak, nurse.'

'You've never been in my head, fireman.'

He nodded. 'Touché. Where to now?'

Chastity didn't know. She had such a feeling, suddenly, that she'd been deliberately led down this path, and that there was only one outcome. She was terrified she'd been played like a puppet, and hadn't even known it until it was too late.

God, she hated the feeling of inevitability. She hated knowing that no matter what she did or how hard she fought, the end would be the same.

And she, of all people, should have seen it coming.

Finally Chastity stirred, looked out to see that the sky had lowered a bit more. The storms were coming. 'Let's go to Kareena's. Maybe my sister called.'

*

301

'You expecting somebody?' James asked a few minutes later as they pulled to a stop.

Chastity looked up to find that they had reached Kareena's. There was a woman up on the porch, pacing like an expectant father.

'Gosh, no,' Chastity said. 'You?'

The woman caught sight of them and sprinted down the steps.

'Are you Chastity Byrnes?' she demanded before Chastity could even make it out of the cab. 'Of course you are. You look just like Faith.'

'When things finally start happening, they start happening very fast, don't they, James?' Chastity asked as she opened the car door.

'Certainly seems that way.'

Chastity climbed out of the cab to face her fourth or fifth surprise of the day. A woman of medium height and build who looked precise and pretty and brunette in her uninspired, tidy attire. Probably forty, definitely not one of the pearls-and-charity crowd. More academic.

'Yes, I'm Chastity Byrnes. How can I—'

'You sicced the police on us!' she spat, jabbing a finger in the direction of Chastity's chest. 'The *police*! I've been working for *months* with New Life to have a baby, and I just found out they're *closed*! Because of *you*!'

'And you are?' Chastity asked, going quite still. She certainly didn't want to scare this woman off.

'Dr. Winnifred Hayes-Adams. Fred. Your sister is supposed to be supplying me with a baby right about now – *twins* – but that's not going to happen as long as you keep screwing things up, is it? Is it worth it? Is he paying you enough to ruin *all* our lives?'

Chastity stilled. 'You know where Faith is?'

'I'm not going to answer you. I want you to tell me what you think you're doing.'

'I'm trying to find my sister.'

'For *him*?'

302

'For him who?'

The woman looked around, skittish all of a sudden. 'You know perfectly well. Her husband. You came down here to see him.'

Chastity nodded. 'What do you want to tell me about Max, Dr. Hayes-Adams?'

'Why should I tell you anything?'

'Because women are being murdered. The sooner I know where Faith is, the sooner we can discover who is responsible for the deaths of at least two other women.'

'I know damn well who's responsible.'

'Then why haven't you gone to the police yet?'

'Because nobody'd believe me. Nobody'd believe any of us.'

'They just might, if you gave them the chance. Please, won't you come in and talk, and maybe we can help each other.'

'No. No, I won't. You go home. That's what Frankie told you to do, and damn it, that's what you *should* do. I didn't take the risk of doing something completely illegal just so you could ruin it all. Especially now.'

Chastity heard James walk up behind her, and ignored him to maintain eye contact with the rather excitable Dr. Hayes-Adams. 'I'm still here because the police won't let me go. Because they think I know something about Frankie's murder. And Susan Reeves and Willow Tolliver.'

Dr. Hayes-Adams's eyes grew wide. 'You know ...'

'I'm going to ask you again. Come in and talk with me. Talk to the police with me. At least make them ask questions, Dr. Hayes-Adams. I promise they can help.'

At which point James leaned in behind her. 'You might want to ask about that completely illegal thing before you make promises.'

'A new identity,' Dr. Hayes-Adams snapped. 'Her *second*, thank you very much, since she just *had* to come back after we'd gotten her safely away, and we couldn't take the chance that she'd be recognized. And that doesn't

303

even count the times we signed her into ERs under assumed names after he beat her like a two-dollar whore. We kept her *safe*, until you came along and screwed everything up.'

'We?' Chastity asked. 'You and Susan and Frankie?'

The doctor suddenly went on alert. She looked around again, as if expecting to see someone else lurking nearby.

'I have to go. Just figure out a way to go home. Please.'

'But if she was safe,' Chastity said, 'why did she come back?'

The doctor had quite a glare on her. 'Because at least *we* care for her. Now, I have to go before I'm seen.'

They were standing out on the sidewalk for anybody to see, and Chastity began to feel as exposed as the doctor. Besides, the clouds were beginning to mass over the rooftops. Another thunderstorm was brewing. The streets were going to start flooding soon. Chastity really needed to get off that sidewalk.

'Please, Dr. Hayes-Adams,' Chastity begged, 'come inside.'

Dr. Hayes-Adams straightened and scowled. 'I will not. I shouldn't be here in the first place.'

'At least give me something I can take to the police. They're looking into the murders. I swear to you.'

For just a moment, Dr. Hayes-Adams stopped, poised to flee. She huffed, shook her head. Looked over her shoulder again. 'All right, you want something? Here. The day Willow went missing, a warehouse in Algiers went up in flames. A warehouse where Willow might have kept your sister for a few days. By the time it caught fire, your sister was safely away. Find out about that fire.'

'You think that's where Willow was killed?'

Dr. Hayes-Adams was already backing away. 'I think nothing. I've told you everything I can. I have to go now.'

'But Faith—'

'I'll ask. I'll ask if she'll talk to you. I'll let you know.'

'No, wait!'

But short of restraints and major sedatives, there was no

way Chastity was going to keep the woman there. She heard the first rumble of thunder as Dr. Hayes-Adams slammed into her Mercedes SUV and drove off. And all she could do was stand there on the cracked and lopsided sidewalk and watch.

'Well, that went well,' James said.

'We should follow her.'

'She's not going to see your sister.'

Chastity slumped. 'You're right. She'll call her. Which means we should probably stay here and wait.'

'Since it's about to rain, yeah. I think so.'

Chastity turned for the front porch. 'Did you hear her? My God, there's a whole group of them. Getting my sister fake documents and getting her out of town.'

'Only to have her show up again.'

Chastity nodded. The trees were dipping now, the smell of rain thick in the air. Chastity shivered with the portent of it.

'She thinks it's Max, James. Doesn't she?'

'You've done everything but say it yourself.'

She sighed. 'She's right. I can't think of one thing that would prove to me that he'd do something that ... that awful. I mean, just because he's an asshole doesn't mean he's a murdering asshole. And I'm the last one to have an objective opinion. But I'm beginning to believe that there aren't any other options.'

'I thought you said he was surprised when he found out about that first body.'

'He was. He really was.' They opened the front door and stepped into the shadows. 'I wonder, though ... '

'Yes?'

Chastity came to a halt on that cool hardwood floor, as possibilities tumbled so fast they ate at what remained of her composure. 'Could it be possible that he wasn't so much surprised by the ring on the body ... '

James stopped to look down on her. 'As the ring being on the *wrong* body?'

305

Chastity couldn't seem to move from where she stood in the middle of the living room. Behind her, lightning forked across the sky. She thought about what had been done to those three women. She felt sick.

'Willow looked so much like Faith.'

'Could a husband have made a mistake like that?'

'Good God, James, I don't know. Besides, if he thought Faith was already dead, why did he ask me to come down to look for her?'

Standing there in the shadows, James didn't answer.

If Max had indeed murdered them, those women who had kept his wife safe, then Chastity had led him right to them. She'd staked them out like goats for him to dispose of at his leisure.

'I need to talk to the police,' she said.

'You need to call Max and tell him you're not coming.'

Chastity stood there, staring into the peppermint-colored kitchen beyond the shadows. 'No, I don't think so. I think I need to talk to him.'

'But you just said you think he murdered those women.'

'He's a bully. I know how to deal with bullies.' She grinned suddenly, feeling tight and brittle and furious. 'Besides, I'll be in plain view in full daylight in a public place.'

'In a thunderstorm. You sure?'

'I'm sure I need to know what he's going to tell me,' she said. '*Then* I'll call the police.'

Jackson Square was all but deserted. Chastity and James arrived a few minutes early to find the trees dripping and the steam rising from the thunderstorm. The rain had stopped, but the clouds still roiled across the sky and thunder rumbled and cracked across the river. The wind was capricious, lifting and swirling the litter that remained from the hastily departed tourists.

Chastity looked, but the psychics had decamped as well. For a second she actually thought she might want to speak

306

to Tante Edie. Find out how this discussion with Max was going to turn out. How the rest of this week was going to turn out, when she had disaster pressing down on her from all sides.

But without tourists, there was no business. And the tourists were at the airport trying to find a way home. The natives were home boarding up houses or in their cars trying to get past Lake Pontchartrain before the hurricane arrived.

Chastity wanted to be with them in the worst way. At the airport, on the highway, on a dirt path – she didn't care. Away from the odd electricity in the air, the constant weather alerts, the dread that crawled in her belly at the thought of her father walking through those wrought-iron gates.

She wiped the water off one of the benches that faced the cathedral and sat down. James prowled a few feet away.

Chastity saw Max first. Clad in a tailored suit, business tie, and shiny loafers, he walked as if he were on a hospital hallway, completely in control. A man to attract attention with his sculpted gray hair and square jaw. She saw that gray hair and held her breath.

Would there be another man with gray hair following behind?

Would Max bring her father?

She was so distracted by the possibility that her father would walk through the gates that Max was almost upon her before she realized that he'd actually come alone. She was so relieved, she damn near melted all over the bench.

She had murders and a missing sister and two women she'd liked who were dead. And she was more distressed by the possibility of seeing her father than by any of that. It was definitely time to go home.

Max gave Chastity a sympathetic smile as he reached her. She knew he'd caught sight of James. She'd seen him stiffen. But he didn't say anything, just settled on the other side of the bench as if they were in his living room.

'Are you all right?' he asked, leaning her way.

Chastity fought the urge to back away. She fought harder to pay attention. She still expected her father to suddenly show up, right about the time Max needed to make a point.

'I'm fine, Max. I have to admit that I'm glad the police are finally paying attention to what's going on.'

She tried hard not to be obvious, but she watched him. She measured him, as if suddenly she should be able to see something in him she'd missed. Could he really be so sadistic and not reveal it? Not smell differently, like Lloyd, or have maroon eyes, like Hannibal Lector?

But Chastity, who lived in the real world, knew that the real monsters were often handsome and appealing.

He smiled and patted her hand. 'The police are paying attention? That's great. I thought they didn't tell you anything.'

'They told me they think that Susan's and Frankie's murders are linked. They're investigating the fertility clinics.'

'Good. I've been so worried about you.' Tilting his head, he oozed anxiety. 'You really don't have *any* idea where Faith is?'

Well, at least Chastity could be honest about that. 'No. I really don't. I assume you haven't heard anything, either?'

'No. Not a peep. I even called your father, just in case she thought to maybe contact him. He was the one who took her to that clinic, by the way. He told me.'

She didn't believe him. Mostly because this time, when he talked about her father, she saw how watchful Max suddenly became. Nothing obvious. There was no gleam, no leer. It was just a curious stillness, as if he was waiting for her reaction.

So there was something she should have seen all along. Something Max had neatly camouflaged with her own fears.

Chastity made it a point to face him, even though she still

308

wanted to watch over her shoulder. 'Thank you for the information. Is that what you wanted to tell me?'

Max dipped his head, his gaze now on his hands where they lay in his lap. His brilliant, manicured, surgeon's hands.

'Are you sure you can't stay?' he begged. 'I really wouldn't ask if I weren't desperate.'

'You don't understand,' she said. 'I have trouble enough driving on a bridge over the river. I'm not going to be able to cope at all with a storm surge.'

'But it's not here yet. Another day or two. I just know you're close to finding Faith.'

'No, Max. I can't.'

He looked away, as if gathering his tact. He sighed, and Chastity felt the tension in her chest begin to coil. What was he about to do?

'I didn't want to have to be the one to tell you this,' he said, not yet facing her.

Chastity didn't answer. She kept James in sight, though. He might not like it, but he was fast becoming her anchor. And she had the dreadful feeling she was just about to need one.

'I imagine you've always wondered why your sister ran away from you. Why she didn't contact you again.'

Well, at least he had Chastity's full attention. 'I imagine you're going to tell me.'

He looked up and Chastity saw distress in those sharp brown eyes. 'I just don't know how to tell you this. But you have to understand, I'll do anything to find my wife.'

His *wife*. There it was again. Chastity wrapped her hands around her purse and held on.

'You know that she had a baby,' he said.

Chastity blinked. Where the hell was this going? 'Yes.'

'Well, I finally found out about it. I found out when she had that baby.'

He expected an answer of some kind, Chastity thought. She didn't give him one. She just watched him.

309

'You were right, Chastity,' he said. 'Your sister is thirty-eight. I guess if I'd known, I might have guessed. At least suspected. Especially knowing your father.'

Chastity blinked. 'My father? What are you talking about? What does he have to do with it?'

This time, Max was the one who waited.

Chastity didn't disappoint him. She knew her jaw dropped and her face drained of color. 'You're saying that Faith had a baby by my father. That that's why she left when she did?'

'Not if you think that she was pregnant then. She'd already had her baby.' He was watching her again. His nostrils even flared, just a little. 'She'd had it sixteen years earlier.'

Should she feel something, Chastity wondered. Should she recognize the inevitability of this moment?

The footsteps in the hall had just stopped outside her door.

'Faith isn't your sister, Chastity. She's your mother.'

Chapter Twenty-One

Thunder rolled over the river. Somewhere a car honked, and the wind caught the trees and set them writhing. More rain was coming. Chastity could smell it. She could see James standing just out of hearing range. She could almost hear her heart thundering in her chest.

Max was lying.

It was the first coherent thought she had. He had to be lying. Her family was dysfunctional. It wasn't gothic.

But Faith was twelve years older than Chastity. She'd always been distant from her. Resentful. As if Chastity had stolen something from her, although Chastity had never been able to figure out what.

Faith and Hope and Chastity.

Chastity.

Well, didn't that just take on a new meaning?

Had it been her mother's indictment? Her ineffectual swipe at the man who controlled their lives, and the daughter who had supplanted her in his bed? Her ultimate denial?

Faith was twelve years older than Chastity, and everything suddenly made sense.

'I'm so sorry, Chastity,' Max said, leaning closer. 'I didn't want to tell you here, right out in the open . . .'

He tried to lay a hand on hers. Chastity yanked back as if she'd seen a snake.

'I understand, Max.'

311

He'd done it on purpose. Set out to hurt her.

Shouldn't she be hurt? Shouldn't she be vomiting up her socks? She'd sure wanted to when she'd thought her father might show up.

Her mother had never expressed affection. Not once in the sixteen years she'd known her. And then, when Chastity had stood up for herself against the man who'd hurt her – hurt them all – her mother had spit in her face and walked way. With her real daughter.

It made so much sense.

'How did you find out?' she asked, sitting quite still.

Max shrugged, his attention never wavering for a second. 'Your mother. When she was dying. I'm so sorry, Chastity. I mean, I know that everything is changed now.'

There it was again, that watchfulness. That flash of expectation in his eyes, as if he was still waiting. Hungry for her reaction.

Chastity had the weirdest feeling that he expected to feed off it. Her fear. Her distress. Her devastation.

She faced him, for the first time immune to his coercion. Bemused by his attempt to shatter her. She thought how precise his hair was, how tailored his clothing. How completely he controlled everything around him.

Until now.

'It doesn't change anything, really,' she said, composed and collected where she sat, her own hands folded around her purse, her focus on the statue of General Jackson at the center of the square. 'The day things changed for me was when I admitted that my father pushed my head underwater while he raped me. And that the first time he did that, I was four years old.' She took a small breath, willing herself to calm. 'I always thought of it as the moment somebody pulls a tablecloth out from under the good crystal only the trick doesn't work. All that crystal is shattered into a thousand shards on the floor, and there will never be any way of making it whole again. That's what I felt that day. But this?' She shrugged, turning now to face him down.

'This isn't really as much of a surprise as you might think.'

Did she see disappointment? A sudden flash of fury, like a glint of red in a gemstone? Did Max seem, suddenly, to coil more tightly into himself with frustration?

She remembered a *Star Trek* episode she'd seen once, where an alien had attacked the ship by feeding off its crew's emotions. How the crew had struggled to maintain calm to starve it out of existence. She thought of that alien now as she caught the quickly suppressed rage in Max's eyes.

He'd brought out the big guns, and she'd just walked on past.

And still he sat there, waiting for her to crumble. To break down so he could offer his help, his comfort, his control.

If only she found her sister for him.

No, not her sister.

Her mother.

But that wasn't Chastity's reaction.

Chastity's reaction was simple. She sat on a slightly damp bench in a park that was already dipping and groaning with the advent of a new thunderstorm, and all she could think of was that she was sure now.

She had no more proof than she'd had before sitting down. Certainly nothing concrete enough to take to the police. She might not ever find a shred of evidence that would hold up in court.

Max was brilliant, after all. He'd certainly kept her bobbing on the end of his line easily enough. She imagined he could probably do the same for anybody else who had questions.

But Chastity didn't have any more questions.

Susan Reeves and Willow Tolliver and Frankie Mae Savage were dead because they'd tried to help her sister escape an abusive husband. They were dead because Max Stanton had murdered them.

And if she betrayed her suspicions, Chastity knew he'd murder her, too.

313

'Thank you for telling me, Max,' she said, steeling herself to pat him on the arm. 'I mean it. It helps explain so much. But it doesn't make it any more possible for me to stay. I'll call the minute I get back to New Orleans. I promise.'

It was a lovely thing she'd learned from her forensics training. The only promise that meant anything was the one made under oath. At least when dealing with a suspect.

'But Chastity—'

But Chastity got to her feet. Max didn't need to know that her knees were so gelatinous they could hardly hold her up. He didn't need to know that she was appalled and terrified and so suddenly sick at the thought of whom she'd been sitting with that she wasn't sure she'd make it off the square before mortifying herself. He didn't need to know that she was looking for James like a life preserver on a high sea.

She was a trauma nurse. A forensic nurse. She was an expert at containing disaster. She knew how to defuse an imminent threat.

'Thank you, Max. I'll call.'

And she just walked away.

'I didn't see your father,' James said quietly as he joined her on the path to the wrought-iron gates.

'You didn't have to,' Chastity said, her eyes focused on the cool white facade of the cathedral across the street. 'Max thought he had enough ammunition without him. I don't suppose you can see what he's doing.'

James looked back to nod, as if saying good-bye. 'Just standing there watching you. He looks kinda . . . '

'Dumbfounded?'

'Feral.'

Chastity fought a new round of shakes. 'I was afraid of that.' She'd hoped for a chance to sneak into the cathedral unnoticed. To slip into a pew in the back and let the incense-rich hush settle on her shoulders. To pray to a God

314

she wasn't even sure existed that she'd come out the other side of this, when even Tante Edie hadn't seen it for sure.

She didn't see it for sure, either.

Especially now.

'Would you drive me to the airport?' she asked, walking on.

Following, James stared at her. 'Thought you weren't leaving.'

'I'm not. But I need Max to think I am.'

He started to look back again and thought better of it. 'And you think he's going to follow us.'

'Oh, yeah. I think he is.'

They walked across Chartres to St. Ann, where James had parked the cab. 'Then you think . . .'

She thought Max would be disappointed that the most intense feeling she had after that meeting was relief that her father hadn't shared it.

'I'll tell you what I think when we're on the way to the airport.'

James must have recognized the less than sturdy condition of Chastity's knees, because he handed her into the cab himself. With his braced hand.

It was unintentional, but Chastity was left with a quick reminder of actions and consequences. Exactly what she needed when she'd just decided to go after a multiple murderer.

She had to find her sister. She had to get her the hell out of New Orleans. She had to find proof that Max had killed those women for no more reason than that they'd helped his wife.

Chastity was amazed that it had taken her this long to figure that out. She was furious that she'd been so fooled.

She was a good forensic nurse. Nothing got by her on her job. Nothing. But Max had made her look like an amateur.

Max the controller. Max the scientist. Max, who hadn't simply tried to get his wife back. He'd taken the time –

he'd taken the unbelievable chance of stopping long enough – to leave the women who'd hidden her from him a message.

You can't stop me.

You can't beat me.

You can't ever again think that you are smarter or stronger or more perseverant.

'You okay?' James asked.

That was when Chastity realized that he'd settled her into the front seat and then slid into his own side. He reached across with that terrible, sore hand and patted her on the arm.

'Don't do that,' she snapped, flinching.

He pulled away, frowning.

She sucked in a quick breath. 'I'm still working on that comfort thing,' she admitted. 'I can't afford to cry right now.'

James nodded. Hooked his seat belt and started the engine. 'All right, then. Let's go.'

She was shaking and sweating again, and damn tired of both. She kept rolling the idea of Faith as her mother around on her tongue, as if the idea of it would suddenly take on a different taste, a more concrete texture.

Max was right. She should be shattered. At least she should feel different: bigger, smaller, unable to quite fit into the same skin anymore. But she didn't. She hadn't been lying. Her biggest change had come ten years ago, the day she'd walked into the police station in St. Louis County. That was the day she'd taken the greatest chance, laying herself out over an abyss she still hadn't crossed. It was the day she'd come the closest to telling the real truths about herself.

Which was the most amusing part of what Max had tried to do today. The only truth that still really ate at her had nothing to do with who her mother was. And if anybody was going to force it out of her, it wouldn't be Max. It would be James.

316

And here she was sitting close enough to him to touch in a car made humid and small in the rain.

Time to get her focus back.

'Do voodoo believers have wakes?' she asked, watching her hands play with the straps of her too-abused purse.

James took a quick look her way. 'You going to Frankie's wake?'

'If it's okay. Are outsiders welcome?'

'Don't worry. Frankie will be buried with all the rites of mother church. The voodoo practitioners will help prepare her, and then hold their own ceremony later.'

Chastity knew that at any other time, she'd have a quart of questions about ritual and belief. Right now, she didn't have time. Max had tried to distract her. She was not about to let him. 'Fine. Maybe somebody there knows where Frankie stashed my sister.'

'What do you think?' James asked, flipping on his blinker and swerving past a slower taxi. 'Is Max a murderer?'

Chastity watched the houses crawl by. She listened to the quick click of the wipers and the low hum of jazz from James's radio. 'Max is a murderer. And I'm not at all sure anybody's gonna catch him.'

'What did he say to convince you?'

'He said that Faith is my mother.'

They almost ran smack into a streetcar. 'Pardon?'

Chastity still watched out the window. 'It explains a lot, really.'

'But she would have been ... '

'Twelve. Makes it easier to understand why we never had a comfortable relationship.'

Poor Faith. Poor little twelve-year-old girl, swollen and frightened and trapped in that terrible place.

For the first time since Chastity had met him, James lit up a cigarette in his cab. Chastity almost asked for one. She almost asked him to stop and pick up a fifth of Jack.

She'd get a couple of stiff drinks at the airport. She'd

317

slam down about a quart of gin and call Sergeant Gaudet. Then she'd wade back into this city on the verge of a hurricane.

Just the sound of water sloshing away from the wheels of the cab made her want to vomit.

'You seem kind of complacent about the whole thing,' James said.

She shrugged. 'As I told Max, I'm not as surprised as I should be. I just wish I'd known a long time ago. It might have made everything easier.'

James shot her an incredulous look. 'Easier?'

She managed a smile. 'A lot of behavior in my family finally makes sense, ya know?'

James shook his head. 'And here I was traumatized by being related to rodeo clowns.'

He surprised a giggle out of Chastity. 'Hell, that'd traumatize me, too. Incest is disgusting. Clowns are just scary.'

They stopped at Kareena's long enough for Chastity to pretend to gather her stuff and haul it back out to the cab. Then they joined the river of evacuees who where trying to get away from the city before disaster struck.

Highway 90 was bad and Highway 10 was worse, bumper to bumper, with taillights flashing in syncopation and lightning stuttering across the sky. The interior lanes were awash, and trucks spewed up a spray that made Chastity flinch.

'I really don't like this,' she muttered, her free arm tight around her backpack and her feet instinctively rising every time they hit a puddle.

'Close your eyes,' James suggested. 'I'm the only one who has to watch.'

'If I don't watch, I could be surprised.'

'Seems to me it never made a difference if you watched or not.'

Well, that took the rest of Chastity's breath. 'You're right,' she admitted. 'It made no difference at all. It's just an illusion of control.'

318

But then, sometimes the illusion was all you had.

An hour later Chastity hefted her luggage in one hand and her cell in the other as she traversed the Louis Armstrong International Airport. It was hard to hear. The concourse was packed with frantic vacationers fleeing and natives making a strategic retreat.

Once again, Chastity stood in line, this time for security. She wasn't taking any chances, especially since James had caught sight of Max's BMW not more than four cars behind them on the freeway. She'd just purchased another standby ticket. If she needed to, she'd walk all the way to the gate before turning back.

She hadn't seen Max yet. She had seen plenty of families, a few gaggles of frat jocks looking very disappointed, and a man with a white rat on his shoulder. The only one not impatient with the length of the security line seemed to be the rat.

During the months she'd spent living out of her car, Chastity used to drive to the airport in St. Louis, just to watch the people. To pretend she was happy and normal and going somewhere interesting. She'd watched anxious young men clutch flowers and restless children clutch patient parents as they walked the halls, and she'd wondered if that was what it meant to be part of something.

She hadn't thought of that in a long time. Good thing she was thinking about it now, when everybody she saw looked cranky and frantic. Nobody looked like they wanted to be going where they were headed, and somehow it made her feel less alone.

'Ms. Byrnes?' a whisky-rough voice asked in her ear.

'Excuse me, Sergeant Gaudet,' she said, shoving her ear bud a bit farther in so she could hear better. 'I got a bit distracted.'

'We need this to be fast, ma'am. I don't have much more time to work on this. We're all getting pulled soon.'

Chastity wished she had a drink. Instead, she had a four-year-old who wanted to jump on her shoes. 'Breaking out the rain slickers and flashlights, are you?'

'Yes, ma'am. Maybe as soon as tomorrow.'

And she wasn't really boarding a plane to escape. 'You don't know how sorry I am to hear that.'

'Me, too. Now, you were telling me how your brother-in-law murdered these women.'

She had told him everything, from the visit of Dr. Hayes-Adams to the moment she'd walked into the airport. He'd listened in complete silence through it all.

'Yes, sir.' Somebody bumped her and Chastity spun around, only to find an old Indian man waving apologies. She swore she saw gray hair at the back of the line. 'That's what I believe he did.'

'Well, there's only one problem with your theory, Ms. Byrnes,' Sergeant Gaudet said. 'There's no way your brother-in-law could have committed those murders. He has an alibi for both.'

Chastity's heart stopped. 'What kind of alibi?'

'He was on the surgery schedule both mornings.'

Chastity went still. 'You checked?'

'I told you I would.'

She nodded to herself, out of reason relieved. He'd believed her. He'd at least taken her seriously. The line moved, and she shoved her backpack forward with her foot.

'Thank you, Sergeant.'

But the alibis. Why hadn't she thought of that?

Because she hadn't suspected Max. Not really. Not of more than being the kind of husband a woman would run from.

But he was the kind of husband who was neat and precise and organized. He was the kind of murderer who'd planned those murders as if they were sacrificial offerings. Of course he'd have an alibi.

'Did you check to see if he finished his cases?' she asked, furious that she'd wasted so much time on the wrong leads. Frantic with the need for action. Now that she knew, she wanted it over. She wanted him caught and her sister safe.

Her mother.

Whatever.

For a moment the sergeant was silent. 'What do you mean?'

Chastity opened her eyes. Focused. Tried hard to pull her suddenly hyperexcited brain into order. 'Tulane is a teaching hospital. It's not uncommon at all for teaching surgeons to let the residents and fellows do the hardest work.'

Sergeant Gaudet huffed. 'Well, that makes me feel more secure.'

'They have to learn sometime, Sergeant. The question is how much supervision they got from Max at critical times.' She was pretty sure she heard the sergeant mutter an oath that would be censored on a talk show. She couldn't help but grin. 'Depending on the surgeon and the staff, it might not even show up on the records that the doctor didn't actually finish the case. If you check from your side, I'll have Kareena do the same from hers, okay?'

'Kareena Boudreaux?' he asked.

'Yeah. That okay?'

'Kareena's a fine woman,' the sergeant assured her. 'Professional and empathetic. Beautiful eyes.'

Chastity damn near laughed. She had no idea what that had to do with anything, but what the hell? 'I'll pass it along, Sergeant.'

'You do that. I'll wait to hear from her. In the meantime, I have a question for you. Have you ever seen the doctor in a black car? A sedan.'

Again it took her a minute to answer. 'Black? No. His car's silver. A BMW, why?'

Was that him, over by the baggage X-rays? Was he watching to make sure she left?

'Yes, ma'am. A 2005 BMW 745i. Another sweep of the Saint Roch neighborhood came up with a witness who saw a late model black sedan parked on Derbigny a couple blocks over from Saint Roch's right about the time of Susan Reeves's murder.'

The hair lifting on the back of her neck, Chastity struggled to concentrate. She had the most unholy suspicion that it was Max there, just beyond the ungainly shuffle of the security line. That somehow he could hear every word she said.

'It wasn't Lloyd Burgard's car?'

'No, ma'am,' Gaudet said. 'The car he drove was white. It was parked right behind the black one.'

Which meant that Lloyd had probably seen the murderer after all. He could easily have identified him. And now, just like Frankie and Willow and Susan, he was dead.

'I don't suppose you found out—'

'If there was a gray-haired doctor seen leaving Lloyd's room about the time of his death? No. I'm afraid nobody saw anything. You're sure you haven't seen a black car?'

Chastity moved up again in line, took another look back. Saw nothing. 'No. Could the car be registered to my sister?'

'No, ma'am. It's not.' He took another of those silences that Chastity was beginning to dislike. 'The cab your friend drives is black.'

'Anybody in that neighborhood would be able to tell a late model sedan from that cab, Sergeant.'

'He did call the cab dispatcher and ask that Frankie Mae Savage meet him.'

'He did not. Somebody else did that.'

'Tough to prove.'

'You've obviously read his history, Sergeant. Do you really think he murdered Frankie?'

This time the woman in front of Chastity turned around. Chastity smiled. 'Working on a screenplay,' she mouthed, hoping the woman didn't see her sweat.

On the other end of the line, the sergeant didn't pause. 'No, Ms. Byrnes. I really don't. But I'm the only one. I'm just trying to tell you.'

'Then we have to catch the doctor, don't we?'

'If you say so, ma'am.'

'Will you help?'

She suffered through another long silence, during which she shuffled forward another few steps and tried to see that gray head over the crowd. Finally, though, the sergeant sighed. 'Makes more sense than anything else we've come up with. Now, you want to give me something on those women you say won't talk to me?'

Chastity actually smiled. 'I thought you'd never ask.'

So Chastity gave him what she had. She even gave him the password to get onto the Arlen Clinic donor page, just in case.

'All right,' he said. 'I'll see what I can do.'

'Thank you, Sergeant. I know it's tough to buy this one. I appreciate your listening.'

'Yes, ma'am. I just hope you're not ...'

'Prejudiced? Shortsighted? Caught with my head up my ass?'

She surprised a quick laugh out of him. 'Well, I wouldn't have put it quite that way.'

'I'm not wrong, Sergeant. I'm just afraid that it took me too long to figure it out.'

She was just about to sign off when Sergeant Gaudet blindsided her all over again. 'One more thing, Ms. Byrnes.'

Somebody walked right over Chastity's grave. 'Yes, sir?'

'Why didn't you tell me that your father was Charles Francis Byrnes?'

That quickly, any equilibrium Chastity had held on to vanished. She actually caught herself looking over her shoulder, as if Chuck would suddenly walk down the hall. And the funny thing was that somebody was indeed watching her.

Standing there right by the X-ray machines, his gray hair dull in the vast lobby, his eyes cold and watchful.

Not her father.

Max.

Chastity almost laughed. She fought the unholiest urge to run. From Max, from the police, from James and Kareena. From every one of them who thought they knew what the worst of her was. Especially from the ones who thought they understood.

They didn't.

They wouldn't.

And there was Max, standing there as if he were trying to impress on her how terrified she should be of him.

Chastity made it a point to turn away from him and focus on stepping forward in line.

'Why do you want to know about my father?' she asked Gaudet, and realized that her voice was no more than a whisper.

'I was checking on your background,' he said. 'And of course, there was the trial. I saw his picture. He and your brother-in-law look quite a bit alike, don't they?'

It took every ounce of control Chastity had not to turn around for another look. She felt him, though, like a shard of glass in her back. 'Yes, Sergeant. They do.'

'Could it be your father?' he asked. 'The man we're looking for?'

She squeezed her eyes closed. Fought through the sudden shakes and sweats. 'No, sir. My father is an opportunist and a predator. But I don't think he has the mind to plan murders like these.'

'Can you tell me why?' he asked, as if it were that easy.

Water. Water and laughter and panic.

And of course the shame. Red, swamping shame that never gave her peace.

'No, sir. I . . . uh, maybe later.'

Not in an airport. Not in public. Not anywhere.

'All right, Ms. Byrnes. I understand.'

Chastity almost burst out laughing. Max had enticed her to a park in an attempt to shatter her, and here the sergeant damn near did it with an innocent question. Because she heard it. The taint of pity in his voice.

He must have read something of the record. He knew what she'd said at that trial ten years ago. He thought he could understand just why she'd be so ashamed to share with him any information about her father.

He didn't, of course. Because he didn't know what she hadn't said at that trial. What she hadn't said to a living soul. He didn't know what had sent her to the streets at fourteen. What had sent her to James's apartment twelve years later looking for absolution and penance.

She was angry at Max. She was afraid that he could harm her friends. But she wasn't terrified of him. Not like she was terrified of her father. And she didn't want anyone to know why.

She didn't want anybody to know that her father, who had made her nights such a living terror, had done much worse than teach her to fear him.

He'd trained her to want him.

Chapter Twenty-Two

At noon the next day the doors to the Clements Funeral Home opened for the viewing of Frankie Mae Savage. A fresh thunderstorm was swamping the city, sending people scurrying for cover and cars skidding for purchase. Thunder cracked and snapped overhead. Wind tortured the trees, and water pooled six inches deep in the roads.

Chastity had to take an extra Xanax just to get in Kareena's car. By the time she ducked under the front porch of the funeral home, she was a bigger puddle than the ones she bolted through on the way from the car.

'You better take some more drugs,' Kareena advised, casting a wry eye at her ashen appearance, 'or they gonna lay you out by mistake.'

'I'm fine,' Chastity insisted, shaking water from her hair, as if that were all that was the matter. She hadn't slept again the night before, even after knowing that they'd fooled Max with the airport gambit. 'I appreciate your bringing me, Kareena.'

Kareena chuckled, her head on a swivel as they proceeded through the front door. 'Well, it's a cinch James wouldn't be let in the front door. Besides, you think Kareena's gonna miss this?'

The room they entered was basic poor funeral home, with tile floors, plastic stained glass windows, and plain walls. Frankie's casket was closed and flanked by branches of blue and white candles. Flower arrangements crowded the walls and floor, and mass cards filled the guest book stand. People of all races and ages and economic levels had come to mourn, and not a few of them wore the traditional white of voodoo instead of mourning black.

In one corner, a thin, wrinkled black man in a pristine white suit was sprinkling some kind of liquid from a Dixie cup at the wall, and in another, a stunning model-sized woman in flowing white poured cheap champagne into plastic glasses.

At the core of the room, though, there was grief, and it was loud and it was heartfelt. A tiny black woman was being picked up off the floor by two hefty young men. She was rocking back and forth and imploring her lord to save her. At least a dozen other people wailed a minor counter-part.

This, Chastity thought, was how to send somebody off.

It struck her that she felt much more at home here than she had with the icy, precise ritual for Susan Reeves. This wake held all the messy, operatic grief that always attended death in the African American community. It was a drama Chastity knew well from her own inner-city ER, and one she envied.

'Do you see anybody to talk to?' she asked Kareena, wishing she didn't feel so responsible for the anguish that ricocheted off these walls.

But Kareena was on a field trip to voodooland, her attention on the guy who was still sprinkling the corners.

'It's rum,' Kareena said, motioning to him. 'Yamaya loves rum.'

Chastity sighed. 'I wonder if she'd mind sharing.'

'Try the champagne. It's another favorite.'

'Not till I've talked to somebody. Do you think Frankie's mother would talk to me? I think she's the one moaning in the front row.'

She was the woman in the front row wearing her best Sunday-go-to-meeting dress and rocking a solemn-eyed two-year-old boy in her arms. Frankie's little boy, Chastity thought. Cossetted and comforted and the center of attention, unlike little Margaret Jane, who'd been banished to the periphery and left beyond family.

'You sure you want to start with her?' Kareena asked.

'No, she's not,' came a voice at Chastity's shoulder.

A hard little hand clamped at her elbow, and Chastity turned to find that she was being glared at by a tiny walnut of a woman in a white suit and gold lamé Sunday hat.

'Tante Edie,' she said, gaping. 'What are you doing here?'

Tante Edie barked an incredulous laugh. 'Well, now, *that's* a funny question comin' from you. I was just gonna ask you the same thing.'

Chastity had to blink a couple of times. For a fortune-teller from Jackson Square, Tante Edie looked amazingly like a Bible School teacher. 'I'm trying to find my sister. And I'm trying to prove who killed Frankie.'

Tante Edie squinted up at her, as if pulling her into focus. 'You ever take my advice?'

'Which advice?'

The little woman gave a great sigh. 'You didn't. You'd look a lot easier, you did. Go jump that boy, girl. He ain't gonna hurt you.'

'Yeah,' Kareena said, 'but she might hurt him.'

Tante Edie squinted at Kareena, which just made Kareena grin. 'I know who you are,' Kareena announced. 'I've seen you at the square.'

'And you haven't had the courage to walk up like a human and ask for a reading. I got no time for you.'

Kareena laughed. '*Mais* yeah, I'll come see you,' she said. 'Then we'll see who's afraid of who. But first we got to finish this, yeah?'

Tante Edie looked right at Chastity. 'Yeah. You do have to finish it. Now, what do you think you can do here?'

Chastity looked right back. 'Ask for any help I can get.'

'To do what?'

328

'I have to find my sister before her husband does.'

Tante Edie looked at her for a long moment. 'Frankie seemed to think you down here to help him, that husband.'

'I was. But that was before I got to know him. Now, I have to stop him before he kills anybody else.'

Tante Edie's eyes went fierce, her little body trembling with emotion. 'You have proof he's the one? The one kill Frankie and my little Willow?'

If she'd had the time or luxury, Chastity might have been afraid of those wise old eyes. 'I'm working on it. But my first priority is to help get my sister to safety. Then I'll have the time to see Max gets his due.'

Oddly enough, Tante Edie smiled. A hard smile, the kind cops use when they hear handcuffs click. 'Oh, you don't worry 'bout that,' she said. 'He'll get his due, and you won't have to wait for the police to do it. He do bad things to a child of Yamaya, he better believe she notice.'

'Yamaya, she not in the business of revenge,' Kareena objected. 'It's not her way.'

'She own the shallow water,' Tante Edie retorted. 'That kind of salt water bein' swept up the swamps right now before that hurricane. She comin' for that boy, I think.'

'That's a hurricane comin', old woman,' Kareena argued. 'Anybody know that hurricanes belong to Oya. Maybe Erzulie Youx Rouge. Not Yamaya.'

'Oh, you know so much?'

'More than you, seems like.'

Chastity couldn't stand it any longer. 'While this is very illuminating,' she interrupted, 'it doesn't help me find my sister. Besides, Tante, last I talked to you, I didn't get the impression you believed.'

The old woman flashed crooked yellow teeth at her. 'I never turn my back on any power, girl. You never know when you might stumble over the truth by accident.'

True words, Chastity thought blackly. Except the truth she kept stumbling over so far hadn't much helped her.

'What I need to stumble over,' she said, holding on to

329

her patience by her fingertips, 'is my sister. Do you think there might be anybody here who can help me?'

Tante Edie squinted at her a few more moments, obviously making her assessment. 'Give me your hand.'

Oh, Chastity didn't want to do that. Not when people had already begun turning their way. People who obviously knew about Tante Edie, and certainly seemed to know the connection between Frankie Mae and the preternaturally blond woman in their midst.

Tante Edie huffed and flicked her hand in Chastity's direction. 'You don't have much time, girl. You want to waste some more?'

So Chastity fought the chills that had started to crawl down her back and laid her hand in that gnarled little palm. She battled the sudden, sharp contact and kept her eyes open by will alone.

Tante Edie wasn't looking at Chastity's hand. She was looking at her eyes. The rest of the room watched Tante Edie, hushed like a church as the host was being raised. Even Kareena stood still, her mouth open and her eyes avid.

Ten heartbeats.

Twenty.

Chastity fought hard to stay still as she endured that tiny woman's scrutiny.

Finally, abruptly, Tante Edie let go. 'Luscious, come here, honey.'

Chastity took a step back to catch her breath. Just then the tall, elegant woman who'd been passing champagne approached.

'Yes, Tante?'

'See these girls to the ladies' room, you hear?'

Kareena opened her mouth. Chastity kicked her. Then she turned to find that the woman who was taking her to the ladies' room had an Adam's apple and big knuckles.

'The ladies' room?' she asked instinctively.

Luscious raised a precisely penciled eyebrow at her.

330

'You got a problem with that?'

Considering the fact that the elegant Luscious had about eight inches and fifty pounds on her, Chastity merely shook her head. Luscious nodded hers and motioned them on like a tour guide.

'Back here. They got fainting couches and real towels and everything. It's real nice.'

The rest of the crowd saw the approval given by Tante Edie and turned back to their conversations.

'You get down to the Quarter?' Luscious asked, her hips swaying off her five-inch heels as she led the way. 'I'm in a lovely gender illusion act at Miss Mamie Eloquence's Club every night. You should stop by.'

'When I have time.'

And the city wasn't underwater. And her sister was safe.

'In fact,' Luscious said, 'I was at Eddie's party when they found that nun. It's all so awful, isn't it?'

'Yes, it is. Could I talk to you about that, do you think?'

Luscious came to a stop in the back hallway right beneath the pictures of the funeral home founders and waggled an elegant set of press-on nails at her. 'Well, you're not *quite* my type, honey, but sure. After my surprise.'

'Surprise?'

The three of them were standing before a closed door that definitely did not say Ladies.

'Why, yes, sugar. Did you know I did magic?'

Chastity was out of patience. 'Excuse me—'

Luscious turned the doorknob with one hand and waved with the other. 'Voilà!'

And then she pushed open the door to show Chastity what was inside.

It was Kareena who reacted first. 'Get down,' she breathed right behind Chastity. 'No wonder everybody mistake her for you.'

Chastity couldn't move. She couldn't quite close her mouth. She kept wondering how bizarre this was all going

331

to get, when it was already beyond any bizarre she'd ever known in her life.

She gulped, and then she gasped, and then she damn near just sat on the floor and sobbed.

'Faith?'

Her sister stood up from where she'd been sitting on a couch. 'What are you doing here?' she demanded.

Faith. Precise, professional, poised Faith. Faith, who had always been the one in charge, the one to aspire to. She was disheveled and wan and fidgety. She was glaring at Chastity as if she'd burst in on a private moment.

But she was there.

After all this time, she was standing right there in front of Chastity. Chastity felt it like a gut punch, just sucking all the air out of her and replacing it with white noise.

And damn it if Faith looked not a day older than the last time Chastity had seen her. Her hair was just as blond, though still in that damn chignon, and her waist as thin, even in the faded red Mardi Gras T-shirt that didn't seem to belong to her and jeans that didn't fit.

If Chastity hadn't seen her sister flinch when that door slammed open, she might have thought that her own suspicions about Max had been wrong. That somehow this was all some big drama concocted by Faith for attention. But nobody could mistake that defensive posture. The quick, protective cringe of a terrorized person.

'Well?' Faith asked, regathering her control. 'Why are you here? Didn't they tell you to go home?'

Chastity blinked. 'I needed to make sure you were okay.'

'I'm okay. Now get the hell home.'

They weren't moving. They stood there on either side of an open pressboard door as if there were a force field between them. Rigid and uncertain and off balance.

Chastity wasn't sure what she'd thought she'd feel when she finally saw Faith again. Closure? Acceptance? Comfort?

She felt none of those. She felt stifled and afraid and impatient.

332

And angry.

She'd spent the last two weeks desperate to find her, and Faith had greeted her as if she'd interrupted her homework. She was feeling disoriented again. Panicked. Overwhelmed.

She just wished she knew which of a thousand questions she should ask first. So she asked the wrong one.

'Should I really be calling you mom?'

At least she got a reaction. Even though it wasn't the one she wanted.

Faith stiffened, her face suddenly showing her age. She breathed in slowly though her nose. She shrugged.

'They wouldn't let me get an abortion.'

Ah. Well, that certainly felt better.

And before an audience.

Chastity just wasn't sure what else she was supposed to withstand.

'Why did you go to St. Louis?' she asked, foundering badly.

Faith threw off another shrug and reminded Chastity of Mrs. Reeves with her posture and her assumed dignity.

'I needed to get away from here. Susan thought Max would never suspect I came to see you.' She laughed, looking anywhere but at Chastity. 'I never thought Max would think of contacting you.'

'Why'd you come back?'

'Where else could I go? I don't know anybody else.'

If Chastity hadn't spent her life within thirty miles of where she'd suffered her own nightmares, she might have thought worse of Faith. But Faith hadn't even left home until she was twenty-eight, and then only because her mother had dragged her. Chastity couldn't really be surprised that she'd run back to the familiar.

'You didn't think to wait there for me?' she asked anyway.

Faith was glaring now. 'You came down here to help Max. What was I to think?'

'You were to think that maybe I'd do everything I could

to stop another man from abusing a helpless female. After all, you sure as hell know I've made it a point to do that before.'

'I know you shattered every—' But she broke off, just shy of saying too much. Especially before witnesses.

But Chastity heard the rest of the accusation. She'd heard it often enough in the weeks during her father's trial. During the days when her mother had wandered the house, not knowing how to fill her days without a husband to tell her what to do. She'd heard it in the years since, when she'd replayed every one of those scenes a million times in her head in her struggle to understand.

But somehow, she thought that after ten years Faith might have understood that Chastity had done what she'd done to save them. Not to shatter them.

The small, hurt girl in her told her to just walk away. Just to leave Faith to her own problems, as Faith had left her ten years ago. The adult she'd worked so damned hard to be kept Chastity standing there long enough to notice that tears were welling in Faith's too-familiar fey eyes. They ran down her cheeks in silence, because Faith simply didn't know what to do.

Faith had never made it away from her abuse. Chastity had.

So once again, it was up to Chastity to try and break the cycle. Whether Faith liked it or not. So Chastity made the first step, and suddenly found herself in Faith's arms.

'I'm sorry,' they both said at the same time, holding on.

'I didn't know what to do,' Faith admitted in a shaky voice.

'How did you get here?' Chastity demanded, pulling back to wipe the tears from her sister's face. 'I've been looking for you *everywhere*. Did you know I've met Margaret Jane?'

Faith's face crumpled a bit. 'I can't look at her. She looks so much like Hope.'

Chastity laughed. 'That's just what I thought.' She shook

her head, overwhelmed all over again. 'God, there's so much we need to talk about. But we've got to get away first.'

Faith pulled away. 'No. No, I'm waiting here for a friend.'

'Yes, I'm sure you are, Faith, but I think I have a better idea. We need time alone. And we can't do that here.'

'You can come to Kareena's house,' Chastity heard behind her, and suddenly remembered they weren't alone.

'Heck, honey,' Luscious offered. 'Bring it down to the club. I think this deserves an audience.'

Chastity turned to see the drag queen had a lace hankie to her eyes. Kareena was grinning like a kid.

'Kareena Boudreaux,' Chastity said with a small smile, 'I'd like you to finally meet my sister Faith. Faith, this is my friend Kareena, who's been helping me find you.'

'Well, at least now I know why they offer you so much money for your eggs,' Kareena said with a sigh. 'You just, like, the middle-class wet dream, huh?'

Faith looked a bit stunned.

'Pay no attention to her,' Chastity said with a chuckle that bordered on shrill. 'She thinks nobody wants an egg with brown eyes. Did you go for yourself, Faith? Just tell me that. Tell me donating eggs was your idea.'

Faith's face fell again. 'At first.'

Chastity nodded, hurting for this woman who still couldn't admit her own abuse. 'Who took you to New Life, Faith?'

Faith blinked. 'New Life? That was Max's idea. He ... well, he needed the money. You know.'

'For his gambling. Yeah, I know.'

'He's sure sneaky about that,' Kareena admitted, a bit of awe in her voice. 'Nobody at Tulane knows about it.'

Faith actually smiled, although it was grim. 'Nobody knows anything Max Stanton doesn't want them to.'

That opened the door to so many questions. But before Chastity had the chance to ask even one, Faith patted her on the arm. 'You shouldn't be here,' she said. 'You should be home.'

'Why?' Chastity asked. 'You never said, nor did any of your friends.'

Faith lifted an eyebrow. 'Who are dead.'

Was it just old habit, or did Faith level a judgment on Chastity with those three words? Would it always be her fault?

'I know, Faith. I was there. But you can help us put a stop to it. You can tell me what's going on.'

Chastity should have known better than to think she was going to get answers. She should have known better than to think that any of this was going to be easy.

She was just reaching out her hand to Faith, a gentle nudge to begin guiding her out to the car and safety, when she heard quick footsteps behind her.

'What did you do?' Tante Edie demanded in shrill tones as she pushed past a stunned Luscious. 'What did you *do*?'

Everybody in the room turned to see the little woman skidding to a halt so fast her hat tipped forward. For a second, Chastity thought she was going to smile. Tante Edie took care of that.

'He's here,' she snapped, right at Chastity. 'You brought that man here *with* you!'

The funny thing was that Chastity didn't get it. She wasn't sure what Tante Edie meant.

Faith was sure.

'You bitch,' she hissed, yanking away from Chastity's touch. 'You traitorous bitch, you've done it again! I *knew* I shouldn't have trusted you!'

Chastity swung back to see Faith reaching for a bundle on the couch. She saw the flight in her sister's movements and got it.

She got it hard.

'Max.'

She knew she sounded sick. She realized just as fast that Faith misinterpreted.

336

'What, did he come too quickly?' she asked, her voice venomous. 'How long were you supposed to hold me here for him?'

Her arms holding her purse and a stuffed athletic bag, Faith whirled around on Tante Edie. 'Help me. How do I get out?'

'No,' Chastity objected, reaching for her. 'I'll—'

Faith yanked away again, snarling. 'You'll go to hell! You helped him!' Her pupils were huge, and her face was suddenly pasty.

'Back this way, girl,' Tante said, grabbing Faith's arm and pulling.

Chastity reached out. Tante Edie slapped her down like a pickpocket. 'You done enough, don't you think? Now come on, Faith, we'll sneak you out the back.'

'No!'

Chastity chased them right out the door to the alley. She tried to grab hold of Faith as she ran, but Luscious, the six-foot tranny, grabbed her arms from behind and held on to her as Faith climbed into Edie's car and sped away.

Chastity was left standing there in the downpour, watching the taillights wink out in the rain. Her sister – no, her mother – whom she'd just found after ten years, was gone.

Chapter Twenty-Three

'Girl,' Kareena said, stepping up next to her, 'we got to go, too. That man can't find us here.'

Chastity couldn't seem to move. She should have chased Faith. She should have grabbed on to her and not let go.

Faith shouldn't have believed that she could be helping Max.

'Chastity?'

She finally turned to find her friend holding on to her arm, as if afraid she'd walk right back into the funeral home.

Hard to do. Chastity and Kareena were the only two people standing in the alley, and the door was closed tight. The rain was easing up already. It didn't matter. Chastity was soaked through, her hair plastered against her forehead and her good slacks and shirt dripping. Kareena didn't look much better.

'I have to go after her, Kareena.'

Kareena took a quick look down the now-empty alley. 'You won't catch her, girl.'

'How could she think I'd bring him here?'

'She scared. But if you don't leave now, that man gonna know you're still in town.'

Chastity finally snapped to attention. 'Jesus, Kareena,' she said, 'we gotta get out of here.'

Kareena scowled. '*Mais* yeah, girl. Why didn't I think of that?'

The air hung heavy and hot. Clouds skimmed low, and the trees rustled with impatience. The drains were overflowing, pouring water right back out onto the streets so that it lapped at Chastity's ankles. She thought she'd vomit.

Swallowing hard, she high-stepped down that alleyway as if escaping prison, all the while with an eye to where her sister might have gone. The shock was wearing off, and she was getting angry.

No, furious.

She'd chanced everything, even her own sanity, to find her sister. And her sister had blamed her for it. Again.

Nothing much had changed. Nothing much probably ever would.

'Well,' she decided, 'at least if Max is here, then that means he's not at home.'

Kareena came to a dead stop, not two feet from her car. 'You are not going back to that man's house.'

Chastity shrugged. 'If I can't get my sister away, the next best thing is to get enough evidence to make sure he can't hurt her anymore. I have a very strong suspicion that I'm going to find that evidence at the house.'

'And if he leaves the wake early?'

Chastity cast a quick grin at her friend. 'Then I know you can figure a way to get him called down to Tulane. Can't you?'

Kareena just glared.

'And while I'm busy,' Chastity continued, 'I figure you'd like to call that nice Obie Gaudet and tell him who we saw today. And where. He says you have beautiful eyes, ya know.'

Well, that at least got Kareena in gear again. She flashed Chastity a bright grin. 'That's one fine-lookin' man, him.'

Chastity snorted. 'Obie? He's fifty miles of bad road.'

'Yeah, but Kareena wouldn't mind drivin' over it a few times.'

They reached Kareena's car and piled into it as if it were the last helicopter out of Saigon.

'I should have run after her,' Chastity said to herself.

Kareena started the engine and pulled out of their space. 'She shoulda stayed where she was. Now come on, let's get outa here before somethin' worse happens. And the way things have been goin' lately, I don't want to see how much worse it can get.'

Kareena didn't have to manufacture a lie to get Max to the hospital. Chastity had been sitting at Kareena's kitchen table for only forty minutes when Kareena called to say that a real patient had demanded the doctor's attention down at the medical center.

Chastity dragged James up from the chair where he'd been doing the *Times-Picayune* crossword puzzle and watching the hurricane reports, and propelled him back into action.

The latest front had passed, dropping about four inches of rain and a couple of tornadoes. The sky, for right now, was calm and flat and uninspiring. The trees drooped and gleamed with water, and the streets were awash. Chastity never again wanted to hear the sound of car tires splashing through water.

Even worse, the traffic was a mess. The official evacuation notice had gone out, and half the roads were closed or blocked or rerouted. Fortunately, nobody was interested in going the wrong way over the Mississippi, so they managed good time, although Chastity did it with her eyes closed.

It was only as they stopped to punch in the security code to open the subdivision gates that it occurred to Chastity that maybe they shouldn't have driven the taxi. It was going to stand out in this subdivision like a cockroach on an OR floor. But if everything went the way she wanted it to, she'd be finished with Dr. Max Stanton after this trip.

Max was an organized man. A precise, thorough man who cleaned to relieve stress. Chastity had a feeling he carried that organizational mania into his personal papers.

Receipts, bills, contacts. They had to be somewhere, and

340

since Chastity hadn't stumbled across any evidence of them in the rest of the house, she figured Max had them carefully locked up in his office, where she could quickly peruse them.

Before the hurricane came.

Before Max showed up.

Chastity wished like hell her sister would call. She'd sure left her number with enough people who could tell Faith how to find her. She had to know by now that Chastity couldn't have brought Max to that funeral home. That a woman who had ruined her own childhood taking an abuser to task would never aid and abet another.

But then, Faith had spent too many years locked in abuse to be logical about her abuser.

'You sure this is legal?' James asked as Chastity unlocked the front door to Max's house.

The neighborhood was still as death, the driveways empty and the streets drying. In fact, every time she'd been here, the atmosphere had been the same. As if the place were a giant movie set waiting for the cameras to roll. Not real at all.

A manufactured security that kept out the real world.

Well, the swamps, anyway.

Chastity was already shivering before she ever walked into that climate-controlled foyer.

'Just as legal as the last time we were here,' she assured James. 'Remember that Max himself gave me the keys and the security codes' – which she punched in quickly to prevent an alarm sounding anywhere – 'and told me to look around. I'm not doing anything different than I did the last two times we were here.'

She actually stood there for a minute this time, just to let the revulsion and shame wash over her like a big wave and then pass. Maybe if she just acknowledged what this place did to her, she could move on and focus on something else.

'You'd think there'd at least be dust somewhere,' James said, looking around.

There was no dust. There was no life in this house. It was as sterile as one of the operating suites Max spent so much time in. Another stage he set for his work.

God, she hated it here.

And she'd never asked Faith if she'd had any hand in the decorating.

'So how do you get into the office, Houdini?' James asked.

For the first time in this house, Chastity smiled. 'There are some benefits to living on the street, fireman. Give me a couple of bobby pins and ten minutes, and I can crack the code on your firehouse.'

He smiled right back. 'You continue to show unheralded talents, nurse.'

'I'm just a font of illicit information.'

She started to walk back toward the bedroom, when it occurred to her that she had the chance to answer one of Sergeant Gaudet's questions. She stopped next to the office door, her focus farther beyond. Past the kitchen, in fact, to where a door led out to the garage she'd never had the chance to investigate.

She couldn't be that lucky. Even Max wouldn't leave that kind of evidence sitting in plain sight. But then, Max might not know what the police had found. And if nothing else, Max was supremely confident.

Without saying a word to James, Chastity stalked off through that silent, oppressive house. Not saying a word himself, James followed.

Chastity opened the door to the garage and found herself holding her breath. It simply couldn't be this easy.

Evidently, for a change, it would be. Chastity flipped on the light to discover that for once in his life Max Stanton had been sloppy.

Max did indeed have a second car. It was sitting in his garage tucked away beneath a protective cover, right next to the empty space where the BMW lived. Chastity walked over and lifted a corner to reveal what lay beneath.

And there it was. An almost new Cadillac Seville. Black.

'I assume this means something,' James said.

'It means we might have our first evidence,' Chastity said, pulling out her cell phone.

She wasn't going to wait to get this information to Gaudet.

'He has a black late model sedan in his garage,' she said without preamble when he answered.

'You're there legally, I know, Ms. Byrnes.'

'Can't get more legal than being given keys, security codes, and the request to search for information, Sergeant. Want the license number?'

It took a few keystrokes on Gaudet's computer and a second or two of silence. 'Ellen Mayhew Stanton?'

'His mother.'

Gaudet huffed like a disgusted teen. 'No wonder we couldn't find it.'

'His mother's in Italy for the summer,' Chastity offered.

'We'll still need more for a search warrant.'

'I'll call you back.'

'I'm sure I don't need to tell you to be careful, Ms. Byrnes.'

'I'm sure you don't, Sergeant. But thank you anyway.'

If nothing else, the discovery gave her an odd sense of power that enabled her to walk back into that house with more impunity. She was right, she knew she was right, and for the first time she felt as if she could prove it.

So when she took a moment back in her sister's room to collect bobby pins from the vanity, she did so efficiently, not once tarrying over memories or expectations or regrets. She did have to remind herself to breathe in this house, though. She might have gained some power, but lavender was still lavender.

'You weren't kidding,' James said a few minutes later as the two of them heard the distinctive click of a lock opening.

343

Chastity straightened from where she'd been bent over the lock and pocketed the bobby pins she'd bent to rake against the pins. Then, with a flourish, she opened the door. 'It's Max's fault. He has such control in this house that he never felt the need to install more than a standard tumbler mechanism.' She took a moment there on the threshold to check the room. No key pads, no surprise alarms. 'He was right, of course. I imagine nobody in his family ever considered walking in here without his permission.'

'Is this still legal?' James asked, standing next to her.

'That door was open, fireman. I'm surprised you didn't notice.'

'Ah,' he returned with a nod. 'I was obviously confused by that door sticking and all.'

'Exactly.'

As far as Chastity could tell, nothing in the office had changed. She hadn't really expected it to. Max would never believe that he was at risk, so why should he disturb his records? After all, nobody would think to look through them.

Especially Chastity. He'd made sure of that by placing the picture of her father right on top of his desk.

Chastity walked up to it and turned it on its face. She wanted to throw it in the trash, but she knew better. So she turned away from it and stood there a moment to assess the room.

Desk, file cabinet, computer. Oh, the opportunities to leave evidence. But Chastity was not quite the whizz at computers that she was at breaking and entering. So she gave James the desk, and she bent to the file cabinet.

'He is the most anal man in history,' she announced, viewing rows of folders marked with household and business accounts. Warranties and school submissions and health records for the boys.

'He may be,' James admitted behind her, 'but I think he's kept his important stuff on the computer. I'm not finding anything like a checkbook or address book.'

'What about the phone bills?'

'Gone. He seems to have gone paperless since we were here last.'

'And I sincerely doubt a knowledge of the begats in Genesis is gonna give us the password to his computer,' Chastity agreed. 'Well, find what you can.'

They found one car. One cell phone bill that had call forwarding, which Chastity kept, just in case it could help blast those alibi times, and a note from an insurance company about a new policy taken out on Faith in the last six months for an additional million dollars. Maybe not a murder incentive, Chastity thought, but definitely the icing on the cake.

They found the contract Max had signed with New Life Associates for his wife to provide eggs for a price determined by auction. And they found an entire thick folder with records of every catalog buy Faith had made in the last five years.

'She addicted to this shit or what?' James asked.

Chastity thought of all those catalogs in Faith's private room and shook her head. 'No. I think it's the only way she could shop. Max wouldn't take the chance to let her shop like a normal person. He certainly wouldn't let her loose with a credit card. Too much freedom.'

'You assume.'

She sighed. 'Yeah. I assume. It's still all pattern and supposition. No proof. But see the jewelry? Expensive, and escalating the last two years or so? That's apology gifts.'

'Apology gifts?'

'Yeah. Classic in the abuse cycle. It's the part where the husband begs forgiveness. 'Here, honey, see what I bought to show you how sorry I am I had to hurt you? Even though it really was your fault, of course.' I sure wish I could get records from those ERs Dr. Hayes-Adams talked about, see if I could match dates. We can already prove he changed the good gemstones.'

'Still not proof of murder.'

345

'Then let's keep looking.'

It was ten minutes later when Chastity opened the file marked Milliken-Powers. She was going to pass right by it since she didn't recognize the name, but it was such a fat folder, she was intrigued. She opened it, and then she froze in surprise.

'I may not have the smoking gun,' she said, her voice tight and her hands trembling just a little, 'but I think I've just found the circumstantial case.'

James looked up from where he'd been searching desk drawers. 'Yeah?'

'Do you know who Milliken-Powers is?'

'Private detectives. They're all the rage for the divorce and alimony crowd.'

Chastity smiled for the first time in hours. 'Oh, good. I smell a subpoena.'

'Because?'

She sucked in a breath and opened the file wider for him to see. 'Because Max evidently used them to investigate every friend his wife ever made. Especially her friends from the Arlen Clinic. And these files go back at least three years.' She smiled, but it wasn't pretty. 'Max knew all about Susan's reliance on Saint Roch, and how Frankie prayed to Yamaya.'

She pointed to the section in the report on Frankie.

'Cornmeal is used to begin any ritual ... as offerings. Yamaya is particularly fond of cantaloupe, honey, white wine or rum, and fish of any kind, especially crab.'

Exactly what had been left with Frankie's body.

James pulled the extensive file from her hands and flipped through it.

'Your sister's in here,' he said quietly.

Chastity looked down to see that Max had compiled it all. Every sordid family secret, every damning detail that had harried Faith into adulthood. Her eating disorder, her obsession with grades, her terrible paralysis around water. Her testimony at the trial.

346

Everything.

That file was seven years old. Max and Faith had been married for six years.

Chastity stood up and walked away. Max, it seemed, knew everything.

Except where his wife had gone.

And Chastity had damn near provided that for him as well.

'Didn't Dr. Hayes-Adams ask us about a warehouse fire?' James asked behind her.

Chastity turned. 'Why?'

He held up one of the sheets. 'The info on Willow. It's eighteen months old and gives an address in Algiers. Describes it as a flop for the local transients.' He waved it a little. 'I think what you have here might get you a search warrant.'

'Good,' Chastity said, surreptitiously wiping at her wet cheeks. 'Let's get the bastard.'

She called Gaudet, but he was on his answering machine again. 'Sergeant, get out your search clothes. We've found the address of that warehouse in Algiers here in Max's file. Also the name of the private investigative service he used to get information on Faith and all her friends. The Milliken-Powers Agency. He's had information on them for at least a year that matches the details of their deaths. Please call me and tell me that's enough.'

His machine beeped, and Chastity thought of calling back to have somebody find him. She needed to know whether or not to take that file with her or leave it where it was.

'Leave it,' James said when she asked him. 'You have the name of the detective agency. They can verify everything.'

Chastity nodded. 'I just hate taking the chance that he's going to destroy everything.'

'If we get out of here in time, he won't know he needs to.'

'Did you find anything else?'

'Just his last credit card statement, which he seems to have maxed out.'

'Any suspicious activity?'

'No gun shops or fruit stands, if that's what you mean.'

Chastity's head came up, her attention straying to the closet. 'Guns . . . '

James sighed. 'I'll look. You stay in the file drawer.'

He found no guns.

'Probably in that damn silver BMW,' Chastity said. 'Or . . .'

She took a few minutes to run out to the garage, but the Cadillac was locked tight and bare of anything in the passenger area. Chastity would have killed to get inside that trunk, but she couldn't find any keys. Besides, the last thing she needed right now was to set off an alarm.

She was so close, she could feel it. She'd found the proof that would bring the police to Max long before he could find Faith. She could finally keep Faith safe.

It was all she'd ever wanted to do. It was why she'd called the police ten years ago. So Faith would finally smile again. Instead, Faith had run away, right into the arms of another monster.

Well, not again. Chastity was just diving back into the file drawer for the coup de grâce when her cell phone went off.

'You still at that man's house?' Kareena asked bluntly.

'Yeah, why?'

'Cause he ain't where he supposed to be anymore.'

Chastity looked around. There was still so much to search. 'Okay,' she said anyway. 'We're leaving.'

'Oh, and girl? Just so you feel better? The girls here say that Dr. Stanton's been getting more and more uncertain about showing up lately. Harder to get hold of, you know? And the case he was scheduled to do the morning that Frankie died was a clinic patient. A real poor clinic patient. You know what that mean?'

Chastity felt the rightness of this bubbling in her chest.

'Clinic patients are for the residents to practice on. He didn't stay, did he?'

'Not past 'Hello, whose turn is it to cut today?' '

'Call your handsome cop. We're going.'

Chastity and James were making sure everything was back in order when her phone rang again.

'I'm going,' she asked without looking at the number. 'I swear.'

'Chastity?'

Chastity stopped dead in her tracks. 'Faith?'

Her sister sighed. 'I'm sorry. I didn't mean to blame you. I just panicked.'

Chastity found herself smiling. 'I know. It's okay. And Faith? It's almost over. I think we finally got the evidence you need. I want you to go—'

'You have evidence? What evidence? We've been trying for *weeks*.'

Chastity laughed. 'Well, it's easy once you have an hour or so in Max's office.'

Chastity had expected her sister to laugh. Maybe to offer congratulations. Instead, she heard a stricken silence.

'What office?'

'The one in your house. By the way, did you have anything to do with the decor here? I have to tell you—'

'You're in the house? You're there *now*?'

'Well, yeah.'

'Get out! Get out now! Jesus, Chastity, he's got cameras everywhere in there. He probably already knows what you're doing!'

'Faith—'

'Get out!'

And then Faith hung up.

For a second, Chastity just stared at the silent phone. 'She says he has cameras in the house.'

Oh, and she said once your sister hated cameras. Didn't make sense to me ...

'Oh, my God,' she said, looking up at a startled James.

'The cameras weren't at the fertility clinic. They're here.'

He held out his hand. 'Come on, then. Let's go.'

She stalled, though. 'No. I need some of those files. If he knows we've been here, he'll destroy them.'

She spun around quickly, pulled the drawer back open. Reached for the Milliken-Powers file, the one she knew could be a nail in Max's coffin. She thought she had enough time. After all, she'd just gotten the call. He had to get through traffic, all that water.

She'd miscalculated.

She knew it the minute she heard the odd, dull little thud and turned to find James crumpling to the ground.

Behind him stood Max, and Max was holding a gun. A .45 with a bore the size of a cannon. It was pointed right at her face.

'Too late,' he said, very calmly.

Chastity felt her heart slam into her ribs. She clutched that file to her middle like a Kevlar vest. She tried very hard not to shake so hard he'd notice.

She couldn't show weakness.

Max backed a bit away from the door. 'Come along, Chastity.' Then he smiled. 'You can even bring the file.'

Chastity edged around his desk. Then she stepped over an unconscious James, where he lay bleeding from a laceration on the back of his head.

'What do you want, Max?' she asked.

He didn't stop smiling. 'I want Faith. But you knew that.'

'Yes,' she said, taking a careful step closer. 'I knew that. I've been trying to find her for you.'

'You lied to me, Chastity. You said you'd be leaving town.'

'I couldn't get there, Max. The flights were booked.'

'I see.' She was so close now, she could smell his cologne, the antibacterial soap he must have used on his hands. She could see his pupils dilate.

'Oh,' she said, suddenly looking down.

350

Making him look down.

Making him look down just long enough for her to act. Lunging at him, she shoved his gun hand away with her left arm. Then she curled the fingers in her right hand and rammed the heel of it straight up at his nose.

His nose crunched. He screamed. The file fluttered to the floor as Chastity slammed into him.

She reached for the gun. It went off, the report thundering in the small space and deafening her for just a moment. She wasn't going to get another chance. Max had a lot of weight on her. She had to get out to get help. It was the only way to save James.

Max was still bent over, blood gushing through his fingers. Chastity gave him another shove, glad to see that his nose was bleeding all over his pristine white shirt. There she spun for the foyer and the front door.

And came to a shuddering stop.

'Chastity?'

Her father was standing there.

She wanted to run. She wanted to scream so loudly somebody on this moribund street would hear her and come to help. She wanted to raise her hands again and fight. The sight of one square-jawed, gray-haired man froze her to the floor.

And she stood there just long enough for Max to recover. He didn't hit her on the head, though. He wrapped his arms around her and shoved a sweet-smelling cloth against her nose.

Ether.

It figured.

It was the last thought she had.

No, the last thought she had was that her father had finally won.

Chapter Twenty-Four

The first coherent thought Chastity had was that she was going to be sick. The second was that she could smell ether. There was nothing else in the world like it, sickly sweet and cloying and more nauseating than the smell of decay. Her third was that she was being dragged by her heels. Up steps. Her head slammed into one and knocked her even dizzier than she was.

She struggled to move, only to realize that she was tied. Hands behind her back, feet together, hog-tied like a beef heading for branding.

She wasn't, however, gagged.

'Shit,' she groaned, trying hard to keep her stomach from heaving as she was dragged across the floor, the rough surface pulling at the old stitches in her back. Wood, she thought, but somewhere inside. She was soaking wet and cold and hurting, but wherever she was now seemed to be dry.

She'd just about gotten her eyes open when her legs were dropped. That was when she smelled cologne over the ether.

Drakkar Noir.

Max.

Chastity opened her eyes to find him bending over her, dripping water onto her face.

'I should have been an anesthesiologist,' he said with a

satisfied smile, panting a bit. 'My timing is perfect.'

'You must be proud,' Chastity managed, wondering what he'd do if she puked right in his face. The way she was feeling, it was a definite possibility. The ether smell still clung to her, unbearably sweet and sticky, her arms were behind her back, and her head hurt like hell. And her brother-in-law was smiling down at her as if she were today's sacrifice.

Then she heard it. The noise.

Water.

Rain beat at the walls. Wind rattled the windows, blowing harder than it had before, gusting so strongly that it seemed to shake the very floor. And if the rain didn't shudder through the floor, the thunder did, deep and persistent and sharp.

The storm was the worst by far, harsh enough that if she'd been in St. Louis, Chastity would have found the nearest basement.

But that wasn't what horrified her.

Not the wind or rain or thunder.

The water that lapped against the cabin. Chastity could hear it right below her head. Against the walls of the cabin, as if they were a boat anchored in a lake or something.

Chastity twitched like an electric shock patient. 'What the hell . . .'

Max, just inches from her face, smiled. 'Like it? It's just for you.'

Chastity finally had enough brain working to look around. They weren't at Max's house anymore. Max had dropped her in the middle of the set of *Deliverance*. Bare wood walls and floors, a couch, two chairs, and a pressboard coffee table. Two windows, a door. The place looked like it was made from two-by-fours and tacks, and it was shuddering with the wind.

And the water.

'Where are we?' she couldn't help but ask, and knew that her voice sounded high and thin.

353

Max laughed. 'Thought you'd never ask. I've been saving this treat for Faith, but ya know what? I think you deserve it more. Actually, this place belongs to a friend of Faith's. A hunting camp named Barataria, as if it were really something special. It's not. Just four walls and a toilet that flushes into the swamp.'

Chastity closed her eyes. 'How nice.'

He nudged her with a shoe. She opened her eyes again to see that his nose was swollen and red. She was glad.

'I'm not finished,' he snapped.

'Sorry.'

'You need to know where you are. You're out off the Chef Menteur Highway, in a shack that's built up out of the water on stilts. Only the water is just a little deeper than usual. In about six hours, this whole house will be gone. Probably blown away, if the water doesn't swallow it in the storm surge. Poetic, I call it.'

Chastity tried hard to catch her breath. 'Why?'

His smile grew cold. 'Justice. It amuses me to think that you'll die in the worst way you could possibly imagine.'

She tried hard to seem calm. 'You know about that, huh?'

'Of course. Faith isn't any better, you know. She can hardly shower. But she won't have to worry about it much longer. Thanks to you, I've finally tracked her down.'

Another gust of wind shook the cabin, making Chastity want to reach out and hold on to something. Hard to do with her hands tied behind her back. Lightning strobed across the bare walls, and thunder made it hard to hear.

And the water lapped right beneath her head, roiling with the wind and rain. Chastity had thought she'd had trouble crossing the Mississippi. Max was right. This was the nightmare of her soul.

'Where's James?' she asked, hearing how thin her control was.

'Behind you. And you probably missed this, considering you were unconscious, but you know that shot I got off? It

354

hit him in his good shoulder. I'd say it's just not your day all-round.'

Chastity stretched around to see that James lay behind her, a small pool of congealing blood darkening the floor beneath his right arm. He wasn't tied, but Chastity figured he probably didn't need to be. His arm looked completely out of order. He was unconscious, but he was breathing.

'You put him out, too?' she asked.

'Why, yes. A little ether, a bit of Versed, and all is manageable. Of course, for him I injected a little more. I'm not as interested in his suffering as I am in his not being around to testify. Besides, it's his cab you two came in. His cab they're going to find here to mark the spot where the two of you perished in the hurricane.'

'Somebody had to hear that shot back at the house, Max. Why don't you just leave before they figure it out and come after you?'

Crouched down on his haunches, Max actually stroked Chastity's hair, as if he were comforting a pet. 'The only person who could have heard that shot was Barbara Rendler, and she's not going to say anything. Barbara thinks I'm a badly misunderstood man whose wife isn't good enough for him.'

'You're screwing her, huh?'

'You don't need to sound so petulant.'

'Tough to sound equable when I'm on the schedule for demolition.'

Was there enough air in this room? She couldn't seem to manage a decent breath. She couldn't hear anything but water.

'I have to leave now,' Max said, patting her again. 'I have an appointment with my wife.'

'You don't know where she is,' Chastity objected. 'Hell, I don't know where she is.'

'I know where she *will* be. I called her, right after you went to sleep. Her number was still on your phone, you know. Isn't technology wonderful? She knows that if she

doesn't meet me at the house at six o'clock, you'll be dead.
She thinks you're there.'

'She won't come.'

'Oh, I think she will.'

Breathe, Chastity. Breathe.

'Why six?'

Max laughed. 'Have you seen the traffic out there? I
have to go against the grain. It's not going to be easy.'

'And you think she's not just going to call the police?'

Max gave her his best smile yet. 'Oh, I know she won't.'

Chastity saw the triumph in his eyes and fought new
shakes. 'You could have saved yourself some time and left
me where I was.'

'I could have just shot you, too,' he said. 'Like the
others. But it's important that you know exactly what it
costs to defy me, Chastity. I made it a point to ask you here
for your help.'

'For your alibi.'

'I told you, don't be petulant. Now I'm sorry I can't stay
to savor your panic, but I have a schedule to keep. But
before I go, I thought I'd tell you exactly what to expect.
You're now on a very narrow strip of land that keeps the
Gulf of Mexico away from Lake Pontchartrain. The hurricane is due in, oh, about six hours. About ten o'clock, they
think, when it's nice and dark. And when it comes, you'll
die – very badly, I think. In the meantime, I'm going to my
house, where I will punish my wife for trying to leave me.'

He straightened, brushing off his slacks. 'Now, as I said,
I've left you here with your friend's cab. You can always
try and follow me, but I don't think you will. Because even
if you managed to start the car without the keys, the only
route left back into the city is over the Lake Pontchartrain
bridge.' His laugh was positively delighted. 'And we know
the chance of your actually doing that.'

He waited, as if expecting her to congratulate him.

'Don't you want to know how I got the cab out here?' he
asked.

356

'Not really.'

He shook his head. 'You haven't even asked about your father yet. Well, here it is. He helped me, of course. He didn't want to. In fact, after he drove Max's cab out here for me, he slipped the cab keys into your pocket, as if that would absolve him. He's standing outside right now waiting for me. So he doesn't know that I've taken them back.' He lifted his hand then, to show Chastity that James's keys dangled from his fingers.

'He didn't want to help?'

'Even he, it seems, likes to think he'd draw the line somewhere. But then, I didn't give him much choice. You see, when he got out of prison, he asked me to help him set up the computer I got him. E-mail, Internet, that kind of thing. Here's a bit of advice, Chastity. Never let anybody you don't completely trust do that for you, especially if you have secrets to hide. Since I knew that your father wasn't about to stop his ... predilection, I helped myself to proof that he's been trafficking in kiddie porn. He goes back to prison, he goes back for good. So? He's very compliant.'

'And you don't feel the need to stop him?'

'No. In fact, just to put the icing on this cake – and I *will* be telling Faith as well – after the two of you have been punished, I'm letting him loose. Well, on a leash, of course. I'll always have the proof. But I really like the idea that you're going to be lying here while the water rises knowing that your sister is about to die and your father is going to be free again to terrorize more young girls.'

Why? she wanted to ask.

She refused to, though. No matter what happened, she was not about to allow this man any bigger a sense of triumph. It was enough that he could see the uncontrollable trembling that had set in, the pasty sheen she knew was on her face.

'The police know it's you, Max,' she said. 'I found the car. I found the evidence. I found the name of the detective agency.'

357

'And didn't have time to share it.' He shrugged. 'But that's neither here nor there. By the time anybody can do anything, I'll be sitting on a beach in a country that forbids extradition, with all the money you seem to think I've gambled away, and my wife will be in an unmarked grave someplace where the alligators won't find her like they did her friend Willow.'

'Learn from your mistakes, did you?'

His laugh was triumphant. 'Mistakes? Are you kidding? I dragged that girl around that swamp for a solid week trying to get her found. Of course, that was when I still thought it was Faith and I needed an alibi. No, this time I'll tidy up after myself. In fact, I already have the body bag and the shovel in my trunk. I've had them in there for days, just waiting till you finally sent me in the right direction. It was a treat telling Faith that it was your fault I'd found her.'

This time Chastity didn't rise to the bait. She just lay there staring at Max as if what he said didn't matter.

It turned out she didn't need to participate at all. He had a script worked out in his head, and he was just about finished with it. He bent again, so close Chastity could smell the mints on his breath. She could see flecks of yellow in his brown eyes. 'Who the hell do you think you are?' he hissed. 'That is *my* house. *My* wife. My marriage. You have no *right* to interfere.'

The song of the abuser. And Max sang it like Pavarotti.

'You forget,' Chastity couldn't help but say, one final spit in the eye of the monster, 'you were the one who asked me to come.'

And for a brief, terrifying moment, Chastity saw Max lose control. His eyes, she thought. Finally she saw what he was in those eyes that grew cold and mad and vicious. 'Well,' he said, 'a good surgeon takes care of his mistakes.' Then, even more terrifying, he just smiled.

That seemed to be all he needed, because he finally straightened, the keys still dangling from his fingers. Giving her one last smile, he took a moment to assess the perfection of the scene, and then he walked out and locked the door behind him.

Even above the rain and wind and thunder, Chastity could hear him start the BMW. She heard the engine rev a couple of times, and then she heard the wet spray of gravel and water as he headed away.

And left her alone with an injured man.

In water.

She dragged in a couple more breaths and fought to stay calm. She wasn't going to make it. Hell, she wasn't going to last long enough to drown. If she could get her hands free, she'd just rip out her own throat before she let herself die in water.

It was still lapping, still peppering the side of this tar paper shack. It was rising; she knew it. Soon it would be seeping in under the door and over the windowsills.

Max was right. He'd found the perfect revenge.

'Windy bastard, isn't he?' she heard behind her.

Quickly she rolled. 'James?'

His smile was a bit wan, but it was there. 'I thought he'd never leave. Want some ya-ya now?'

Chastity laughed. She was damn near sobbing, but he made her laugh. 'You're not supposed to be awake yet. I'm not even sure you're supposed to be awake at all.'

He huffed with impatience. 'That guy obviously never treated burn patients. I throw that crap off like water.'

Chastity could hear that he was still slurring a bit. She could see that his eyes weren't focusing quite right. But he was awake. And he was suffering for the chance he'd taken for her.

'God,' she said, 'I'm so sorry. I got you kidnapped, I got you shot. I got you drowned in a hurricane.'

'Not yet, you didn't. And just so you know? He's full of shit. That shot didn't hit me. He did it himself. Stood over me and shot me point-blank right before dumping me in my own cab.' He shook his head a bit. 'Talk about being full of yourself.'

He seemed so calm. Chastity sucked it in like fresh air. She focused on it like a mantra. He was calm. She could be calm, too.

Well, no, she couldn't. But maybe she could manage.

'I don't suppose you could figure out a way to untie me,' she said, trying to keep her voice from wobbling like a bad soprano's.

He seemed to think about it, as if he were assessing his available resources. 'I can try.'

'We have to get to the police, James. He's going to kill Faith.'

'Well, of course he's going to kill Faith. Isn't that what this has been about all along?'

Another gust of wind rattled the windows, and Chastity came within an inch of shrieking. Her heart was thundering and her breath rasped through constricted airways. She could feel her bowels turning to water. Oh, yeah. *That* was good.

'Please, James.'

James was already doing his best to lever himself up on his stiff left arm. 'Nag, nag, nag. I'm coming.'

Chastity turned so he could get at her hands.

'Well,' he said from behind her, 'the good news is that our friend the surgeon was never a Boy Scout. The bad news is he's a hell of a shot. I have absolutely no strength in this arm.'

'He just knew where to place it. All that anatomy he took.'

'Yeah. He must have had the reception for those cameras in his frickin' car to get there so fast.'

'Could he do that?'

'How the hell do I know? I don't know anything about technology.'

'Oh, yeah. I forgot.'

More wind. More rain. Chastity was sure the hurricane was there. She could almost hear that damn storm surge headed their way, just like that big-ass wave in *The*

360

Poseidon Adventure. This cabin was going to turtle and she was going to be dumped headfirst into the water and tumbled around like laundry in the spin cycle and . . .

'Yo, Chastity. Focus.'

'I am.'

'Yeah, but not on the water.'

His one hand was scrabbling at the rope, and Chastity could feel something wet drip over her wrists. More viscous than water. Warmer.

'How much are you bleeding?' she asked.

'Enough to ruin my good T-shirt. Hold still.'

'I am holding still.'

'You're shaking like a can in a paint mixer.'

'Think about how you'd feel if it were fire out there, James.'

For a moment, there was just silence. 'Yeah. Okay.'

It seemed to take him an eternity. Chastity tried hard to hold still, but every time the cabin moved, she flinched and James lost hold.

'I'm sorry,' she kept saying, fighting tears, fighting panic, fighting the swell of inevitability.

She should never have called Max back all that time ago. She should have respected her omens. Once she'd started down this path, there could be no end but this. She'd heard those footsteps approaching down the hallway. She should damn well have known the door was going to open.

'We only have so much time,' she said. 'It's already after four, I think. Are we going to be able to drive out of here?'

'We don't need to drive out. We can get my dispatcher on the radio and have them send some help.'

Chastity's arms were aching hard and her shoulders cramping. Better to think about that than what her intestines threatened to do.

'By which time we'll be fish bait. I'm driving out of here.'

'I thought we didn't have a key.'

Chastity actually laughed again. 'Key? We don' need no stinkin' key. That taxi's a GM. I can steal it in my sleep.'

James huffed a bit. 'You need a higher class of hobbies.'

'Those *were* my higher class hobbies. I'm not even going to tell you what I can do with a pair of panty hose and a lightbulb.'

'If it doesn't involve untying wet ropes, don't.'

Five more minutes.

Ten.

And then, suddenly, Chastity was free. Her arms shrieked as she pulled them around to get the rest of the ropes off.

Then she saw the blood.

'Oh, shit, fireman. We got to get that hole plugged before you just pass out on me.'

'Yeah,' he said, his voice a bit weaker. 'I think we do.'

Chastity managed to get around to see him lying back on the floor, his face so pale that his scars looked as if they were painted on. He was sweaty and open-mouthed, a fish out of water. A man short on blood and flush with sedatives.

'Any hospitals close to wherever the hell we are?' she asked, instinctively checking his pulse to find it fast but fairly strong.

James didn't bother to open his eyes. 'Not that we can get to today. Traffic's all going the other way.'

'Yeah, but there have to be police somewhere. We'll get help.'

She untied her feet and wiggled them a bit until the pins and needles announced the return of circulation before she attempted to stand. Then she stood for a minute to shove back the leftover ether nausea. James stayed where he was.

Chastity searched the cabin until she found a couple of clean white T-shirts and a bottle of Jack Daniel's. Oh well, beggars couldn't be choosers. She ripped the shirts into bandages and then applied the Jack, half to the wound and half to the patient. James hissed with pain as she wound the best pressure dressing she could.

The wound was through-and-through, just below his shoulder, where movement of any kind would hurt like hell and set it to bleeding again. It didn't involve a major vessel, but Chastity imagined that had been Max's intent. Max had wanted James to be just weak enough to watch helplessly as he drowned.

Which was when Chastity realized she couldn't put off checking weather conditions any longer. Leaving James the bourbon, she struggled to her feet and forced herself to approach the window.

She moaned like a castle ghost. Her gut threatened to humiliate her. Her heart just stopped in place.

Water.

It was all she could see, rippling through the tall grasses that stretched out about fifty feet from the back of the cabin before there was nothing but water, all the way to the horizon. Water, rising, swirling, stalking her like a vandal.

'We're trapped,' she rasped.

James managed to climb to his feet, although he was holding on to furniture. 'Other side,' he said. 'The cab's still there.'

Chastity ran to his window and looked out to see the cab.

Surrounded by water.

It looked like a houseboat sitting there, with water up to its hubcaps and a few weeds sticking up higher. Some ground was visible just past it, and then a bare shoulder of gravel about a hundred yards on. Beyond that, she could see a line of trees about half a mile off. Other than that, it was nothing but swamp.

Swamp and water.

'The cab's not a boat,' Chastity said, shaking.

James settled his left arm around her shoulder. 'Hell, nurse. This isn't water. You'll see water when that hurricane hits. That cab ran through higher puddles than this yesterday. You say you can get it started? Okay, prove it.'

Chastity couldn't stop shaking. 'I have to go out there?'

'Unless you can figure a way to get that car in here.'

She couldn't take her eyes off the water. But his arm was oddly warm where it lay, and it gave her a bit of courage.

'We only have so much time,' he nudged gently.

Chastity nodded, feeling that clock ticking away in her head. They had less than two hours until Max expected Faith, and Chastity had a feeling that she had to be there to stop it herself. And she had no idea where the hell she was or how she was supposed to get back. She just knew that Max had been wrong. Pontchartrain bridge would not be involved.

'Okay.' She looked around again, distracted by all that water. 'I wish Max had left my purse. I have everything I need in it to heist a car. Not to mention a phone.'

James patted himself down with his semiworking hand and shook his head. 'No phone here, either. Plan B?'

'If it includes burglary and grand theft auto, yeah. Plan B.'

'It's not grand theft. I'll be in the car. Which also has a radio.'

'Then that's where we're going.'

After settling James into one of the chairs, Chastity went back through the cabin. It took her another ten minutes, but she unearthed not only a coat hanger, but a screwdriver. No phone, though. No computer. On the other hand, if she'd wanted to fish, she would have been set.

But she didn't want to fish. She wanted to get out. And Max had locked the door. So Chastity left her cache with James and walked over to the window he'd been leaning against. Then, knowing that they didn't have time, she just lifted one of the chairs and hurled it straight through.

Listing badly where he lay, Gumbylike, in the other chair, James lifted an eyebrow. 'Feel better now?'

'The door's locked and I don't have time to pick it,' she said, shoving out the remaining shards of glass. 'I'd kick it, but it opens in.'

'You could have just opened the window and climbed out.'

364

'Not in the mood I'm in.'

James struggled to get to his feet, but Chastity just shoved him back. 'Stay there. I'll be back.'

She refused to look past the narrow porch as she swung her leg over the windowsill. Instead, she focused on the weathered, warped boards beneath her feet.

There was no key, of course. Max was nothing if not organized.

She stood there a moment, fighting the panic. Trying to think. She could hear the water behind her. Below her. Sucking at the supports of that fragile little house. Battering at her fragile self-control.

She had James inside and a limited amount of time to get the cab out past all that water. So she gathered all the rage Max had incited in her and reared back. Then, like an action hero, Chastity kicked the front door in.

It took three tries, and her right foot would probably never be the same, but she thought she'd never heard a more satisfying sound than the sudden splintering as the door slammed in on itself.

Well, maybe James's chuckle as he shook his head at her. 'I just love a strong woman,' he greeted her when she stepped through.

She couldn't help but grin back, breathless with effort and exultation. 'Amazing what a little outrage can do for a girl.'

'I could have climbed out the window, though.'

'Nah. It'll play much better this way when they make the movie about us.'

Carefully pulling James up out of his chair, Chastity wrapped one arm around his waist and grabbed her purloined tools with the other. Then she led James out onto that rickety porch and right off it again into the water.

'You guide, I'll support,' Chastity said, closing her eyes.

'Come on, nurse. You just punched out a house. You can do this.'

'Houses are easy, fireman. Water's hard.'

365

But she managed to get them both as far as the car, the water pulling at her calves and splashing around her knees. Propping James against the hood, she bent the coat hanger and slid it down alongside the driver's side window and popped the lock. It took her one more try than her attempts on the front door to achieve success.

'Hmm,' she said, taking hold of James again, 'I'm slowing down.'

'Shameful.'

She actually grinned. 'Humiliating.'

But she got him into the car. She even got him belted in. Then she reached for the mike on his radio, only to find that it wasn't there.

Not just the mike. The entire radio.

'My God,' Chastity breathed, stunned. 'He took it.'

James shook his head. 'I'm going to have to call my insurance company.'

'We're going to have to go looking for that help after all.'

Chastity closed her eyes a second, just so she didn't have to see the water. Then she forced her attention to the job at hand.

The lovely thing about ten-year-old GMs was that you didn't need to waste your time digging wires out and crossing them. All you had to do was wedge a screwdriver in at the base of the steering column and pop the ignition loose. Then you used the screwdriver like a key.

'God bless you, fireman,' she said as she did just that. 'You didn't go for one of those fancy new cars with all that computer shit on 'em.'

'I couldn't afford one of those fancy new cars with all that computer shit on 'em,' he assured her as he melted back against the passenger seat. 'I don't see your purse here, either.'

'If he stole your radio, I sincerely doubt he's going to be sloppy enough to leave my cell phone and drugs.'

James lifted an eyebrow. 'Drugs I don't need right now.'

366

'Me,' she said. '*I* need the drugs.'

The engine roared to life and Chastity tried to breathe. 'Tante Edie said I'd have to wade through water. She didn't say I'd have to drive through it.'

'At least you can keep your ankles dry now.'

She was shaking so hard again it took her a couple of tries to get the car into gear. 'You're sure you know where to go?'

'Sure. Point for the trees. Beyond that is the traffic.'

She pointed. She kept the car in a straight line, even as the water pushed at the bottom of the doors. She kept her eyes on those trees like a saint seeking heaven. She held her breath.

'I don't suppose you have airsickness bags in here,' she said, keeping the bile down with nothing but will.

'You're doing fine. You're almost at the traffic now. Hear it?'

'I hear the shrieking in my head. You listen for the traffic.'

Then, suddenly she was through the trees, and it was there. All she could think of was the scene in *Lawrence of Arabia* when Lawrence slogged up the desert hill, dying of thirst after weeks in the desert, to suddenly see the Nile on the other side.

It was a two-lane road. Both lanes were packed with cars, trucks, campers, and trailers, all going the same way. It was like the rush hour from hell, like a scene from every disaster movie Chastity had ever seen, with the entire world trying to escape the asteroid.

'What do we do now?' she asked, overwhelmed.

James considered the scene for a few minutes. 'I was hoping we were closer to the city. I think we're way past Bayou Savage, though. Follow the traffic for a bit. Let's see if I'm right.'

Chastity wanted to cry. 'We'll never get back in time.'

'Oh, ye of little faith, nurse. If I'm right, we're not that far from the north end of the lake. In no more than a few miles, the rest of the traffic will keep going north and we'll go west. In the meantime, take the shoulder.'

'What if I just stopped a car and asked to use their cell phone.'

'Okay.'

She tried that. She climbed out of the car and began banging on doors, begging for help. People treated her like a homeless woman with a hand out. After a few minutes of it, she actually heard car doors locking.

She could stand there. Or she could get in motion. Because even if she did get hold of the police, she had a feeling that Max was going to murder Faith anyway.

She had to get to them. She had to stop it herself.

That was what kept going through her head every time she saw a person turn their head and drive by as she begged to use their phone.

Then a couple in a Volvo stopped.

'Please,' Chastity begged as they cracked their window against the rain that she suddenly realized had drenched her. 'I need to call the police.'

The man was already shaking his head. 'We've been trying to call out for the last twenty miles. The circuits are jammed.'

Chastity damn near fell on the ground and wept. 'Can you keep trying? Please. A life is at stake. Call nine-one-one and ask that Detective Gaudet of the Cold Case Department go to forty-one River Bend Estate Road. Tell him that Faith Stanton is going to be murdered if he doesn't get there in time.'

'Murdered?' the man retorted, his voice a mixture of suspicion and distress.

Chastity held on to her patience by her fingertips. The guy was old, bald, and sweet-looking. And she'd just asked him to play a bit part in a suspense movie.

'On my honor,' she said. 'Please. Try and keep calling.'

The window started sliding up. He was wide-eyed, and his wife was leaning over, even more wide-eyed than he. But he was nodding.

368

So Chastity climbed back into the cab.

'I hope he actually calls,' she said, starting the engine.

'I think you scared him. You're looking a little wild-eyed.'

'No kidding. Well, the rest of these people didn't help, so they'd just better get out of the way.'

She revved that engine like a pace car, pointed it in the right direction, and drove.

It was another thing about driving a big, honking cab instead of a Mini Cooper, Chastity realized as she pushed her way into the traffic. A Mini Cooper could certainly find the little spaces to slip into, but a big Caprice could just muscle its way through to where it wanted to go.

And that was precisely what she did. It even felt pretty good. Like throwing a chair through a window. The level of honking escalated precipitously as she pushed her way into the flow, but Chastity didn't care at all. She had to get the hell back to New Orleans, and there was only one way to do it.

In the passenger seat, James managed a wry laugh. 'Now I'll close *my* eyes, nurse. Your driving positively terrifies me.'

Chastity could actually laugh back. 'And you haven't seen me on an open road yet. You should be afraid, fireman. You should be very afraid.'

She could at least breathe again. They were on dry land. She could mostly ignore the encroaching swamps that stretched out to the right of the road, the open water that stretched away just beyond. The rain was even letting up again, just a little, although the thunder and lightning had returned, syncopated and insistent, as if pushing her on to get her sister. She'd made it out of that cabin before it collapsed into the water, and she was moving. She could only see one problem.

'Where the hell are the police?'

James, leaning more heavily against the far door, did his best to shrug. 'Think they're all already in Mississippi?'

'They should be here directing traffic,' she insisted, pulling the car over in front of a refrigerated shrimp truck. 'We've got to get hold of somebody to get down to Faith.'

'I'll look for phone booths.'

Chastity couldn't help but laugh. 'Out here? The only thing out here is herons and fishing boats.'

'A house then, with a phone.'

'More breaking and entering?'

'You telling me you can't break into a house?'

'Of course I can break into a house. I'd just rather not have to.'

Chastity huffed and yanked the wheel again to pull out to the narrow shoulder. Hitting the accelerator, she ignored more outrage and outdistanced another couple of campers and a length of cars.

It went that way for at least fifteen minutes, until Chastity's blood pressure redlined and her chest felt full of acid. She knew that James was slumping farther and farther down in his seat. She felt the seconds ticking away in her head. She fought the traffic and the panic and the clock. She fought the water and the time, and still she didn't see one goddamn cop on the road.

She saw bridges, though. She crossed at least two, sweating harder each time she saw one, saw the water beneath waiting for her. She came damn close to telling James that she just couldn't do this. Her hands were going to slip off the steering wheel from the sweat, and they were going to end up in the water after all.

And then, after she had crossed another flimsy metal bridge over yet another wide bayou that swept out to sea, James suddenly came to attention. 'Okay. Here's one ninety. We turn off here.'

And finally they escaped the traffic. Chastity slammed her foot onto the accelerator and took the road back along the northside of the lake like a Grand Prix driver getting a white flag.

And still there weren't any cops. They passed Slidell and

370

found that evidently everybody there had already left.

'Should we break into one of these buildings?' Chastity asked as they sped past a small collection of structures.

'Not unless you want to waste perfectly good time. Those aren't just power lines lying along the side of the road.'

'Okay, then, that's one less option. Wish we had a radio. See if Bob's coming.'

'Your brother-in-law said six hours.'

'That wind looks pretty high to me right now.' Which was when she had to swerve to avoid another set of sparking lines. 'I don't suppose there'd be somebody standing on the side of the road with a damned phone!'

She was getting even more afraid. The good news was that she wasn't near open water anymore. The bad news was that they were driving through thick woods that seemed to catch the wind. Twice they had to skirt downed limbs, and twice more fallen lines. The wind seemed to be howling now, gusting hard enough to drive the rain sideways.

'Where *is* everybody?' Chastity moaned, fighting a fresh gust of wind as they hit an open area.

'Going the other way.'

'But shouldn't, like, the National Guard be here or something?'

'They said they'd be here about six tonight.'

Chastity really did laugh. 'This is all a cosmic farce, isn't it? It's like the whole thing's been choreographed to drive me completely insane.'

James managed a grin. 'It's all about you, is it?'

Chastity was surprised into another laugh. 'Inside my head it is. My father was with him, you know.' She sucked in a lungful of air and still felt suffocated. 'My father.'

'I know. I heard.'

'I can't believe he'll go along with Max. No matter what.'

'Why not? Isn't he evil incarnate?'

'Yes, but he always seemed to like Faith best. I just can't
. . . ' She shook her head, not at all sure this was the time
for family psychology. 'I just hope he's gone before we get
there. I can handle a murderous psychopath. I'm not at all
sure I can handle my father.'

'Maybe the police will get there first.'

'That's if we get the police. This thing drives like a tank,
you know.'

'All the better to fend off other taxis.'

'There *are* no other taxis out here, James. Just rain and
trees.'

Two more of which they had to swerve around. But it
seemed that the storm was easing, the wind not sounding
quite so demonic, and the rain falling down now instead of
sideways.

'How far do we go?' Chastity asked.

'Almost there.'

'Almost where?'

'Where we're going to find a policeman.'

'And where's that?'

It took James a moment to answer. Chastity was just
about to look over to make sure that he hadn't finally
passed out, when she saw him lift his burned arm.

'There.'

She looked up to see road signs. Her eyes opened very
wide.

'There where?' she demanded, suddenly sounding shrill
all over again.

James pointed. 'Follow that sign. I promise you'll find a
cop there.'

'The Lake Pontchartrain Causeway? Is that what I think
it is?'

Water. All that water.

And only one bridge.

'Yeah. But with the wind this high, cops'll be at the
entranceway pulling people over. I think they close it when
the wind tops forty or something.'

'Okay.'

And James was right. There, right by the tollbooth that led to the bridge, that led to the water, sat a car with a light rack on it. But beyond it Chastity saw a steady line of cars approaching from the far expanse of the causeway. Nobody had closed anything yet.

Chastity froze at the sight. How could anybody do that? Just drive over water as far as the eye could see? What if the bridge broke? What if a boat slammed into it? What if the wind just blew them off into the water?

'Okay,' she said, focusing on that cop. 'Now we can get help. After we talk to him, how do we get back off the highway?'

'We don't.'

She actually stopped the car right in the middle of the road. 'What?'

'The lake is forty miles around, Chastity. The bridge is only twenty-three miles long.'

'You said they'd close the bridge.'

'I might have forgotten to add that it's one of the hurricane evacuation routes.'

She shook her head. '*I'm* not going over that bridge.'

He leveled a hard look at her. 'Then you're not going to get to your sister in time.'

'The police are!' she shot back. 'That's what we're calling them for!'

'And if they can't get there in time?'

Chastity opened her mouth. She closed it again. It was what she'd been thinking for the last half hour. She shouldn't be surprised James said it.

'He's got a head start on us, Chastity,' James reminded her. 'The police have a hurricane to contend with. We don't have a choice.'

'You always have a choice,' Chastity snarled.

But you might not always be able to tolerate the consequences of the choice you made.

Chastity sat there so long that the cop finally noticed,

373

some hundred yards away. He climbed out of his car, watching her.

And still she sat there, her attention riveted by the endless vista of water. Roiling water. White-capped, angry water. Her heart stuttered badly. Her hands were sweating as if she were a woman in labor. She was dripping with it, hands and forehead and the small of her back.

She had to get to her sister. She had to somehow save her. She had to cross all the water in the world to do it. And then she had to face her father.

Chastity reached over and shut off the engine.

'No.'

James looked over at her, his expression unreadable. He looked back out over the water, where the policeman waited. He shook his head. 'Then it's over.'

Yes, Chastity thought, sitting there like a stone. He was right. After all that effort, all that pain and grief and trauma, she'd reached her limit. Right at the edge of a lake she couldn't see across.

Her sister was still in danger, but Chastity simply couldn't summon the strength to go a step farther.

It was over.

Chapter Twenty-Five

For the next few moments there was dead silence in the cab.

'Are you quiet because you have no argument?' Chastity asked, her attention on the horizon, her hands wrapped around the steering wheel as if it were Max's neck. 'Or because you're unconscious?'

'You made your decision,' James said simply.

Which made her turn, of course, to see that he was slumped against the far side of the cab, cradling his freshly injured arm in his lap. And bleeding through her bandage.

The rain was falling again, still only a sprinkle. The wind started to dance across the road. Chastity felt the panic surge in her chest, choking out any kind of logic. She noticed that the police officer had stopped only a few feet from his car, and that he was watching her, his hand positioned near the gun on his hip.

Just beyond him, three tollbooths stretched across the road. The police unit blocked the only open lane. The others were barricaded with orange cones. Beyond that the causeway swept out across the lake, a double span of concrete that dipped and rose and finally disappeared into the horizon.

The horizon of water.

Chastity couldn't believe it. There were cars on that bridge. Moving slowly with wipers and lights on, they crept toward her like a funeral procession. Just seeing that it could be done made Chastity sick all over again.

'If we tell the police officer what's going on, he'll help,' she said. 'Then we can just stay here.'

James didn't bother to open his eyes. 'We could do that.'

And James could then comfortably bleed to death in the front seat of his cab.

'There have to be hospitals on this side of the lake.'

'I'm sure there are.'

'And, I mean, what could I really do against a murderer? I don't have a gun. Hell, I don't even have a good nail file. The best I could do is kick him with my tennis shoes.'

'Did a nice job on his nose.'

She actually managed a smile. 'Yeah, I did. Didn't I?'

'Whatever you decide to do, you have to do it soon. It's already almost four-thirty, and even the bridge is gonna take a while.'

'Okay,' she said with a sharp nod. 'Okay. I'm deciding. We'll talk to the cop. Then they can intercept Faith and we can go the long route. Okay?'

'Sure.'

'Besides. I don't have the toll. Do you?'

'Probably not.'

She nodded again, trying to tell herself that she really was going to let the police handle Max. That she had the luxury to circle the entire lake to get back to the house.

She couldn't breathe again. She couldn't think. She couldn't get the image of Faith out of her head, of Margaret Jane, who'd lost a mother and had the Byrnes eyes. Of her father, standing there in Max's house. She couldn't get over the idea that no matter what she did, the police wouldn't get there in time. But that somehow, she could.

She couldn't do this.

She *couldn't*.

James shifted in his seat. 'Chastity?'

'Oh, shit,' she moaned, turning the engine over.

James didn't say a word.

'Let's go talk to that cop,' she said.

He smiled, his eyes still closed.

The cop was standing just a few feet away in a bright yellow rain slicker. Chastity tried hard to keep her attention on him. But he was so close to where the water was.

An entire world of it stretched beyond those tollbooths, and it was all angry and frothing, a sickly green-gray color that mirrored the roiling clouds. Lightning flickered along the horizon, where the sky was even darker. Another storm was sweeping over the water, and with it the wind. The wind that would tear at a car up on the heights of that span and send it spinning off the road right into that churning water.

Chastity sat there shaking. She needed to get closer to the cop, but she was already too close to the water. She sat idling no more than fifty feet from her goal.

'Come on, Chastity,' James said. 'There's that phone we've been looking for.'

Chastity sucked in a breath. She nodded. 'Okay.'

She could see that the cop was watching them. So she pulled up until she sat at an angle to his unit as if she meant to go past onto the causeway, and then she put the cab in park. Her hand shaking, she rolled down the window to let in a gust of fetid wind from the storm.

The policeman, scowling at them as if they were trespassing, walked on up to them. 'Probably not a good idea to try the causeway today, ma'am,' he said, his voice pitched to be heard above the rising wind. 'Storms are getting stronger, and the wind is causing problems. Besides, evacuation order's gone out for the city. Hurricane Bob's on his way, or hadn't you heard?'

'We heard,' James said, because Chastity was still looking at the water.

The cop leaned a little farther over to answer James and caught his first good look at him. He suddenly went very still. 'You folks wanna tell me what's going on?'

'I hope you don't want the long version,' James

377

answered, barely moving. 'I don't think I have time.'

'We need your help, Officer,' Chastity said, not budging. She wanted to get out of the car, but cops tended to see that as aggressive behavior. Let him stay in control. She just wanted him to make a phone call.

'And how's that?'

And just how *did* she explain the mess she was in in twenty words or less?

'I need to get hold of the New Orleans police. My sister is in danger. Her husband is on his way to kill her, and he has to be stopped.'

'And just how do you know that?'

'He told us.'

'Right about the same time he shot me,' James said.

'Look,' Chastity said, finally facing the cop. 'Check me out with Detective Obie Gaudet of Cold Case. We've been working together on this. But everything blew up today, and we don't have any more time. My sister is going to be at forty-one River Bend Estate Road at six o'clock, and her husband is going to be waiting there for her. He's going to kill her, I swear to you.'

'And you are?'

'My name is Chastity Byrnes. My sister is Faith Byrnes Stanton. Her husband is Max Stanton. Please . . . '

'Do you have some identification, ma'am?'

Chastity damn near did get out of the car then. It might be quicker for her to make the damn call herself. 'No, sir, I don't. My brother-in-law has my purse with him. He abducted James and me and left us to die out in a swamp someplace.'

'And you just happened to pop the ignition on this car?'

'It's my cab,' James said quietly, reaching into his pocket. His hand stalled there. 'He took my wallet.'

'I see.' The cop straightened. 'Can you step out of the car, please?'

'Look at my hack license in the back,' he suggested. 'Run the plates.'

378

The cop actually looked, his hand now resting on his gun. 'The only thing back here is a Marine Corps Etch A Sketch. And there are no plates. Get out of the car.'

James sighed. 'I just don't think I can.'

'Can't you call Detective Gaudet?' Chastity pleaded. 'He'll tell you who I am.'

'Yes, ma'am. Step out of the car.'

Chastity really couldn't breathe now. She'd been right all along. They were going to get stuck here playing a round of dick-pull with a cop while Faith died and James bled out. Chastity just couldn't let that happen.

She couldn't wait that long. She couldn't think of what she had to do. So she just did it.

Whipping the steering wheel around so she'd miss the cop and his car, she slid the car into gear, slammed her foot on the accelerator, and ran right over the orange hazard cone that blocked the second tollbooth. Then she smashed through the lowered gate like the defensive line sacking a quarterback and sent wood splinters flying at least twenty feet.

'Oh, God,' she moaned, seeing the cop jump into action in her rearview mirror. 'I'm a fleeing suspect.'

'So much for the toll.'

'I'll make it up to them later.'

'Well,' James said, curiously unmoved, 'at least you got his attention. He'll certainly check out your story.'

'After he has me locked away in a cell somewhere.' Chastity fought hard to keep her eyes on the road. But even if she did that, she was faced with water. Water everywhere, stretching as far as the eye could see.

And behind her, the police. He was standing outside his car, excitedly talking on his radio.

'He's not following us,' she said.

'He'll let the guys on the other end stop us.'

'Oh.'

'Hopefully they'll have called Gaudet by then.'

'Well, at least we'll get you some help.'

379

Which was right about when Chastity realized just what she'd done. She was already a couple of miles out onto the bridge, sweeping up into thin air over the water and heading for that terrible horizon.

'Oh, my God,' she moaned, her foot slipping off the accelerator. 'What did I just do?'

'Keep your eyes open, nurse.'

She really had closed them. And the cab was still moving.

Her heart was thundering in her throat. She was sweating like a malaria victim and shaking even worse. She was on water. She was trapped by it, surrounded by it, and she couldn't do this.

She just couldn't do this.

'Can't you drive?' Chastity begged James, her voice impossibly small as the car coasted aimlessly onward. 'Please?'

James managed to shake his head. 'Even if I had two arms, I'm still half bagged. He really shot some shit into me. I can't even read the road signs. And I swear the bridge is undulating like a snake.'

Chastity groaned, squeezing her eyes shut again. They'd rolled to a stop, just beyond the land where she couldn't get back.

'It *is* undulating,' she retorted. 'I can see it, too.'

'Nah. That's just panic talking. Come on, nurse. We have to get off this water before it bites us.'

The wind was gusting. Chastity felt it tug at the car. She was cold all of a sudden in the cab air-conditioning. Her shirt was soaked with sweat, and she thought maybe there was glass in her lungs.

'We're running out of time here, Chastity.'

Chastity pulled in a breath that wheezed with fear. 'Well,' she said, opening her eyes. 'If you can't go back, you go ahead.'

'That's the way, baby.'

She got the car rolling again and pointed it down that

too-narrow line. She tried hard, but she couldn't take her eyes off the water. It pulled her like a drug. It settled in her chest until she couldn't sit up or sit still.

'You don't want to go too fast,' James said. 'Especially over the high points of the bridge. Nasty crosswinds up there.'

She focused on keeping the wheel pointed straight. 'Uh-huh.'

Silence.

'You might want to go just a bit faster, though. We have a ways to go, and I don't think twenty miles an hour is going to get us there in time.'

Chastity tried her best not to close her eyes as she eased down on the accelerator. The car bucked against the wind, fighting her hold on it.

'How far is it to the city?' she asked.

'Twenty-three miles. And then about seven more to the Mississippi.'

Another bridge. Chastity nodded, her attention on the road. The road that seemed to stretch into nowhere. The water that waited for her.

The rails were too low, weren't they? Wouldn't it be too easy to roll over them? Shouldn't there be some kind of wall? A roof? *Something* that kept her from seeing all that water?

'I have this recurring dream,' she said, trying not to notice that her heart rate was redlining again. 'I'm driving across a bridge just like this one. Over so much water that it eats up the world. But the bridge doesn't go all the way across. When it almost reaches the horizon, it simply sinks straight into the water, and I sink with it. I can't stop it.' Were those tears on her face? She couldn't stop to think about it. 'Please tell me this bridge goes all the way across.'

'It goes all the way across. We'll get there.'

Chastity let go a sharp, manic laugh. 'We have to. I need to get you to a hospital.'

381

'After you make sure Faith is okay.'

'Yeah.'

The rain started again. Chastity turned the wipers and lights on, just like the people who were passing on the other side.

They were so close to the water. Suspended right above it, as if caught between reality and nightmare. And she had no choice but to keep driving farther and farther into it, away from the safety of land. Far from the possibility of rescue.

She was heading into hell, and there was no way to turn back.

'Have you considered what you're going to do when we *do* get there?' James asked, his eyes closed, his head back against the seat.

Chastity thought about it a second. Better than thinking about the fact that the wind was tugging at the car like a kid pulling on a kite string.

'I don't know,' she admitted. 'I don't suppose you're packin' heat in this thing.'

'I don't even have a tire iron. I lent it to somebody and haven't gotten it back.'

'How 'bout a cloak of invisibility? I have to figure out how to get into that house.'

'We still have some time left. It's only ten after five. Maybe we can head her off.'

'Maybe.'

They were rising now, on one of the high arches of the causeway, where Chastity guessed ships could pass under. The wind was waiting, swirling and hard and hungry. Chastity held on, despite how much her hands were sweating, and fought it. She was *not* going into that water.

'We have the element of surprise,' James said, and Chastity knew that his voice was thinning out.

'Yeah, until we show up in that neighborhood in a black cab.'

'You want to leave it outside the wall and climb over?'

'The way Kareena talks, the subdivision is built up out

382

of that swamp. You might float away while I'm busy.'

James was distracting her. Chastity knew it. But for the moment, it was working.

Mostly.

She still kept watching that water. It still filled her chest like acid and tumbled in her stomach until she just knew she had to pull over and puke. She felt her father closing in like death, and it terrified her, almost as much as the water. No, maybe more.

Yes, more.

Because without him, water would have just been wet.

But it wasn't. It was a living, predatory thing, and Chastity couldn't bear it.

'Pay attention,' James snapped.

Chastity pulled her eyes back to the road.

'You're doing fine.'

'No I'm not. There's nothing but water. Nothing in the world. And it's all mad at me.'

'Well, you're probably right there. But you don't want to give it the satisfaction of winning.'

Chastity's laugh was as shaky as her hands. 'I don't think I'm going to have any choice.'

'Then don't give Max the satisfaction.'

She'd say she was living a nightmare, but who could imagine a nightmare like this? There was no land anywhere. No solid ground. No sanity. Just roiling, smashing water and the eerie howling of the wind as it built over the lake. The clouds, skudding fast.

And the water.

She really was going to puke.

'Oh shit, oh shit, oh shit . . . '

Hours.

She drove for hours. Right into the darkness that held New Orleans hostage. Right into the hurricane that was eating up the coast and swamping the streets. Chastity held her breath until she saw spots in front of her eyes, and then she gasped like a fish.

383

She rubbed her hands against her pants and then she held on again. She listened to James in the passenger seat as he slipped further away.

And she kept driving.

At least, though, the terror of the endless road took away the more awful fear of her father.

She just didn't have time for it.

Not yet.

'How's our time?' she asked.

'Go faster.'

And then she saw it. Rising like Oz from the end of the poppy fields. Like the first sight of land after the Atlantic.

New Orleans.

She saw the buildings rise, a geometric miracle, from the horizon.

She felt the tears again, flooding her eyes and spilling down her chest without stop. She couldn't believe that she might actually make it.

'Where do we go when we get there?' she asked, her voice wobbling like a bad coloratura.

'Six-ten to ten east.'

'Okay.'

'But that's if the cops don't stop you first.'

Chastity blew off a pent-up breath. She'd managed to forget to do that, too.

'Don't worry,' James assured her. 'If you just keep going, they'll follow you.'

'What if they shoot at us?'

'Baby, this is New Orleans. The cops don't actually *hit* anything.'

Another shaky laugh. 'I'll hold you to that.'

But weirdly enough, there weren't any cops to greet them. There was just empty roadway, sweeping down off the causeway and into Metairie, where the traffic was all coming the other way and the streets were filling again with water.

Chastity rolled off Causeway Boulevard and onto 10 east

toward the city, and thought she could accomplish anything now.

She'd driven right across her nightmare and made it out the other side.

She'd found land.

Well, mostly. The puddles were still deep enough to drown a truck, and the thunder was cracking again. The wind had taken to keening, tugging at the car, and the rain was falling sideways again. They were in imminent danger from flying street signs and downed power lines, but at least she'd conquered the water.

She saw police, of course, now that she didn't want to stop them. They were in the evacuation lanes, directing traffic in their slickers and flashlights. Chastity watched them with longing as she sloshed by.

'We might just make it,' she said.

Forty minutes later, she knew they wouldn't.

They did reach Max's subdivision. After crossing Pontchartrain, Chastity even managed to cross the Mississippi bridge without so much as a tremor. She sailed through the flooded streets like the Ark. She even ignored the debris that was starting to fly with the fresh wind gusts. She had to get to Faith in time.

She actually thought she would. She pulled up to the gates of Faith's subdivision with ten minutes to spare. It was when she punched the security code in that she realized she'd run out of luck.

The gates didn't open. Chastity looked up through the storm darkness to realize that there weren't any lights on anywhere.

'The power's out,' she said, sitting on the wrong side of the wrought-iron gates.

'Can you climb?'

'How much do you like this cab?'

James just sighed and closed his eyes. Chastity slammed through that wrought-iron fence like a tank. James still refused to open his eyes, even as the heavy gates screeched and crashed across his hood before falling away.

'You're getting way too comfortable smashing through things,' he informed her.

'Think of it this way,' Chastity said with a nervous chuckle, 'the police won't have any trouble finding us now.'

Then they turned onto Faith's street, and Chastity thought maybe she'd been wrong. Maybe she hadn't run out of luck. She didn't see any car in the street.

But Max was there. She realized it as she coasted past the house to see that the garage door was half up. The power must have gone out just as he'd parked. Both cars were tucked away in the garage, right where the police could find them.

If the police ever got there.

If anybody had ever managed to call Obie Gaudet.

At least Faith wasn't there.

Chastity was just about to turn the car around and wait for Faith out by the subdivision entrance, when the storm paused, just for a second. Just long enough for Chastity to hear the gunshot.

And the scream.

Chapter Twenty-Six

Chastity's first instinct was to throw open the cab door and run for the house. But she knew it wouldn't do any good. She still didn't have a weapon. She had James bleeding all over the passenger seat. And she had no idea what was going on inside that house. She couldn't even see the front door from where they sat, just beyond the garage at the bottom of the downhill slope.

'Chastity . . . '

She couldn't take her eyes off the cars in that garage. Max had said he'd stashed shovels in those cars.

Those cars were one doorway away from the inside of the house, and Max still didn't know she was coming.

'Anybody comes, James, flag 'em down,' Chastity said, as if he really would be able to.

Throwing open the cab door, she sprinted through the rain for the garage. She was drenched by the time she got there, the rain running in small streams down the street and pooling by the curbs. She didn't notice. She only had eyes for those cars.

Skidding to a sloppy halt at the garage door, she dropped into more water and squirmed beneath the half-open door. At least the floor was clean. Hell, the entire garage was clean, with nothing more than a lawn mower and an extra bag of grass seed tucked into a corner to show it was used.

Max could have made it easier for her, Chastity thought

as she surveyed empty walls and small drawers filled with nothing but nails and screws. Not even a hammer.

She shook her head. Another stage he'd set. The suburban husband, who really didn't live here.

So it was to be the shovel in the trunk after all. Chastity approached the BMW, prepared to get complicated, only to find that the doctor had finally made a mistake.

God bless men who thought they were superior. He'd left the damn car door unlocked. Chastity was just about to reach in and find the trunk release, when she heard voices on the other side of the door into the house. She stopped, her heart stuttering all over again, terrified that the door was about to open.

It didn't.

Edging closer, just for a moment, Chastity listened hard for a woman's voice. For Faith's voice. For the proof that she wasn't already too late.

There.

The words were sharp, high-pitched. Desperate. But they were Faith's. Chastity didn't waste another moment. She returned to her search so that she could, please God, stop Max before he hurt Faith.

He wouldn't hurt her in his own house, where he'd leave evidence, even if he was going to flee. He'd spent too much time eliminating evidence to get sloppy now. He'd have to come into the garage so he could force Faith into a car.

Well, Chastity would be waiting.

With a shovel.

Taking a tight breath and wiping her hands on her slacks again, Chastity returned to the BMW. It took her mere moments to find the trunk release. Her hands were shaking, and she was wheezing again, something she thought she'd never done in her life, but she heard that click and knew that Max was about to meet the surprise of his life.

She crept around to the trunk and lifted it, and almost swore out loud.

Luggage.

Shit. Of course. Max had been tailing everybody in the black car. He wouldn't have left any evidence in his own. He'd much rather prepare that for his trip to the country that didn't extradite.

Chastity had thought that once she got past all that water, her heart would settle down. She'd stop sweating. Her stomach would right itself. Instead she felt as if she'd been thrown blindfolded onto a roller coaster. She was a veteran of stress, of surprises, of danger. But her body had been in fight-or-flight mode for at least six hours, and she was just wearing out from it.

And then there was the pesky problem of her murderous brother-in-law, who probably had at least one gun, if not two pistols and a shotgun, in that house.

She kept searching anyway. There wasn't anything else she could do. Keeping an ear out for any activity on the other side of the door into the house, Chastity crept over to the Cadillac.

Max had obviously finished his preparations. The cover had been taken off and carefully folded away. The car itself was not only unlocked, the trunk was already popped. And inside, just as Max had promised, lay a shovel, some rope, a cinder block, and a folded-up body bag. The complete Lacey Peterson Disposal Kit.

Chastity ignored the rest. She hefted the shovel in her hands and headed for the door into the house.

She'd just reached it when she heard the slam of another door.

The front door.

'Help!'

Faith.

Chastity spun on her heel and made for the garage door.

'Get back here, you stupid bitch! You're not going anywhere!'

Faith raced across the lawn like a track star, screaming. Max evidently had no desire to leave the front porch.

'Are you kidding?' he taunted. 'Nobody's here anymore.

Nobody's going to—'

There was a sudden total silence and the sound of shoes skidding across the grass.

'Son of a bitch!' Max growled. 'Where did *you* come from?'

The element of surprise was obviously gone.

Chastity crouched to peek under the door and saw Faith hurtle toward the cab.

'Let me in!' she screamed.

She was bleeding from the scalp, and the rain plastered her clothes against her. She was shaking and swearing and tugging on the driver's-side door. And ten feet away, Max was standing there with a .45 in his hand, looking at the cab in stunned disbelief.

Well, that wasn't going to last long.

At least, Chastity thought, he hadn't seen her yet. She might still be able to surprise him. Sneak up behind him and whack him up the side of the head with her shovel, and then whack him again. Then whack her father, because she knew he had to be here, too. This nightmare simply wouldn't be complete without him.

Chastity bent low to keep Max in sight. She lifted the shovel clear of the ground so it wouldn't make any noise. Holding her breath, she waited as he walked down the lawn, his attention on the cab. He didn't even see that there was someone not ten feet away peeking out from beneath the garage door.

She didn't move until his back was to her. Then, with another quick peek to the porch to make sure her father wouldn't appear and check her forward momentum, she slithered out under the door.

'What do you think you're going to do, Faith?' Max jeered as he stalked his wife. 'Escape?'

Faith had finally yanked the cab door open. James was still sitting slumped in the passenger seat, his eyes half open. Max slowed, bent over to peer inside. At his wife. In the driver's seat.

'Where is she?' he yelled, straightening.

He'd obviously realized that Chastity was missing.

Ten feet behind him, Chastity had just gained her feet. Straightening, she hefted the shovel in both hands. Inside the cab, Faith yelled something. She'd obviously just realized that there was no ignition key. One of the few moments in life when it paid to have lived on the streets, Chastity figured. Faith would never be able to boost that cab.

Well, at least they had some kind of protection in there. Chastity had none. And Max was finally getting the idea that he wasn't the only one on that driveway. Sniffing, as if catching her scent in the air, he began to turn.

Chastity didn't wait for him. She only had ten feet to cross. She had a shovel in her hands. She shifted it so she could start her windup. Eyeing the side of his head as if it were a major league baseball, she started to run.

Max swung the gun around at her just as she started her backswing.

'You are the most *annoying*—'

Chastity felt the thud before she heard the report. Then the clang, simultaneously, as the shovel damn near flew from her hand.

He'd hit the shovel and it had ricocheted and hit her.

How stupid, she thought. Her left arm. He'd shot her left arm, so she'd be a matched set with James.

It just about stopped her.

Not quite, though. She wasn't hurting yet. She knew she would, so she had to act now. She had to stop him before he killed her.

Max was sighting again. Chastity could see James struggling to get the door to the cab open, as if he could help. She could hear Faith shrieking, as if that would help even more.

She couldn't think of that, though. Max was pointing the gun again and he was smiling. That smile a man got when he knew a woman wasn't going to stop him.

391

Chastity *hated* that smile.

Max figured she couldn't win. After all, he had a gun. She had a shovel and one good arm. He was going to take his time and kill her long before she could do anything to prevent it.

But then, he only knew how Faith reacted to things. He really didn't know Chastity. He didn't know that she'd just driven a car right over the Lake Pontchartrain Causeway.

He did when she swung.

Screw her bleeding arm. Screw the rain that pelted down on them, and the wind that whined along the chimneys, and the thunder that rolled up and down the river only a few miles away. Chastity swung for the fences. And Max, tightening his finger on the trigger, thought he had time.

Chastity heard a bone crunch when she slammed that shovel against his right hand. The gun flew free, skidding across the driveway toward the garage. Max howled, both in pain and outrage. He lunged for her.

Chastity planted her feet and shoved the point of the shovel into his chest like a lance. He howled again. He fell back, just enough. Chastity hoped like hell she'd broken at least a couple of ribs, if not his sternum.

She swung the shovel again, and she swung it with everything she had. She slammed it against the side of that square-jawed, gray-haired head so hard that Max not only fell, he rolled right off the lawn and lay still in the street a good fifteen feet away.

'Oh, good,' James said from where he was half falling out of the cab. 'I don't have to save you after all.'

Soaked and shaking and suddenly hurting like hell, Chastity laughed. 'Faith!' she yelled. 'Get back inside and call nine-one-one.'

'I ... can't!' Faith wailed, still curled up on the front seat of the cab.

Chastity dropped the shovel in exchange for the .45 that was still lying by the garage door. She almost passed out

392

from the pain, but the weight of the gun was reassuring. She picked it up.

'He's not going to hurt you, Faith,' Chastity promised. 'I have the gun. He can't beat a gun.'

'Have you ever actually shot anybody?' James asked, eyes closed, elbows on knees.

'It's a forty-five, James. I only have to be in the general vicinity.

C'mon, Faith! I have to watch Max. You have to call for help!'

Chastity didn't want to admit that she was only barely still on her feet. She couldn't imagine how James had lasted this long if he felt any part of as hurting as she did. And she was bleeding. It dripped off her hand onto the driveway and washed away in the rain.

But she balanced that .45 in her right hand and lifted it until it pointed right at Max's unconscious head.

'Faith, come on!' she yelled again.

Faith was whimpering. Chastity could see that her face was bruised and her head bleeding from several places. She was shaking. But she finally pulled herself from the safety of the car and splashed through the water toward the house.

'You think you should check and see if he's still alive?' James asked, looking back at the crumpled form of Chastity's brother-in-law.

'I'm not getting that close.'

She didn't need to. She had a gun, and Max didn't. She had Faith going to get the police. She'd made it through the water whole. She felt the success of it begin to swell in her throat. She watched Faith trudge up the lawn, and she thought, finally, it's over. She'd made it.

She was just about to say that to James, when she was forcefully reminded that she wasn't finished after all.

'Is he dead?' a new voice demanded.

Chastity spun toward the front door, and her stomach hit the ground. Her throat closed up all over again, and she suddenly felt five years old. Small and shivery and afraid.

393

She had a .45 in her hand, and she felt helpless.

Her father was standing there, just out of the rain on the porch, and Chastity was frozen in place.

In the end, Max had been easy. It was her father who was hard.

'Chastity?'

She realized when she heard James's voice that she was pointing the gun directly at her father.

'Chastity, you don't want to shoot him.'

Chastity started at that. No, of course she didn't. She just wanted to protect herself. For once in her sorry excuse for a life, she wanted to make sure he didn't touch her.

He was standing there on the porch in his white shirt and black pants, his same old square-jawed, handsome self. Innocuous. He'd always been innocuous, so that it even took a jury five days of deliberation to convict him of destroying his children. And even then some of the jurors had looked uncertain.

But then, Chastity had long since realized that the most terrible evils wore a familiar face.

It was his hands, though, that most terrified her. Those broad-fingered, manicured hands that had splayed out over her face and pushed her down. Held her as he'd laughed until the water rushed into her nose and mouth and choked her, until she'd closed her eyes and her mouth and prayed for an escape that never came.

If she shot anything, it would be his left hand.

Faith ran right by him, patting him on the shoulder as she did so, and Chastity fought a fresh wave of betrayal.

'Chastity?'

Her father was watching her now, his eyes wide and disbelieving, his hands up a little, as if warding her off. As if protecting himself from her, when she was the one who was helpless.

'Chastity,' James said behind her, 'somebody must have gotten hold of the police.'

Chastity didn't turn to him. But she heard. Sirens.

Swooping close. Coming to save her, finally. Coming to put an end to the whole fiasco.

She'd thought she was finished, and now she wasn't so sure.

Because her father still stood there.

'I tried to help you,' he said, his voice almost a whine. 'I tried to save you.'

Just beyond him, Faith stopped and turned. 'You did not.'

'Chastity,' he amended. 'I tried to help Chastity. I couldn't just let him leave her out there.'

'But you could let him pummel me like a punching bag?' Faith shrilled.

He didn't meet her gaze. 'I've tried my best.'

Which was, oddly, when his power shattered. Chastity was standing there pointing a gun at him, terrified of him, wanting so hard to run from him, when he said that.

When he lifted his hands like a supplicant and whined.

That was when she realized just how pathetic her father was.

Here she'd been running from him her whole life, this monster who was too big to ever escape, and he was the one who was the failure. He wasn't just innocuous. He was ineffectual. A coward and a loser. He preyed on children because he didn't have the courage to face adults.

He would never be different. But she'd crossed the Pontchartrain Causeway.

Chastity was just making up her mind to drop her gun, when Faith screamed.

'Chastity!' James yelled behind her.

Chastity heard it at the same time. She spun and fired and hit Max just as he reared up for her. He staggered, a hand lifting to his side as it blossomed red.

'You know,' Chastity said almost conversationally, 'you just don't want to piss me off right now.'

'You *shot* him!' Faith screeched, running back down the lawn.

Max scowled, as if he couldn't believe Chastity had actually won. 'Stupid ... bitch ...'

Then he fell right back where he'd been before.

'Yeah,' Chastity answered, 'but right now, the stupid bitch is in charge.'

Faith stopped within a couple of feet of Chastity, her hands fluttering about as if she could somehow do something.

'Leave him there,' Chastity said, turning back to her father and leveling that gun once again.

Savoring the flinch in his features.

It *was* nice to finally feel as if she had the upper hand, she realized. Maybe James wasn't so far off the mark. Maybe she did want to kill her father. Or maybe she just wanted to geld him.

She thought about that for a few minutes as they all stood there facing her father and waiting for the police cruisers to swing through what was left of the wrought iron gates a block away. She heard tires screeching and car doors slamming and weapons cocking. Somebody even racked a shotgun.

'Ms. Byrnes?' that familiar gravelly voice asked. 'That you with that gun?'

The police were here. Obie Gaudet had come to play.

'So, somebody did get hold of you, Sergeant,' she said, still facing her father, whose hands were now up as if she were robbing him of his wallet.

'They sure did. We've been tracking you across the city like Bonnie Parker, Ms. Byrnes.'

'Nonsense, Sergeant. I've just been driving a wounded man around in a boosted cab. Not robbing banks.'

'You just shot a man.'

'I did. But as you can see, he shot me first. And James. And he beat my sister.'

'Oh? Isn't the man you're pointing the gun at your brother-in-law?'

'No, sir. I know you haven't met, but you probably

396

recognize him from his photo. This is my father, Sergeant. Charles Byrnes. My brother-in-law is the one lying in the ditch. You should probably get an ambulance for him. Not to mention James.'

'And you, I think, Ms. Byrnes.'

She shrugged. 'Okay. I guess.'

'There's nobody in the ditch,' somebody said.

Everybody looked, and damned if he wasn't right. There was a wash of blood against the curb, but no Max.

'Might have seen him trying to climb that wall when we pulled in here,' one of the uniforms offered.

'Then you might want to go find him,' Chastity suggested, not moving. 'He's got a lot of money in a nonextraditing country and at least three capital murder charges, not to mention kidnapping, assault with a deadly weapon, and blackmail.'

'Why don't you do that, Paissant?' Gaudet said. 'Go find the man.'

There was some reorganizing, and a couple of the cops hotfooted it back out the gates.

'Now, how 'bout you, Ms. Byrnes? Can we do something for you?'

Chastity nodded, her focus still on her pasty-faced father, who was standing there shaking in the rain. 'Yeah. Okay. We should probably get out of this hellhole before the hurricane hits.'

'Haven't you heard the news?' Sergeant Gaudet demanded. 'This is it. Most of the hurricane hit land down the coast and slid off west. Not only that, but it's weakened to about a two.'

'So the big threat is just a worthless blowhard?'

'That's what they're saying.'

Chastity started laughing again. It fit so beautifully, really. The perfect coda to this farce.

'Wanna give me the gun before these other police get nervous?' Gaudet asked. 'Then we can let the rescue people in.'

'Sure. But before you just let my father walk away, Sergeant, you might want to know that if you search either the computer here or the one at my father's house, you'll find proof that my father has been downloading quite a bit of kiddie porn. Which I'm pretty sure cancels his Get Out of Jail card.'

At that, Faith swung on her father. 'You *what*?' she demanded.

'She's lying, baby,' their father swore. 'I promised I'd never do that again.'

'I let you in my *home*,' Faith shrieked, suddenly ramrod straight. 'You *promised*!'

Chastity finally let the gun drop. She didn't need it after all. The police all uncocked their weapons and straightened. Chastity's father took two steps toward her, his face furious and frightened at the same time.

'Why did you do this to me, Chastity? Why!'

Chastity stood there, gape-jawed. Why did *she* do that to *him*? God, she'd been right. She wasn't helpless after all. In fact, considering what she'd accomplished today, she'd have to say she was pretty damned strong. Stronger than this monster had ever been.

Chastity felt unholy laughter bubbling up in her chest. It would feel so good, she thought, just to laugh right in his face. Just to finally tell him how little she thought of him.

She didn't have to. Faith did it for her. With the shovel.

Nobody thought to stop her. Not even when they saw her swing. Chastity saw that big-ass shovel heading for her father's face, and finally laughed until she was sick. She didn't think she'd ever seen anything so funny as the look in his eyes right before he got his comeuppance.

Epilogue

She screamed like a B-movie actress. She screamed like a hockey fan. She screamed like a woman who was experiencing the first ever, no-holds-barred, four-star orgasm of her life. She screamed, and James, sweaty and gasping, smiled back.

The room was still sparse, the neon flickering over the walls like a scene from *Blade Runner*. From four stories down Chastity could hear the raucous celebration of a Wednesday night on Bourbon Street. But for the first time in her life, she wallowed in the surreal feeling that she'd just been lifted right out of that world.

Of any world.

Exhausted, she sank back into the tumbled sheets on James's bed and tucked herself nicely beneath his left arm. He was using his healed right one to stroke her hair away from her face. He was chuckling, too, that kind of self-satisfied sound a man makes when he's just proved himself right.

'*That*,' he said, 'was good ya-ya.'

Chastity chortled right back. 'No kidding.'

'You stay down here, you can get it often as you like.'

'I stay down here, I'll become a sybaritic wastrel.'

His hand was starting to stray again. Chastity wiggled her ass a bit at the surprising shivers that were starting to skitter through her.

399

'Yeah, baby, but you'd make a damn cute sybaritic wastrel.'

Chastity smiled. How odd. She was in a tumble-down apartment on Bourbon Street with an ex-felonious cabdriver listening to 'Born to Be Wild' and working herself up for another round of hot, nasty sex, and she felt cherished.

She'd never felt cherished. Not in her entire life.

But James managed to do it with one good arm and half a smile.

But then, it was positively indecent what James could do with one arm.

And half a smile.

'Well,' Chastity said. 'I have nothing better to do.'

'Not since your father went back to the joint and your brother-in-law died.'

'I still can't believe he drowned in seven inches of salt water. That's just not right.'

'That's justice. Tante Edie told you so.'

They had still been there on Faith's lawn when they found out. It had been Kareena who told them. She'd pulled up right behind the paramedics and sashayed out of that T-bird of hers like the prom queen.

'Where've you been?' Chastity demanded from where she was seated on the lawn. The rain had let up and the thunder was passing. Her father was tucked inside a cruiser and James was being given fluids.

'I've been savin' people, just like the good nurse I am! Hey, ain't this hurricane a big letdown? Me, I expected houses to fly by an' everything!'

'Come see a tornado, you want to see that, Kareena.'

'I did see a drowned man,' she said. 'Right outside those walls.'

Even Obie Gaudet turned to hear that. 'A drowned man?'

Kareena smiled like a shark. 'Dead as disco, Sergeant. And how are you this fine evening? You like dancin'?'

'I'm sure I do, Mizz Boudreaux. But first, I'd like to hear about that drowned man.'

400

Kareena planted a hand on her hip and smiled big. 'Well, I'm surprised no police came to tell you. It seems somebody was running from all you and fell in the water 'bout half mile down the road. I saw 'em drag him out.'

'Did you recognize him?'

'Look a lot like that Max Stanton, who fixed the police commissioner's heart.'

'I *killed* him?' Chastity asked, feeling even more light-headed.

'Nah, girl. You just winged him. He drowned right in the swamp. Now, ain't that just some kind of poetic justice, yeah? I think ole Yamaya, she got him after all.'

Kareena was now Obie Gaudet's new fling, and Mrs. Ellen Stanton was on her way back to Italy with her grandchildren after burying her only son. It was only left for Chastity to figure out what she was going to do with herself and her dog.

'What about that job Kareena got set up for you?' James asked.

'Senior death investigator?' she asked. 'You really think they're gonna let a woman do that in a city this hidebound? I thought the guy now was somebody's cousin or somethin'.'

'But so am I. And you have the recommendation of everybody at Cold Case.'

Chastity smiled. 'Yeah. That was awfully nice of them.'

'Since you put a multiple murderer away and all.'

'And sent a sexual predator back to prison.'

'Liked that, huh?'

She smiled. 'Most of all. Why, since his hearing, I've been able to cut my drugs down by half, and my therapist says that she's gonna miss me.'

'And just think how much better you're gonna get now that you have all this good ya-ya.'

'Yeah. That and my pretty bracelets.'

It was, even though James didn't know it yet, what had tipped her decision. He'd had his cousin the jeweler take her treasure out of that small velvet bag and set it into a couple of bangle bracelets. Chastity had a feeling she wasn't going to take them off for quite a while. They gave a very satisfying clink as she set off on her own exploration to find that those scars of James's didn't extend to any vital areas after all.

She was feeling aroused again. Really excited, not crowded with shame and hunger and loss. She was just horny and happy and expectant. She'd turned a corner back at Faith's house. She'd walked away from her past.

And now, her toes still tingling from what James had just done – and was starting to do again – she was stepping into her future.

She really hadn't known that a man's touch could feel so good.

But then, she'd never known a man who could cherish a woman with nothing more than a smile.

'I'm just sorry that Faith hasn't done as well.'

Faith had definitely swung that shovel. She'd given her father a whack worth thirty years of rage that left his nose flat against his cheek and his mouth split like a melon. But after such a promising start, she'd faded. She'd packed up her house and packed up her life and moved back to St. Louis. And she'd done it without once talking to Chastity.

But Chastity understood. She'd even passed along the number of her own therapist. She hoped that one day her sister would heal as much as she had. She hoped she'd come back down and help raise funds for the brand-new Reeves-Savage-Tolliver Women's Shelter that Chastity and Kareena were putting together along with the survivors of that group of women who'd banded together to save Faith.

But that was for another day. For today, Chastity was going to find out how many other ways James could make her scream.

And how many ways she could make him smile.

And then, come summer, she would be the one to host the Annual New Orleans Hurricane Parade and All Day

Party. Because, she realized, there was nothing wrong with hurricanes. After all, they swept away a lot of broken and useless things. And left behind the things that were strongest.

'I hope you like dogs,' she murmured against his chest.

'I love dogs.'

'How 'bout baseball?'

'How 'bout concentrating on what I'm doing?'

She concentrated.

'They should name a hurricane James,' she sighed an hour later. Then, for the first time in her life, nestled in a safe place, she slept all night long.

Also available from Piatkus Books:

With a Vengeance
Eileen Dreyer

Maggie O'Brien is a medic on a SWAT team in St Louis who has always lived in the shadow of her father, a famous – some would say notorious – cop.

But Maggie has begun to suspect that there is something seriously wrong within the city's emergency services. On the back wall of the nurses' lounge there is a list that names every person who has ever annoyed the staff, police or paramedics in the city. Only what has started as a way for overworked people to let off steam has taken on quite sinister connotations. For a growing number of the city's lowlifes and criminals are turning up dead, often after receiving non-life-threatening injuries after skirmishes with the police. Their only other link – a guest appearance on the nurses' infamous wall.

But if someone is dispensing their own brand of rough justice in the city, Maggie isn't entirely sure where her loyalties lie . . .

Praise for Eileen Dreyer:

'I raced through this thriller, devouring every page. I just couldn't get enough of heroine Maggie O'Brien' Tess Geritsen

'A smart, provocative, page-turning thriller. An absolutely terrific, hair-raising read' Tami Hoag